GALLOWGLASS

Gallowglass is the concluding Douglas Brodie novel in the *Glasgow Quartet*. The three earlier books in the series are *The Hanging Shed, Bitter Water* and *Pilgrim Soul*. All three are bestsellers and have been shortlisted for numerous awards including Scottish Crime Book of 2013, the CWA Dagger in the Library and the CWA Historical Dagger. Discover more at www.gordonferris.com.

Also by Gordon Ferris

DANNY McRAE SERIES

TRUTH DARE KILL

THE UNQUIET HEART

DOUGLAS BRODIE SERIES

THE HANGING SHED

BITTER WATER

PILGRIM SOUL

GALLOWGLASS

GORDON FERRIS

CORVUS

Published in hardback and paperback in Great Britain in 2014
by Corvus, an imprint of Atlantic Books Ltd.

10 9 8 7 6 5 4 3 2 1

A CIP catalogue record for this book is available
from the British Library.

Hardback ISBN: 978 1 78239 075 6
Paperback ISBN: 978 1 78239 078 7
E-book ISBN: 978 1 78239 077 0

Printed in Great Britain by
TJ International Ltd, Padstow, Cornwall

Corvus
An imprint of Atlantic Books Ltd
Ormond House
26–27 Boswell Street
London
WC1N 3JZ

www.corvus-books.co.uk

For Sarah

Gallowglass (Gaelic: *gallóglaigh*):
An elite Scottish mercenary warrior

'The merciless Macdonald,
Worthy to be a rebel, for to that
The multiplying villainies of nature
Do swarm upon him, from the Western isles
Of kerns and gallowglasses is supplied.'

Macbeth, Act I, Scene II
William Shakespeare

PROLOGUE

e was dead. It was announced in his own newspaper, the *Glasgow Gazette*. Instead of the usual crime column, there was a brief editorial. It described the tragic death of their chief crime reporter and staunchly defended him against the unproven charge of murder. It was a brave stance to take, given the public outcry and the weight of evidence against him.

Finally and conclusively, his death was confirmed in the tear-streaked faces of the women by the fresh-dug grave. It was spelled out in chiselled letters on the headstone, glistening oil-black in the drizzle:

Douglas Brodie

Born 25 January 1912
Died 26 June 1947

'A man's a man for a' that.'

In the circumstances there were only four mourners: two women and two men. Of the black-garbed women, the taller held an umbrella aloft in two hands. Only the tufts of blonde hair on a pale neck showed beneath the hat and veil. She sheltered her smaller companion: a veiled and stooped figure clutching a bible and dabbing at her face with a lace hankie.

Alongside was a human water feature: one man clutching the handles of a wheelchair while rain cascaded off his hat on to the rubberised cape of the man in the chair.

Bit players lurked off stage. A man and a boy leaning on their shovels in a wooden bothy, staring despondently at the mound of earth as it grew heavier and more glutinous by the minute. Further down the green slope, a man in the dog collar of the Church of Scotland, scuttling for home, dreaming of a hot toddy after his desultory oration by the graveside. It had taken some persuasion even to get Douglas Brodie consigned to this cemetery. There had been an embarrassed debate with the kirk and Kilmarnock corporation about using a Christian burial site for the interment of a man who'd committed two mortal sins: murder *and* suicide. But Agnes Brodie's quiet insistence was not easily denied.

The two women had had enough. They turned and started to shuffle their way back down the path towards the metal gate in the high sandstone wall. They clutched each other for support on the wet gravel. The standing man birled the wheelchair round and fell in behind the women. Pusher and passenger struggled with brake and shoe leather to keep the chair straight and stop it careering down the slope. Behind them the straight rows of stones marched towards the horizon of lush green Ayrshire hills.

Their transport was waiting, chugging out a pall of grey smoke into the dank air, wipers thumping back and forth like a metronome. For the needs of the mourners, they'd hired a converted Bedford van, painted black, with windows and two rows of facing seats. It took a while and considerable manoeu-vring to get the four ensconced on the benches and the chair crammed into the rear. Once seated, they were off into the steady downpour. They closed the window between them-selves and the driver and were free to talk.

'Are you all right, Agnes?' said Samantha Campbell. 'It's over now. We can get on.'

Agnes Brodie sniffed and wiped her nose and eyes with her hankie.

'Ah never thought Ah'd see the day. It's not right for a son to go before his mother.'

Sam patted her hand and turned to the men sitting facing them.

'You're drookit, the pair of you. I hope you haven't over-done it, Wullie. Can you get that cape off him, Stewart? Dry out a bit?'

She reached to help him pull it over his head and drop it on the floor. The smell of wet rubber tanged the air. His face was blanched and he took in two shuddering breaths to settle himself.

'That's better. Thanks, hen.'

'I said you shouldn't have come. You're barely out of hospital.'

'I'm fine, lassie.' To prove his fitness, Wullie McAllister, sometime doyen of crime reporting at the *Glasgow Gazette*, reached into his jacket, pulled out his pack of Craven A, lit up and drew luxuriously on his cigarette. Stewart, his companion, slid a window open an inch.

'Ah should have brought a half-bottle,' Wullie said wist-fully. 'Will you be having a wee bit of a wake? Raise a glass to him? Even though we're so few.'

Sam and Agnes exchanged glances.

'Surely we should get you straight home? Get you into dry clothes?' asked Sam.

'Inner warmth. That's what Ah need.'

Sam smiled at Agnes and lifted an eyebrow. 'Of course, Wullie. A dram it is. And I've got some soup on the go as well.'

They were quiet for a bit, then Agnes spoke.

'Such a poor turnout, as well.'

'You can hardly blame them, Agnes. We asked for privacy in the *Gazette* and the *Kilmarnock Standard*.'

'Ah suppose so, Samantha. A' the same.'

Wullie flourished his fag at the thought. 'He wouldnae have wanted a fuss. You know what Brodie's like.'

Stewart joined in. 'They all wanted to come from the *Gazette*. Wullie talked them out of it. Said he'd represent them.'

Sam nodded. 'And I was approached by half the synagogue at Garnethill. You know what Douglas did for them. I said it just wasn't right. It would have felt wrong somehow.'

Agnes persisted. 'Not even his old regiment. There should have been a piper.'

Wullie blew out smoke. 'Mrs Brodie, funerals are dreich enough affairs without "The Flowers of the Forest" making our ears bleed.'

Again, silence left them with their thoughts all the way across the sodden Fenwick Moors and back on to the rain-lashed streets of Glasgow. It was only as they began the climb up to Park Terrace and Sam's home that Wullie spoke.

'Ah'll fair miss him, so Ah will.' He unfurled a huge white hankie and gave his nose a good blow.

Sam pursed her lips. She reached out and touched his hand.

'Wullie, I have a confession—'

'Wheesht, hen, Ah know you blame yourself.'

She hesitated as the car drew to a halt by the kerb. She nodded.

'You're right. It would never have happened if he'd got through to me that night.'

Agnes shook her head. 'You cannae blame yourself, Samantha. Douglas wouldn't have listened to you anyway. He was as stubborn as his faither.'

'I might have persuaded him. It could have turned out differently . . .'

ONE

It was as if I'd had a blood transfusion. Or perhaps it was just the warm June sun on my brow after the longest, coldest winter in Scottish records. Rising with first light, strolling through Kelvingrove Park down the winding paths lined with new-minted leaves. Then across to the Western Baths Club to carve out spluttering lengths in the great echoing hall. Something was making my blood sing, as though – and I scarcely dared hope – I'd finally emerged from festering anger and self-pity.

They say the best blades are toughened by heat and hammering. Time and again over the past eight years I'd been fired in the furnace, pounded flat, and quenched. In blood. I was at last rising from the dust of the African campaign, the damp of the Ardennes, and the soul-shrivelling scenes from the death camps. Last month, in merry May, a line had been drawn in my personal ragged history when the death penalties had been carried out on the Nazi overseers of Ravensbrück. It was as if the hangman had performed an exorcism with every pull on his lever.

Or maybe it was the couple of sessions I'd had with a head doctor. Sam had cajoled me into seeing the husband of an old pal of hers: Dr Andrew Baird. There was no couch, no tweed and pipe, no inkblot tests or unravelling of my childhood. Baird – about my own age, intense and engaging – was even prepared to come to me. We sat in Sam's library, each nursing a glass of whisky, while he gently plied me with questions.

'When the war ended you were commanding a company of Seaforth Highlanders?'

'I'd been given Acting Major. We'd fought our way from Normandy to Bremen.'

'But you didn't come home with them?' he said casually, taking off his specs and cleaning them on his tie.

'Sam's briefed you well.' I smiled. 'No, I studied languages at Glasgow before the war, French and German. The top brass found out and I was assigned to sift Nazi goats from Wehrmacht sheep and send the former off to military courts.'

'Harrowing?'

'They weren't nice people. They'd done bad things.'

'You saw?'

'Yes. Belsen.'

He nodded. 'When did they let you come home?'

'November '45.'

'Back here?'

I shook my head. 'Couldn't face it. All too ... normal, somehow. I just needed time off. I was demobbed in London and hung around there for a few months.'

'Doing?'

'Drinking mainly.' I hefted my glass and swilled its golden contents. 'Then I began pulling myself together. Started getting work as a reporter.'

'When did the nightmares start?'

'Oh, mid '45, I suppose. It figures, doesn't it?'

'Yes. Very typical. I'm seeing a lot of men like you, Douglas. They called it shell shock in the Great War. Now it's combat stress, or battle fatigue. But you know what I'm talking about?'

'I was fine during the battles, Doc.' I smiled again.

'That's how it works. We're only just appreciating how deep the trauma runs when a man is subjected to horror on a continual basis, such as war, or recurring acts of violence. Seems like you received more than your fair share.'

We met for a second time a week later and I told him about my recent experience of getting dragged into the hunt for the war criminals who'd used Scotland as a staging post to South America.

'And this January you ended up in Hamburg with Samantha. Back in uniform?'

'Ridiculous, wouldn't you say?'

'Asking a lot of a chap, I'd say. And the nightmares began again.'

'They never really stopped.'

'While the drinking got worse.'

'Never really stopped either, Andrew. But, yes, I suppose I was hitting the bottle a bit harder.'

'Is that when you . . .?'

'Cracked up? I'm not afraid of the term. I've seen it in some of my men. I was exhausted. We'd been in Hamburg for weeks. A city of rubble. An ice city. Minus thirty degrees. I was questioning the same swine about the same foul deeds. An endless loop. Into the bargain, I lost a good man. A soldier. Between the booze and the . . .'

'Trauma?'

'Is that what it was? I suppose so. But, yes, I fell apart for a bit. But I'm through that, Doc. As you can see.' I raised my glass in a toast.

He looked at me over the top of his specs. 'So it seems, Douglas. So it seems. Good for you. But I must warn you that even the toughest finds it hard to shake it off completely. It could take a while.'

'Months?'

'Years. They saw a lot of this after the last war. Some chaps never got it back together. Nothing to be ashamed of. It's like a leg wound that never quite heals.'

'That's comforting. Are you saying I could crack up again?'

'Let's say you should avoid situations that could trigger a relapse.'

'Makes sense. No more chasing war criminals. I'm all for the quiet life.'

He gave me one of his looks again. 'That's another thing. Douglas, you've been in action of one sort or another since you went to France in '39 with the British Expeditionary Force. That's nigh on eight years of fighting. And before that you had a tough job as a Glasgow policeman. It is astonishing what the mind can get used to. How many jolts it can take. It becomes natural to the point where the mind misses it when things are quiet. Begins to *need* it.' He paused. 'Do you get bored easily?'

'Wish I had the chance!'

'Watch out for it when you do. Let's keep in touch, Douglas.'

I promised I would, but in truth I was feeling more and more that I was back in control of my life. Sure, grief and anger still rose in me like bile when I walked across Glasgow Bridge into the Gorbals and passed the Great Synagogue. But as my loss moved to the background like a nagging toothache, I found myself sleeping better, and drinking and smoking less. I'd been given new responsibilities at the *Gazette* and even my relationship with Samantha Campbell seemed to have moved on to a surer footing. Sam was winning most of her cases at the bar, although it took her to Edinburgh every day and some nights. More, her chambers had hinted at some relaxation in their stance on married women taking silk. Perhaps I could make an honest woman of her before we were both too old for it to matter.

Capping it all, my erstwhile mentor and drinking pal Wullie McAllister had broken from his dwam, like Rip Van Winkle, and was now his former cantankerous self, albeit wheelchair-bound while his unused muscles – mental and physical – got working again. I heard that the ward sister in the Erskine convalescent home had come to his room wondering what all the noise was and found Wullie roaring and shouting and banging his bedpan. As though some Scottish Frankenstein had jolted a monster back into life. The day we got the phone call from Stewart, Sam and I leaped into her Riley and drove out to Erskine. We found him sitting up in bed behind a newspaper, fag in mouth, with a pile of discarded papers on the floor. After our squawking reunion had subsided he demanded to know everything that he'd missed.

'What was your last memory, Wullie?' I asked across his ash-stained blanket.

'Getting hit ower the heid by that bastard – sorry, hen – Charlie Maxwell. His goons grabbed me from behind and chloroformed me as I was coming oot the pub. See, if it had been a fair fight . . .'

'You'd have slaughtered them, Wullie. I know. Sam and I found you in the stables at his castle. They gave you a good hiding. Do you remember that?'

He screwed up his face. 'Bits. Those sods – the twa side-kicks of Slattery? They were there?'

I nodded. 'They got their come-uppance. I'll fill you in when you're out of here.'

He was like a child, his red eyes dancing with unslakeable curiosity.

'Aye, aye. You surely will. But Stewart was telling me you've been fighting Nazis again?' He turned to Sam. 'You as well, lassie?'

Sam nodded. Neither of us wanted to pick at this still raw wound. Sam gave him a crumb.

'I was asked to help prosecute some of the guards from Ravensbrück. In Hamburg.' She turned to me to carry on.

'And I was trying to catch a thief. Someone was burgling Jewish homes in Glasgow. Some of the loot they stole turned out to be Nazi gold, taken from the poor Jews just before they gassed them. I followed the trail to Hamburg with Sam. It led back here. *Ratlines.*'

He leaned forward and grabbed my hand with his claws.

'Did you get them? Did you get the bastards?'

'Some. It's a long story. And there was a price.' I held up my hand to say enough. 'Later. Don't want to send you back into a dwam, Wullie.'

I didn't admit that it was as much for my sake as his. I'd taken on board some of Andrew Baird's advice; I didn't want to stir up old nightmares. Wullie fell back on his pillows.

'Christ, Brodie, Ah leave you for five minutes and you kick off World War Three. Whit are we tae dae wi' you?'

'Give me a quiet life?'

He chewed his tobacco-streaked moustache and squinted at me.

'A quiet life? That's no' in your stars.'

TWO

A month later Wullie blundered into the newsroom of the *Gazette*, a tetchy Boadicea in his chariot, causing mischief and hilarity and wanting his old job back. As I was now occupying it, I was filled with a mixture of delight and bolshiness. Glad to see him back but not ready to give an inch. Eddie Paton – our editor in chief – had ducked the decision as usual and simply assigned me to broader duties as well as covering the crime circuit in tandem with Wullie. It suited me fine; I was happy to spread my wings and give rein to my opinions on politics and world news, though in the lightest possible way to avoid reader indigestion over the porridge.

Whatever was driving my good mood these days I wasn't going to question it. I'd vowed never again to take for granted a sunny day or a good night's sleep. On the wireless this morning I'd heard a new song by Sinatra and couldn't shake the dratted thing out of my head:

> *What a day this has been!*
> *What a rare mood I'm in!*
> *Why, it's almost like being in love.*
>
> *There's a smile on my face*
> *For the whole human race.*
> *Why, it's almost like being in love.*

It might have earned me funny looks from my fellow Glaswegians if I'd tried to serenade them first thing on a workday morning. So I stuck to just whistling the tune as I stalked down Mitchell Street and climbed the stairs to the newsroom.

I strolled to my corner desk across the office. The room was already filling up. The early secretaries were clashing and tinkling away at their typewriters and a few of my fellow journalists were sucking on first fags and mugs of tea, hoping for inspiration to arrive with the nicotine and the caffeine. The small and increasingly rotund figure of the editor was loitering with intent over one of the desks. Bum in the air, elbows on the desk and fag hanging from his lips, Eddie was hunched over the vacant desk of Jimmie Livingstone, the paper's football reporter. Eddie was picking away at the scraps of paper – Jimmie's handwritten notes of the weekend's results – seeing if there was any mileage left in any of the triumphs and disasters. Between them, Eddie and Jimmie could milk a full week of polemics out of an iffy offside decision at Parkhead. Eddie lifted his head and removed his fag.

'Morning, Brodie.'

'Good morning, Eddie. No sign of the wild man yet?'

'Your pal, McAllister? Wheesht, Brodie. To speak his name is to summon the de'il. Let's enjoy the quiet for as long as we can.'

'Can you no' just remind the man he's supposed to be retired?'

Eddie stubbed out his fag, drew himself erect to his full five feet two inches and pulled down his tartan waistcoat. I noted it was filling out nicely again. Soon he'd be back to his former stature and we could start calling him 'Big Eddie' again. At least in circumference.

'It's no' that easy, Brodie. McAllister took an awfu' hammering in the line o' duty, so to speak. We cannae just throw him on the scrap heap. And technically, of course, he didnae actually get round to retiring before his heid got bashed in.'

'Well, it all adds to the gaiety around here. Is he really knocking out a column or two? I mean, how does he get the stories? Has he commandeered his own tram?'

I knew his companion-cum-brother, Stewart, had a full-time job as a teacher and was nobody's Man Friday.

Eddie visibly shuddered. 'Taxis. He's got a deal with one o' the taxi boys. Costing us a bloody fortune, him whizzin' aboot like a dervish. Chasing crime, he says. But if you're worried about being edged oot of a job, Brodie, dinnae fash yersel'. Wullie is just part time for a while until he works oot his notice. Once we gie him it, of course. Besides, you've got this new column to play wi'.'

World affairs, was how Eddie had explained it. The bosses of the paper thought it was time to raise the profile and quality of the paper and expand the readership by tackling the big events in the world outside Glasgow. Outside Scotland even, if that wasn't too big a step. The *Gazette* had taken an ad hoc approach to it in the past; when something big happened, like dropping the first atom bomb or the Nuremberg trials, they'd run special columns. Now they thought there was enough incoming material from the wireless and ticker tape to merit a section on its own. Snippets, they said. A round-up of major news items from across the continents. I was their guinea pig. When I'd asked why me, Sandy Logan, our lanky sub-editor, chewed on his inner cheeks for a while and then explained:

'You're seen as somewhat more worldly, Brodie. If you take a glance over the last twelve months or so, I think you'll agree that you've been at the centre of some of the more *outré* events round here. Is that fair?'

'Do I detect a wee hint of accusation, Sandy?'

'Naw, naw. I wouldnae say that. Just that you seem to be singularly good at attracting exotic headlines. Usually violent.'

'You mean the hunt for Nazis in Glasgow?'

'There's that. Then there's the number of senior polis you've managed to get banged up for corruption. Not to mention the councillors that began dying like flies just as you began delving into their wicked ways.' Sandy shook his long head. 'You're not so much a reporter of news, Brodie. More the instigator.'

'And that's what the bosses want from me? For this new column? Someone to stir things up?'

'Good God, no. Just report, laddie. Just report. You've got a broader world view than some. And then there's your degree. Other than the fair Elspeth you're the only man on the staff wi' one. The bosses like a man of letters. As for your writing ...' He paused, took a pull on his fag. '... I've seen worse.'

'I've had more ringing endorsements for my talents, Sandy. But it sounds interesting; it should be fun.'

'Fun? You've got the wrong idea, Brodie. This is a serious column. But of course not *too* serious. And absolutely nae Latin. We don't want to lose our old readership. Think of it as an everyman guide to foreign parts and foreign doings.'

'No big words.'

'You know fine that good journalism is about simplicity. Just tell the story. Like that fella you rate, Hemingway. Though I'd encourage the odd adjective or two to gie your piece some colour.'

'And what about the crime stories? Are you taking me off those?'

'Not a bit. The management want to give Wullie a few months to see out his time properly. Besides,' he sighed, 'there's enough crime oot there to warrant the attention of the pair of you for a while.'

I made my way to my desk where I was working up stories that neatly covered both camps. On the larger scene, I was trying to find something exciting to say about America's Marshall Plan. In terms of newsworthiness, the timing could hardly be bettered. The plan was coming into being on this very day, 5 June 1947. But high finance and international economics had little relevance to the average *Gazette* reader struggling to muster enough ration coupons to feed her family on powdered milk and Spam.

The details had still to be hammered out with participating nations like Britain, France and Germany but essentially it was an aid programme for the reconstruction of Europe. The idea was George Marshall's, the US Secretary of State. One of their better generals – and a visionary. It wasn't altruism. America recognised that her own prosperity and democracy would only thrive if the other Western nations did. Moreover, America wanted a solid bulwark against Communist expansionist plans across Europe. They were even offering aid to the Soviets, but Stalin didn't want to be in anyone's pocket. Not if it curtailed his plans to fulfil Churchill's prophecy of installing an iron curtain across the Continent 'from Stettin in the Baltic to Trieste in the Adriatic . . .' The endless machinations, double-dealing, back-stabbing and power grabs by the Communists made Glasgow councillors seem like models of fair-mindedness and graciousness.

More parochially, I had a column half written about the resurgence of gang warfare in Glasgow; the walking wounded were still trickling into the Royal after the Old Firm match on Saturday. But there was nothing new in that. I needed something fresh.

At lunchtime, I took my paste sandwiches to my favourite bench in George Square to enjoy the sunshine and admire the girls in their summer frocks. It lightened an old man's heart. But as I sat there, trying hard not to gawp too much, I was treated to one of my favourite acts from Glasgow's repertoire of street theatre. It was a one-man show with unwitting audience participation. I only knew this strolling player by his nickname, Sticky.

Sticky didn't get his name from the adhesive quality of his manky donkey jacket and greasy bunnet. Brutally and inevitably, as per the mores of the streets, he was named for his most prominent feature: the loss of both legs above the knee in the Great War. A medal for courage under fire was scarcely fair exchange, but Sticky wore it proudly on his threadbare breast pocket. His chosen method of propulsion was a pair of sticks: cut-down brooms that kept the stubs of his thighs just a couple of inches above the pavement at the apogee of his swing and allowed their leather pads to take his weight as he rocked forward on to them. A human crankshaft.

Sticky's physical loss had made no dent in his humour or his enterprise. He made a living from his own form of green-grocering. He'd pester stallholders in the Barras until they filled his knapsack with their over-ripe, about-to-be-jettisoned produce and then Sticky would click and stump his way to wherever punters gathered. Today it was George Square at lunchtime.

I heard him clacking towards me. He rocked past, pistoning away, and chose a sheltered spot by the Scott column. He settled down and produced an old rag from his inside pocket. He spread it carefully in front of him. Then he dug into his knapsack and laid out his wares on the suspect cloth, and waited. His eyes flicked across the passers-by until he spotted his prey. He went still. A middle-aged woman was hirpling towards him, carrying a string bag filled with her messages. Not too filled, Sticky would be hoping.

'Hie, missus,' he called out. 'Has yer man still got his ain teeth?'

The wee woman froze in her gait, alarmed by this seer's insight. Sticky knew his clients, knew their afflictions.

'Naw, he husnae a wan.'

Sticky nodded in sympathy, carefully surveyed his cornucopia, and selected two squidgy handfuls.

'Then, hen, these pears are for him.'

His performance deserved applause but I knew Sticky would appreciate a more tangible tribute. I walked over to him.

'Any apples left?'

He squinted up at me. 'I've been keeping one back. Just for you.' He grinned and held out a mottled Granny Smith. I took it and gave him a florin. He began sifting through his small pile of coppers.

'Naw, that's fine.' I smiled at him. He flung up a smart salute. I reciprocated, then left him to ply his trade.

THREE

My good humour lasted until I left the office at six, contributions to both world and local crime news fulfilled. Wullie hadn't come in but I expected to find him in his new favourite perch in the Horseshoe Bar just round the corner. It was opening time and Wullie had nearly nine months to make up. I stepped into Mitchell Street. It was a dry bright evening and I thought briefly about skipping the pub and strolling home early with the chance of phoning Sam in her Edinburgh digs.

She was summing up for the jury today and hoped to persuade them that her client was a lost soul, led astray by his poor choice of friends rather than the dyed-in-the-wool villain suggested by the Procurator Fiscal. It was an uphill job given that the well-known defendant had only been out of prison for three months and that his face had been plastered over the papers three years ago for the armed robbery of the very same post office. It confirmed my experience as a reporter and former copper that Glasgow criminals were creatures of habit and stilted imagination.

As I turned to head up to Gordon Street I saw a man walking purposefully straight towards me. He wore a smart suit and carried a cap. His face was set and serious. As though he'd been waiting for me. We stopped and stared at each other some two yards apart. I waited, ready to throw a salute or a punch.

'Mr Brodie?'

'Yes?'

He looked nervous, shifty. My brain ran through a selection of possibilities; something had happened to Sam? An upset reader with an axe to grind? More likely a messenger from Percy Sillitoe, head of MI5. I still carried the King's commission as a reserve officer. I'd been warned that it could be activated at any time. My stomach flipped. Whatever it was, it looked like bad news.

'Sir, would you kindly step this way? Lady Gibson would be grateful for a moment of your time.'

Lady Gibson? That rang a bell. He nodded up the street towards a big Humber Pullman. There was a figure in the back seat but I couldn't make it out.

'What about?'

'Lady Gibson will explain, sir.' He kept glancing away, wrestling with his cap. I now saw it had a peaked brim: a chauffeur's cap. He took a pace back, turned and expected me to follow. Like a peewit trying to lure a fox away from its nest. Why not? What did I have to fear from a smart car and a title? My reporter's antennae were twitching. I followed him to the car. Its chrome glittered and its spotless grey flanks reflected our approach. He got there first and held open the rear door. I peeked in.

A stylish woman crouched in the far corner wearing a hat with the veil pulled down. All I could see was a pair of perfect red curves of lipstick and a smooth jawline. A scarf hid her neck. Her smart grey frock stopped just above nylon-clad knees – nice knees. She held a handkerchief in her hands. It was twisted and knotted. The woman spoke. Her voice was strained and breathy as though she'd only just stopped crying.

'Mr Brodie? I need your help. Badly. We don't have much time. Would you please join me?'

She lifted her veil and dabbed her cheeks. Her dark eyes were red and the mascara lightly smudged. But it scarcely detracted from her looks. Waves of dark hair fell from her hat and framed strong features. A woman in her late forties, I'd say, more handsome than lovely, more interesting than pretty. Just past her peak.

She patted the seat beside her. Next she'd be offering me an apple: *Bite this, try me*. I looked around. If this was a trap I was a sucker for the bait; I liked an older woman's poise and hint of a dangerous past. And if my life were at risk rather than my reputation they'd do it from a van not a chauffeur-driven Humber. I ducked down and slid on to the capacious slab of leather. I sank into the soft coolness and heard the door close behind me with a nice expensive clunk. The subtle waft of her perfume breached the remainder of my meagre defences.

'Lady Gibson, I presume?'

'Yes. Sheila Gibson. My husband . . . My husband—' Her breath caught in her throat and choked off her answer. She dabbed her eyes and tried to regain her composure. I heard the driver's door close and the next thing we were in motion.

'Hie, you! Driver! Stop!'

I leaned over and grabbed his shoulder. The car began to slow down and then stopped. Her light fingers touched my arm. Light sparked off the diamond ring next to the gold band.

'Mr Brodie. Please.' She'd found her voice again. 'I want to explain. But I need you to come with me. To my home.'

Her grip tightened. Small but powerful hands. I thought for a second. It was a very elaborate way for a married woman to pick up a man. And looking at her tortured eyes, I doubted she was after my body.

'Just tell me what this is about. Then maybe I'll go with you.'

She took a deep breath, gathered herself. 'My husband is Fraser Gibson. Sir Fraser.'

'Scottish Linen Bank?' I asked, now understanding the Humber Pullman.

She nodded. 'Fraser is the Chairman and Managing Director.'

I knew that; I banked with them in their head office in St Vincent Street.

'What about him?'

Her face contorted again. 'He's been kidnapped.'

I sank back in the leather. Why was she telling me this? What did she want from me? Among the many fragrant notes of her perfume I smelt trouble. And it stirred interest in me. An alcoholic sniffing a single malt. But, hell, this was a scoop. Eat your heart out, Wullie McAllister.

'All right. Let's go, driver.'

I could see his eyes in his mirror. A small smile lifted the corner of his mouth. He nodded at me and pressed the accelerator. The Pullman's big nose rose up and we sailed off. As we drove, Lady Gibson began to let it pour out.

'Fraser comes home for lunch every day.'

Lunch? *Dinner*, where I come from.

'He came home as usual today. About half past twelve. We'd just sat down when the doorbell went. Janice took it.'

'Janice?'

'Our maid.'

'And the *we* . . .?'

'Just Fraser and me. We'd had a glass of sherry in the lounge and had come though to the dining room.'

How nice. How different from my own house and how its master – my father – came and went. Depending on which shift he was working, Dad would set off with his battered piece-box, a treasured tin that once held Rothesay Rock, my parents' only souvenir from a three-day honeymoon. Apart from me. He'd come home ten hours later, blackened by coal dust and ready for his grub, be it tea or breakfast. But first the tin bath would be hauled out and kettles boiled until there was enough water to sit in and sluice off the grime. I'd help carry out the filthy water and pour it away while Dad got towelled and clothed in his faded collarless shirt and trousers. He'd sit by the fire, legs roasting, with a huge mug of tea in hand, fag in the other, hair wet and flattened as though with Brylcreem, while Mum magicked food over the range.

The picture her ladyship had flashed up was a Hollywood set: gleaming cutlery and glasses on a white damask table-cloth; exquisite small glasses drained of their sherry, the crystal decanter standing on the sideboard in case either fancied a second libation *pour aider la dégustation*. Sir Fraser in his starched collar and tails as befitted a senior banker. Or perhaps he slipped into a velvet smoking jacket until the car picked him back up again for another hard afternoon counting his money? Lady Gibson, freshly made up and perfumed, would be directing kitchen operations from a distance to avoid sullying her soft hands or scraping her perfect nails. A smiling servant would deliver steaming bowls of vegetables and plates of finely cut meats.

Were they happier than Agnes and Matthew Brodie in their kitchenette with the bed-in-the-wa'? Impossible.

'Who was at the door?' I asked.

She clasped her hand to her mouth. 'Them. Two of them. Janice opened it and they burst in. We heard this shriek. Fraser was on his feet in a flash. He grabbed the carving knife but before he even reached the door they'd barged into the dining room. Masked, you know, with balaclavas. And in overalls.'

'Were they armed?'

She nodded. 'Both of them. They'd dragged Janice along and pushed her in first. They made her sit down at the table. I thought they were going to rob us. They waved guns at us and told us not to move. Then the men pointed to Fraser and told him to drop the knife. They would kill him if he didn't. For a moment he looked like he would have a go at them. He's like that. He's not afraid of anyone or anything. But he could see that Janice or I could get hurt. A stray bullet or something.'

'So, your husband dropped the knife. Did they take him then? Did they say anything?'

She nodded. 'They shouted at Janice and me to shut up and stay seated. Then they grabbed Fraser, put a gun against his head and marched him out of the door. The one that was doing the talking turned to me as they went out. He said' – I saw her searching her memory – '*Don't, whatever you do, phone the police. This is a kidnap. It's about money. It's only money. Just do as you're told and your husband won't be harmed.*'

'What exactly were you told?'

'To wait for a phone call. This evening at seven. With instructions. And not to phone the police. Or else.'

'Else what?' Though I knew the answer.

Her face crumpled. 'They'd kill him. They said they'd kill him.' She dissolved in tears.

I waited till she got a grip. 'So did you? Did you call the police?'

She shook her head vigorously. 'Of course not! Why would I risk my husband?'

'Because that's what every kidnapper says. You need the police. This is what they're trained for.' I said it, but I didn't believe it. Not the amateur blunderers that comprised Glasgow's finest.

'I couldn't risk it.'

'Do you want this in the *Gazette*? Is that why I'm here?'

'No! For God's sake, no!'

'Then why did you pick *me* up?'

'You're . . .' She struggled for words. 'I've read about you. You know these sorts of people.'

Right. She meant they were *my* sort of people. What a reputation to have. My pain must have registered.

'I don't mean that in a bad way. It's just you're used to dealing with them. You're a have-a-go hero, Mr Brodie.'

Have-a-go Brodie was how my old army boss had described me after I'd taken out the Panzer unit that had kept my platoon bogged down for days outside Caen. There was nothing heroic about it. I'd just got fed up and angry. A moment of madness that led to a medal. This character flaw had been much in evidence this past year in one scrape after another. But it was wrong to confuse heroism with pig-headedness and impetuosity.

'Hardly, Lady Gibson. But what do you want me to do if I can't write the story?'

'I want you with me at seven, when I take the call. I need you to help me decide what to do.'

FOUR

Lady Gibson levelled her dark eyes at me, and I saw the steel behind the fear. Whatever happened, this woman would get through this. There might be more tears shed, but she'd pull herself together. It was one of the redeeming features of the upper classes. I glanced at my watch. We had half an hour. I was filled with misgivings about being dragged into a new mess. So much could go wrong with kidnappings. They rarely ended happily or without someone getting hurt. But I suppose I could at least hold this poor lady's hand this evening. More selfishly, what was wrong with having a dash of spice in your soup? A kidnapping would certainly be more interesting to write – and read – about than international finance or vote-rigging in Budapest.

'All right, Lady Gibson. I'll sit with you while you take the call. Then we'll see.'

I was already clear in my own mind that my advice would be to call the police. Sooner or later, they had to be involved. Regardless of their incompetence or the outcome. This was their business.

'Thank you, Mr Brodie. Thank you.' She again reached out and touched my arm. I wished I'd rolled my sleeves up.

All this time we'd been heading south, over the Clyde and then out on to the Kilmarnock Road. Soon we were in the Glasgow suburbs of Whitecraigs, the natural habitat of

25

wealthy bankers and their ilk. Wide tree-lined streets. Proud bungalows and massive red sandstone Victoriana with deep driveways. We pulled through the gates of a detached version of the latter and I admired the lions *couchants* perched on each. A variation on the wally dugs either side of our tenement fireplace.

We stopped with a crunch of gravel in front of a solid wood door framed by stone pillars. The door wouldn't have looked out of place behind a moat. I got out and looked up at the house. Mansion might be a better word. I followed Lady Gibson inside. The hall was spacious and wood-panelled. Faux-baronial. But when does *faux* become *fait*?

An expensive central carpet cushioned our feet from the privations of the polished parquet floor. Soft lighting studded the panelled walls and illumined seascapes and mournful glens. At the far end of the hall one portrait stood out. In pride of place, and inspecting visitors as they arrived, was a glowing oil of a slim young woman with the eyes and lips of Lady Gibson. She sat at regal ease in a velvet gown holding a single red rose across her lap. Her proud eyes quizzed the visitor, asking why riffraff like me had been allowed in her exquisite home. I bit my tongue just before I asked Lady Gibson if this was her daughter. I followed her into a lounge off the hall. A maid scurried after us collecting the gloves, hatpin and hat of her mistress as they were shed.

'Excuse me? Are you Janice?' I asked.

The girl bobbed. 'Yes, sir.'

'Are you all right?' Her face was white and strained. 'It must have been terrifying today?'

Janice looked to her mistress for direction. Lady Gibson nodded.

'Aye, it was. But Ah'm fine, sir. Ah'm OK now.'

When Janice left us, Lady Gibson walked straight over to a tray of crystal glasses and decanters.

'Is Glenlivet all right, Mr Brodie? Pre-war, J. G. Smith.'

'It works for me.'

It certainly did. The distillery had been mothballed during the war but I heard they were pumping the golden stuff out again. She splashed generous measures into two glasses and lifted a syphon with an enquiring eye.

'Just a dash of water please,' I said.

She fizzed a stream of soda into her glass, and handed me my whisky and a small jug of water. I inhaled deeply. Bliss. But it could be a difficult evening and I needed my head clear enough to tender sensible advice. I diluted to half and half. Lady Gibson took a deep swig of hers. It seemed to settle her.

'I shall be back in a moment.'

She was back in two moments, her mane of dark auburn hair brushed and gleaming like the pelt of a cosseted cat. Now the hat and veil had gone I could admire the expertise which had brought it within a hue or two of the portrait in the hall. The smudges had been removed from under her eyes and the mascara subtly retouched. Her lips glistened redder as though she'd just licked them. Her figure was fuller than the one captured in oils but none the worse for that. Lady Gibson might have eased past her best years, but would still turn heads.

She strolled to the table, picked up a cigarette box and opened it for me. I took one of the oval beauties. Passing Cloud. An expensive habit. My first sight of them had been at a regimental ball in the officers' mess of the Seaforths. I'd thought our supply officer was offloading flattened fags until he'd put me right.

We both lit up and raised glasses to each other. No cheers. This wasn't a cheery moment. I sipped. She paced and swallowed the remainder of hers. I looked round. She saw me searching.

'The phone's over there.' She pointed to a small table by the wall.

I took in the rest of the room. Soft lighting, sumptuous

furnishing. Like Sam's could be if she could be bothered. I checked my watch. Quarter to seven. She was going to pace for fifteen more minutes.

'While we're waiting, Lady Gibson, can you show me how the masked men came and went?'

'Follow me.' She strode to the door and walked into the hall. 'Janice heard the bell and went to the front door. Then she was dragged in and down to the dining room, along here.'

She walked down the hall and turned into a room on the right. We walked in and my conjecture came true. A picture-perfect dining room at whose heart was a rosewood table and six matching chairs. The mirror-polished surface held a centrepiece of flowers surrounded by four willow-pattern plates. The walls were papered a warm shade of red. A sideboard in the same opulent wood held a cutlery tray and table mats. A door led off, presumably to the kitchen.

'Sir Fraser and I were sitting at the table when they rang the bell.'

'Did they come straight in from the front door?'

'What do you mean?'

'How did they know where you were? It's a big house.'

'I told you. They grabbed Janice.'

'You said she shrieked. And that got Fraser to his feet. With the carving knife.'

She nodded. 'That's right. But after that I'm sure I heard voices. A man's. They made Janice bring them here.'

I took one long lingering look round the room; then we went back to the lounge to wait. She poured herself another hefty drink. I declined and we sat and listened to the clock on the mantelpiece beat out the passing of time in a steady toc, toc, toc. We'd been expecting it but we both still jumped when the phone rang on the dot of seven.

FIVE

'**P**unctual anyway,' I said.

Lady Gibson gave a weak smile. She walked to the phone and picked it up.

'Whitecraigs 2139.'

I heard the buzz of a distant, male voice.

'Yes, this is Lady Gibson. Who is this?'

The buzz sounded again. Sheila was shaking her head.

'But is my husband safe? I need to know.' Her voice edged higher.

Buzz.

'*How* much? We don't have that much. Nothing like it.'

Buzz.

'It's impossible! I need more time. No, of course I haven't called the police.'

Buzz.

'All right. I'll do what I can. But, really, it's . . .'

No buzz.

Sheila hung up the phone and turned to me. She lifted her glass and drained it in one toss of her head.

'Noon tomorrow.'

'What?'

'We have until noon tomorrow to find twenty thousand pounds.'

I whistled. 'Or?'

Her hand went to her mouth and her body spasmed. Her eyes filled with terror.

'Or they'll kill him. Like Salome did to John the Baptist. I don't – I don't know what—' Then realisation hit her as to what they'd do if the money wasn't forthcoming. She collapsed on the couch and her body convulsed in great heaving waves.

As usual I was at a loss in front of a crying woman. Should I go over and pat her and go *there, there*? Pour her another drink? Give her my hankie? Tell her to pull herself together? But soon enough the grief stopped. She pulled herself upright and took deep breaths. Then she got up and walked out. She was back in a few minutes. Her face was red but the tears had gone. She'd washed and towelled her face. She walked over to the drinks tray and replenished her glass. She sat down facing me.

'What now, Mr Brodie?'

'Tell me exactly what they said.'

She took a gulp. 'They want twenty thousand pounds by noon tomorrow or he's dead. Tell the police and he's dead. Instructions to follow.'

'How? I mean how will you get further instructions?'

'Phone. Tomorrow morning at ten. They'll call with instructions and then we have to take the money to . . . somewhere. Wherever they say.'

She kept saying *we*. Maybe all titled folk used the royal plural.

'Lady Gibson? You make it sound like you're thinking of paying them. You mustn't. Kidnappers never know when to stop being greedy. Give them anything and they'll ask for more.'

She turned her dark eyes on me with fury.

'Then what should I do? Just let him die?'

'I think you should get the police.'

She shot to her feet. 'No! No! Never! Not while there's a chance.'

'But it's impossible. How can you get your hands on that amount by tomorrow?'

She waved her hand, as though her knight's ransom was loose change.

'Not easy. But not impossible.'

I looked at her standing there nursing her glass. Poise returned. Ramrod back. Tough lady in a crisis. A dark-haired sister of Samantha Campbell.

'Then pay the ransom and hope for the best. But, Lady Gibson? One thing. How do you know he's still alive?'

She stared at me as though I'd made a clumsy pass at her.

'I'd *know*,' she said simply.

I got to my feet and placed my glass down on the coffee table.

'I wish you luck, then.'

I started to head for the door, hoping she'd get her man to give me a lift back to town. I didn't fancy the walk and knew nothing about the buses this far out.

'Mr Brodie? I know you think I'm mad. But it's all I can do.'

I looked at her. I nodded.

She went on: 'Will you do it?'

'What?' Though I knew what was coming next. Knew my search for a story had just taken a wrong turn.

'Will you hand over the money for me?'

'I'm sure your man – your chauffeur – can drop it off. He just has to follow instructions.'

She'd lost her air of confidence. Back to looking vulnerable. She shook her head.

'I don't want anything to go wrong. You're more used to . . . this sort of thing. Please. I'll pay you.'

It's not flattering to be told that you're a shady character and that you can be hired to do dirty work. Was that who I'd become? High time I dropped the crime column and concentrated on becoming a world affairs man.

'Look, I offered you my advice. I think you should get the police involved, but if not, call me in the morning after you've heard from them. First, ask the kidnappers for proof your husband is alive. Tell them you must speak to him before you'll do anything. If you hear from him and it sounds straightforward then your man could make the drop. *You* could. If it sounds tricky, then . . . we'll see. OK?'

She looked hard at me for a moment then nodded.

'I'll get Cammie to give you a lift. Where will I get you in the morning?'

'At my desk. Phone the newsroom.'

Cammie, the chauffeur, took me home in silence. He dropped me right at Sam's front door. The first thing I did was call her hotel, but she was out. I left a message asking her to phone me. I wanted some advice of my own. I went to bed and she still hadn't called. But what would she have said if I'd asked her? Don't get involved? That wasn't how Sam worked. She knew it would be my call.

I set off the next morning all set to rebuff Lady Gibson. This wasn't my problem. I'd prepare the story and watch it unfold from a safe distance. Then I'd write the unhappy ending. Kidnaps are always unhappy: you either lost money or a loved one; often both.

SIX

Wullie was already at his desk and bashing away at the keys like a demented xylophone player. It was good to see the familiar roll-up stuck in the corner of his cynical mouth. The smoke curled up through his narrow moustache leaving a yellow streak and making him close one eye as though he was winking. I could see he was in mid-flow and we just nodded at each other as I went to my desk. Shortly after, he scudded across to see me in his battlewagon. I kept expecting to see flailing blades poking out from the wheel hubs. But his attacks were usually verbal.

'Whit you up to, Brodie? Anything juicy?'

I'd already made a shorthand note of the kidnap to date and was working on a new world affairs column. I pulled off the foolscaps and carbon and handed them over. Wullie's eyes tore down the page, his head nodding as he read. Viscount Louis Mountbatten had just announced the intended partition of India and the creation of the two independent states of India and Pakistan. It meant the loss of the shiniest jewel in our imperial crown. Violence was already erupting as the citizens of these nascent states took sides. I'd given it a local spin by suggesting it might put up the price of Lipton's. That would trigger storms in the nation's teacups.

'The world's gawin' to hell in a hand basket, is it no',' he said.

'Ever since Kilmarnock got relegated this season.'

'They'll be back up. If only fitba' solved everything, eh. Anything criminal going on?'

I paused. I almost mentioned the kidnap. It would be good to get his advice. But who knew what the old rogue would do with it? There would be a column on Eddie's desk with Wullie's name on it before the morning was out.

'Nothing much. I've got one lead but it's probably going nowhere. You know what it's like.'

We nattered a bit longer and then Wullie trundled off, claiming he'd got the nod about some shenanigans at the Barras. A gang was trying to impose a protection racket on stallholders and meeting bloody resistance from the independent-minded entrepreneurs of the East End.

At quarter past ten I got a signal from Elaine, one of the secretaries. She was waving a phone at me. I walked over and took the call, wondering if it was excitement or dread that was flipping my stomach over.

'Brodie, it's Sheila Gibson.' Her voice was slurred and higher. I wondered when she'd started this morning.

'What's happening?' I didn't use her name, far less her title. I would keep the lid on a bit longer around the newsroom.

'They called me.'

'Did you speak to your husband?'

'Yes. He's OK. Alive anyway.' Her voice choked.

'What do they want you to do?'

I heard her take a deep breath.

'Take the money to a phone box in Govan at twelve o'clock.'

'You have it?' I was incredulous. 'All of it?'

'Yes. Our bank brought the cash out first thing this morning. It's all here.'

Wish my bank manager was so accommodating. But then why would he personally deliver my pittance to me?

'Tell me exactly what's to happen.'

Her voice broke. 'Brodie! I need your help. It's all too much.

34

I can feel it's all going to go wrong. Please, please help. I'll give you fifty pounds if you'll deliver the money. Cammie could come round to your office right away.'

I thought for a long moment. My life was back on an even keel now. I wanted to keep on enjoying sunny days and restful nights. I wanted to prove Andrew Baird wrong that excitement had become an addiction. On the other hand, being entirely practical, fifty quid has a certain persuasive quality too. For just being a postman.

'Get Cammie to set out now. Come to my office, where he parked yesterday. I need him to run me back to my house for something. Send him now. We need to leave plenty of time for the drop.'

'Oh, thank you, thank you!'

For giving away £20,000? Maybe I should have asked for a percentage. Scott Fitzgerald was right: the rich are different.

I gave him twenty minutes, enough time to wonder if I was being stupid. These events rarely went to plan. And I wasn't doing the planning. Even if it did, and I had a front-page story, I'd get hell from my pal Inspector Duncan Todd for assisting in the payment of ransom. It would only encourage the kidnappers. I had some sympathy with that.

When I emerged I heard a short beep. The Pullman was waiting at the road end. I walked to the car and waved to Cammie to stay seated. I could manage the door. I slid on to the wide leather bench in the back and we set off. There was a bulging briefcase on the seat. I sought Cammie's gaze in his rear mirror.

'Do you know what this is, Cammie?'

His eyes flicked between mine and the road ahead.

'Yes, sir. The money.'

I nodded and hefted the case on to my lap. The straps were on their furthest setting. Twenty grand has substance to it. I opened the case up and pulled out a slim brick made up of twenty-pound notes bound by a rubber band. I counted twenty notes. Four hundred pounds. A year's salary. The brief-case was packed with another forty nine. I'd never seen a twenty before and now I had a thousand of them. Blank on one side and on the other the arms of the Scottish Linen Bank and a promise by the chief cashier to pay the bearer twenty pounds sterling on demand. Cammie wasn't my type or I'd have suggested we elope.

I picked out each bundle and flicked through it, making sure Sheila wasn't short-changing the kidnappers. It was the sort of stupid thing that could get folk killed. Get *me* killed. I stuffed the money-bricks back into the case and tightened the straps. Unless the notes themselves were forgeries, the full amount was there.

Cammie drove me to Park Terrace. He parked and waited while I went into Sam's. I went upstairs to my room and pulled out the bottom drawer of my dressing table. I rummaged among my socks until I felt the Sam Browne belt and the heavy leather case. I pulled out my service holster and revolver: an Enfield No. 2 Mk 1. I slid the gun out and filled the cylinder with six .38 cartridges. For good measure I stuffed a further half-dozen shells in my pocket. The Enfield didn't have the stopping power of the old Webley that had belonged to Sam's father but it was lighter to carry and just as effective at close range. I couldn't imagine having any sort of Western-style shoot-out. I tried the gun in my inside jacket pocket but it wasn't deep enough and bulged too much. I tucked it into the rear waistband of my trousers and went back out to the car.

'You know the address, Cammie?'

'Yes, sir. Over in Govan.'

'Let's go.'

We rolled down North Street, picked up Argyle and then over the George V Bridge. The big Humber seemed to float on its well-sprung chassis. We turned west along the Paisley Road and into the sprawling tenements and industries of Govan. No matter which way we turned the backdrop always seemed cluttered with swivelling cranes dipping in and out of the shipyards and graving docks. The residential streets contained more than their fair share of pubs. Thirsty work, shipbuilding. We followed the tramlines down the Govan Road itself then cut into Hamilton Street, lined by blackened tenements. There was a grubbiness about the buildings, and a tiredness about the few people negotiating the cracked pavements, as though everything and everyone was just too weary to care. Entropy writ small. One gaping hole through a run of tenements still showed the legacy of Goering's raids six years ago. The council would get round to it eventually.

'It's quiet, Cammie.'

'It's Govan Fair, sir. First Friday in June. Been going on for ever, so it has.'

'Of course. I'd forgotten. A big parade?'

'Aye, doon at Elder Park. A motorcade wi' the Fair Queen. They're going past the new Vogue cinema, I hear. They're even doin' a film o' the parade.'

'That should be worth seeing. Can we avoid the traffic?'

'Depends where we're going. This is Hamilton Street, where we were telt to go. There's the phone.'

He pointed through the windscreen. About a hundred yards down the deserted street was the red outline of the solitary phone box. I could see it was empty.

'Stop here, Cammie. We're ten minutes early.'

He pulled up by the kerb and I stared at the box and all around it. No sign of anyone lurking in a close ready to rush out and nab the cash. No parked car with Sir Fraser Gibson tied and gagged in the back seat. Only a few kids playing peevers on the pavement, one wearing callipers on his wee bent legs. Too young for the parade or not interested?

'Stay here, Cammie.'

I got out of the Humber and tucked the revolver more securely into my waistband. I reached in and dragged out the briefcase. I closed the door and began walking towards the phone box. As I neared it I checked the time. A couple of minutes to go. I assumed there would be a phone call with instructions. I stood outside the box and waited. It was noon. Still no sign of either kidnappers or kidnapped.

'Mister? Mister?'

I turned round. A small boy had broken off his game with his pals and now stood looking up at me. His face was dirty, his grey shirt and short trousers holed and stitched, his feet bare.

'Look, I'm busy, pal. I've got no sweets and I'm waiting for a phone call.'

'Naw, mister. This is fur you.' He held out his grubby paw. It contained a crumpled bit of paper. I reached down and took it. The boy scarpered before I could ask him who gave him it. I looked up and round. Still nobody. And all the kids had vanished. I put the briefcase down between my feet and flattened out the paper. In childlike capital letters it read:

KELVINHAUGH FERRY. NORTH SIDE.

BE AT THE PAY BOOTH AT 12.30. COME ALONE.

WE ARE WATCHING. NO POLICE!!!!

SEVEN

I looked up again. There were a hundred windows looking down on me. A score of entries either side of the road. The kidnappers could duck down a close, through the back greens and be on their way in seconds. To our next rendezvous. Clever move too. It would put me on the far side of the Clyde and would lessen the chance of anyone following me. I checked my watch. I had twenty-five minutes to get to the ferry and across the river. I knew the little passenger boats ran all the time but it was cutting it fine. I signalled to Cammie. The Humber sailed towards me and drew up. I jumped in.

'It's a game. A treasure hunt. They're being careful. I have a new address. Can you drop me as close as you can to the Kelvinhaugh Ferry without ending up stuck in the Govan Fair?'

'Sure. We're heading away from the parade. Hold on.'

He put the foot down and the big car surged. We drove up on to Langlands Road and then right on to the Govan Road heading back to the city. After a couple of hundred yards we forked left on to Main Street. It must have earned its name a long time ago. It was a poor offshoot cousin of the Govan Road and was lined by more cranes, pubs and timber yards than tenements. We pulled up facing the huge graving docks that fed Prince's Dock.

'Up there, sir. Just at the end.'

'Head back to Lady Gibson. With the parade it'll be easier for me on foot. Tell her where you left me. This is going to be a long day.'

I got out with the briefcase and walked along Highland Lane. Directly ahead the Clyde glistened dull grey. I passed two dry docks on my right. Two small liners sat high and dry having their bottoms cleaned and painted. I came to the river. The far bank seemed closer than any other part of the Clyde running through the city. Perhaps it was the solid mass of the Yorkhill Quays lining the north bank; they seemed to squeeze the river at this point and make it look like a canal.

The ferry was just bobbing towards us. A tiny ungainly boat with awnings across the mid-section. Two other folk were waiting to cross. We hopped on. The ferry backed out and then headed towards the wharf that jutted out from the Queen's Docks to the right of the Yorkhill Quays. From mid-river, as I swung my gaze round, I had a sudden wide perspective on the scale of industry prompted and supported by the Clyde. The smokestacks and funnels of a host of ships jutted up from every wet and dry dock. Cranes swung back and forth like gossiping dinosaurs. The clamour of steel on steel resonated from the Freshfields yard and triggered echoes from the sawmills and foundries up and down the bustling river. Glasgow was well back on its feet.

We were quickly on the north bank and I was climbing the broad stairs up to ground level. I had a spare five minutes before my deadline at the ticket booth. I tucked the case under my arm and lit a cigarette. There was just me and the ticket man. The two other passengers were already well on their way up Sandyford Street heading to Kelvinhaugh.

'Are ye waiting for somebody?' asked the ticket man.

'I was supposed to meet a fella here.'

He just nodded. 'Would that be him?' He pointed up the road. A cyclist was swooping towards us. A kid. He came straight at us and skidded to a stop next to me. He was in a sweat.

'Gibson?' he asked.

'Well – yes – I suppose . . .'

'Here.' He thrust his hand in his pocket and pulled out a folded paper. He stuck it in my hand, grabbed his handlebars and hauled his front wheel about. He was off.

'Hie! Hie, you!' But he was gone, pedalling like a mad thing. I opened up the paper.

GOVAN FERRY. SOUTH SIDE.

PAY BOOTH. WATER ROW. 1.30. ALONE!!!

Bastards! I was really being given the run-around.

'Bad news?' asked the ticket man.

'More annoying than bad. How do I get to the Govan Ferry? Fast as possible.'

He looked at me as though I were daft.

'Which wan?'

'There's more than one Govan Ferry?'

'Oh aye. There's the big yin, the vehicular ferry, and then further along there's the wee yin, just for passengers.'

'It says Water Row.'

'That's the big yin. Ye can see it frae here.' He pointed west along the river.

'Is it quicker to take your ferry back over or walk up to the Govan Ferry and cross?'

The ticket man sucked on his teeth as though I was asking him whether it was quicker to get to Australia round the Cape or via Tierra del Fuego.

'It depends on the timetable. As it happens ye've just missed the wan going back frae here. So it micht be a wee bit quicker to tak' the Govan Ferry.'

'How do I get there?'

41

'Ye go up here to Pointhouse Road, bear left and keep walking till ye come to Ferry Road jist afore the Kelvin. Cannae miss it. Go doon Ferry Road and there ye are.'

'Thanks.' I started off, cursing the Gibsons, the kidnappers, and myself for being stupid enough to get involved in this rigmarole. I toyed briefly with the idea of continuing to walk north. I'd soon be in Kelvingrove Park and home for tea. But what would I do with a bag full of money and a pricking conscience?

It was a long hot plod along the rear of the Yorkhill Quays past a seemingly endless line of goods sheds. I was hot and testy by the time I trudged down the slipway of the Govan car ferry. At least foot passengers didn't have to pay and I was wafted over the river to Water Row by quarter past one. I'd gone round in a circle and crossed the Clyde twice – three times if you counted the first traverse by car. I was now within spitting distance of Hamilton Street again. I took up position by the railings near the little wooden ticket booth and waited. The next kid who ran or cycled up to me with a message was going to get a gun up his nose and told to describe who'd sent him. One thirty was showing on my watch when a man called from the booth.

'Are you waiting for a Mr Gibson, sir?' It was the Govan ticket man. They seemed cut from the one roll of dull cloth. Slow of speech and thought, but steady.

I called back yes.

'There's a phone call for you. Says it's important.'

I threw my cigarette away and walked over. He handed me his phone.

'Hello?'

'D'ye huv the money?' It was a deep rasping Glasgow brogue.

'Do *you* have Gibson? Alive?'

'Marr Street tenements. Number twelve. Top floor. House on the left. You've got fifteen minutes. No polis. If we see anyone following you, Gibson's had it. Clear?'

'What do I do when . . .?' But the line was dead. I was about to hand the phone back to the ticket man when I wondered if I should dial 999. I was tired of this game. I should dump it on Chief Inspector Sangster and his pals. Get Duncan Todd in. But they'd take longer than fifteen minutes to get here. Hell, it would take longer than fifteen minutes to explain what I was doing here with a bag filled with twenty-pound notes. And what if the kidnappers carried out their threat?

'Do you know where Marr Street is?'

'It's just doon the road. Cross over the Govan Road and then doon Helen Street. Marr is . . .' He pictured it in his head. '. . . third on your right. There's a factory and some tenements.'

'Thanks, pal.'

I set off with the avowed intention of this being my last stop. Unless the handover took place in Marr Street, I was calling a halt to the whole fiasco. It was amazing how heavy a briefcase of twenty-pound notes could be. I kept changing hands as my grip grew slippy with sweat. The morning cloud cover had parted and it was getting hotter by the minute. I licked my lips as I passed the odd pub. But they were closed anyway. Maybe, like the rest of Govan, the publicans were all at the fair. Or knew their customers were there and were grabbing a long lie-in.

At last I came to Marr Street. I stood at the entrance. It was a short road. On my immediate right, a waterworks followed by a brief run of three-storey tenements. On my left, a high wall shielding a factory building. It was silent. All at the fair. Not a soul about. I checked my gun was in easy reach and walked forward into the deserted street.

EIGHT

It was the third entry along. I paused in front of it and looked up at the blind face of the tenements. No twitching curtain. No flickering shadow behind a window. I turned and looked around. No cars. No pedestrians. As though the whole area had been evacuated pending some awful catastrophe: earthquake, blitz, plague of frogs, shoot-out. Sweat chilled and ran down the small of my back. I shivered despite the heat of the day. I walked into the dark close, my feet echoing loudly on the solid slabs. I switched the briefcase to my left hand and took my gun in my right. I paused, waiting for my eyes to adjust. Then I began to climb, up and round, treading softly on each step.

I passed the first landing and continued to the top level. I stood poised on the last step facing two doors. I listened. From the door on the left – *my* door – came the faint sounds of music. The Andrews Sisters belting out 'Don't Sit Under the Apple Tree'. Silence from the right. I moved forward, feet coming down first on the outer edges.

I reached the door. No nameplate. What was the protocol for handing over a ransom? Stand and wait? Knock? Barge in shooting? I listened. It sounded like a wireless. I took a breath and used the butt of my gun to knock loudly, twice. On the second hard thump the door moved. I stopped. A chink showed. I pushed and the door swung open.

A hall beckoned. Two doors led off it. One to my left and one further down. Both doors closed. Light under each. I stepped over the sill and turned to the first door. The singing was coming from further down, from the next door. My grip tightened on the gun. I put the briefcase down on the floor and turned the handle of the door. I pushed and then shoved it hard. It banged back against the wall. A scullery. Empty. Not even a chair or a kettle. I backed out and started along the corridor. Next door, same routine. I turned the handle and flung the door wide. I had my revolver up and cocked. Bare wood floor. A wooden table lying on its side. And a wireless burbling on a mantelpiece:

> '... *with anyone else but me,*
> *till I come marching home.*'

I took one step forward and heard the squeak of boards behind me from the hall. I began to turn—

I was face down. Scared to move. Scared to find out how badly I was hurt. My mouth tasted of iron. Blood tastes of iron. I dragged my hand up to my face and winced at the movement. I wasn't in a pool of blood, although my head felt as though a lump of concrete had crushed it. Some blood dribbled from my mouth and when my tongue probed, I found I'd bitten it.

Where was I? What had happened? I remember entering the tenement and climbing the stairs, but then nothing. Wait. Gibson. Had I found him?

Nothing. Just a blank.

I touched the back of my scalp. I heard a groan and realised it came from me. The back of my head was a huge tender throbbing mass. No blood, though. I began to push myself up on to hands and knees. A wave of nausea coursed through me. My vision blurred and I thought I'd keel over. I dropped back on all fours. The pain pulsed through my skull like jolts from a bare power cable.

When my eyes focused again I got slowly and gingerly to my feet, grasping the wall for support, trying to remember where I was. How long had I been out? I turned round, eyes squinting and vision fracturing. An empty room apart from a bare wood table against the left wall. To the right, a man lying on the floor. On his back. I stumbled across and peered down. A dead man. He had that special fixed look of horror of someone who knew he was about to die – savagely. The pale eyes were open and already filming over. The other clue was the hole in his forehead. Blood had oozed from it and was still congealing. Recent.

What the hell had happened? I had no recollection of walking into this room; just scattered images. Like a broken kaleidoscope. A song: . . . *the apple tree* . . . I looked back towards the door where I'd been lying. And saw the gun. It looked familiar. Looked like my service revolver. I walked over and picked it up, and immediately regretted it. Had it been used? Had *I* used it? Had someone else? If so, had I just buggered up the prints? I checked the cylinder. One fired. Shit!

I looked around. What for? Something was missing. The song. The wireless had vanished. Something else. Something on the table? Wait. I'd come with a briefcase full of money. Where was it? I walked into the hall. Gone. So had £20,000. I groaned. Not just because my head was gowping. What a bloody mess. I went back into the room where the body lay. I was sorely tempted to simply walk out, walk away and pretend all this was a bad dream. But I couldn't. I needed a phone box. I needed my pal, Inspector Duncan Todd. Fast.

It seemed I only had to wish and it was true. I could hear the distinct sound of a police car's agitated bell rushing towards me. How had they found out? There was a screech. Then doors slamming and shouts from out in the street. I walked back down the corridor to the front door. It was wide open, so I could hear the calls and the pounding boots of coppers coming rapidly up the stairs towards me. I stuffed my gun in the rear of my waistband and waited nonchalantly at the door for the much too late cavalry.

The first head that poked its way round the corner belonged to Detective Chief Inspector Walter Sangster. Oh good.

'Brodie! What the fuck are you doing here!' He panted to a halt on the landing. His uniformed pals crowded up behind him, all gasping for air. All staring at me. Accusingly.

'You need to take more exercise, Sangster. Or cut out the fags.'

Sangster went even more purple. 'What are you doing here, Brodie?'

'I might well ask you the same question.'

He pushed his face close to mine. 'Because Sir Fraser Gibson's been kidnapped. Oot ma road!'

He shoved me aside and his minions charged after him. Maybe I should slip away now.

'Fuck! Brodie!' came the call from the back room. 'Get your arse down here!'

Something in his voice suggested this wasn't going to go well. I could just tell. I walked down the hall. Sangster was standing over the body.

'Do you know who this is, Brodie?'

'I assume it's—'

'It's him! It's Sir Fraser Gibson! The chief of the Scottish Linen Bank. Dear God!' Sangster seemed to be having a seizure. Then his law-enforcer's reflex cut in. Pavlov should have experimented on Glasgow cops. Sangster pointed at me. 'Arrest this man.'

'Sangster, you're an awful hasty man. Let me explain.'

But by then two young constables had pinned my arms. 'Search him!'

'Sangster, will you just hang on a minute.'

'Sir! Sir! Ah found this!' The excited young officer held up my service revolver as though he'd found the grail. In Sangster's eyes, he probably had.

NINE

'**D**on't get your prints all over it, ya eejit! Here, gie me it.' Sangster had taken a big hankie out of his pocket and reached for the gun. He grasped it by the barrel and inspected it. It didn't take him long.

'It's been fired!' Then he pointed down at the bullet hole in Gibson's head. 'You shot him, Brodie!'

'Don't be ridiculous, Sangster. Why would I do that?'

'Well, we're going to find out, aren't we?' He pulled himself erect. 'Douglas Brodie, Ah'm arresting you for the murder of Sir Fraser Gibson. You don't have to say anything but anything you do say will be noted and may be used in evidence. But Ah'm sure you know a' that, Brodie.'

There was a malicious light in his eyes. I was equally certain he didn't really suspect me, but he was sure as hell going to enjoy every turn of the screw.

'I've nothing to hide, Sangster. Sheila Gibson employed me to deliver a ransom and free her husband. Just ask her.'

He looked at me sceptically. 'Funny, *Lady* Gibson didn't mention that. And where's this ransom then?'

I stared at him. What? Her ladyship called the police after all? While I was out trying to deliver the ransom? Did she think I'd run off with it? What was she playing at?

'Sangster, whoever did this coshed me and stole the money.'

'Convenient, Brodie. Is that a' you have to say? What else have you found, Constable?'

Not to be outdone by his pistol-finding buddy, cop number two stuck his palm out to show off the glinting pile of bullets. He passed them to the other cop and dug back into my pocket. He pulled out some papers and scanned them.

'Sir! These look like ransom notes.'

What? What the hell was he talking about? Couldn't he read? They were surely just the slips of paper from the kids sending me running round Govan? Sangster grabbed them with glee.

'Ah see. So let's think now. You've always been a bit of smart-arse, Brodie. A bit of a wide boy. Thought you'd make a few bob from a spot of kidnapping and ransom?'

'Sangster, you are aff your heid! Even by your pathetic standards that's the most preposterous deduction you've ever come up with.'

He flushed and his lips became thin lines. That may not have been the most tactful way of putting it. Not in front of his impressionable men. I started again.

'Look, Sangster, this is crazy—'

'Enough! Cuff him and take him away. Book him at the station. Ah'll interview him in the morning after he's spent a night in our cells.'

They wrestled my hands behind my back and clipped the cold steel cuffs round my wrists. I fought down the panic and made one last effort as the bobbies began to march me to the door.

'I was coshed, Sangster. I've got a lump the size of an ostrich egg on the back of my head. Take a look.'

He turned my head, glanced at it and grinned triumphantly.

'Nae sign of blood, Brodie. Any injury ye could have got wrestling wi' pair Gibson here. Ah'll see you later.'

As well as Sangster's squad car they'd come with a Black Maria, ready to fill it with kidnappers. I was hauled into the back of the van and made to sit facing one of the coppers. The ride was long and hard. My wrists were aching and chafed by the time I stumbled down the van's step on to the pavement outside Central Division in Turnbull Street. I hoped none of my pals was around. Then I hoped for one pal at least to appear: Duncan Todd. He'd sort this out. I went through the laborious and demeaning booking procedure in front of the desk sergeant – no one I knew, thankfully.

'I'm allowed a phone call to my lawyer, sergeant.'

'Oh, ye've yer ain lawyer, huv ye? Go on, make the call.' He plunked the black handset on the counter in front of me.

There was no point phoning Sam at home. She was still in Edinburgh. But I had a number for her chambers. I could at least get a message to her. Though God knows what to say. When I got through to her clerk I told him where I was and – in very sketchy terms – why.

They released the cuffs, removed my belt and tie, then took me off down the cold corridor to the cells. The solid-steel door groaned on its hinges, clunked shut and I was left to contemplate my sins. They were mainly of stupidity and naivety. Stupid to get involved with the ransom drop in the first place. It was just the sort of thing Doc Baird had warned me about. Naive not to spot I was walking into a trap. But who had set it? And why? Naive about puncturing Sangster's tender but inflated ego in front of his men.

I sat on the hard bench and put my head in my hands. My mind was spinning. My head throbbed from the blow and from the turmoil of fractured memories and unanswered questions. Why had Sheila Gibson called in the police even as I was delivering the ransom? Why hadn't she mentioned me to Sangster? How did Sangster know to come to Marr Street? Had Cammie been following me around, picking up information from the people I'd met? Why did the kidnappers kill Gibson and not me? They couldn't have known I'd have a gun, if indeed it was my gun that killed him. Was this a set-up from start to finish?

Finally, the most tormenting question of all: if my gun had shot him, who had pulled the trigger?

Could it have been me?

TEN

'Well, you've excelled yourself, Douglas.'

'I expected a wee bit more sympathy from you, Sam. Not to mention some top-class legal advice on getting me out of here.'

'As for the sympathy, you could have said *no* to Sheila Gibson!'

'It was a story. Just a story.'

'*Scoop, Brodie,* was it! That would have been fine, but then you had to get involved.'

'Is that your top legal advice? I should just have walked away?'

She coloured, always a pretty sight on her pale complexion.

'Not walk away. Just not jump in *heid first*. Like you usually do. Was she pretty?'

'You think I'm so easily seduced?'

She raised a withering eyebrow.

'She might have been. Once.'

'Ha!'

'How about the legal advice then?'

She shook her head. 'My legal advice is to say nothing until we find out where the bullet came from and hear what *Lady* Gibson has to say. If it's as you say, she'll corroborate your story and you'll be out of here in a trice.'

'If? If! My *story*? Do you think I'm making it up?'

'No, of course not. It's just how it looks to the likes of your pal, Sangster. You know he's never forgiven you for showing him up last year. In fact this year too, come to think of it. You're no diplomat.'

'He's an eejit. I don't think he ever quite worked out which were the bad guys: the Glasgow Marshals or your old flame the dishonourable Charlie Maxwell.'

'He was never a *flame*. Barely a damp squib.'

'Talking of pals, I'd hoped Duncan Todd would have stuck his smiling face round the door. Just to see how I was doing. Maybe bring me a fish supper.'

'I spoke to him. He's been told, on pain of instant reduction to the ranks, not to come near you.'

I wasn't surprised. 'Sam, I tried to call you last night to sound you out. After Sheila Gibson picked me up and asked me to help. I needed your advice. I couldn't get you.'

The spots of pink on her high cheekbones widened.

'We were working all the hours preparing for today's trial. I got your message this morning but I was on my way to the court.'

'How did it go? I need to know I'm hiring the best.'

'Oh, he went down.' She smiled ruefully. 'The prosecution case was watertight. I think he missed being inside. All his pals were there and at least he was getting fed. I did get him down to the lower end of the tariff. I swear he looked disappointed.'

'Why didn't he just plead guilty?'

'He thought he was entitled to a trial. Didn't want to make it look easy. Crooks have their pride.'

'Hmmm. I'm not sure that convinces me I've got the right advocate. Assuming I need one.'

She reached across the table and squeezed my hand. All her bluster was worry.

'I can't get you out on bail tonight. But things will look better in the morning. I'll be here first thing. Try and get some sleep.' Her voice softened. 'I'll miss you. I was looking forward to coming home tonight.'

I gripped her hand. 'Me too. Look, it's late. Grab a taxi. I'll be fine. This is all stupid and we'll clear it up in the morning.

She left and I lay down on my side on the thin mattress and gazed at the rough concrete walls and steel door. I couldn't switch off the overhead light. It would be put out in half an hour. Not that I could sleep. Sam had provided me with some aspirin and had demanded and got a cold damp towel for my swollen head. The physical pain had receded somewhat but my brain was whirling with anxiety and questions. And a sheer, raw anger at being dragged back down into the pit again. That'd teach me to be happy.

I lay nursing my grievances for a while, trying to convince myself I'd be out in the morning after Lady Gibson had cleared the air. Yet those little gaps in my memory still niggled. What had happened in Marr Street? Why couldn't I recall for certain whether I'd used my gun or not? Why does the old Scots saying always seem so apposite when it comes to me: *Enjoy it the noo, it'll no' last . . .*

Somehow I slept.

I woke several times in a lather of headaches and bad dreams. I thought I'd scoured those demons from my head. Seems they'd only been hiding, waiting for some new turmoil in my life to pounce. Just as Doc Baird had predicted. Christ, I was fed up with this yo-yo existence.

I was allowed a shave and a basin to wash in. Sam had left me a clean shirt and underwear. They gave me breakfast in the form of a mug of tea and a buttered roll with slice sausage. No sauce, otherwise a decent enough start to the day. I made myself smile in the steel plate that passed for a mirror and tried whistling:

> *There's a smile on my face*
> *For the whole human race.*
> *Why, it's almost like being in love . . .*

But the words stuck in my brain and no sound came out.

They took me along to the interview room. Sam was waiting, freshly scrubbed and in her smart dark business suit. She also wore her don't-mess-with-me look. It would be needed. Across from her side of the table were Sangster and a constable with a pad and pencil. Sangster's gaze swept over me as if he'd rather have me for breakfast than a slice sausage sandwich.

'Over there, Brodie.' He pointed at the vacant seat next to Sam.

Sam bridled. 'It's *Mr* Brodie, please, Chief Inspector. My client is innocent until proven otherwise and deserves common courtesy.'

Sangster's grin vanished. 'Innocent, you say. We'll see. Anyway, *Mister* Brodie, sit doon and let's get on with this.'

He turned to his constable. 'Yesterday afternoon at precisely three fifteen, *Mister* Douglas Brodie was arrested and formally cautioned. He was taken into custody and charged with the kidnap and murder of Sir Fraser Gibson. This interview is the first to establish the case for bringing Douglas Brodie in front of the Sheriff Court. Are we all agreed?' He waited for Sam.

'Let's establish some facts here, Chief Inspector. You claim that Sir Fraser Gibson was murdered. What proof do you have that it *was* Sir Fraser?'

'Whit? Of course it wis him. Ah've seen his face in the papers. He was kidnapped, wisn't he?'

'Has there been formal identification?'

Sangster swallowed and then he got his confidence back.

'Aye, there has, if you must know. His wife, Lady Gibson, identified his body this morning. At the police morgue. Does that satisfy you?'

'Thank you. Has the police doctor established how he died?'

'It didnae need much medical training. He'd been shot in the head at close range by Brodie's gun.'

'That's a rather sweeping and unfounded accusation, Chief Inspector. Would you care to withdraw it, please, unless you have independent evidence that A, the cause of death was a bullet to the head, and B, that the bullet came from the gun found at the scene, and C, that the gun found did indeed belong to Mr Brodie here.'

Under different circumstances I would be enjoying Sam's gentle evisceration. Sangster spluttered.

'Aye well, we'll soon have proof enough of yer A, B, C.'

'But in the meantime, you don't have any proof that links Mr Brodie with Sir Fraser's death?'

'He was there, wasn't he? He had a gun. We took it off him. It had been fired. Fraser Gibson was lying wi' a hole in his heid from a bullet. Q. E. D., you might say.'

'But you don't know when, and you certainly don't have proof that it was that particular weapon that killed Gibson.'

'Look, Miss Campbell, if you think Ah'm letting this yin oot o' here just because we huvnae exactly dotted a' the Is and crossed a' the Ts, you have another think coming.'

'Chief Inspector, the rules of arrest are quite clear. Unless you have solid grounds for holding a suspect, you must let him go. I want my client released immediately or I'll get a court order this morning to force you to follow the procedure.' She kept cool and waited.

Sangster sat back and lit himself a fag, before delivering killer blows.

'Ah do have solid grounds.' He waved his thumb at me. 'For one, he was hinging aboot the crime scene. What was he doin' there? How did he get there before us? Then – *coincidentally* – we find a gun stuffed up his jooks. Said weapon had just been fired; I smelt it masel'. Lastly, his pockets were fu' o' bullets and kidnap demands.'

'They weren't kidnap demands, Sangster!' I'd had enough.

'It's a simple fact. My constable found them.'

'Then they were planted on me!'

He sucked in his cheeks and leaned forward. 'They a' say that, don't they?'

'Look, it's easy. I was acting for Lady Gibson. Just ask her.'

'In due course. She's no' fit to be questioned. You can imagine how the pair wumman is feeling after seeing her man with a bullet hole in his heid. She's taken to her bed.'

'Well, ask her chauffeur, Cammie. He picked me up two days ago, when Fraser Gibson was kidnapped. He ferried me around yesterday with a bag full of money to pay off the kidnappers. Or Lady Gibson's maid. She'll tell you.'

Sangster was nodding in that infuriatingly patronising way of his.

'Oh, we'll get to them. But they're looking after Lady Gibson. We've been asked not to disturb the household. They're in mourning.'

'But you're happy to disturb me, Sangster!'

He grinned. 'Oh aye. Anything else, Miss Campbell, before we tuck *Mister* Brodie back in his wee cell?'

ELEVEN

The cell *was* wee. And getting wee-er, as I paced its six by six concrete floor and contemplated the tiny high barred window from the bunk. I could push my cot close to it and reach to pull myself up to look out. But all you could see from any of the cell windows was the inner courtyard. At least it allowed some daylight to angle in.

The sense of injustice burned. Why was everybody lying or hiding? I kept trying to piece together a clear consecutive run of images of the events in the tenement but I couldn't bridge the gaps. My brain wouldn't let go of the puzzle that was Sheila Gibson. Why hadn't she simply confirmed I was working for her; that I'd been carrying the ransom? Pure and simple grief at the loss of her husband? She'd seemed tougher than that. Or was she terrified that the murderers were still out there, might come after her? Maybe she was confused; what story had Sangster spun her? Had he blamed me for letting the kidnappers kill Sir Fraser?

Sam came to see me later in the day. She didn't bring good news. When she entered my cell her tight face said it all. It was no surprise.

'Forensics say the bullet came from the gun they took from you. And of course the serial number of the gun matched the War Office records of the gun issued to Lieutenant Colonel Douglas Brodie, six months ago.'

I could only nod, sitting hunched forward on my bed-bench.

They seemed to be pulling out all the stops. Unusually competent for this lot.

'OK, it was my gun. What else?'

'It has your prints on it.'

'Of course it does. It's mine.' I didn't add that I'd stupidly handled it after I picked myself off the floor.

'Well, it doesn't need much else to prove a prima facie case, does it?'

I shook my head. She continued.

'Then there're the ransom notes they found on you. Drafts, they said, for the real thing.'

'That *proves* this is a set-up. All I had were scribbled directions from a couple of kids, sending me on a wild-goose chase round Govan. Conveniently timed for the Govan Fair, I might add. I didn't have *ransom* notes per se. There were no notes. The demands were all done by phone. The notes must have been planted. When I was out cold on the floor at Marr Street.'

Sam just looked at me, tight-lipped. She didn't have to say how far-fetched that would sound to a jury. And suddenly the thought took shape, became live. Me in the dock and a jury. Alice in Wonderland: 'Sentence first –verdict afterwards.'

'This is madness, Sam. What possible motive did I have? Sheila Gibson and her maid – probably her bloody chauffeur too – saw two masked men burst in and take away her husband. Are they saying that was *me*? I'm sure I can prove where I was at the time.'

Where was I? Lunchtime on Thursday. Sandwiches in George Square. Great. I'll get a couple of pigeons to vouch for me. Or Sticky. Right. That would work. Sam seemed to be reading my thoughts. She shook her head. Her face took on lines round her eyes and mouth.

'Sangster is presenting a case to the Procurator Fiscal that suggests you were the ringleader of a group of at least three men. That you decided to kill Gibson once you knew his wife had refused to pay the ransom and called in the police.'

I was spluttering now. 'But they found me nursing a broken skull. What was that about?'

'Thieves falling out? You killed Gibson; the others panicked and coshed you. Left you to take the blame. And anyway, Sangster says they found no sign of your injury. Far less ransom money.'

'Christ! Feel! It's still a big lump.' I stroked the back of my head.

She reached forward and took both my hands.

'Douglas. Douglas, my dear, they see it differently. Or choose to. They've built a case. This will be enough for the Procurator.'

'Enough?'

It was a stupid question. I knew the answer. Could see the concern written in her eyes. The last thing a defendant needs is an anxious advocate.

'You're appearing on petition on Monday in front of the Sheriff.'

TWELVE

It was a long weekend made almost bearable by sweaty exercises and by the book Sam left me. She knew I'd go daft if left to sit and ponder my fate. She'd carried it in her handbag, and cleared it with the desk sergeant. It was good to see she still had a sense of humour about this stupid business, and expected me to share it. *The Count of Monte Cristo* by Dumas, the tale of a man wrongfully imprisoned, who escapes and then metes out justice and revenge on the men who'd arranged his incarceration. My plan exactly.

But I struggled to concentrate and found the book bleak in its parallels. I wanted to be out hammering on doors, following leads, lining up testimonies. The hours and days after a murder are the key ones for uncovering evidence, and squeezing every drop from witnesses before their memories grow clouded or distorted. Before anyone has been got at. I was desperate to be out there, hot on the trail. As a poor substitute for action I started doing my army exercises: push-ups, sit-ups, running on the spot and squats. I hung by the window bars and did pull-ups till my shoulders screamed. My old drill instructor would have been proud, except for the location.

The nights were bad. I lay tossing and fretting, my brain seething with questions. None of them getting answered. I felt the old clammy sense of being caught up between giant stones, trapped in my own head. It was both purgatory and a blessing not to have access to alcohol. But it meant there was no release, no let-up, except when I'd exhausted myself into twitching sleep. Twice during the first night and again the following, the guard banged on my door and told me to stop shouting.

While I was grinding out the seconds in my cell, Sam was choosing a solicitor to handle the initial call and response between defence and prosecution. The three of us convened in my new abode first thing Monday morning before the court hearing. I was heartened to see it was John Dalziel, a Glasgow lawyer whom Sam had worked with before. A short round man with bottle glasses, and sharper than he looked. His pudgy mildness hid a lightning brain and a knowledge of the law that tested any prosecuting team and, occasionally, the Sheriff.

'Tell me in your own words, Mr Brodie, the whole story.' Dalziel smiled encouragingly. I recounted my tale while he scribbled notes. At the point where I was explaining waking up next to the dead man, he looked up.

'Are you saying you have no precise recollection of the events surrounding the shooting?'

'I can't even remember going into the room. Not really. I recall hearing music, the Andrews Sisters, on a wireless. It was coming from the flat where they found Gibson. Then, things get blurred. I don't have a clear sequence. Like missing photos in an album. I went from standing outside to waking up with my head on fire next to Gibson's body.'

Dalziel took off his thick specs and looked even more like a bewildered forest animal that has blundered into a searchlight. He polished them on his tie while shaking his head.

'Not that it matters. Even if you could remember everything, and it showed that someone coshed you and killed Gibson, we'd struggle to get a jury to believe you.'

'What! Are you saying *you* don't? Time you found me another solicitor, Sam.'

He sighed and his fat chest heaved and rippled.

'I'm just commenting on the story itself. What *I* believe is neither here not there. There will be no stinting of my efforts on your behalf, I assure you.'

'Well, it's material to me, Dalziel! And if I can't rely on you being fully on my side, then we should part company.'

I knew I was being unreasonable but I had every cause. Sam leaned over and touched my arm.

'He *is* on your side, Douglas.'

'Of that you can be sure, Mr Brodie. And – for the record – I do actually believe you're *not* guilty.'

I studied him. He seemed to be telling the truth. But I was suspicious. 'Why? Even to my ears it sounds fanciful. And if so, do you think you could persuade fifteen jurors of the same truth?'

'Why? It doesn't fit. None of this rings true for Douglas Brodie. Not with your past record. Not with how you've been talking. And there are too many leaps of imagination by Sangster and his crew.'

'Such as?'

'How they knew where to come, for one. And their claim that Lady Gibson, her maid and her chauffeur have been so flattened by this tragedy that they've been unable or unwilling to confirm your employment on her behalf. Miss Campbell has already raised the latter with the Procurator Fiscal and we hope to obtain some clarification this afternoon. It ought to lead to a quick dismissal of the case or at least get you out on bail until we can kill the charges. As it stands – unless we get Lady Gibson's testimony of support – they have enough evidence to get you through all the preliminaries to full trial in the High Court.'

Full trial? Dear God. I'd felt so dazed from lack of sleep and from turning the situation over and over that I hadn't let the thought of a High Court grilling enter my mind.

'No need to sound so enthusiastic, Dalziel.'

He had the grace to look sheepish. I suppose a juicy murder case made a nice change from petty theft and traffic violations. But as the notion digested in me I knew he was right. I'd seen enough of these procedures in the past to know appearing on petition is pretty much a formality on the path to a full trial. But surely I'd prove the exception? We'd soon find that this was all a silly mistake and that Sangster had acted like an over-eager amateur again.

That afternoon, I was marched through the rabbit warren of Turnbull Street from the police cells to the District Court. There in a small closed room with no members of the public and certainly no press, the Sheriff listened to the charges. Dalziel sat on a front bench next to the Procurator Fiscal's man. Two rows behind Dalziel sat Sam, trying to look as though she was there by accident or mere curiosity. The Sheriff knew her, though. His eyes scanned the court as he came in and we all stood. I saw a brief nod pass between them as he sat down.

I sat to one side, in the dock, a bystander to the discussions and ruminations about my own fate. I listened with growing disbelief and irritation to the charges being read out and a brief description of the chain of events – as seen by the prosecution – leading up to the kidnap, the imprisonment and the murder of Sir Fraser Gibson. Alexandre Dumas might have made better use of such a plot, but it sounded pretty damning.

The prosecutor was drawing to a close.

'We therefore petition the court's approval to take the next steps in investigating this crime. This will involve gathering all evidence, interviewing all witnesses and arranging for written reports on the accused's background and character ...'

The prosecutor stood back and left the field to Dalziel. Normally at this point – as I recalled it – the accused's solicitor makes no plea or declaration about innocence. But this time Dalziel – prompted telepathically by Samantha Campbell, silent advocate – was all set to get the case thrown out.

'If it please, my lord, we have just listened to the charges by the prosecution. We submit that these charges are without foundation.'

The Sheriff leaned over. 'I'm sure you think that, Mr Dalziel, but the charges have been made and must be examined. Such examination cannot happen in this court, can it?' He smiled indulgently.

'My lord, we well understand that, but this case is exceptional. The accused is the chief crime reporter for the *Glasgow Gazette*. His involvement in the tragic case was purely tangential in the course of his investigative duties. There appears to be a fundamental error in this petition. The charges claim that Mr Brodie was the chief instigator of this dreadful crime when in fact he was acting *on behalf of* Lady Gibson in trying to resolve the kidnap without loss of life. A simple question to the tragic widow of Sir Fraser Gibson would elicit this fact and we are sure his lordship would immediately set aside the whole case against my client. This is something we have been actively pursuing with the Procurator Fiscal.'

The prosecutor got to his feet. 'My lord—'

'No need, just give me a moment,' said the Sheriff, peering at the sheaf of papers in front of him. He picked one up and brandished it at the prosecutor. 'Is this properly signed and witnessed?'

'Yes, my lord.'

He then waved it at Dalziel. 'Have you seen this, Mr Dalziel?'

Dalziel stepped forward, took the single page and read it slowly once and then again. His jaw muscles tightened under his jowls. He swallowed.

The Sheriff asked, 'This is the sworn testimony of whom, Mr Dalziel?'

'It purports to be from Lady Gibson, my lord.'

'And what does the good lady say?'

Dalziel coughed and glanced round at me before replying.

'Lady Gibson claims that she has never met the accused and did not appoint him to help her. She states that she knows only of Mr Brodie through his work as a reporter, but has never communicated with him either by telephone or in writing.'

I heard Sam make a stifled *no*. My world dropped away. The bitch!

THIRTEEN

D alziel returned the letter to the Sheriff and turned to go
back to his bench. He took off his glasses and his big unfo-
cused eyes turned my way. He raised an eyebrow as if to
say: We're stuffed. But he turned to face the Sheriff and had
another crack at it.

'Clearly there is some confusion here, my lord, and we are
sure it will be easily cleared up. I imagine Lady Gibson is
distraught at this time and naturally will not be quite herself.
But while accepting that the petition might indeed contain
sufficient weight for you to send my client to trial, we would
in the meantime request bail for the defendant. We would
remind the court that Mr Brodie is a former detective
sergeant in the Glasgow police and served with distinction
until called to the colours. During the war he rose through
the ranks to became a decorated officer who fought valiantly
for his country. Furthermore, in the first quarter of this year,
Mr Brodie worked closely with the police in the successful
disruption and capture of escaped war criminals hiding in
this very city.'

The Sheriff was nodding, apparently sympathetically.
Apparently.

'I am well aware of Mr Brodie's exploits in this matter. He
wrote vividly about them and he is to be congratulated on his
endeavours. However, brave deeds by themselves do not exon-
erate anyone from a criminal charge.'

'That's as may be, my lord. But Mr Brodie's war record and his public profile are such that there is a negligible chance of his absconding before a trial. We would even accept a requirement for his reporting weekly to a police station.'

The prosecutor pounced. 'My lord, the charges are so serious as to make bail almost unseemly. The public will neither accept nor understand how someone accused of such terrible crimes could be allowed to walk the streets. Particularly as Lady Gibson herself – poor lady – has made a sworn statement which completely contradicts the defendant's version of events. This leaves her open to possible harassment by the accused if he were out on bail. We therefore request that the defendant be remanded in custody pending trial.'

The Sheriff was nodding again. Shit! I was going to be banged up for months while awaiting trial! I couldn't do this. I'd go mad.

'My lord?' All eyes turned to the body of the court. Sam was on her feet.

The Sheriff nodded to her. 'Miss Campbell, I believe?'

'Yes, my lord. I ask you to excuse my addressing you from the body of the court but I have something material to contribute.'

The prosecutor was on his feet. 'My lord, this is completely irregular . . .'

The Sheriff raised a hand. 'I know, I know. This whole case is. I'm sure Advocate Samantha Campbell would not presume to waste the court's time unless she had something of substance to bring to the attention of the court. Miss Campbell?'

Sam took a deep breath. 'May I approach, my lord?' She held out a piece of paper.

The Sheriff beckoned her forward and took the piece of paper. Sam stood back and spoke.

'As you will see, my lord, this is a letter couriered from London late yesterday evening. You will be glad, I am sure, that this court is cleared to the public. The letter is from the Sir Percy Sillitoe, head of a *particular* Government department.'

My heart lightened. Brilliant, Sam. She'd never even mentioned it to me; it was a card only to be played *in extremis*. Then my stomach lurched; *extremis* was exactly where we were.

The Sheriff read it. 'It would appear so.'

Sam continued: 'I would add that the information contained in the letter – indeed even to acknowledge the existence of Sir Percy and his department – must go no further than the personnel in this court.' She looked round the court officials to make certain they had understood and felt bound by what she was saying. She went on.

'This letter tells the court that Mr Brodie – or rather, *Lieutenant Colonel* Douglas Brodie – is a serving member of His Majesty's Security Service.'

Both Dalziel and the prosecutor stepped forward and read the letter in turn. The prosecutor was first to react.

'My lord, this revelation is entirely irrelevant to these charges. In the same way that Mr – Lieutenant Colonel – Brodie's distinguished war record is irrelevant. Perhaps it makes the accusations all the more tragic, but it does not nullify them.'

The Sheriff thought for a long moment while I held my breath.

'I'm afraid I agree, Miss Campbell. Unless you have anything to add, simply being a senior member of the intelligence services is not material.'

'My lord, I accept that trial is the only way forward to resolve this complicated matter, but my point is to underpin the case for bail. Colonel Brodie is hardly likely to attempt to flee the country. His good name is at stake and he has the personal backing of Sir Percy Sillitoe who, I would remind the court, is a former chief constable of this city.'

For a second, I thought she'd won, but the Sheriff, after a further mulling, shook his head.

'It is a powerful argument, Miss Campbell. However, a knight of the realm has been cruelly kidnapped and murdered. There is a public interest in seeing justice done. We will take this case on to the next stage. There will be a private hearing in no less than eight days' time at which point this court will decide on whether or not to commit the accused fully to trial. Both sides have this period of eight days to bolster their arguments. But in the meantime, the accused shall be remanded in custody.'

Knight trumps knave. As I was led down, I nodded at Sam. She and I had discussed this possible outcome and we'd agreed she'd head straight off to Kilmarnock to tell my mother the whole dismal story. I'd hoped the matter would have gone away at the hearing and I could have driven down to Kilmarnock myself and had a good laugh with her over a silly misunderstanding in the middle of a horrendous and tragic murder. But now the press would be full of it and my name – and hers – would be dragged gleefully through the midden. It was essential that Mum heard the real story from Sam before the first neighbours offered their 'sympathies'.

Later in my cell, I lost the place with poor Dalziel. I was pacing from side to side, slapping the wall at each turn.

'You've got to get me out of here!'

'We did everything we could.'

'Clearly you didn't! I'm still here!'

'The sworn statement from Lady Gibson was the killer. We weren't told about it. Even if we'd known it would still have taken the feet out from under us.'

'She's lying! It's clear she's lying.'

'Why? Why would she?'

'Oh, so you think *I'm* lying!'

Round and round we went, getting nowhere. I knew I was being unfair but I couldn't stop myself. The Procurator Fiscal's man was right; I would be straight round hammering on Sheila Gibson's door, lying in wait for her bloody chauffeur, rounding up witnesses. Anything to get me out of here. But there came a moment when I realised I'd switched from slapping the walls to punching them; my knuckles were bleeding. I sat down on my bunk and grew still. Was there just a chance that I'd lost my mind? That the combat stress Doc Baird warned me about had exploded again? And what *had* happened in that room? Could I have shot Gibson?

Dalziel took the chance to slide out of the door vowing all the time that he'd leave no stone uncovered to prove my innocence. He would have his work cut out. I turned back to my book to see if I could steal some hope and ideas from the Count of Monte Cristo. But the pages were a blur.

FOURTEEN

From then onwards, the days dragged by. I'd check my watch and find that only ten minutes had passed instead of the two hours I thought. I sank further into myself, into a despondency about my character shortfalls. I seemed condemned to repeat my mistakes, climbing a ladder and slithering down the snake. Was this what Nick Carraway was talking about? 'So we beat on, boats against the current, borne back ceaselessly into the past.'

Could I just blame the war or had I always carried this flaw? Either way there seemed no way of ridding myself of this self-destructive tendency. I couldn't resist a challenge. I was always the first to volunteer. An impetuous child who had to feed his addiction to thrills and spills. If this was all I'd become, there seemed little point going on.

Sometimes I stirred myself. My mood would change and I'd engage in a sweaty bout of press-ups, star jumps and running on the spot until I fell on my bunk exhausted. Other times I tried burrowing my way deep into the canon of Alexandre Dumas. But where were the four musketeers when you needed them?

My only visitors, apart from the constable who brought me grub and water, were Sam and Dalziel. And I was doing a fine job of encouraging them to pop in and keep me company.

'Speak to Lady Gibson! You *must* be able to get hold of her.'

'How do you suggest we do that, Douglas? Grab her as she

leaves the graveside of her husband? It's the funeral today. They expect a big crowd. But I'm sure Sheila Gibson will have time to stop and chat.'

Oh, bugger. I buried my head in my hands.

'Sorry, Sam. Sorry. I forgot. I've no idea of time. But why did she lie?'

'Confusion? Grief? Maybe she actually thinks you killed him. By accident, of course.'

'That's really encouraging. But what about Cammie the chauffeur? Can't Dalziel summon him? Can't you speak to Janice, the terrified maid?'

She sighed. We'd been round this a dozen times.

'Douglas, we can't get near them. It would be harassment. It's exactly why the Sheriff wouldn't give you bail.'

I was pacing the interview room, wearing a groove in the concrete. Sam sat with her face between her hands waiting for me to calm down. It was impossible. My brain was racing with frustration. I wanted action!

'Are you sure you didn't mention being waylaid by Lady Gibson to anyone at the *Gazette*? Eddie? Wullie? Any of the secretaries?' she asked, not for the first time.

'Not one of them. It all happened in less than twenty-four hours. I didn't have the full story, so I kept quiet.'

'And you didn't want to share your scoop.' It wasn't a question.

I stopped and leaned against the wall letting its cold hard surface grate my face.

'No, I didn't,' I said softly.

'And you can't account for where you were at lunchtime on the day of the kidnapping.'

'No, I can't,' I whispered. 'Unless you can find an old tramp called Sticky I slipped a couple of bob to. But you couldn't exactly call him a character witness. And don't tell me: the two ferrymen don't remember a thing.'

Dalziel said quietly, 'The police got there first. They took statements in which they claim to have no recollection of you and your briefcase. The police also told them not to say anything to the press or defence team. Said it would prejudice the case.'

'That's bloody convenient! What about the kids who passed me the notes for the treasure hunt?'

He shook his head. 'Do you know how many kids there are in Govan? *Thoosands*. There's only me, they all look alike, and the police won't help.'

I sat down at the table and reached out to touch Sam's hands.

'I'm sorry, Sam. I'm growing desperate. Sangster thinks he's got his man and can sit back. Is he even trying to trace the others? If I'm the so-called ringleader where are the rest of my gang?'

She shook her head and squeezed my fingers.

'All I get from them is that *enquiries are continuing*.'

'But they're not, are they?'

'I don't think so, Douglas. No.'

The eight days stretched to an interminable ten because of weekends, so that it was mid-June before I had my next change of scenery. It was more than enough time to go mad or slit my wrists. It brought back the boiling desperation of being corralled in a foxhole for a week outside Caen, pinned down by a line of Panzers and their chattering machine guns. But at least back then I had occasional sun on my face, and the option of going down fighting with a gun in my hand. This airless cube was squeezing the life out of me. I thought longingly of the cool depths of the Western Baths.

When I at last stepped back into the dock I felt a brief and stupid sense of release – surely justice would out – until the dead weight of hopelessness crushed me again. It was a rerun of the first petition. If anything, the prosecution case had hardened, while my defence arguments sounded more and more hollow. *My* gun, *my* bullet, and *I* were placed at the scene of the crime without an alibi. Furthermore, the prosecutor smugly offered a motive for my heinous acts:

'My lord, we would like to submit this letter from the defendant's bank, the Scottish Linen Bank.'

He handed two pages to the Sheriff who passed them to Dalziel.

'Continue with your point,' the Sheriff requested.

'For the record, my lord, the first letter states that the defendant had two accounts with the St Vincent Street branch – a current account and a savings account – and both were overdrawn on the sixteenth day of May, some three weeks before the murder. The second letter is a copy of a letter notifying the defendant of this state of affairs.'

I couldn't hold back.

'That's impossible!' I leaped to my feet. 'I didn't have much but I was in the black. I got no letter! They've got the wrong account!'

The Sheriff leaned over. 'The defendant will take his seat and be quiet. Mr Dalziel, please ensure we hear no more from your client.'

'Yes, my lord.' Dalziel turned to me and flapped his hands up and down to get me to sit. The prosecutor tried to look grave but I could just tell the smug bastard was holding in a smile.

'It seems clear from these bank statements that the defendant had financial problems. We also understand that he had a drink problem.'

Dalziel shot up. 'I protest, my lord. That's hearsay.'

'I withdraw the last point. But leaving aside the drinking, the facts are clear about the state of the defendant's finances. That alone would provide motive enough for the kidnap of a senior banker and the associated demand for a ransom. And it is probably no coincidence that the banker in question was the chief of the very bank used by the defendant.' He paused for effect. 'Financial gain *and* revenge.'

I was flabbergasted, but all I could do was sit open-mouthed. How can you argue against the rectitude of a Scottish retail bank? The prosecutor piled it on, accusing me of living beyond my means and turning to crime instead of doing an honest day's work. Crime reporting clearly didn't count as such, and perhaps contributed to my going off the rails; all those bad examples turning my head.

Hammering home their case, they'd got Lady Gibson's staff to add to her own sworn testimony that they'd never seen hide nor hair of Douglas Brodie. They still didn't have to testify in person so I couldn't confront them. But their statements were written with such damning certainty that even I was beginning to doubt my own evidence – not to mention my sanity. How bad had my concussion been? Had it left me doolally and imagining things? The fragments of memory surrounding my entrance to the flat and waking up next to Gibson's body still refused to join up. The more I tried to fill in the blanks the more elusive the memories seemed to become.

But apart from that brief interlude, everything else was crystal clear in my mind. The fact that so many key people were denying ever meeting me, and that Sangster had miraculously and inexplicably arrived on the murder scene just after me, convinced me I was being framed. Conveniently for the framers, my memory was blank at the crucial moment; it just made it easier for them to make their case. But why? Why *me*?

Unsurprisingly the hearing had the same outcome as the first, except this time the Sheriff committed me to full trial. For fear of witness harassment – *you bet your life I would* – I was again remanded in custody pending the next stage of the proceedings. The saving grace was that my former life as a Glasgow copper and my present MI5 affiliation kept me from being transferred to Barlinnie. The Sheriff accepted that old lags would take a dim view of cops and spies.

When they escorted me back to my cell I found it had shrunk to coffin size. Sam and Dalziel squeezed in with me and I pressed them for the details I'd refused to hear about, until now.

'The next thing is a preliminary hearing?'

'In the High Court, Douglas. Yes.' Sam said it in such a downbeat way that my already crushed heart sank like a stone. It lodged somewhere in my bowels.

'When? How long before we get to it?' I had a rough idea from my police days but I was stupidly hoping the court system would have speeded up in the last eight or so years. Seems it hadn't. Sam and Dalziel glanced at each other.

Dalziel ventured, 'Well, the maximum wait is a hundred and ten days.'

'One hundred and ten! That's nearly four months!'

'That's the maximum, Douglas. It could be sooner.' Sam reached for my hand.

'How do we make it happen quicker?'

'By getting our case together, but it depends on the other side. They will want as long as they can. It puts pressure on us.'

'To do what?'

Again they exchanged glances.

'To plead.'

'Guilty? You're kidding me. They'd hang me.'

There. I'd said it. The unthinkable. At the back of my mind, buried as deep as I could dig it, was that single thought: I could be hanged if convicted.

'No, no, Douglas! That won't happen. You could plead manslaughter. Say it was an accident. The gun went off. Your pals slugged you and made a run for it.'

I looked at her, astonished. She'd actually been thinking about it. Trying to come up with a story that would fit. That would let me off with life in prison instead of having my neck stretched. Perhaps buy time to find out what really happened.

And maybe she actually believed I did it? Why wouldn't she? It was possible that in some series of supremely clumsy events – a fight? a wrestling match? – I'd shot poor Fraser right between the eyes. It didn't add up, but I couldn't prove it. I squeezed her hand back.

'I'd rather be found innocent or face the drop, if it's all the same to you, Sam.'

Her face screwed up and I thought the tears would come. *That* would set me off. I hate being pitied. I was providing enough for myself as it was. I hugged her and patted her until she got control. Then I pushed her gently away from me and examined her reddened eyes.

'Sam, *no plea*. Do you understand? No. Plea. I'm innocent.'

She nodded, and sniffed. 'Of course you are. We'll prove it.'

'That's the spirit. Once we get Lady Gibson in the dock at the hearing it won't run to full trial.'

Sam winced and shook her head. 'The hearing will be in public but any witnesses we might want to call at the full trial will be asked not to attend. It might prejudice the case. That would certainly cover Lady Gibson and her staff.'

'Bugger. All right, we'll have to wait for the full trial. What's the maximum delay between the preliminary hearing and trial?'

'A hundred and forty days,' she said.

I did the sums and clenched my fists. 'So including the wait for a preliminary hearing it could take about eight sodding months just to come to trial!'

She nodded unconvincingly. 'In theory. But . . .'

'But?'

'Even when we get to the preliminary hearing the prosecution could say – or *we* could – that they're not ready for trial and seek a continuation. We'll only get a trial date set when both sides say they're ready.'

'What's the *average* delay between preliminary hearing and trial?'

She bit her lip. 'It could be up to a year.'

A *year*? Plus four months for the hearing?

I couldn't take sixteen months in this concrete tomb.

I looked at them both. Pictures of concern. If I told them what I was thinking they'd be even more concerned. I bluffed some heartiness into my voice.

'Well, Sam, good job you've got a big library. After Dumas, we can move straight on to Dickens. Or maybe just start with A and see how far we get? But we'll skip the Ks if you don't mind. Kafka's too close for comfort.'

FIFTEEN

That was the day I stopped shaving. What was the point? I wasn't going to be seen in public for months. Besides, they never left me alone with the safety razor. They handed it over with the blade already locked in. There wasn't enough time to unscrew the handle, pull out the blade and slice an artery before a minder grabbed me or got me to hospital. I'd have to think of something else.

As my brain ran through the permutations it was as though I was watching myself from outside, a disinterested observer of my last days. Until the hearing I hadn't thought I could go lower. Seems I was wrong. Some part of me – the last sliver of optimism – had been hoping for a different outcome.

Over the weekend, that last hope was excised, ground underfoot and swept away. I had a visitor. He snuck into my cell like a thief. I stirred from my fugue as the door creaked open. I sat up.

'Well, if it isnae my old pal Detective Inspector Duncan Todd. At last.'

'Wheesht, Brodie. If Sangster found out Ah was here Ah'd be back wearing ma boots oot on the streets as a constable. That's if Ah still had a job at a'.'

'You care more about a bloody pension than a friend?'

He coloured and I was glad it stung.

'It's no' like that, Brodie. If Ah could've done anything, Ah would've.'

'So what have you brought me? A decent meal? A bottle of Red Label? Some good news that it's all been a stupid mistake and Sangster will be apologising to me in person? Just before he commits hara-kiri in George Square?'

'Sadly old pal, nane of the above. Can Ah sit?'

I shrugged and he pulled over the small stool and sat facing me.

'Fag?'

I took one and we both lit up.

'I like the whiskers, Brodie. A new look?'

'It gives me something to do. So tell me, why is Sangster doing this?'

'Ah don't think you realise how much you upset him. Now's his chance.'

'To frame me?'

Duncan shook his head. 'He disnae see it that way. He actually thinks you did it.'

'Why? Why the hell would I have done something like that?'

'He disnae need to know. He disnae care much why folk do things. He thinks everybody's capable of foul deeds. And Ah suppose he's right. But he's got a particular automatic suspicion about folk that are smarter than him. Ca' it an inferiority complex, but he jist assumes clever dicks are up to something.'

'So he's going to try and nail me for being a clever dick?'

'Sort of. For making him look stupid.'

'It's not hard.'

'See whit Ah mean?'

I sucked on my fag. Duncan might be my last chance. I needed to calm down, see how I could use him. I spoke steadily.

'Sangster's case is full of holes. I'm being set up.'

'Ye think so? That's no' the way it looks. Christ, Brodie, it was a bullet from your gun they dug oot o' Gibson's heid. No one else's prints on the gun. That's a fairly compelling argument, is it no'?'

'So *you* think I did it, too!'

'No, no. Not at a', Brodie. Ah'm just telling you how it looks. Tae the casual observer.'

'I'm more concerned about the casual jurist. What about Sheila Gibson? Is she changing her tune yet? She's going to have to face us at trial.'

'She refuses to say anything more to a soul, including the press. Too grief-stricken apparently.'

'She gave me twenty thousand pounds in ransom money, Duncan!'

'That's no' what she says.'

'Has Sangster checked with her bank?'

'Ah could get into real trouble wi' this, Brodie.'

'Well, has he?'

'Aye, apparently. And her bank says no money was handed over.'

My attempt at calm wasn't going to last long.

'The lying bastards! Let's not forget that it was *his* bank! Gibson's. The Scottish Linen. Whose side would *they* be on, do you think? They even emptied my own accounts. Bloody crooks!'

'Calm doon, old pal. Ah believe you. But what's in it for them? Why would they lie aboot losing twenty thousand quid?'

'Maybe they're embarrassed. Or don't want to encourage other kidnappers?'

'Who knows, Brodie. Ah just know how a bank manager would come across in the witness box. Swollen wi' righteousness. Wi' his fingers crossed ahint his back and his tongue going black.'

I tried a different tack. 'Do you know the coppers working for Sangster on this?'

'Aye, sure. But Ah cannae go near them. Cannae interfere.'

'All I'm asking is that you have a quiet word with one of them. Ask him to talk to the ticket collectors at the ferry booths of Kelvinhaugh and Govan. Ask them if they remembering talking to me. I mean why would I be charging backwards and forwards across the Clyde if I was a kidnapper?'

'It disnae prove anything, Brodie. You could be laying a false trail or something. There's nothing there that would get you aff the hook.'

'What about the weans?'

'What weans?'

'The ones that gave me directions. It was like a treasure hunt. I was sent round and round like a dafty, following instructions. The last one was a phone call at the Govan Ferry booth. He told me to go to the tenement in Marr Street. How else would I have got there?'

Duncan raised his eyebrows. He almost had no need to say it out loud.

'As Sangster will put it – has put it – *because you were one of the kidnappers.*'

Duncan's visit simply underlined the strength of the case they'd rigged against me. I'd be held in custody for a year, have my name and reputation – such as it was – dragged through the papers, and be found guilty. I'd either be locked away for good or face the gallows. I was determined to do neither. The first would be a living hell. The second ... Years ago as a trainee copper we'd been sent to Barlinnie to have a ghoulish tour of the hanging shed. Not a separate building, far less a shed; simply a room on the third floor of D Hall with a rope dangling from the room above and a trapdoor through to the second floor. The thought of it froze my marrow.

It wasn't so much the moment of death I feared – I'd seen how efficient the hangman was and knew my neck would break in a trice. Ending it all. It was the dread of it, the waiting and the build-up with all the ceremony and paraphernalia of ritual execution. The short walk from the condemned cell across the landing and through the white door. Guided into position on that hinged hatch. The bag pulled over my head so I couldn't see, couldn't breathe. The noose tightening about my neck. Like the end for my old pal, Hugh Donovan.

I didn't want to be unmanned.

So why wait? Only the occasional visit by Sam kept me from tying a sheet to the high bars and round my neck. But even her presence was provoking smaller and smaller sparks of interest. It's hard to go on loving someone who thinks you're guilty – of something. The arguments inside me had resolved themselves. I'd become numb. It was no longer a question of would I or wouldn't I. It was a case of how and when.

SIXTEEN

My zen-like journey to perdition was interrupted a few days later by another visitor. I was led to a small interview room, annoyed at having to leave my familiar box. He'd come with Sam. A distant part of me was glad to see her. In front of the duty officer who'd ushered them in Sam introduced him as a new member of my legal team. Reinforcements, she joked. He looked like an insurance salesman: colourless, bland, specs, someone you'd meet at a party and have to be introduced three times before his name and face stuck. He was tall, my height but skinny, though there was a hint of wiry strength. I saw no point in him.

'Harry Templeton. Nice to meet you, Mr Brodie.'

A languorous English accent accompanied the requisite flop of hair. He stuck out his hand. I gazed at it, then studiously ignored it. I took in the tie. Unless he was a fraud, the distinctive maroon and navy stripes with the repeating gold crest proclaimed Grenadier Guards. Christ. That's all I needed. Some poncy Sassenach with a top club tie. What was he? A trainee lawyer come to slum it, inspect the hard-core villains? I certainly looked the part.

Sam must have seen my boiling frustration. She gripped my arm and put a finger to her mouth. I took a deep breath and tried to get hold of myself. She waited till the door was fully closed and the three of us were left alone, then sat back. At that, Harry came alive, as though his spirit had returned to his body. Or an actor had cast aside his stage character. He stuck his specs in his breast pocket and leaned forward. Suddenly his blue eyes were focused and full of intelligence and intent.

'Templeton isn't my real name, but it'll do. Call me Harry. Sir Percy sent me.'

For the first time in two and a half weeks I felt a surge of something other than despair. It couldn't be hope. Curiosity? My boss at MI5 hadn't forgotten me. His letter to the Sheriff at the first court hearing hadn't got us anywhere and I'd thought that was it. That he didn't want MI5 involved any further in something so dirty. He'd activated me at the start of the year to track down the fascists infesting Glasgow, but he'd always made it clear that if I got into trouble, in public, I was on my own. I looked at Sam. She was smiling faintly now. Also for the first time in weeks. I shrugged. So what? Harry Templeton – was either a real name? – pulled out a silver cigarette case and passed it round.

'Seems you're in a spot of bother, Mr Brodie.'

'I love your English understatement, Harry.'

'We need to get you out of here.'

I stared at him, then at Sam. She nodded.

'Music to my ears. But I think you'll find that the Procurator Fiscal intends keeping me here until they can send me to the gallows.'

'Don't, Douglas!'

'Sorry, Sam. Just being realistic.'

I was sorry to see Harry nodding in agreement.

'It does seem a pretty watertight case, Mr Brodie. Almost like a set-up, don't you think?'

'Just Brodie. I *do* think.'

'So do we. What do you know about Gibson, Brodie? Other than that he was head of the Scottish Linen Bank?'

'Nothing. I was aware of him in a general sense, as one of the Scottish establishment. But that's it.'

'We've been watching him for the past few months.'

'"We" being you and our mutual boss?'

He nodded. 'We've been watching Gibson personally and his bank in general.'

'Why?'

'Rumours. Nothing much. Straws in the wind. Drinking, women, that sort of thing.'

'Sounds suspiciously normal for Glasgow.'

'But not if you're head of Scotland's largest retail bank. And an issuing bank to boot. The timing is – how shall I put it? – inconvenient.'

I paused to think what he might mean. Just lately world affairs had taken a back seat to my own affairs.

'The Yankee loans?'

He nodded. 'Early last year, just before he died, John Maynard Keynes – bless his soul – managed to persuade the US of A and Canada to lend us nearly four and half billion dollars. It culminated in the Anglo-American Agreement of the fifteenth of July 1946 and saved our bacon just after the end of Lend-Lease. '

'A lot of dough.'

'But of course you'll recall it came with strings? One of the biggest – more a noose actually – was that sterling would become convertible exactly a year later, on the fifteenth of July 1947. About three weeks' time.'

'Remind me why that matters? I recall a lot of noise in Parliament last year. Accusations flying about the end of Empire. The Labour Government selling the nation's silver to pay for its Welfare Bill. Etcetera.'

'Britain stays afloat – just – by virtue of our overseas colonies. We can buy and sell the goods we need from abroad because we have favoured-nation deals. And because we didn't permit the colonies to swap the pound for something more tradable.'

'Like the dollar.'

'Exactly. In three weeks' time, that barrier will be lifted and there is a real possibility that countries will convert some or all of their sterling holdings to the dollar. I know I would. The dollar is becoming the de facto gold standard internationally.'

'And the result in Britain?'

'A run on the pound. Britain's dollar reserves depleted. And we find we can't pay our way in the world. Treasury nerves are frayed. Smelling salts at the Bank of England. The last thing we need is for one of our main banks to get into trouble. Especially an issuing bank. It's amazing how quickly the international markets can lose confidence in a country if they think we're printing money without collateral. News of trouble at Scottish Linen could open the flood gates.'

'You think there's more to this than the kidnap and murder of the boss?'

'We don't know. And we don't want to send the troops in because it will have the same effect of undermining confidence. We've already had some delicate questions raised by our friends across the water. They read the papers in Washington too.'

'Bit of a problem then, Harry.'

'It gets worse.'

'That already sounds plenty.'

'You know about the Marshall Plan?'

'Hah. It was the last column I wrote just before I ended up in this mess. An aid programme for the reconstruction of Europe.'

Harry nodded. 'Just as we hit the date for convertibility a crucial meeting takes place in Paris to decide on the loan amounts.'

'And Britain will be setting out its alms bowl.'

'Quite. A banking scandal could leave it empty. Or at the very least embarrass the Government. They don't like losing face. Admitting that Britain is an upper-class pauper.'

'What do you think's happening at Scottish Linen that's so damning?'

'We don't know. That's the trouble. During the war and its aftermath, there wasn't quite as much supervision as we could have hoped. Tempting opportunities for a rogue banker.'

'You think that's what Gibson was up to? Embezzling?'

He shrugged. 'Something pongs a bit. There's plenty of opposition in America to pouring more money into the bottomless pit of Europe. If they thought it was going into someone's back pocket, we'd never get it. The Chancellor is personally looking to Sir Percy to sort this out. Fast. And *quietly.*'

That was it. I'd heard enough.

'*Something pongs?* The Chancellor wants it sorted out, *quietly*? I don't care if you make a noise like Krakatoa going off! Sorry to be so parochial about this, Harry, but if you've got all these suspicions, why the bloody hell have you let me end up in the frame?'

He had the grace to wince. 'Apologies, old chap, but it's not that easy. We don't think it's coincidence that the head of the bank is bumped off and you get the blame. Someone is pulling strings and we want to know who and why.'

'Mean time, *old chap,* I'm banged up facing a murder trial!'

Harry began signalling I should calm down by flapping both hands up and down in front of my face. If he didn't pack it in I was about ready to bite his fingers off. Sam read me again; she reached out and squeezed my forearm. I swallowed and tried to get my composure back.

'Well, Harry, can you kindly lift the pace? I'm getting stir-crazy. And, unlikely as it sounds, I'm running out of Dickens.'

He was nodding furiously. 'Trouble is, the firm has no one up here with local knowledge or cover. And we absolutely must avoid any scandal, which would be inevitable if we blunder around the bank's back office arresting people. Particularly if we don't know whom to arrest or why.'

I switched from shouting to sneering. 'Well, I'd love to help, but as you can see, the bad guys are out there and I'm in here.'

There it was; MI5 knew something dirty was going on and that I'd been made the fall guy. But they were hamstrung by fear of bad publicity, and Glasgow was a bridge too far to mount an operation. Templeton had been sent all this way to tell me to keep my chin up, that I wasn't alone. Really? It didn't feel like it.

The black dog began snapping at my heels again.

SEVENTEEN

The next day, at half past ten, Advocate Samantha Campbell and her colleague Harry Templeton returned to Turnbull Street and asked to see the prisoner. His cell would do. No need to set up the interview room. The tall Englishman was the first through the door. The prisoner's advocate was right by his shoulder and screamed as she entered.

Harry shouted, 'My God! Officer! Get an ambulance!'

The constable tried to push past to see what the commotion was about. He took one look and saw enough.

'Och, no!'

'Officer, quick! Get an ambulance. We'll get him down. Fast as you can!'

Harry, in full command of the situation as only a former Guards officer could be, grabbed the young constable, spun him round and pushed him out of the door. Then he turned and stepped up on the bunk. He tugged at the torn sheet tied carefully through the window bars and just as carefully looped round the neck. Then he and Sam lifted and then lowered the prisoner down on the bunk. Sam knelt beside the bunk and flung herself over the still body.

'No, oh no! Douglas, you can't! Don't go! Don't leave me!'

The young constable came running back, followed by the puffing desk sergeant. Both in a lather. Sam leaped up, tear-stained face contorted. She blocked their way and began screaming at them.

'When did you last see him? How could you leave him alone! Douglas Brodie's dead! He's dead! And you lot will pay for this!'

She began flailing at the chest of the sergeant. He stepped back in panic at this assault by the blond harridan.

'Miss Campbell, we didnae think he was a risk! We check every hour. Jamie here was round to see him just a wee while back. Is that not so, Jamie?'

Jamie looked as though he'd drop. 'Ah did, Ah really did. Ah thocht he was fine. Quiet, of course. He's been in a dwam for some days noo. But Ah didnae ken he'd dae sic a thing!'

Both uniforms were pushed back to the door but they had a clear view of Douglas Brodie lying on his back, not breathing, the pallor of death on the face, the bare neck a mass of red contusions, tongue poking out. Dead all right. Harry sprang up. Grenadier Guard issuing commands again.

'Never mind who's to blame. Where's the damned ambulance? There's no sign of life, but I won't give up. Constable, go and see. Miss Campbell, please take the sergeant back to his desk and check the log. We need to see if anyone is at fault,' he said with heavy meaning. He turned and looked down at Brodie and shook his head. 'There's nothing you can do here.'

For a few minutes it was quiet in the corridor, then shouts arose and two figures in white ran into the cell carrying a rolled-up stretcher between them. They were followed by a white-coated man with a stethoscope round his neck. They clustered round the still figure on the cot. Harry moved to the door and kept the police uniforms at bay. Sam clung to Harry's arm and watched from the doorway. The doctor stood up and hung his stethoscope back round his neck.

'I'm afraid it's too late. This man is dead.'

Sam gasped and hid her face. 'No! Oh, no. This can't be right.'

'I'm sorry, miss. Are you his wife?'

'No, I mean yes. No. I'm his advocate. But he lives with me. I mean I'm his landlady.'

The doctor became less brusque. 'I'm very sorry. But we need to clear the cell now. My men will take— What did you say the prisoner's name was?'

'Brodie. Douglas Brodie,' Sam whispered.

'We will take Mr Brodie to the hospital. We'll do a post-mortem, but the cause of death seems fairly apparent.'

A muttering crowd had gathered in the foyer of the police station, a mix of uniform and plain clothes. They fell silent and watched with ghoulish curiosity as the two ambulance men brought the heavy stretcher out from the cells. A white cloth was draped over the body. Behind them came the distraught figure of the prisoner's lawyer, helped by her colleague. The double doors were held open and the men solemnly carried their burden through and out into the street where another crowd was forming. They lifted the body into the back of the ambulance and helped the grieving woman inside. The two ambulance men got in the front. The white-coated doctor climbed inside with Samantha Campbell.

The tall Englishman who'd taken charge of events closed the doors and watched as the ambulance slowly drew away. The urgency had gone out of the situation. There was no need now to ring the bell. The onlookers lapped together in the wake of the ambulance to gossip and dissect what had just happened. The Englishman straightened his tie, buttoned his jacket, shot his cuffs. Job done. He did a smart right turn and strode briskly off, arms swinging in time to an internal but spirited rendition of 'The British Grenadiers'.

Inside the ambulance all was quiet, until:

'Can I breathe now?' I asked.

'Wait a minute.' Sam pulled the curtains over the windows. 'OK now.'

I sat up. Then I held her tightly to me. 'You were brilliant, Sam. You can stop crying now.'

'Och, they weren't real tears.' More fell.

'Wheesht. Wheesht. It's all going to be all right now.'

'Don't you ever die on me again, Douglas Brodie.' She sniffed and dug out a hankie.

'I promise.' I turned to the 'doctor'. He was grinning.

'How did it go? No problems?'

'All fine, sir.'

'Did you come up from London overnight?'

'We slapped some paint on one of our vans yesterday, changed the plates and drove through the night. Doesn't bear too close an inspection.'

Sam prodded me. 'Talking of paint, I hope you've got my make-up? That lipstick was expensive.'

'And better on your lips than my neck. In my pocket. What happens now?'

'We change transport. And you go into a safe place.'

'Where?'

Sam grinned. 'You've still got some friends.'

EIGHTEEN

We drove for a while and I keeked out between the curtains to see where we were. Suddenly we were pulling into a yard somewhere in the East End. We stopped and the doors were opened. One of the ambulance men stood there, smiling.

'All change,' he said. 'God, you look poorly, sir. I'd take something for that.'

'I had a whisky in mind.'

'I'd take a couple. Be on the safe side.'

They threw their white coats in the back of the ambulance and I stepped down on to the cobbles. I could now see where the white paint had been slopped on the van's sides and how the overnight drive had marred its surface. One of the men drove it into a garage in the forecourt. He emerged in a smart Morris Ten. Sam and I climbed in the back and we were off. I pulled a hat down on my head and sank down in my seat. I was so low I could only see the top half of buildings but knew we were heading back to the city centre.

We bumped down one of the narrow back lanes that ran parallel to the main streets throughout the centre. Tradesman's entrance. We stopped and sat for a moment. The driver turned.

'Clear. Good luck, sir.'

Now I knew where we were. We ducked out of the car just as a door opened up in one of the back walls of a building. We were inside in a second, into pitch dark. The door closed behind us and I heard the car drive off. A faint light came on from somewhere up ahead. A big bear of a man stepped forward with both hands held out. His great black beard emphasised his glowing eyes.

'Shalom, Douglas.'

'Shalom, Shimon. It's good to see you.'

We shook hands, double-handed, like long-lost brothers. I nearly embraced him.

'Shimon, I'm sorry, you're taking a great risk.'

'Nonsense, Douglas. After what you risked for me? For us? This is nothing. Come through. Your quarters are waiting. It is a poor thing but you are most welcome.'

Despite his smoky colouring and his yarmulke, Shimon Belsinger's accent was posh Glaswegian: born and bred in Hyndland. His parents had made the thousand-mile trek from Estonia fleeing the Tsar's pogroms. Shimon was as Scottish as Sam or me.

Did he owe me? I didn't see it that way. Six months back I'd helped Shimon track down a burglar that was pestering his community. But in the process I'd stirred up a wasps' nest. Or, more correctly, a rats' nest of fascists fleeing judgment for war crimes. Before I could bring an end to the bloodletting, five people had died, including one of my oldest friends. Shimon himself had barely escaped with his life.

It was a bad period for me and until the roof fell in on me on the day of the Govan Fair I thought I'd put it behind me. But some good comes out of even the darkest hours; here I was, reaping what I'd sown. I took it, gladly. It was astonishing how my heart was lifting at such kindness, at someone taking such a risk for me. And I was also simply grateful to get out of my concrete holding pen.

Shimon led us both through a maze of crates and piled furniture to a clear area. It was a snug little corner of his warehouse at the back of his furniture shop in Candleriggs. I looked around. A lamp glowed on top of a crate. An army cot was neatly set up with blankets and a pillow. Beyond, against the wall, was a sink and tap. Incongruously, in the small open space between the cot and us was a table covered by a white cloth and surrounded by three upturned boxes. The Ritz. We each chose a box.

I looked around me hardly believing I was here. I suddenly felt overwhelmed by it all. I realised my legs were vibrating and pushed my hands down on to my thighs. If anyone had asked me to speak just then I'd have choked. My throat was constricted. Sam saw what was happening and pulled her crate closer to me and squeezed my hands. She took out a cigarette and lit it for me. I took a deep drag, felt dizzy and sick all at the same time, and bowed my head till it had passed. After a while Sam and I held hands without a hint of self-consciousness. Shimon smiled indulgently. I took some deep breaths and found my voice. It sounded shaky.

'This is cosy, Shimon.'

'It is the best I could do. But you will be safe here. For a while.'

'It's a thousand times better than my recent quarters. Thank you.'

Just then a bell rang from somewhere behind us. I jumped, my heart thudding in my chest. It rang twice, stopped, then two more times. Shimon got up.

'We have a visitor.' He disappeared among the packing crates and came back with Harry Templeton in tow. I got up and shook his hand. We grinned at each other. He found a fourth box and we formed a conspiratorial circle. I was beginning to think this was real. I was out, but what now? Had we got away with it? What could I achieve?

'What now, Harry?'

'In a way, that's up to you, Brodie. Sillitoe sends his regards and says you're back on the payroll. Though he also said the usual rules apply: he would deny it if things go wrong. You understand?'

'Perfectly. But how much worse could they get? Don't bother to answer that. What does he expect us to do?'

'Not "us", Brodie. You. I'm heading south tonight. So are my colleagues. Job over for the moment. We'll leave a contact number for emergencies but 'fraid you're on your own, old chum, for the time being.'

'To do what?'

He raised his fingers one at a time. 'One, find out who killed Gibson. And two, why. Three, find out what's going on at Scottish Linen – we presume the two are linked. Four, in the process, clear your name and hence the Service's.'

'Is that all?'

He just smiled and handed round his cigarette case. I ought to get one.

'The clock's ticking on the financial time bomb. We need to find out how bad things are at Scottish Linen and prevent an explosion in international – make that American – confidence in British finances. The drop-dead date's the fifteenth of July. But we must have answers before then. The Yanks are asking more questions. And the panic's rising.'

'What's today's date?'

'Thursday, twenty-sixth of June. You've less than three weeks, Brodie. Call it two.'

I drew a deep breath. My first thought was that I had a fortnight to find a way of disappearing. Maybe follow the fascists to Argentina. Perón seemed happy to take anyone. My second thoughts were:

'The police saw a body leave their nick. Doesn't there need to be a burial? An autopsy? Paperwork? How much of this charade do we have to complete?'

Harry exchanged glances with Sam.

'All of it, I'm afraid. To be free to pursue your mission, Brodie, you need to be dead. Moreover, you need to be *seen* to be dead.'

What a bloody mess. Sam put on a wry smile. She squeezed my hand again.

'We can do this, Douglas. We have to. Let me tell you, Sangster and his pals had a nigh-on watertight case. I don't know who was behind this or why, but they stitched it up good and proper.'

'Stitched *me* up. Well, it wouldn't have been Sangster, that's for sure. He doesn't have the talent.'

'Whoever it was lined up the evidence and the witnesses to virtually guarantee conviction.'

'And execution?'

Now she gripped my hand tightly. 'So it's just as well you're already dead.'

'All we need now is last rites. How am I going to explain *this* to my mother?'

Sam said, 'I'm going to see her right now. I'll drive down to Kilmarnock before she hears it on the news. And it *will* be on the news. You've already caused enough of a stir. This will be sensational.'

I winced. 'And will it say I committed suicide?'

She looked rueful but nodded.

'Not much of an epitaph.' I sighed. 'You'd better get going, Sam. My mum will kill me when she finds out.'

It got smiles all round, except from me.

NINETEEN

I spent the next four days regaining some equilibrium and doing some planning. I heard from Shimon and Sam that the furore was dying down and I was moving off the front pages. I asked both to spare me the details. It was time to get going. But there was one last piece of public deception required.

On the last night of June, Sam drove into the unlit back lane serving Shimon's store. I slipped out of the back door and into the Riley. Reversing the flow, Sam drove up to Park Terrace and down her own tradesman's lane, and I sneaked into her house.

First thing I did was luxuriate in a hot bath. Sam insisted on it before I was allowed near her. She kindly scrubbed my back but declined my selfless offer that she should join me. It made it all the more delicious and surprisingly naughty to share a bed with her again. I was a schoolboy sneaking into his girlfriend's house while her parents were out. We didn't seem to have forgotten how to make each other happy, though I'd have settled for just holding her in my arms all night through.

Lying there listening to her breathe, I looked back with shame and wonder at my suicidal self of a week ago. See what I would have missed. My emotions were on a Big Dipper ride. Come morning I holed up in the kitchen while Sam went off to pick up my sore-pressed mother from Kilmarnock.

It was an emotional reunion: the first time I'd seen her since I'd been jailed. I'd refused point blank to have her visit me in a cell.

'I like the beard. It suits you.' She rubbed her face, then mine. A deep red mat was already thickening round my chin.

'Camouflage, Mum. Sorry.'

I was more sorry for the hot tears I felt running down her face, and I took a moment to dry them off with my hankie. It didn't stop the flow but Sam had done a fine job of preparing her for my 'death' and what was to follow.

'I didnae mind hearing about you on the wireless, for Samantha had warned me. And it didnae seem real. But see oor neighbours!'

'I thought they'd be kind, Mum?'

'Oh aye, kindness mixed wi' nosiness. They couldnae wait to get the facts so they could a' sit around and gossip about us.'

'They always did, Mum. You and Dad were different.'

'That's the truth. Some o' them see it as comeuppance.'

'What for, Agnes?' asked Sam.

'For sending my boy to university instead of down the pit like the rest of the lads in Bonnyton. *Ken your place* are the local watchwords.'

Later, I hugged them both in their black ensembles and watched them set off into the downpour. A suitable backcloth for a bleak pantomime. The rain had been pelting down for hours, compounding my guilt. On a day like this, on a venture like this, an old woman could catch a chill – pneumonia ...

They were picking up Wullie McAllister and his companion, Stewart, en route. Despite Sam's best efforts to put off mourners – I still struggled to cope with the pain and bother I was causing – Wullie had stubbornly insisted on paying his respects. Shame he'd saved them till now. Neither man knew I was alive, so it loaded added pressure on Sam and my mother to go through with this terrible charade.

102

To while away the time, I made a phone call. I knew from a recent letter they'd had the phone installed. Business was so good on Arran they needed one to handle the enquiries. The response was everything I could have hoped for and took the edge off a bitter day.

Now I stood peering out of a slit in the heavy curtains in the first-floor lounge, impatient for their return, checking my watch, calculating the mileage to Kilmarnock and back, and the possible length of the rituals. I'd insisted it was kept simple. No church, no hymns, no mourners. My mother had argued; despite the sham nature of the ceremony she felt it wasn't seemly. I patiently explained that there was nothing about this whole business that was seemly, and that the quicker and simpler the process, the better. In that sense I could have wished that Wullie had kept his distance. I only hoped that Sam would have been able to put him off coming back for the ritual drink and sandwiches.

At last I saw the converted Bedford creep up Park Terrace and pull up outside. It stopped tight against the kerb, tyre-deep in the gutter coursing with water. I wanted to rush out and help but had to stand and watch as the driver got out and held up a huge umbrella as the van disgorged. Damn! Wullie and Stewart were climbing out. What the hell should I do? Stay upstairs till they'd gone? Had Sam already confessed? What could I say to him? Could I trust Wullie to keep silent? I was neurotic enough about being on the run. It seemed only a matter of time before I was recaptured.

I closed the curtains and took the stairs down to the hall and then along into the back dining room. I couldn't be seen at the front door. The curtains were drawn here too, as per the custom and, in this unusual context, to shield the pacing corpse from prying eyes. It also meant I could look down the hall to the front door without being seen myself.

I could picture the driver handing the two black-clad women to the front door under the protection of his umbrella. He'd then have to help Stewart carry Wullie McAllister and his wheelchair to the open door: two trips. The door opened and grey light tumbled down the hall. Sam and my mother stepped in and shook off their hats and veils and their soaking coats. I watched them hang up their clothes, receive Wullie and get him seated on the stairs while he waited for his wheels. Then Sam broke off, holding my mother by the arm and dragging her towards the dining room. She marched in.

'Douglas?' she whispered.

I stood forward. 'I'm here,' I whispered back, at the same time giving my mother a quick embrace.

'He doesn't know. You need to tell him.'

'I could hide behind the curtains.'

'Don't be daft. You need to face this.'

'Can we trust him?'

'Do we have a choice? Listen. They're coming.'

The wheels creaked along the hall.

'Give him a warning. We don't want to stop his heart,' I hissed.

Sam turned and stepped through the door.

'Wullie? And you, Stewart. Just a minute please. In the van there I was trying to tell you something. But I couldn't, in case the driver overheard.'

'Whit is it, hen? Have you run oot of whisky? I'll send Stewart to the off licence.'

'No. It's not that. We have plenty. And you're going to need a big glass. It's about Douglas.'

'Oh aye. You'll be telling me he's no' deid?'

'How . . .?'

'I knew it. Are you there, Brodie?'

I stepped forward into the light and shook their hands. Both were grinning like fools. So was I.

'How did you guess?'

'Suicide? Douglas Brodie? And I'm the Emperor of China.'

Behind him, Stewart, beaming, added, 'He tried to put a bet on with me. I wouldn't take it.'

My mother slid out from behind me. 'Are you two saying you didnae believe Samantha and me? I'm fair hurt.'

'Naw, you were great, Agnes.' He stroked his thin moustache. 'Maybe there could have been more tears for your only-begotten son.'

'Was that all?' she asked.

'I've been a crime reporter for forty years. I've seen every scam. This felt like one. Especially the ambulance bit.'

'What do you mean?'

He touched his long thin nose. 'I have contacts in every hospital in Glasgow. I taught Brodie to trawl for stories in the accident wards on a Sunday morning. After I heard the terrible news, I made a few calls to see where they'd taken him. Nobody knew.'

'God, Wullie, I hope you haven't blown my cover.'

'Naw, naw. When I began to suspect, I pulled right back.'

My mother persisted. 'So why did you insist on coming to the cemetery?'

'To assist with the verisimilitude, Agnes.'

'You old devil. You might have said.'

'Well, I didnae want to upset the pair of you if I'd got it wrang. But listen, this is a gie dry wake. I was promised a dram.'

Tea was made, sandwiches produced and whisky drunk. Just like a proper funeral, apart from the increasingly cheerful corpse in their midst.

We sat round the dining table in the gloom and I heard how it went from my mother.

'I was saying to Samantha, it was just terrible. I kent fine it wisnae you going into the ground but it felt like it. As for that minister . . .'

'He was a miserable git.'

'Wullie!' said Sam.

'Sorry, hen. That's the only way to describe him. He couldnae get oot o' there fast enough.'

I shrugged. 'You cannae blame him, I suppose, given my reputation.'

My mother was unforgiving. 'But where was his Christian charity? I should have pressed harder on my own minister to come and do it.'

'But let's not forget, Mum, it wasn't actually real.'

'It felt gie like it. As for mourners – apart from this pair – nary a one. Shameful it was.'

I touched her arm. 'Mum, it's what I wanted, what we agreed. It would have been too embarrassing to have had loads of folk greetin' and bawlin' while all the time I was ensconced in Sam's house with a big whisky in my hand.'

'Loads? Well, maybe wan or twa, eh, Brodie?' Wullie's eyes twinkled.

My mother gave him a look. 'Aye, well, I hope when the time comes for real, you get a better send-off.'

'It's not something that will worry me, Mum, come the day. But I suspect the eventual number of mourners will depend on whether or not I can clear up this mess. Which reminds me, Wullie, I need your help. I'm stuck in Shimon's store but I need some eyes and ears out on the street.'

'In my pomp, I'd have been glad to help, Brodie, but as you can see . . .' He tapped his wheels.

'Can I help, Brodie?' asked Stewart.

'It's good of you to offer, but I need someone with a particular set of low-life talents. I want Wullie to contact one of my old snitches, Weasel Watkins. I want you to run him, Wullie. He'll report to you and you to me.'

'Weasel?' said Sam. 'He sounds dependable. Are you sure, Douglas?'

'Oh, you can count on Weasel. He's a snitch whose chief talent is hanging about, watching and clyping. He's a natural spy. Weasel doesn't have enough imagination to get easily bored. He's a wind-up toy: point him, set him loose and he'll keep doing what was asked until his spring runs down. His "spring" being alcohol. It makes for dedication but uncertain results. His other talent is that he's invisible. No one notices Weasel. Which makes him perfect for the job.'

'Which is?' asked Wullie.

'I want Weasel to watch Lady Gibson and report to you each day.'

'What are you looking for?'

'I'm not sure, Wullie. All I know is that she dropped me in this mess either willingly or unwillingly. I want to know where she goes, who she sees, who visits her, anything at all. At some stage I need to confront her, but I'd like to be as prepared as possible.'

'I could talk to her,' said Sam. 'She doesn't know who I am. She's been pointed out to me at the odd function in the past but we've never met. She won't connect me with you.'

'She may not know your face, Sam, but she'll know who you are. Let's see what Weasel comes up with. You all right with that, Wullie?'

'Aye, sure. Ah'm used to hobnobbing wi' low life.'

'I also want to find out more about Fraser Gibson. I don't think he was murdered for the ransom money. Or not just for it. It doesn't make sense. The Government is terrified his bank was pilfering American aid. I want to know everything about Gibson. Who his pals were, where he hung out, what he got up to, what his background was, etc.'

'Ah can make some calls, Brodie. And maybe get the lovely Elspeth on the case.'

'Who's she?' Mum asked.

'Elspeth MacPherson. A bonny lass with a huge brain,' Wullie replied. 'Our literary critic and chief researcher at the *Gazette*. Has a first in Classics from Edinburgh. Knows the Encyclopaedia Britannica off by heart. Possibly wrote it.'

'Great idea, Wullie. See what you can get in a hurry. Can we meet tomorrow with your first findings? I'll tell you where and when.'

'Aye, sure.'

'That's another thing. I need to move. I'm putting Shimon at too much risk. He's having to keep his staff out of the back store and it's only a matter of time before someone finds me skulking there.'

'You could skulk here in the scullery?'

'I'd love to, Sam.' And sneak up to your bed every night, was my unspoken wish. 'But that's even riskier. It would be catastrophic for your career if you were found harbouring an alleged murderer and had helped engineer his escape. God knows what crimes we committed this afternoon.'

'Well, let's hope it is only God who knows. OK, where are you going to move to? Where's safe?'

I smiled. 'I made a phone call. It's all fixed. You'll be amused.'

When I told her, she was. Sort of.

TWENTY

It was two in the morning, and the night sky was darkened by cloud. Though the early July night was warm, I had my cap pulled down over my face and my jacket collar turned up. I clutched a small holdall. I took the byways and back streets and avoided the pools of light round the soft hissing gas lamps. Like a cat burglar, I slipped down the shadows and walked softly until I got to the Clyde. It seemed appropriate and ironic to rendezvous at the Kelvinhaugh Ferry. Only this time I'd arranged my own transport.

The ticket hut was in darkness and only a faint glow from a street lamp reached as far as the steps down to the water. I stared into the darkness. I thought I could make out the hull and rigging of a boat. A few steps nearer and I confirmed it. It wasn't ferry-shaped but long and sleek. It had two masts, fore and aft, one taller than the other. I knew its make and its name, or rather its old name. It was a gaff-rigged ketch called the *Lorne*, though its present owner might have renamed it, given its shifty provenance. I began stepping down towards it. Still no lights from the boat. Then finally, just as I got to the foot of the steps, I saw a glimmer from behind a curtain, and made out the bulk of a man sitting outside on the deck. He'd seen me and was moving towards me, grinning. I stepped on to the gunwale and Eric McLeod's big hand gripped mine to steady me down to the deck.

'You're a sight for sore eyes,' I said.

'And you've been causing trouble again.'

Neither of us spoke names out loud, just in case. We talked no more until Eric had cast off his moorings and let the river carry us out into the channel.

'Where to, Brodie?'

'Downriver, Eric. Find us a quiet spot.'

He nodded and raised the furled mizzen sail, then the jib. I remember him saying she handled just fine without needing to hoist the mainsail. The canvas picked up the breeze, filled, and pulled us sweetly down the black flow. I looked back to see a small tender slipping along in the silver wake. I smiled at the sensation of gliding along the deserted Clyde in the wee small hours. It tasted of freedom and I was permanently greedy for that these days. Insatiable.

I thought of the last time I'd been on board the *Lorne*. Over a year ago. Sam was lying battered and chloroformed on a bunk below. I'd freed her from hostage and was cack-handedly steering the ketch back to Arran. Its owners were both dead; one by his own hand, one by mine. The Slattery brothers, drug-running between Ireland and Arran and on to the mainland, had framed my childhood friend, Hugh Donovan, for murder and seen to his hanging despite the best efforts of Hugh's advocate, a certain Samantha Campbell.

Big Eric – former Black Watch, and 51st Highland Division like me – had lent me, a desperado with a shotgun, his motorboat. I'd chased down the *Lorne* and consigned Slattery to the depths. Him or me. It seemed only fair that Eric should acquire a new boat for his unquestioning help. Besides, I was no sailor and had no use for a yacht – until now. If I ever got out of this fix, I'd ask Eric to take Sam and me for a sail round the islands for old times' sake.

We'd exchanged the odd letter over the past year. Eric's were effusive with thanks. His small boat-hire business at Kildonan on the southern tip of Arran had been considerably augmented by the big ketch. As well as fishing for his family and selling the catch locally, he skippered it out for day trips and longer through the sailing months. Business was growing and – luckily for me – had necessitated the installation of the phone.

We anchored by the south bank well down the estuary and beyond the lines of houses and shipyards. At last we could talk. Eric made us mugs of tea spiced with Navy Rum and we sat out under the warm clouds. He pulled out his pipe and I lit a companionable cigarette.

'You're beginning to look as much like an old seadog as me, Brodie.'

'I've a way to go before I match your burning bush.'

I stroked my tufts. Barely two weeks' growth, but already a solid mat. One of my meagre talents. The difference between Eric's and mine – apart from the length – was that his beard and hair were in matching shades of fiery red. My whiskers honoured my mother's once flaming locks, but my head kept to my father's dark hue.

'Is this your idea of camouflage?' he asked.

'I need all the help I can get.'

'It seems you do.'

'You'd heard about the Gibson murder?' I hadn't been able to tell him much in my brief phone call. But for Eric McLeod, it was enough that a pal was in trouble.

'Oh aye. Almost sent you a postcard.'

'To say?'

'To wish you luck.'

'Did it cross your mind I might have done it?'

'Naw. Not your style, Brodie.'

I smiled at this big man. We'd barely met, yet here he was making judgements about whether or not I'd kidnapped and murdered a man. I'm not sure I could be that confident of my fellow man. Unless that man was Eric McLeod.

'Thanks.'

'And I was sorry to hear you were deid,' he said solemnly.

'So was I, Eric. So was I. But I had to get out.'

He nodded. 'To find out who did do it.' It wasn't a question.

'That, and why. There's more to this.'

Sitting there rocking gently in the soft night, I would have told him my life story and every secret. I knew it would go no further than the hull of the ketch. So I told him about MI5 and what was at stake. He whistled when I told him of the deadline racing towards us for Britain avoiding bankruptcy via handouts from US Secretary of State George Marshall. Mostly he just listened, asking no questions, and occasionally sucking on his pipe. At the end, he asked:

'How can I help?'

'What are your commitments these days?'

'Catch fish. Take trippers round the bay. Put up the wi' wife and weans.'

I smiled at the last point; I knew Eric doted on his family, which made my request all the harder. He already had a daughter when I first bumped into him. In his last letter he had been bursting with pride at the safe delivery of a son. They called him Douglas, or just Dougie.

'How's wee Dougie?'

'Not so wee. I think he's taking after his namesake.' He grinned.

'And Mairi? How's she keeping? It must be a handful.'

'She was made for this. She's well.'

A big smile split his face at the mere thought of his magnificent wife. I'd met her when I brought the *Lorne* into harbour. A big capable woman with the blonde hair and blue eyes of her Norse ancestors. I was asking too much of him.

'What do you need, Brodie?'

'I needed a favour. But it's too big.'

'Go on. Ask.'

'I need a base. A safe base.'

He nodded. 'Moored or mobile?'

'Mobile's better. Safer if I keep moving.'

'How long for?'

'Couple of weeks at most. After that, it's too late. It may already be too late.'

'The Marshall plan deadline you were talking about?'

'Exactly. And I could pay you for your loss of business. Or rather Harry Templeton will.'

'No need.'

'There is. You can't fish and you can't take day trippers out round the bay. But really – can your wife and weans spare you?'

His broad grin said it all. 'I'll be glad of the sleep. I'll get her sister to stay. Tell her I've gone fishing.'

'And that's the truth, Eric. That's the truth.'

I lay awake for a long time in one of the bunks, feeling the ketch stir and rock beneath me. It was the first time in days I'd felt truly safe. In Shimon's storeroom I'd been on tenter-hooks waiting for a police raid or one of Shimon's men finding me lurking among the crates and giving me away. Partly, too, it was the feeling of claustrophobia, sealed in the dark among the boxes and smells of wood and textiles. Out here on the river, under the stars, I was free.

It gave me time to think, to wonder again about how life turns, how choices made long ago cascade down the years. All you can do is be true to yourself and take what happens on the chin. How could I have reacted any differently to Sheila Gibson's request for help? It wasn't the fifty quid. I'd forgotten to ask for it. It was how I was made, how I was shaped. I didn't always like the results; often I wished I could react differently to events, offer a more measured response. But I would be a different man. I wasn't so sure that Dr Andrew Baird had it right: that I'd become some sort of junkie for excitement. I suspected that 'the fault, dear Brutus, is not in our stars, but in ourselves'.

Whatever the cause, here I was, a vilified outcast floating in the Firth of Clyde, in some sort of metaphor for my life. Can a dead man be an outcast? The saving grace was that I was couched in a safe haven provided by a man I knew only a little, but who understood honour and core decency. A friend in need, prepared to throw his lot in with a man accused of murder, based solely on gut instinct and – as he saw it – repayment of a debt. He ignored the fact that my gift of the ketch was to repay *him* for the loan of one of his small boats and his best engine in the first place. It was a simple and clear strain of morality that I recognised for my own but which seemed all too rare these days. It gave me back hope. My life was in turmoil again, but this night, for the first time in weeks, rocked in Eric's cradle, soothed by the clinking of the rigging, I slept like a baby.

Next morning we breakfasted on fried oatcakes and herring caught on lines trailed behind him as Eric sailed from Arran. It beat the hell out of prison bacon rolls. After, as we sat and enjoyed a cigarette:

'Brodie? I've been thinking.'

I was half expecting this. 'I've asked too much of you? Of course I have. Look, just drop me off and I'll go to ground in Glasgow.'

He waved his big hand dismissively. 'Not at a', man. Look, we're on a boat, right?'

I nodded.

'She's seaworthy enough to get us all the way down the west coast. Wales and England. All the way to France. It would take a good few days and it would depend on the weather. But if you don't think you can pull this off . . . Or even if you thought, the hell with it, they all think I'm dead and I might as well disappear . . . You and your lady, Samantha of course.'

I looked at him. I could hardly reply. 'A safety net, Eric. An escape route. *Moran taing*, Eric. *Moran taing*.'

'I didn't know you had the Gaelic.'

'Some key phrases are useful when you're in charge of a bunch of Highlanders. But thank you, Eric. It's good to have options. Let's see how things go.'

We put in at the pier at the Erskine Ferry and made some phone calls. Eric had already told his wife he might be gone for a few days; now he confirmed it and told her to get her sister over. I stayed out of hearing but could tell by his actions that he didn't have to coax her but that he'd miss her like mad. I resolved to take her an armful of flowers if I got out of this mess in one piece.

My own calls were first to Sam to say all was well, then to Harry Templeton. During my days of planning and thinking ensconced in Shimon's store, I concluded I needed to get to the heart of this whole sorry mess. All roads led to the Scottish Linen Bank. But though I had handled some basic bookkeeping in my army days, I wouldn't know the workings of a retail bank from the workings of a Chinese laundry. I needed help. Preferably someone with a flexible grip on morality. From my pre-war days pounding the beat I knew just the man. If he wasn't banged up. If he wasn't dead.

'Harry, I need you to find someone. A certain Archibald Higgins, a Glasgow accountant – until he was struck off. Which takes some doing for Glasgow accountants. Airchie's also done time. Indeed, he may be doing a stretch currently. But if he's available I'll need cash to persuade him.'

'We have funds to overcome most scruples.'

'Scruples isn't a word I'd associate with wee Airchie.' I told Harry where to set up a meeting if he managed to track down Higgins. 'I need to do my own research too. I know it's risky but I need to get out and about. Can you fix me with some papers?'

'What do you need?'

I told him. He wasn't fazed.

'They'll be with you tomorrow. How will I get them to you?'

We agreed on the drop.

We hung up and I handed the phone to Eric. I had him call the *Gazette* and ask to speak to McAllister. When he was put through I took back the phone.

'Wullie, it's me. Have you got hold of Weasel?'

'He's on the payroll.'

'Well done. How about your banking enquiries?'

'A wee bit of progress. Some desk research and face to face. Shortly, in fact. I'm just on my way there now. I've a couple of interviews lined up.'

'Could we meet this evening?'

'Where?'

I told him.

TWENTY-ONE

Just as twilight eased into night, Eric steered the *Lorne* alongside the steps at Anderston Quay downstream of the Clyde Street Ferry. It was as far upriver as he could take her without chopping down the masts to get under the road and rail bridges running up to Central Station.

The sails were furled, and we were moving under power, the four-stroke marine diesel steadily throbbing throughout the hull. I was down below and peeking out from behind the curtain. I saw two figures waiting, one in a wheelchair, one behind. Wullie and Stewart.

Eric tied up and climbed the steps. With Stewart's help they carried Wullie and then his wheelchair down on to the deck. Quickly, Eric brought the ketch round and out into the river. When it was dark enough and we were far enough out of plain sight, I came out of hiding. Wullie was perched as far forward on the deck as possible, by the forestay. Like an unbraw figurehead. He turned and waved at me, his lit fag carving a glowing scimitar against the night sky. His eyes gleamed in the light from the boat's lamp. Stewart stepped towards me and shook my hand.

'A fine night for a trip, Brodie.'

'It surely is, Stewart. I hope you don't mind being dragged into this cloak-and-dagger stuff.'

'More fun than trying to get a class of Govan weans to learn their twelve times table.'

'If this is fun, frankly, I could do with a wee bit less of it in my life.'

'I bet.'

'I assume you're pleased and astonished at how the old rogue has recovered?'

'In some ways. It was quieter there for a while.'

He peered forward at the old rascal and smiled fondly. Wullie just grinned and waved. They called themselves brothers for appearances' sake. They'd been together most of their adult lives and exhibited all the best signs and symptoms of the long and happily married. I left Stewart to talk to Eric at the tiller and to enjoy the ride. I walked forward and hung over the bows on the other side to Wullie, and proceeded to probe him about what he'd learned. Not that Wullie ever needed much persuasion to talk. He was chuffed with how clever he'd been and how much he'd achieved.

'You've got Weasel Watkins on the job?'

'He was between jobs, so to speak, and seemed happy to get started. I told him it was for the paper. He didnae seem to care what it was for as long as he got his ten bob a day.'

'Where's he basing himself? Weasel's a wee scruff – unless he's had a makeover. He'd stand out in a nice neighbourhood.'

'Scruff still, but he's playing to his strengths. Camouflage. He's got himself a big brush and wanders up and down the road pretending to be a sweep. They'll have the cleanest street in Glesga.'

I laughed at the image. 'But he knows the house and knows what to look out for?'

'Ah took him there masel' in a taxi. We went past a couple o' times to make sure. Then Ah dropped him at the road end. Him and his brush. He knows he has to watch for comings and goings by the lady of the hoose, and any strangers.'

I nodded. It was a long shot but it was the best we could do for the moment.

'What have you got on Gibson?'

'Let's start wi' the public stuff. I asked our fount of all knowledge, the fair Elspeth, to trawl through the clippings. But she already had a load at her fingertips. Pure curiosity, she said, but facts seem to stick to the inside of her heid, like midges to a roll of flypaper.'

'Let's hear the basics. Where did he come from?'

'Keep mind, this is all the public stuff, the stuff that Fraser would have allowed to come out. Great men are gie handy at managing their public images.'

'Well, it's a start.'

'He's a south Ayrshire boy. Down by Maybole. Nothing special about the family, except the mother died while the boys were young and the man took another wife. Younger model, I suppose. Other than that, jist ordinary working class, him and his younger brother.'

'Not a privileged start? I thought he'd be part of the Gibson merchant clan. The tobacco barons.'

'Far from it. Went to local schools, left at fourteen but Fraser managed to get a job in his local bank branch running messages. He made a big thing of the humble beginnings for the press. Then he just worked his way up, probably ower the dead bodies of the competition. No' quite rags to riches but certainly a self-made man.'

'Ambitious then. Anything untoward?'

'Not that Elspeth knows of. But a strong impression of a man in a hurry. A streak of ruthlessness – more of which later. Anyway, as the money got better the houses got bigger. He married above himself if you like; Lady Gibson was Sheila McKechny, daughter of the owner of the big stores in Edinburgh and Glasgow. Private education, the whole bit. They've moved in charmed circles for some years now. Especially when he got knighted.'

'Pals? Who does he hobnob with?'

'He's a gowfer. But then it goes wi' the territory in the

upper echelons. A lot of business done on the nineteenth green. Gibson's a member – *was* a member – of Whitecraigs Golf Club. Private, exclusive and very expensive.'

'Of course he would be. You could swing a seven iron from his back garden and put a ball on the fairway. Any other clubs? Positions?'

'A yacht club out by Gourock. Rangers. He's on the board. His bank's a supporter.'

'You mentioned a ruthless streak. Tell me more.'

'Elspeth says the papers over the years have oblique references to a man larger than life, disnae suffer fools gladly or otherwise, quick temper and always gets his way. Nae surprise there. You don't get to be top dog without biting a few folk on your way up.'

'But?'

'But it's more than normal pushiness and ambition. I said I'd lined up to interview a couple of folk at the bank, the day. One was his old private secretary; the other was the new boss, Colin Clarkson, formerly the number two.'

'I wish I'd been there!' I realised how much I meant that, how strongly I felt cut off from my normal life. From being able to carry out my own digging. 'Did you have any difficulty? I mean in the circumstances?'

'The circumstances in which a *Gazette* reporter bumped off the Managing Director?'

'Exactly, Wullie.'

'Eddie had to get his boss to put in a personal request. Director to director kinda thing.'

I nodded. 'Good for Eddie. Who did you see first?'

'Talking's thirsty work, Brodie. Have ye anything that would wet a man's thrapple?'

I went down into the cabin and came back with a bottle of Eric's rum. I poured us both a large shot. Not Wullie's usual tipple, but it tickled his fancy to be sipping a sailor's ration. He'd want a parrot next.

'Let's start wi' Clarkson. Ah telt him we were doing a kind of memorial piece for Gibson in the *Gazette*.' Wullie described it so vividly I felt I was there beside him taking notes . . .

TWENTY-TWO

A uniformed doorman met Wullie and wheeled him to the executive lift and then up to the top floor, the senior management floor, marked by thick carpets and hushed conversations. Along the corridor lined by oil paintings of past head men and into the outer office of the Managing Director. An obligatory wait until the great man deigned to buzz his secretary, then into the imposing inner sanctum: wood panelling, high ceilings and silken Persian carpet.

Colin Clarkson came out from behind his massive oak desk to shake Wullie's hand. It was as though the room and furniture had been built for a grown-up and this wisp of a man was there under false pretences. But to counter that illusion, Clarkson sported the full dress uniform of a senior banker: tails and stiff collar, striped trousers, gold watch chain straddling his waistcoat pockets. Only the bowler was lacking. A quick glance showed it perched on a coat-stand by the door.

Tea was brought and they settled down round a low table, Wullie in his wheelchair, Clarkson in a throne-like chair on the other side. Wullie detected someone who could hardly believe his luck but was trying hard to seem suitably grief-stricken for his old boss. He suspected that the moment Clarkson had heard about the murder he'd sneaked in, fingered the furniture, admired the view and tried out the big leather swivel chair for size. Maybe punched the air a few times. Now it was his, all his.

'You must have been gie upset, Mr Clarkson, to hear about the kidnapping, not to mention the murder?'

'Upset doesn't go near it. We were traumatised, Mr McAllister. Traumatised.' He rolled the word around his mouth as though he'd used it frequently lately and loved the taste of it. 'The head of our bank, abducted from his own home? Then murdered in cold blood? What's the world coming to?'

He wrung his small hands as though it was cold in his barn of an office. The rest of him was in proportion: neat, slight build, owl eyes behind thick glasses. More accountant than top manager; but of course he'd come up through the post of finance director.

'What indeed? It's as well you were able to step quickly into his shoes.'

Clarkson looked grave. 'I was his second in command, so I was able to pick up the reins. The bank had to move on. For our customers' sakes.'

'Tell me about Sir Fraser. Tell me about the *man*. My paper wants to do a piece on him. Something beyond the obituaries.'

Clarkson looked worried. 'I trust this won't be some sort of hatchet job, Mr McAllister? Given that it was one of your paper's reporters that is alleged to have been behind the murder?'

'I'm glad you said "alleged". The *Gazette* always stands behind its employees. In the same way that we stand for unbiased and accurate reporting.'

Clarkson inclined his head.

'What we're looking for is the human angle. Our readers want to know more about this self-made man. How it was possible to come from such humble origins to lead this great bank. Like you yourself, Mr Clarkson. And in due course, I might add, we'd like to return and do a feature on you, if that's appropriate?'

Clarkson preened and smoothed his waistcoat. 'I suppose you could say we're cut from the same cloth, Sir Fraser and I.'

Clarkson was already dreaming of kneeling at the feet of his monarch, head bowed, awaiting the tap on each shoulder from the King's sword.

'Is that him over there?' Wullie pointed to an oil painting on the far wall. It looked like a colour version of the newspaper archive photo.

'It is indeed. A great man.' Clarkson shook his head in sorrow.

The painting was a head-and-shoulder study. It showed a heavy-jawed man with blazing eyes, a stubborn nose and chin, and a thin line for a mouth. The hair was a slicked dark brown, and the shoulders meaty and powerful. Like a second row forward gone to seed but still hoping for a last call-up to the Scottish team.

'I wouldnae want to get on his wrong side, eh?' Wullie all but winked at Clarkson. The little man thought for a second and then nodded. The *Gazette* wanted the human angle; this was part of it.

'You could say that. Knew his own mind. Spoke out.'

Wullie took a chance. 'I heard he had a temper.'

Clarkson stole a glance round the room, as though Gibson might be listening.

'Some days it was like walking on eggshells.'

'What set him off?'

'Oh, it depended.'

'On?'

'Off the record, it could be anything. A typo in a letter, someone late for a meeting, cold tea, poor annual results. Anything.'

'Would it be fair to conclude, Mr Clarkson, that he was a bit of a bully?'

'Gosh, I wouldn't go that far.' *Too* human. Clarkson moved to his seat edge and his hands became increasingly jumpy.

'How far *would* you go?' Wullie put down his pencil and pad. 'Let's keep this off the record. I just want to get the sense of the man. What he was like. We can agree what we'll put in the paper later.'

Clarkson thought for a second, glanced at the closed notepad on the table and nodded.

'Aye. Right. We all walked in fear of him. Especially if he was in a mood. And lately he was often in a mood. He was a big man and liked to use the fact. He'd get up close to you so that he was looking down on you. Then he'd start quietly and work up the volume until he was shouting at the top of your head. We used to say that someone had been Gibsoned.' The small man shivered, obviously remembering his own roastings.

'You said he was in a mood lately. Why, do you know? Worries about the bank? Home life? Golf handicap?'

That got a smile from Clarkson.

'Any of the above. He likes the racing too. I mean *liked*. Always had a bet going about something. Didn't like losing.'

McAllister nodded and left it a beat.

'How did he leave the bank? Are the accounts in good shape? Any problems?'

The sudden switch threw Clarkson for a second. His guard came up. He started prattling.

'The bank is in very good shape. No problems whatsoever. All good . . .'

TWENTY-THREE

Wullie finished his graphic account and waved his empty glass at me. I refilled it.

'You did well, Wullie. You haven't lost your touch. Gibson sounds like a bully under pressure and losing control. I wonder who was applying it?'

'Well, I got a bit of a clue from the next wee chat wi' his former PA, Miss Pamela McKenzie.' Wullie preceded his account by drawing an hourglass shape in the air with both hands. This would be interesting.

'Miss McKenzie was no longer personal assistant to the Chief. Clarkson had kept his own girl. It took a while to track Pamela down. For a while there, when we couldnae find her, I wondered if she'd been obliged to commit corporate suttee. Finally they located her and brought her into one of their wee interview rooms. She made quite an entrance. A real looker. Mair Mae West than Loretta Young. And of course, no' really my taste.' We grinned at each other; then I sat back and let his account draw me in . . .

She'd come in, flags waving, full of the poise that came from the steady barrage of admiring glances and wolf whistles that had followed her since she was sweet sixteen. But with a few sympathetic words from Wullie, her heavily made-up face crumpled and her large eyes filled.

'I'm sorry to hear about your boss, Miss McKenzie. It must have been devastating.'

'That's the word. That's exactly the word, *devastating* so it was.'

Her voice was street Glasgow with applied polish. Instantly classifiable as someone on the rise, and therefore scorned and disowned by the sneery folk either side of the class divide.

'What are you doing now, Pamela? May I call you Pamela?'

'Pamela is fine. Ah'm back in the pool, so Ah am. It's a comedown, Ah tell you.'

'How long did you work for Sir Fraser?'

Her face screwed up again. 'Nigh on five years.'

'How did you get on with him? You must have been quite close?'

She completely lost it. Her chest heaved and rippled with sobs, and tears flooded her make-up. Her West End accent slid off with her mascara.

'Ah'm sorry. Ah cannae take it in. That he's gone.'

'It shows remarkable devotion, Pamela. Especially as I'd heard he could be quite hard to work for. Very demanding.'

'Oh, he was. Wi' everybody except me.' She smiled bravely at the thought. 'He could be a real tyrant but he was different wi' me.'

'Pamela, I hope you don't mind my asking this. And it's completely off the record. But just how close were you and Sir Fraser? I just have a sense about these things. Were you and Fraser more than just boss and *personal assistant*?'

Her crying stopped. She reached into her purse and pulled out a hankie. She dried her face, applied some lipstick, dabbed some powder on her cheeks and sat up straight. Had Wullie badly offended her?

'Ah'm not ashamed, neither Ah am. He was gontae leave that bitch o' a wife. We were planning to run away thegither. So, there! Print that in your paper!'

'No, no. It's off the record, this bit. And we'd all get into that much bother if I did, it wouldnae be worth it. When was this supposed to happen? Had you made plans?'

'Soon. We were just waiting for the right time. Fraser had some stuff to deal with. Then we were for off. Maybe to France. Or even America.' Her voice caressed the new world. Her eyes glowed, then switched off and filled, at the realisation the dreams were over.

'You said his wife was a bitch. In what way? Did you know her?'

'Well, for one thing, she wisnae fulfilling her conjoogial duties.'

'No sex?'

'If you must put it that way. No' for years.'

'For another thing?'

'She could spend money like watter. Jewels and claithes. Fancy hoose.'

'That's not a crime.'

'Naw, but it was draining Fraser. He couldnae keep up.'

'Was he in debt?'

Pamela sniffed. 'Ah've said enough. It was jist a' pressure. He used to say Ah wisnae his secretary, Ah was his *sanctuary*.' The word triggered tears. Wullie handed her his handkerchief and she dabbed at her face.

'I can understand that, Pamela. Was this pressure getting to him lately? I heard he was in a bit of a mood this past wee while.'

'Who telt ye that? Ah wouldnae say a *mood* exactly. But he was a wee bit mair touchy than usual. But that's because me and him were jist wanting to get away. *Be* thegither. You know?'

Then she broke down completely and Wullie's hankie was lost for good.

*

128

'Wullie, Torquemada would hire you like a shot. It would save all that nonsense with thumbscrews and the rack. This throws new light on the case.'

Wullie pushed his glass over for a refill. I'd need to do a run ashore to restock if we were going to be a mobile hostelry.

'It disnae explain why he was kidnapped and murdered,' he said.

'Unless his wife found out about the lovely Pamela and engineered his demise?'

'It's a helluva roon' aboot way of dealing with a love rival. Cheaper and simpler to hire one o' the Glasgow gangs to gie him a good hiding or finish him off.'

'But this way they had a scapegoat. Me.'

'What if you'd said no, Brodie? What if you'd called the polis?'

'I keep wondering that. Maybe they chose a reporter because they were certain I'd not want to spoil a story by bringing in the cops too soon.'

'Could be. Maybe they knew of your propensity for diving in? It's no' much of a secret.'

'Thanks, Wullie. I thought my personal esteem was at its lowest. You've just taken it down a notch.'

'On the other hand, you tend to dive in for the best o' reasons. It's why I didnae believe for a second you were up for kidnapping.'

'I'm touched. I mean it. There were times back in my cell when I was beginning to doubt it myself.'

'You're past that?'

'The only uncertainty I have is what happened between walking into Marr Street and waking up with a split skull. The rest I'm clear on. The tapestry of charges against me is so much string and chewing gum. Liars and eejits working hand in glove. A conspiracy of ravens.'

Wullie nodded in agreement. 'Anyway, I'm enjoying this wee jaunt by moonlight. Are we off to Rothesay?'

'We're taking you and Stewart back to Anderston Quay.'

'Could you drop us off on the other side? At Govan? Anywhere near Summertown Road and we're home and dry.'

'I know just the place, Wullie.'

Eric brought the *Lorne* round and we motored back upstream. We moored at Highland Lane by the steps of the Kelvinhaugh Ferry. Eric and Stewart carried his majesty McAllister up to the landing on his portable throne and then Stewart wheeled him off into the night, Wullie softly and ironically warbling: "'Give me the moonlight, give me the girl . . .'"

Then we moved off again downstream to find a quiet mooring. I had a lot to digest and needed to plan how to marshal my thin forces.

TWENTY-FOUR

In the morning, we fired up the diesel and began motoring up towards the centre of town. We took the *Lorne* as far upstream as our masts permitted: just past Anderston Quay where we'd picked up Wullie and before the three arches of the King George V Bridge. Eric barely skimmed the passenger dock between the towering estuary ferries and passenger ships blocked from travelling further upstream. I was poised on deck so that as the *Lorne* glanced off the fenders, I was stepping off and vanishing into the crowds. With a two-week growth and a flat cap pulled well down, I was unrecognisable. And I was dead, wasn't I?

It was noon, and I strode up Oswald Street and into Kirkham's Bar. I'd made the arrangement with Harry by phone the night before and hoped it would come off. I was looking for a man reading a copy of today's London *Times*, a feat only achievable if he'd picked it up at Euston before catching the early morning train.

Kirkham's was a sliver of a pub crushed between office blocks. It made for a select and a limited number of lunchtime drinkers. My man – or rather one of Harry's – was at the bar conspicuous by his choice of reading and by his trilby among flat caps. I squeezed next to him and ordered a pint.

'Anything worth reading?' I asked over the top of his paper. He lowered it.

'Depends what you're interested in.'

'I have broad tastes.'

He folded it and pushed it over to me. 'Then you should enjoy this. I've done with it.'

I thanked him, he supped the last mouthful of beer and left, and I began to read the still-folded paper. I had a cigarette, finished my pint and went to the toilet. I took out the slim packet tucked into the paper and slipped it into my trouser pocket. I stuck the paper under my arm and walked out of the pub, heading towards the river. I strolled along the Broomielaw to Anderston Quay where the *Lorne* was tied up just along from the Clyde Street Ferry. I glanced around me, and then climbed down the ladder on to the deck of the ketch and into the cabin.

I opened the packet Harry had sent, very special delivery. It contained a pair of specs with plain glass and a warrant card in the name of Chief Inspector David Bruce, CID, Edinburgh. The card held a black and white photo of me but cleverly touched up. They'd used a print from my army days, presumably on file in MI5, and forged beard and glasses. It was like looking at my short-sighted brother who played accordion in a folk band. It would be tricky if anyone asked why Edinburgh was exporting its detectives to other regions, especially if they queried it with the Edinburgh police. A huge gamble but what was the choice?

It gave me more than a moment's pause, not so much at the transformation, but at the fact I was now – at least on paper – back in police harness again. The irony of rejecting Chief Constable Malcolm McCulloch's offer of such an appointment while I was 'alive' made me smile. In a rueful sort of way.

I scrubbed up in the cabin's washroom and donned the good navy suit, the white shirt and tie I'd brought with me. I creamed and flattened my hair, bushed my beard, gave my shoes a polish with a rag and put on the specs. I inspected myself in the small mirror against the photo in the warrant card. Close enough. I'd been worried about the beard for a police officer, but the collar, suit and tie and accountant's glasses made the look respectable. An ex-Navy man perhaps? Back to his old pre-war job but still bearing the hairy legacy of his years before the mast? Had I acquired enough of the gait in two days afloat? It would have to do. It wasn't as if anyone knew me where I was heading.

I climbed back up on to the dock and walked smartly away. I glanced back to see the *Lorne* swing out into the current for Eric to take her downstream and beyond the gaze of onlookers. He'd be back for me at dark. Provided I hadn't been caught.

The trains run every half an hour from Central Station to Neilston, and stop at Whitecraigs. One was just leaving. Twenty minutes later I was stepping down from the carriage on to the bucolic platform of a quiet Renfrewshire station in summer. Bees droned, birds warbled, the green hedges crowded in, and at any moment the railway children would dash on to the Victorian platform to welcome home their errant father.

A short walk along the somnolent Ayr Road and I was gazing down a tree-lined driveway at the long, comfortable shape of Whitecraigs Golf Club, like a very large bungalow, white-painted and solid. A gentleman's club. Amidst rolling lawns and under a cloud-speckled blue sky like this, I had a sudden urge to slip into plus fours and take a three club to an innocent wee ball.

I walked down the raked gravel and up the steps into the clubhouse. A few members in smart Pringle were about, with that serious mien of men about to go over the top or into the bunker.

'Excuse me,' I asked one man, 'I'm looking for the club secretary.'

He sized me for membership material and wasn't convinced, but he nevertheless pointed the way down the corridor lined with photos of former captains and famous victories. They even had the odd woman in the frame: scone- and sandwich-makers no doubt. I came to a door open on to a small but comfortable office. A man sat behind the desk. Bald, showing the skin on his head and hands mottled with sunspots; that's golf for you. He was on the phone, but indicated I should come in and take a seat. I did. He put the phone down.

'Good afternoon. I'm James Harding, club secretary. What can I do for you?'

'David Bruce. Detective Chief Inspector. Edinburgh division.' I leaned over and showed him my warrant card. He inspected it and handed it back. It worked.

'You don't see many police with whiskers these days,' he said.

'Skin problem.'

'You're well out of your area, Chief Inspector. What can I do for you?'

'As I'm sure you know, Edinburgh is our main financial centre. So we've centralised all police work dealing with banks and investment companies and insurers.'

'Makes sense.'

'I'm involved with some delicate investigations. It concerns one of your club members. Or should I say former club members.'

He leaned back. 'I assume you're talking about Sir Fraser Gibson?'

'Correct.'

'Nasty business that. Poor Sheila.'

'You know Lady Gibson?'

He nodded. 'She's been here often. Functions, dinner, etc. Used to help out with our medal days. Lovely girl. Very popular.' Said wistfully as though Lady Gibson would be sorely missed by some of the local Lotharios. 'Must be going through a terrible time. But I assume the Glasgow police are dealing with the murder side. Which means you're . . .?'

I nodded. 'Scottish Linen is one of our major banks.'

'Are you saying there was something funny going on?'

'Mr Harding, can I be direct with you? This is all highly sensitive.'

'Of course, Chief Inspector. The club sec. job at Whitecraigs requires the utmost sensitivity. Our members are mostly pretty senior chaps. Captains of industry, top professionals, you know the kind of thing.'

'I do, Mr Harding. It must require a great deal of tact. I can imagine there might be the occasional incident, the odd chap getting out of line – we've all been to Burns Suppers eh? Whisky flowing like water? The guard slips. Things get said. Someone's wife goes off with another chap? That sort of thing? Good breeding doesn't always mean good behaviour.'

Harding looked at me, not sure how far he should confirm that this select little enclave might be a hotbed of alcoholism, temper tantrums and infidelity. Monthly dinner dances that led to surprising foursomes. He stood up and walked to the door and closed it. He came back and sat down.

'I'm not going to tell tales out of school, Chief Inspector, but you wouldn't believe some of things that happen round here.'

'I think I might. But can I bring us on to Sir Fraser?'

Harding was agog. He could almost taste the scandal. It was what stirred his blood. I needed to head him off.

'Please do.'

'I want to assure you of two things. First, that whatever you tell me will be in strict confidence. Second, this is not about the Scottish Linen Bank per se. We're *not* investigating the bank. It's purely about Sir Fraser. I want to emphasise this.' I laid it on thick. The last thing Harry would want is for rumours to start over a glass or three in the club bar . . . *Had a senior policeman in the office today. Mustn't say too much, but if I were you, old boy, I'd find another home for the savings, be on the safe side. For God's sake, don't say where you got this.*

'Lord, no.'

'I understand Sir Fraser wasn't a man to cross?'

'A bit of a powder keg, actually.'

'Just lately or that's how he was?'

'This past year he's been a bit touchier.'

'How so?'

'Example, about a month back he accused one of our chaps of cheating. Said he'd not counted a stroke on the twelfth. Long hole and loads of rough, so you're always lucky to get par.'

'Normal enough?'

'It wasn't the first time. It was getting to the point he couldn't get anyone to play him.'

'Just over a game?'

'More to it. Chaps round here like a flutter. Sir Fraser was a big betting man. Seems he was pushing chaps to double or quit. Meantime his own game was all to pot.'

'Not enough practice?'

Harding lowered his voice. 'Bit too much of the Black Label. I've had to pour him into his car some nights.'

'I thought he had a chauffeur?'

'Sometimes. But sometimes he just drove himself. Insisted. Not much anyone could do. Wrote it off about six months back. Put it in a ditch.'

'Who were his pals? Anyone special?'

'He ran with a small group. Lawyers, businessmen. Called themselves the *Chanty Wrastlers*. Used to meet before sun-up on the first tee on a Sunday morning.'

'Lively blokes?'

'Boisterous, I'd say. Liked a good drink. Liked a party.'

'Gamblers? I mean as well as betting on the holes?'

'Matter of fact, yes. They were always betting on something. Horses, football results. Always had a card game going in the locker room.'

'I thought gambling wasn't allowed on the premises?'

136

'Oh, no money changed hands. All done on bits of paper. Reckoning done elsewhere. But look, Chief Inspector, where's all this going? I mean, what's the connection?'

It was a good question and one I hadn't fully thought through. But the signs were writ large: an affair, gambling, booze. Any one of them could garner ill will from some quarter. But if you had all three, a full house, you were guaranteed trouble. Whether it amounted to kidnapping and murder was what I was trying to find out.

'Sir Fraser was kidnapped and murdered and my unit wants to know if there was anything related to the workings of the bank that we should know about.'

'You're not saying Gibson had his hands in the till, are you?' Damn, another juicy comment to be dropped into a bar conversation, preceded by: *Of course I don't believe it myself . . .*

'Not at all. It's all standard procedure. Call it extreme due diligence. We like to rule out any such activity no matter how unlikely. So we're working our way through the books of the bank. Just to make absolutely sure. And I'm checking the character side of the matter, looking for motivation.'

'Like gambling debts?'

'You'd make a good detective, Mr Harding. Yes, that sort of thing. But as I said, this is all belt and braces. We have no proof of any wrongdoing. We have a duty to the public to make sure our banks are properly controlled and funded.'

'Glad to hear it, Chief Inspector.'

'Good. Now if would you be kind enough to give me the names and any contact details for these so called Chanty Wrastlers . . .'

TWENTY-FIVE

After my session with Harding and walking back to the station I was sorely tempted to drop in on Castle Gibson to have a wee tête-à-tête with the chatelaine. But much as I'd enjoy seeing her expression, she didn't strike me as someone easily persuaded to rewrite her statement. It would be the end of me without any proof of anything. However, I couldn't resist a small diversion to check on Weasel Watkins.

It was a ten-minute walk to the wide leafy street I'd last seen from the back of Sheila Gibson's Humber. That was in another life; was I now in the afterlife? Her house was about two hundred yards from the end of the street and I could only make out the gateposts with the lounging lions. The street was empty and I was about to find a phone box and call Wullie to tell him Weasel was absent from his post without leave when a drooping figure appeared from a cul de sac halfway along. He was dragging a big broom as though it was a ball and chain. I smiled and thought about walking up to him and having a wee blether. Would he remember me? Not worth the risk.

I got the train back to Glasgow, slid on my specs and clamped my hat on to walk through Central Station. Even so, it was amazing how furtive and vulnerable I felt out in the open. There was no price on my head, no wanted posters up – and none would have my present image – but the concourse seemed full of policemen with searchlight eyes. All it would take for the hunt to start up would be for me to run into someone who knew me.

I had a couple of hours to kill before the Eric McLeod river taxi service showed up. I needed to lie low till then. It would be hard work. I was conspicuous in my suit and red beard, not to mention standing taller than my average Glasgow cousins. I needed to be somewhere a man could linger unnoticed. I knew just the place, and I could makes good use of my time. While I'd been incarcerated I'd hardly seen a newspaper. Partly I didn't want to. Partly Sam didn't want me to. Partly the cops didn't provide a daily delivery service.

I set off for the Mitchell Library and enjoyed stretching my legs up and down the hillocks of the city centre. Entering any library always feels like coming home. I went into the reading room and settled down with back issues of the papers covering the period of the kidnap. It was a salutary experience.

Apart from the *Gazette*, which began in outrage and denial and became more circumspect as evidence mounted against me, all the other dailies were as good as marching me on to the scaffold for my foul murder of this poor banker who'd been held in such high esteem by his friends and colleagues. My own black and white photo blazed out from the front pages. Fortunately it was from ten years ago and I was in police uniform. Sangster must have unearthed it from the Tobago Street files. He really seemed to have it in for me. The Douglas Brodie of 1937 looked so young, so very young. Keener and less world weary. But back then I hadn't been to war.

It was pointless, I knew, but as I read, I felt consumed by the sheer injustice of my treatment, despite the festering worry about the gap in my memory. Like waking in the morning with a towering hangover and no recollection of how the night ended. Just a nagging guilt. About something.

I felt sick at what my mother might have read about me, and what her neighbours would have thought about me. And said to her. In poor homes – and my mother had the pension of a sparrow to live on, supplemented when I could by the odd ten bob slipped on to her mantelpiece – sometimes all you had was your good name. They'd taken that from her and my dad. And me, come to that. I made a vow then and there that someone would pay.

I realised my heart and head were pounding and that it showed in my rustling of the paper and my tsks and pahs. Some of my fellow readers were glancing at me. I got hold of my emotions and turned to the text. I paid particular attention to what the police said about the kidnap and killing of Gibson, and how they'd known to go to Marr Street. A police spokesman said that it had been the result of fine police intelligence. An oxymoron if ever there was one. What they meant was a snitch, a clype, a stoolie had whispered in someone's ear. Whose ear? Who clyped? Was Lady Gibson involved? If so, how? The papers were silent.

They claimed to have arrived at the scene of the murder in Marr Street shortly after the dirty deed and found the merciless and ruthless killer holding a smoking gun over the body. They'd arrested the suspect – me – and charged him with kidnapping and murder, claiming that my fellow kidnappers had fled out of the back entry. No mention of a ransom being paid. Lies or fantasies!

But flicking forward through to the present day I could find no mention of the police looking for my fellow conspirators. Conveniently, I was dead and I was the ringleader; that seemed to be all that mattered to them. It fair made a man feel unloved.

I skipped quickly past the eulogies and photos of Gibson's funeral. There must have been a couple of hundred mourners – a couple of hundred more than mine. I noted that the widow's plight had been softened by a large life insurance payout. Most papers had the same photo of the dead man all dressed up for business – presumably an official one from the bank. Even in black and white, the power of the man's personality shone from the eyes and could be seen in the set of the jaw. I stared hard at the image, until it became overlaid with my memory of a face with a hole in the forehead and eyes of milky glass.I returned the papers and sat for a while quietly mulling. I could do with having my own snitch, someone inside the force getting me answers. The clear choice was Inspector Duncan Todd, drinking pal and fellow ranter against bigotry, cronyism and corruption, but how far could I really trust him? I'd accused him of being more concerned about his pension and position than his pal's life. Unfair, but a reflection of how low I was at the time. But I still wasn't certain whether he sided more with the arguments of his boss, Sangster, than mine. And, to put it mildly, it was asking a great deal for a serving officer to act as informer for an accused murderer – a dead one at that.

There was one route in. Risky, and I didn't like playing this particular card. But these were desperate times. Needs must. I left the Mitchell and headed down to the Clyde. I had to rendezvous with the *Lorne* and ask Eric to make a call for me.

TWENTY-SIX

After Eric had left his message we pottered down the Clyde and moored up for the rest of the afternoon and early evening. During our wait we talked.

'I'm sorry you're having to hang around so much, Eric. What do you do with yourself?'

'Repairs. It's good to catch up. Ropes fray, sails rip, varnish dries and cracks. Always something on a boat. Oh, and I've been doing a wee bit of reading. I hope you don't mind?'

'My pile of Dickens? Help yourself.'

'It's rare enough to get the chance.'

We'd never talked about his life before the war. I asked him.

'Och, a bit of this, a bit of that. Always messing about in boats, I suppose. That's what you do in Skye. Either that or sheep. I don't like sheep.'

'Spoiled for choice. Then you joined up?'

He shook his big hairy head. 'I came down to Glasgow looking for work before the war. Laboured in the yards for a couple of years, then joined the Black Watch. I'd met Mairi six months before, at the dancing in '39. She's Orkney but her folks lost their holding and came south.' He stopped and stood erect from his rope coils. 'They lived in Clydebank.' His eyes were distant.

'The Blitz? In '41?'

He nodded. 'Mairi had a wee job as a waitress. She couldn't

get home that night. When she did, the next day, the house was gone. Everything. Everyone. She wrote to me. When I had some leave I came back and we got married.'

'Then off to war again?'

'Like you, Brodie.' He smiled. 'North Africa with the 51st.' He shook his head. 'A long time ago. I'm not sure the world's any saner now. Look at what's happened to you.'

The long summer night and the cloudless sky meant we had little or no protection from curious eyes as we sailed up alongside the pier at the Govan Ferry. I crouched below and watched Eric glide in alongside the steps just abandoned by the little ferry. As we nudged the pier, the lone woman waiting at the top of the flight stepped neatly down and on to our deck. This was her first time back on board since she'd been abducted, knocked out and bashed around in the bilges of the *Lorne* by mad Gerrit Slattery. It was asking a lot of any woman. But not – apparently – of Samantha Campbell. She stepped down into the cabin and into my arms.

'Stop it. You're tickling me, you big hairy oaf!'

'I thought you liked it.'

She pushed back from me and eyed me up.

'Sort of. It's so – so different. Like being carried off by a Viking.'

'Every girl's dearest fantasy.'

'Not mine!'

'I can make it real.'

'Behave yourself. Eric's just there.'

'I can close the door.'

Her eyes were shining with the temptation. But—

'Not here, Douglas. Not here.'

I nodded and smiled and let her go with a chaste kiss on the forehead.

'Sit down, Sam. I'm sorry to drag you back to this – this scene of the crime.'

'It's all right, really. I hardly remember a thing. Other than you boarding us like a pirate and rescuing me. Oh, and me throwing up. Lots of that.' Her nose wrinkled with distaste. She looked around. 'It's different now. Better. Who's the woman and the bairn? Eric's, I hope? Unless you've something to tell me?'

She pointed at a small framed picture on the wall of a buxom blond lass, smiling and holding a baby.

'Mairi, his wife. And Eileen, now two. They have another one, a boy. Three months. Called Dougie.'

A look crossed her face. We didn't talk about it. But it was there, always there. Back in April she'd turned thirty-eight and it seemed fairly certain that we'd missed that tide in the affairs of men and women.

'Bonny. Both of them.'

'And when this is all over, you and I are going to sail over to Arran on this fine boat and have a wild ceilidh with Eric and Mairi. Agreed?'

'It's a date. In the meantime, what have you found out?'

I told her about my new identity. She pursed her lips at the forged warrant card but thought the rank was suitable. I told her about Gibson's ruthlessness and recklessness as reported by Wullie and the Whitecraigs' club secretary.

'Who were these pals of his?'

I ran through the half-dozen names. She blinked at one.

'Roddie Adams? I know him. One of the most sleekit, arrogant, slimy solicitors in Glasgow. Possibly Scotland.'

'Don't hold back, Sam. Tell me what you really think.'

She took a breath. 'He's been around twenty years. Built his own practice. Fancy office in Blythswood Square. Clientele mainly crooks and shifty businessmen. Twice – that I know of – up before the Law Society accused of malpractice. Money laundering was one. Pilfering from client accounts was another.'

'But?'

'He got off. They couldn't prove it. But everybody knows he was guilty.'

'"By your friends are you known."'

'It's certainly a character reference. You've been busy. You and Wullie. What do you want *me* to do?'

'Have you spoken to Duncan Todd since . . .?'

'Your funeral? He came round the day after in an awful state. He'd wanted to come but we'd made it clear we didn't want mourners. He was still blaming himself for doing nothing to help you, but Sangster was on the warpath. Nothing was going to get in Sangster's way of getting you convicted. Duncan kept saying he should have disobeyed orders and done something. He was quoting the Bible: "For what is a man profited if he shall gain the whole world and lose his own soul?"'

'Ouch. I don't know if a job as detective inspector equates to the world but I know it meant a lot to Duncan. I should have told him. You didn't, did you?' I half wished she had. It seemed wretched leaving an old friend grieving for nothing. For no . . . body.

'It was hard. I felt really bad. But I just couldn't. Could I? Not while there's a chance.'

I looked at her and loved her for her optimism.

'Sam? What if there's no chance? What if I can't prove my innocence? And, Sam – what if I'm *not*? Not totally. I told you, I don't have complete recall. That whack on the head. I could have shot him by accident.'

'Don't be so daft! You think you shot him while you were out cold? You would have to have been facing him to shoot him square in the temple at the exact second someone hits you on the back of the head. The alternative, that you shot him on purpose because you'd masterminded the kidnapping is just – just – ridiculous! Why would you? Why would *you*?' She punched my chest. Hard. For punctuation.

'OK, it's OK. Sorry to raise it. But if I can't find out what happened, if I can't prove who did it . . . Then it's back to a condemned cell or life behind bars. I couldn't take that, Sam. I just couldn't.' I grasped her shoulders with both hands and made her hold my gaze. 'Look, Eric is prepared to sail the *Lorne* all the way to France. If it comes to it – if I can't fix this – I'm going to take him up on his offer. Will you . . .? I mean would you . . .?'

'Run away with an escaped murderer? A *penniless* escaped murderer? Just say the word. France would be nice. The weather's much better. So's the food. You speak the lingo and I took it for five years at school. Or maybe Spain— You're breaking my ribs, Douglas!'

'I was just saying thank you.'

'Well, that's nice, dear. Any chance of a drink round here?'

'We're down to our last mouthful of rum.'

'Good job I brought this, then.' She dug into her copious bag and pulled out a half-bottle of Johnnie Walker.

'Samantha Campbell, have I asked you to marry me?'

'Not lately. Do you have glasses on board or do we just pass the bottle?'

'How about these?' I picked up my specs and put them on.

'My God. A short-sighted Viking. Now I've seen it all.' When she'd stopped giggling, and I'd found tumblers and poured us each an inch, she asked, 'What's my task?'

'I need someone inside Turnbull Street. Someone who knows what's going on. Or can find out. I need Duncan's help. Could you give Duncan a call and ask to meet him? Could you say you're still trying to clear my name? As my advocate. Ask him to help you find out what really happened.'

She was nodding. 'I was already thinking about it. It all stank, but I couldn't get a thing out of Sangster and his crew. They seemed to have all their answers worked out in writing. I'd hoped to take him apart on the stand, but you up and died before we got to trial. I've been twice into the station to demand an interview but no one was available. I tried to get through to Malcolm McCulloch but his secretary kept stalling me. Duncan is our best hope. What do you want me to find out?'

She took out a pad of lined paper and her silver propelling pencil, and sat poised for dictation. I reached over and touched her hand.

'Sam, you're amazing. Haven't you ever doubted me?'

She looked down for a second, and then held my gaze. 'Honestly? I have never had a single doubt about the kidnap and murder accusations. But for a wee while there, until I got my head round the actual dirty business itself, I thought it was vaguely possible that my own dear Douglas Brodie had thrown himself into the fray – righting wrongs as usual and careless for his own safety – and somebody got hurt. Accidentally. But the more I look at this the more it's clear you were a stooge, a fall guy, a . . .'

'An eejit? But you'd still run away with a penniless eejit?'

'Shut up, Douglas. What do you want me to ask?'

Later, we dropped her off at Anderston Quay and, despite her protestations, I walked her up as close to Central Station as seemed sensible. I stood and watched until she climbed into a taxi and set off up Hope Street towards home. I wanted to run after her. For a moment I had a pang of self-pity that I should be denied her company this night. But unless I pulled my finger out and tracked down the men who'd set me up for a hanging, the loss of a night of passion was the least of my worries. I turned and walked back to the river, keeping to my new life in the shadows.

TWENTY-SEVEN

Next morning, I asked Eric to put us into the yacht club at Gourock. His big face opened in a wide grin.

'A pleasure. The *Lorne* could do with stretching her legs.'

He turned her head round to the open mouth of the Clyde and we began to haul up the sails. The fresh morning breeze filled them one by one until we had a full set and the ketch was jumping forward in the water like a salmon. We ran down the widening estuary and rounded the head at Gourock. We were out in mid-channel. Away in the distance, framed between the isles of Bute and Cumbrae, but much further south, was the grey hump of Arran. I could see Eric fight against the desire to keep on soaring with the wind to where his wife and children would be waiting. I wouldn't have blamed him. I felt like running away myself.

But suddenly I saw him push on the tiller and felt the boat heel round on to a bearing that would bring us into the far-off yacht club. I walked up to Eric, clinging to the rail on the tipping deck, and clapped him on the shoulder. We exchanged looks and nodded in full understanding. How could I repay this man?

We began hauling down sails so that we were slipping forward on just the jib and mizzen as we cut across the wide bay towards the club. As we closed on the shore I could see the attraction of its position. It was a solid building perched on a promontory. Behind it passed the road that ran along the

Gourock coast. The club was framed by rows of sandstone houses set all along the foreshore. It gave convenient access by road from Glasgow while offering unparalleled views across the whole Firth, up Loch Long and to the Gareloch.

Apart from golf, I'd been told sailing had been one of Gibson's passions – unless all he wanted was a private club-house and bar rather than pottering up and down the Firth getting cold and wet. We tied up to a visitor's mooring and dragged the tender alongside. I was about to clamber down into it when Eric stopped me.

'Are you going like that?'

I was in suit and glasses again.

'Too formal?'

'You look like a Revenue man. They'll never talk to you. Try these.' He flung a bundle at me. I caught them and the accompanying reek of smoke and fish and oily wool. I went down into the cabin and changed. I emerged wearing a worn pair of brown corduroys and an Arran sweater.

He nodded. 'Better.'

'I'm short of a fiddle.'

'You'll do. Just don't go talking about bowlines and clove hitches.'

'I know the difference.'

'But not how to tie them.'

It was only a short row so we didn't bother with the outboard. Despite this being my first outing I only missed a couple of strokes. I certainly felt more the sea-dog in my smelly sweater. I pulled on to the shallow beach and walked up to the clubhouse and into its corridors. I tracked down the club secretary – John Grant – to a corner of the small dining room. He seemed a different kettle of fish to the Whitecraigs' smoothy. Grant was as blunt as his name, and more guarded. Even though we shared a taste for facial hair and smelly sweaters, Grant showed a clear preference for facing a force 10 off the Hebrides than an inquisition from an Edinburgh policeman. We sat outside watching the yachts and stroking our beards at each other. He puffed on his pipe while I fired unanswered questions. I was getting nowhere and was tempted to call for Eric to see if he could exchange smoke signals with the dour Grant.

'Well, I couldnae really say,' was his standard response to most of my probes about Gibson. He finally opened up when I asked about Gibson's sailing. Was he an expert helmsman, a brilliant man with a sextant?

'Huh. A gin palace. A floating gin palace, that's what he had.'

'Did he take it out much?'

He almost spat. 'Oh, he took her out. A complete waste of a fine yacht.' He pointed with his pipe at the *Lorne*, rocking gently on the buoy. 'Not like yours. Saw you coming in across the bay. Well handled. I love a gaff rig.' Then he moved his pointer over. 'Gibson moored just out there. He'd drive down at the weekend, load his poor craft up with booze and drinking cronies and fire up the engines. He'd anchor half a mile out in the Firth or maybe sail over to Dunoon. When I say sail, I don't think he raised them once in the past two years.'

'Who did he drink with? Club members?'

Grant shook his head. 'He brought his pals with him. From Glasgow. Right bunch they were.'

'How so?'

'Not our sort. Loud, flashy. Cigars and directors' box at Ibrox. Some wi' fancy accents.'

'Same bunch each time?'

'Two mainly. Adams and Elliot. Sometimes they'd bring a couple of lassies. Tramps.' He spat out a thick black gob on to the pebbles.

'Not his wife?'

'Ha!'

'Catch any of *their* names?'

'One of his favourite bits of stuff was a burd called Pamela. A right tart. It was Pam this, and Pam that. Often enough just *Sir* Fraser and his tart. You could see the boat rocking from a mile off.'

He paused, mulling.

'There was another yin. Classier. A real beauty.'

'Catch her name?'

'Something like Candy. Too guid for him.'

'Did his behaviour change much in the last – say – six months?'

'How do you mean?'

'Still bringing his pals down for a boozy weekend? Still bringing Pam? Or Candy?'

'Mostly. But they didnae seem to be having as much fun. Arguments. Him and his pals. You could hear them effing and blinding. Booze and women – a potent mix on a boat.'

'Was it women they were arguing about?'

'Gambling debts. Heard it all the time . . . fights over who'd lost at the races. They'd bet on which way the wind would blaw in the next half-hour.'

I used the phone in the club before re-embarking on the *Lorne*.

'Harry, it's me.'

'You got the package?'

'Perfect. And it works. So far.'

'Don't overdo it, old chap.'

'Time's running out. I need to take risks. It's beginning to get results. I've got some names for you. Can you check them out? See what you might have on them?'

'My pen is poised.'

'First batch is from his golf club, the so-called Chanty Wrastlers. Two of the names that crop up are also associated with the yacht club: Frank Elliot and Roderick Adams. We should start with that pair. Sam knows Adams. He's a bent lawyer. Sounds like a good lead.'

'Leave it with me. Call me tonight. By the way, we've found your man Higgins.'

'Wee Airchie? Alive, I hope. Not banged up?'

'His last stretch finished four years ago. But we don't think he's learned his lesson. Just hasn't been caught. He's still consorting with the wrong people. Still in Glasgow.'

'That's a relief. It would be a pity to find he'd gone straight. Where can I find him?'

'You're going to blow your cover?'

'I need a breakthrough. Or, more accurately, a break-in.'

'When do you want to see him?'

'As soon as poss. Tomorrow? Ten o'clock.'

'Where?'

I didn't want Eric McLeod to be dragged into illegalities any more than he already was. I wouldn't use the boat.

'Glasgow Green. Nelson's Column. Tell him to find a seat and wait till he's contacted. The forecast is sunny, so he'll have to fight for a bench with sunbathing pensioners.'

'Consider it done.'

TWENTY-EIGHT

Eric took us back up the Firth to moor overnight at a cove near Rosneath up the Gareloch. It would be an easy sprint up the Clyde in the morning for my rendezvous.

I was curious to meet wee Airchie again. I'd last encountered him before the war when we'd rounded up a cartel of soft-fruit providers who'd been keeping prices high despite a glut of produce from a great summer. Airchie was the rate setter and central 'banker' for nine companies and had made them handsome profits at a time of rationing. He was one of those local legends, a man whose myths had long since eclipsed the reality. When it came to cooking the books Airchie Higgins was considered a master chef.

I knew that even the Scottish accountancy profession had a set of standards for practitioners of their black arts. Fall below them and you could be struck off. Airchie entered their hall of infamy for keeping too many parallel sets of books for his various crooked clients. But it was precisely such inventiveness and flexible morality that I needed.

He was also a likeable wee rogue. If he hadn't yielded to temptation so often, he could have known esteem and financial security among the professional classes of Glasgow. I led the arresting team that picked up him and all his dodgy books, and even as I was cuffing him, he seemed more resigned than angry.

Normally – if I hadn't been quite so personally constrained – I'd have been able to buy Airchie's talents with a modest cash offer. But to gag him about my existence, at least for a few weeks, would require more than just a bucketful of bawbees. That's where Harry could help.

Next morning, Eric delivered me as neat as ninepence to the dockside at Anderston. I wore the specs and was in an open-necked shirt and Eric's brown corduroys: a compromise between a Revenue man and a rum smuggler. As I walked along Clyde Street to the Green I stifled an urge to run past the corner with Saltmarket; just two hundred yards from my recent prison cell. A fast walk later and I was in the park and strolling towards Nelson's Column at the centre of the great city green.

I spotted him from a good way off. Airchie was sitting in the sunshine perched on the end of a bench pretending to read a newspaper he'd probably found in a dustbin. He kept sticking his head above the pages to see who was coming. He looked older, fatter and shorter. But then none of us was wearing too well.

I didn't head straight at him, but took a stroll round the monument and came at him out of the sun. Even when I sat down beside him he still didn't recognise me. In fact he put down his paper and turned to me:

'Excuse me, pal. Ah'm waitin' for a couple of folk. We're havin' a bit of a confab about a new statue we're putting up. So if you wouldnae mind . . .'

'Airchie, I'm glad to see you haven't lost your talent for telling fibs.'

Behind his wire-rimmed glasses, his small round face looked startled. Close up he looked nearer sixty than the fifty I understood him to be.

'Ah'm sorry, pal. Ah don't know who you are. Though the voice is kinda familiar. Am Ah supposed to be meeting you?' He peered at me, struggling to bring his memories into focus.

'You are, Airchie. But before I prompt your memory, let me say that what you will be asked to do will be very worth your while.'

'Oh aye, how much worthwhile? And nae violent stuff, mind. Ah've got a low threshold for pain.'

'Agreed. Answer me a couple of questions first. Are you going straight now?'

He looked affronted. 'Here, you, Ah'm as straight as a die. Who do you think you are, asking me that?'

'I mean, you're legal, on the straight and narrow, reformed?'

He peered at me, wondering whether I was trying to trap him. 'Aye, all legal, now what—?'

'Let's leave that. Who do you work for the now?'

'Ah'm actually between jobs at the moment, but Ah huv a number of folk Ah'm having discussions with, wi' a view to taking on an engagement. If the work and the remuneration are appropriate.'

'Fair enough. OK, I'm going to tell you who I am and then we'll talk. You can walk away from this job. No one will stop you, especially if you're going straight. But you need to know that if word gets out about me and anything I'm going to say to you, not only will I personally come and rip your head off, I'll hand over the bits to the British secret services to put through their mincer.'

'Whit! You're joking, right? C'mon, pal, naebody needs work as much as that. This is no' for me. Ah'm away.' He got up, folded his ragged paper under his arm and made to leave.

'Airchie? I'm Douglas Brodie.' I took off my specs.

He stopped, stared, went to say something, peered closer.

'Fuck! Ah heard you were deid!'

'I am. Sit down, Airchie. Let's talk.'

He sank beside me on the bench, as much stunned as intrigued. I explained what I knew of the kidnap and murder, and how I'd been set up. He shook his head.

'Christ, Brodie, who can you trust these days? Ony idea who's behin' it?'

'Some, but not enough. And here's the thing, Airchie, we think there's some dirty goings on at Scottish Linen. But if you breathe a word of what I just told you, my pals will lock you away and lose the key.'

His wee face screwed up. 'These pals o' yours? Are you sayin' they're the fly boys, the spy boys?'

I nodded.

'Fuck.' Then he thought for a minute. 'How did you end up working for them?'

'Airchie, I see you read the paper. Were you reading it earlier this year when we were chasing Nazis in Glasgow?'

'Oh aye. That was rare, so it was. Who'd'a thought it? And you did the reporting on that. Are you saying you were working with the spy boys at the time?'

'I'm a sort of a part-time officer in the army and an even more part-time employee of the said outfit. So when I ran into this bit of trouble, my friends were concerned and helped me play dead. They're helping me now and they are willing to pay you well for helping me.'

He fiddled with his fingers and pulled at his collar as his mind ticked over. He was calculating just how much to ask for.

'Would Ah get a medal?'

I laughed. 'Is that what would make you do this? What good's a medal to you?'

'You wouldnae un'erstaun'.'

I studied him. 'Try me.'

He looked down at his hands and then out across the park. 'See, it's like this. Ah was inside for half the war. An' when Ah came oot in '43, they wouldnae huv me. Ah wanted to fight the bloody Hun but they wouldnae let me. This would kinda make up for it, would it no'?'

I didn't point out that even if his criminal record hadn't excluded him, his age and health would have.

'You wee patriot, you. I'll have a word with them. But are you saying you're up for this? I haven't even told you what we want you to do.'

'Ah guess it's something sneaky and un'erhaun'. Something that uses ma talents?'

'You and I, Archibald Higgins, are going to break into the Scottish Linen Bank and take a look at their books.'

'Fuck.'

'Fuck, indeed.'

TWENTY-NINE

U sually it's best to be bold. I told Airchie when and where to meet me that night. Then – with my beard and specs to protect me – I strolled as casually as I could up through the city centre to St Vincent Street, the business centre. Halfway along stood the Scottish Linen Bank, its solid red sandstone façade proclaiming rectitude and propriety. *Your money is safe with us and we might let you have some of it back if you ask politely and do a bit of grovelling.*

That's what I'd thought when I opened an account there last year. I'd liked its air of permanence and liked walking into its banking hall knowing I was also walking into the headquarters. I liked it right up to the point a couple of weeks ago when I found out in court that the tiny sum in my savings account had disappeared and my current account was in deficit.

From the front the building was impregnable unless you had a battering ram for the massive central doors and a really big fretsaw for the barred windows.

Inside, up a set of marble stairs, the banking hall opened up, wood-panelled, high-ceilinged and patrolled by doormen and clerks with neck-strangling hard collars. They polished their Dickensian image. I'd been inside it a few times in the past year to set up my accounts, change my address and withdraw cash that had barely spent the night in my savings account. The last time I'd visited was to change a fiver and had been treated as if I'd come to deposit a barrow-load of gold ingots.

If I recalled right, a short side corridor led to the back offices where the bulk of the clerks worked and where the books would be kept. That was the target for Airchie and me.

I walked round the corner and headed uphill. Within twenty paces I turned sharply into St Vincent Lane. Like most of the great arteries of Glasgow, the main street was customer-facing and very smart. But running in parallel, all along the back of the grand buildings, is a service lane, the tradesman's lane. Rough and cobbled, the lanes give access to the storerooms and staff quarters.

Scottish Linen was no exception. A ten-foot-high lane wall protected its rear but I could see that there was a small yard between the lane wall and the rear of the bank itself. I could clamber over the lane wall but I'd then be facing heavy locked doors and barred windows into the bank. I saw holds in the rough lane wall where I could get a grip and scramble up and over, but wee Airchie would need a full set of steps either side. Preferably with a handrail. For a moment I was daunted. This was never going to work.

The lane was quiet but it wouldn't do to be found loitering outside the back door of a major bank eyeing up the walls and entrances. I started to walk along the lane, as though simply using it as a convenient passage to the next street. As I walked I studied the layout of the neighbouring buildings. Each shared the dividing wall with the next, and though the heights varied, there was more or less a contin- uous roofline right down the row. On my return trip I confirmed that the building next to Scottish Linen – a multi-level department store called Faulds – had a lower wall by the lane and, more interestingly, on the back wall of the building itself, a fire escape zigzagging from the roof to the ground.

I made one last pass down the lane to check what I was seeing. It was hard to tell from the ground, but it looked like the angled roofs of the Scottish Linen Bank and its neighbour fell to a gulley and parapet. Each roof had tall chimneys. Each seemed to have skylights. It might be possible to reach the roof of Faulds via the fire escape and then to climb over the short dividing wall on to Scottish Linen's roof. And then to penetrate the bank through one of the skylights. It was a lot of ifs.

I made my way out of the lane and, as pre-arranged, met a very nervous Archibald Higgins at the corner of Argyle Street and North Street.

'You can relax tonight, Airchie. We're not raiding the bank. Well, *you're* not. I just need some quick lessons from you about bookkeeping.'

His head lifted. 'It took years of training, Brodie.'

'To get where you are?' I saw his look and was immediately sorry for my sarcasm. 'I just need some basics. Some distilled wisdom.'

'You've come to the right man.'

'I know. Come on, let's find a seat.'

I walked us up North Street and into the little graveyard behind the church. It was twilight and warm enough to sit on one of the benches scattered among the paths between the rows of headstones. We took a seat and lit cigarettes.

'Right, Airchie, you worked for one of the banks years ago. Correct?'

'Correct. The Royal.' Said with pride.

'But you left under a bit of a cloud, if I recall?'

His brow puckered and he took off his specs to give them a rub against his worn jacket.

'You micht say that. Ah got nicked for trying to take a wee bit on the side. Hell, naebody would have missed it. Loose change for them. But there you go.'

'Tell me about the bank books. How do they keep records?'

'Simple, really. You go into a bank, go up to the counter and ask to take oot your money or put some in. You provide some identification unless they really ken you, and the guy behind the counter makes a note of it on a chit and puts it in his basket.'

'That's the start of it, the customer transaction.'

'Aye, then throughout the day, and especially at three o'clock when they close the doors, they collect a' the baskets and take them into the back office. The place is fu' o' clerks – maistly girls – who sort the transactions and then record them in their ledgers. Double entry, of course. So it all balances.'

'So they keep accounts for each customer? But presumably they need to add it all up? To know what a branch has taken or given out each day?'

'That's right. That's where the accountants come in. The two sides of the ledgers need to add up. Double entry. They copy the ledger information into branch ledgers and do their calculations. At the end of every day, each branch has to make sure the books balance. They summarise the results and send their messenger to head office with them. Then head office consolidates the lot of them either once a week or once a month.'

'So Scottish Linen head office – up the road here – would keep all the summary details of all their branches. You could look at the books and see how much money has come in and how much has gone out, and to whom? Every day?'

'They'd only have the summary information from the branches. You wouldnae know about individuals unless there were big amounts or very important folk.'

'What about if you banked at head office, like I do. *Did.* I suppose they closed my account after stealing my money.'

'It would be like they were a branch but within head office. They'd have the individual accounts' details and chits. And every week we – the accountants – would consolidate the books and report to the treasurer how the bank was doing.'

'If we got our hands on the Scottish Linen ledgers could we see if there were any holes in the accounts?'

'Wi' a bit of digging, sure.'

'Could we also see where the money was going? For example, if a company or individual was getting sizeable amounts each month from the bank but without any corresponding deposits?'

'You mean pay-offs? Back-handers? That kinda thing?'

'That kinda thing.'

I spent some more time questioning Airchie until my head was throbbing with numbers and procedures. He seemed to know what he was talking about. It might become clearer to me when I actually saw the ledgers in front of me. Maybe. But first I had to get my hands on them. It was finally dark enough for nefarious activities. I left Higgins sitting among the graves contemplating his own mortality and set off towards St Vincent Street and its back lane.

THIRTY

It looked very different by night, away from the soft-hissing street lamps lining the main streets. I gazed up from the lane. The fire escape zigzagging up the neighbouring department store and the step across the two roofs looked even more challenging in the dark. And who knew what lay under the skylight in the pitch dark? If I could even open it. A fifty-foot drop into a stairwell?

I scaled the Faulds' wall and lay on its rounded top for a moment to peer into the small courtyard. To see what I was getting into. No mad dogs with glittering jaws waiting for me and no pointed railings. No nightwatchman that I could spot. I slid over and into the yard and waited till I had better night vision. When I had, I could see that the fire escape stopped at the level of the first floor. There was a pull-down segment of ladder. Just out of reach. Damn.

I looked around and saw a couple of packing crates. I edged them over until I was under the ladder and climbed up on my shoogly base. I stretched and grabbed the bottom rung and started pulling. It screeched. I stopped and waited to hear running feet. Nothing. I had no choice. I yanked firmly and pulled it all the way down in one long tortured grind until the legs hit the ground with a bang. My heart was hammering. All I could do was wait and hope. I counted slowly to sixty. Then another sixty. No pounding feet. No shouts. No whistles. No dog barking. I started climbing.

It was easy enough. When I reached the roofline, I stepped over the parapet and into the two-foot wide gutter between it and the slate roof. I looked back down into the darkness and could see nothing of note, and certainly nothing moving. I edged along the gutter and reached the brick barrier between the two roofs. It was topped with a glazed curved tile which followed the roofline at a height of about four feet; low enough to scramble over, high and slippery enough to set the blood pounding. I pictured myself as a kid sliding down the long polished bannister of the central stairs in the Dick Institute, housing Kilmarnock's library, and sprawling on the tiles. Painful enough. But this time I'd simply sail off the end into the abyss.

This wasn't the time to think. In one wild, heart-hammering moment I put my hands on the rounded top and jumped up. As I gained height I swung my leg up and over so that I was astride the rounded top. An uncertain cowboy clinging on with fingernails to the rougher bricks below the smooth top. I could feel sweat oozing from the pores on my hands. The inexorable pull of gravity was winning against the smooth rounded surface. I was being tugging backwards and downwards. I had no time to check where I might land on the Scottish Linen side. I flung my other leg round and dropped.

It seemed a long way but only in my head. My feet hit and skidded and jarred my spine. But it was the same height on the bank's side. I fell on to my side and lay clutching the tiles shaking and panting. Not relishing the return trip. And without any clue as to how I'd get wee Airchie over this hurdle. Maybe I could just tie a rope round his middle and fling him over.

When I'd got my heart rate down, I rose to my feet and began to sidle along the inner gutter, hugely conscious of the great space to my right. Conscious too that I would be in profile against the grey sky to anyone walking down the lane.

My army training about avoiding such ridges and my primal instinct for self-preservation screamed at me to cower against the roof tiles, but I kept pushing on to a point below the first skylight. When I reached it, I found a small maintenance ladder fixed to the roof running up from the gutter past the skylight and on up to the chimney breast. I climbed up the first rungs and lay flat, peering down through the glass. It was like looking into a coal mine. I gave my eyes a long while to get used to the dark but I still couldn't see any floor.

I began feeling around the rim of the skylight, pushing and pulling as I went. There was some movement and, at the top, I found hinges. It was designed to be pushed up and back from the inside so that it sat against the roof. I half stood, half knelt, and tugged. Something gave inside. It came up with a jerk and I almost fell into the gap. I steadied myself and gently lowered it backwards on to the roof.

An updraught of stale air swept over me as I peered into the depths. Now I began to make out objects. I was about fifteen feet directly above a bannister, which meant I was halfway over a stairwell. Underneath me would be the landing. If I could clamber into the hole and hang by my hands and swing my body, my momentum should carry me safely beyond the railing and on to the landing. Getting back was the bigger test. I had to hope that the maintenance crew normally left a ladder nearby. And didn't bring one with them and take it away afterwards.

By now I was beyond fear. In full attack mode, the adrenalin pushing me onward. I got my legs into the hole, swivelled round on my belly and slid my body inside. My legs now dangled in space and my stomach rested on the ledge. I eased off my perch and slid down into the darkness until I was dangling at full stretch from the frame. There was no going back. Then I began to swing, commending my shoulder muscles for the hours spent ploughing up and down the pool of the Western Baths Club. Not to mention all the press-ups in my prison cell. After a couple of to and fros I let go on the forward swing and dropped, praying I'd avoid breaking my back on the bannister.

I sailed forever through the air and wondered briefly if I'd let go on the wrong swing. Then my feet hit ground and I tumbled forward in an ungainly sprawl. I flattened out on the cool lino and got my breathing under control again. I looked up and around me and smiled. Facing me was a ladder hooked horizontally on the wall. On the underside of the rim of the skylight, above the void, was a curved metal hook to hold the ladder in place above the drop. I got to my feet and began to pick my way down the staircase into the body of the Scottish Linen Bank.

Did money smell? I was stepping down the wide wood staircase into the heart of the bank and was aware of a growing mustiness. Paper certainly, like a library. But banknotes? All tainted by a thousand hands shuffling and fingering, rubbing and pocketing. Or polish on wood panelling and parquet floors? Mixed with the cloying aroma of generations of clerks toiling over great ledgers.

The staircase wheeled round in a great descending spiral with a void in the centre, plunging four floors down to the level of, but behind the banking hall. Off each level I could see corridors. On each of the top two floors, set in one of the walls, a single barred window peered out into the back yard. The lower floors were blanked for security. I assumed there would be a locked and reinforced basement where they kept the cash and gold sovereigns. I imagined a great safe with fancy locks and tumblers. I wasn't interested in the money. Where would they keep the ledgers? Would they be as protected as the cash?

I kept my eyes and ears sharp for signs of a night-watchman. But I was gambling that with all the heavy doors, locks and barred windows, they saw no need.

My eyes grew sharper now as they drew in the light from the rear windows. I descended to the first-floor landing and peered down. Desks. Rows of them. All cleared and ready for the start of business. Along every side were rack upon rack of open wood shelves, all filled with tall books. The books of records. The bank's ledgers.

I followed the staircase down. It opened out on to the floor of the hall and I began to wander between the desks. The fustiness crowded round me, as though I'd stuck my head in an ancient book and was inhaling dead words.

I walked to the sides and started to peer at the spines of the books. This was it. Bank ledgers, some by branch, some by customer, some by period. Inside, pages filled with neat script, carefully blotted, numbers carefully transposed from one ledger to another, carrying the details of Mr McKay's five-pound deposit on 20 June in Paisley through to the weekly balance of a million pounds in and a million pounds out. Telling the fortunes of the bank and its customers, day by day, month on month, year by year. In turn, telling a story to shareholders of how well the bank had used their money, and how much dividend they would be receiving.

Somewhere in here, among these yards of inked-in volumes, were clues about what Fraser Gibson was doing with his own money, the bank's money and Government and USA loans. But I didn't know where to start. I could only hope that Archibald Higgins, crook and swindler, struck-off accountant and former jailbird, was better equipped. My daunting challenge was to get his creaky middle-aged body over the wall, up a ladder, over a roof and into this bank without breaking his neck. Or mine.

I reversed my steps. At the top of the stairs I looked long-ingly at the ladder on the wall, but how would that look in the morning propped against the skylight? I could kick it back and let it fall on the landing, so that people would think it had simply dropped off its hooks. But it might just tumble into the void. How would you explain that? When I next came with Airchie I didn't want to find a grinning man with a slavering Alsatian waiting for us. But there was a simpler answer.

I brought the ladder down and placed it against the skylight rim. I climbed up and out. Then I pulled the ladder up behind me, through the skylight, and laid it against the roof. I carefully closed the skylight, moved down the fixed rungs and manoeuvred the ladder down into the gutter. For at least a day or two no one from the bank other than a maintenance man would notice the ladder was missing. Or if they did, they'd think it was in use elsewhere. And it would solve at least one of the barriers to getting Airchie into the bank.

Getting out was another matter.

THIRTY-ONE

I n the morning we put in at the Erskine Ferry pier in a smooth exhibition of steering and furling of sails. I was finally getting the hang of the ropes and beginning to be a half-useful member of the crew. Anyone glancing at us would have seen two red-bearded old salts happily and easily working together. I went ashore and phoned Harry to tell him what I was up to. I was glad to find him at his desk on a Sunday. Showed commitment. Like me.

'Higgins will play ball?'

'Yes, but he had conditions.' I explained what they were. Harry laughed but promised to see what he could do.

'Any results on Roddie Adams and Frankie Elliot?'

'Sam's description of Adams bears out. Apparently a very dodgy lawyer in a very dodgy corner of the profession. As for Elliot, he runs a drinking club in Glasgow. On the face of it, all clean. But we're pretty sure it's a cover.'

'Drugs, sex trade, laundering? The usual?'

'The usual. Good luck, Brodie. And don't forget, old chap . . .' The apology was in the tone.

'If I'm caught, I'm on my own. I know, Harry.'

'Sorry and all that. And clock's running, Brodie. We have nine days. The Chancellor is being pressed to make a statement about how sterling will hold up and whether we'll get a big enough slice of the Marshall Plan cash.'

'I'm sure I should be feeling the weight of history on my

shoulders, Harry, but just at the moment, I'm a wee bit more concerned about my own skin. If this all goes tits up, and I need to go on the run, can I count on HMG? Get me out of the country? Honorary Consul to Mongolia or the like?'

'Depends if we've got any money left. We might afford *Outer* Mongolia, but if you had your choice?'

'Anywhere that's still pink on the map. Canada or New Zealand might work. They're full of Scots running away from something. And that would be papers for two, Harry.'

We collected Sam further upriver at noon and whisked her off back down the Clyde. Once we were out in mid-river I emerged from the cabin to enjoy the air and her company. Eric waved from the helm. We were sailing on mizzen and jib; he didn't need any help. And I didn't need to show off my rope lore for Sam. For a while we sat side by side on cushions just forward of the main mast holding hands like a courting couple. The sun and warm breeze bathed our faces.

'A Sunday jaunt to Arran?' I asked.

She smiled ruefully. 'No time, my dear. But when we get out of this . . .'

I didn't say 'if' back to her. I got us on to business.

'You saw Duncan?'

'I met him this morning. He's still in a bad way over you. Castigates himself for not coming to see you.'

'He was ordered not to.'

'He thinks he should have told Sangster where to get off.'

'And lose his job? He's got a wife to look after. I wish I wasn't duping him like this. Will he help?'

'Oh yes. In fact he's already been doing some digging. He said it all reeks of the midden. Said he's seen it before when the boys are up to something, trying to hide something. He said they go quiet and go around smirking.'

I nodded. 'Like kids. Have you ever been with a gang of other school pals and suddenly they're avoiding you? You catch them huddled together, whispering and glancing your way?'

A look flashed across her face. 'Once. I must have been about fifteen. I'd fallen out with my best friend at the time – Shona – God knows what about. But she sided with some others to get at me.'

'Did they?' I studied Sam. It had obviously rankled for – what? – twenty-three years.

'One of them clyped to my form teacher that I'd been smoking.'

'Had you?'

'At a party. Everybody tried it, including the wee clype.'

'What happened?'

A wicked smile thinned her lips. 'I tearfully confessed and got off. The wee nyaff that told on me got four of the belt for being a tell-tale.'

I grinned. 'Your personal motto, Sam: *Nemo me impune lacessit*.'

'For me and mine. That includes you, my dear.'

'Other than the feeling he's being ganged up on, what's Duncan found out?'

'Two things. You won't like the first at all.'

'Try me.'

'Seems that after you were pronounced dead, Sangster held a wee party in his office. They kept the door shut, but they polished off half a dozen bottles of Whyte & McKay.'

'Poor choice. I deserved a good Glenlivet. A toast to my memory, I'm sure. Who was at this party?'

'I've got the names. Here.' Sam dug out a slip of paper with four names on it. I read them out.

'Inspector Geddies, and Sergeants Hamilton, Caldwell and Gillespie. A fine bunch. They've been around a while.'

'Did you work with them?'

'No. But I knew of them. All I'd say is that like attracts like. Funny, I knew Sangster didn't like me, that I'd made him look even more stupid than usual. But I wouldn't have bet on him dancing on my grave.'

'I don't think you realise how annoyingly talented you are, Douglas. For someone like Sangster, who's smart enough to know it, but too thick to do anything about it, it must grate.'

'To the point he'd be happy to see me swing? That seems a bit of an overreaction.'

'Don't underestimate the driving force of an inferiority complex.'

'You believe that Alfred Adler stuff?'

She shrugged. 'It fits. I think that was Shona's problem.'

'What was the other thing Duncan found out?'

'That they've closed the Gibson case.'

'What! How can they? Sangster knows two men abducted Gibson from his house. Unless that was completely made up? Sangster even claims that while they were handcuffing me, my fellow conspirators were vaulting the back wall. Even Sangster – if he really believed I was involved – should be out looking for at least two other kidnappers.'

'Unless he got orders not to?'

'From the top? You think my old pal the Chief Constable would take him off? After what I did for him?'

'Malcolm McCulloch thought highly of you and what you did. Perhaps even to the point of saying stop, enough raking up dirt.'

'To spare my good name? But?'

'But he's a politician as well as a cop. This case was dynamite. A senior member of the establishment, kidnapped and shot on his patch? Life becomes much quieter if there's a dead scapegoat to hand.'

'Hmmm. That sounds more likely than being concerned about my image after death. You don't think there's more to it than that? McCulloch is straight, isn't he? He's not in anyone's pocket?'

Sam frowned. 'I've never heard anything.'

We let that notion simmer.

'Back to Duncan. What can he do?'

'I told him I was determined to clear your name. I asked him to find out who warned Sangster about Marr Street. Who was the informer? And why Lady Gibson denies ever meeting you? I suggested he has a quiet word with Cammie the chauffeur and Janice the maid.'

'Will he?'

'He's knows he'd be taking a big risk. He's wound himself up to try. But he said the widow's in mourning and has let it be known that she's talking to no one. Everything's being done through her lawyer.'

'Not Adams, I hope!'

'No. A big aggressive firm though. Armed with writs.'

'I need to talk to Duncan. I'm going to have to face him. Soon.'

'Let's give it a day or two. See what he comes up with.'

We basked for a bit longer before she said, 'Douglas, I can feel my nose burning and I didn't bring my bonnet. Besides, I have to get back. I'm in court tomorrow. I need to prepare. And not show up with a peeling neb.'

I squeezed her hand. 'I need to prepare too, Sam.' But my appointment was with a bank.

THIRTY-TWO

I was in much better shape for my second assault on Scottish Linen that night. I carried a range of makeshift tools in an old gas-mask case. If it had been just me, I'd be near to brimming with confidence, except for the small matter of making sense of the ledgers. It was eleven o'clock when I entered the graveyard on North Street. I peered around but couldn't see Airchie. Then I caught a cigarette glow between the headstones. I found him sitting, head in hands on top of a flat stone. A small ghost taking the air.

'You OK, Airchie?'

'Ah suppose so. Huv ye had a word?'

'About what?'

'Aboot ma medal?'

'I spoke to London this morning. It should be no problem.'

'Did ye?' His voice lifted. 'Yer no' bullshitting me, ur ye, Brodie?'

'I'm perfectly serious. There's a bloke called Harry in London. He's our contact. He said he'd raise it with the boss. My boss. *Your* boss in head office. He thought the only problem might be the need to keep quiet about it. For a bit anyway. They don't make public awards in the Security Service.'

'Whit's the point o' that? Ah want tae flaunt it. Doon the pub. Among ma' pals.' His voice lowered. 'Show ma wee mither Ah'm no jist a nae user.'

174

'We'll sort something out. But first, you need to earn it. Let's go.'

It wasn't much of a battle cry, but it got him on his feet.

The back lane was quiet and shadowed. It was important that I didn't allow Airchie time to think about the dangers or size up the obstacles. I told him to wait in the doorway in the lane wall, shinned up the stone dyke and dropped down on the other side. I knelt down on the inside of the door and searched in my bag. My last action the night before had been to inspect the lock carefully. It was a very standard lock screwed on to the heavy wood. I pulled out a couple of screwdrivers and three long nails bent at the end. Eric and I had angled them to slightly different specifications on the ketch this afternoon. If none fitted, I'd at least be able to unscrew the whole block. I told Eric it gave me a rueful reminder of my former pal, Danny McRae, who'd pitched up earlier in the year to stir things up. Lock-picking and stirring were two of Danny's special talents.

'I thought he was helping you, Brodie? Against those bloody Nazis?'

'He was. Sort of. Turned out he was doing it for a woman. Lust trumps friendship.'

'An old story. Are they happy?'

I shook my head. 'I don't know. But she was using him. She might well have dumped him after she got what she was after.'

'Women, eh?'

After a poke or two, and a change of nail, I felt the lever give and the lock slid back. I was inordinately pleased with myself. I opened the door. Airchie fell in. We tiptoed across the dark yard and I dragged the crates back under the fire escape. I felt in my bag and pulled out a tin. I opened it, dug into its viscous contents, stretched up and smeared the grease on to

175

the runners of the pull-down ladder. I tugged and had the satisfaction of having the section slide down with barely a moan. I turned to Airchie. He was staring up through his specs, mouth agape. Paralysed. It was what I'd feared when I saw his face as I'd described how we were going to get in.

'Ye didnae say we hud tae sclim up there, Brodie.'

'There's no actual climbing. It's just a ladder.'

'Ah'm feart o' heights. Ah cannae dae this.'

I wiped my hands on the rag I'd brought and pulled out a half-bottle of Teacher's.

'Here. Take a big sook.'

He grabbed it and sank several mouthfuls of raw whisky. He gasped as it scoured his throat.

'Better?'

'Better. But Ah'm still feart. Ah cannae even see the top.'

'Turn round.' I took out a strip of sacking and tied it round his eyes.

'Oh, Christ, Brodie. That's worse. It's left tae ma imagination noo.'

'Hold the sides and start climbing. Pretend you're a commando.'

He reached out blindly and gripped the ladder. I prodded him.

'Get on with you. I'm right behind you. And go quietly.'

He began climbing and I followed him on up. At each landing, he'd ask, is this it? No, nearly there. Until finally we were at the top.

'Christ, Brodie, Ah can tell we're high up. Ah can feel the wind on my face.'

'You're doing great, Airchie. Just step over this wee wall. Then it's easy.'

I pulled on his leg and got him to step on to the department-store roof. I looked down and decided it was better to keep him blindfolded until we were on the Scottish Linen roof. I got behind him and steered him gently along the wide gutter towards the divide of the roofs. I had him sit down with his back against the roof and his feet braced on the parapet.

I gave him another slug of whisky and a fag, and took out the last bits and pieces from my gas-mask case: a four-foot strip of jute sacking and a can of varnish. I unrolled the foot-wide cloth and sprinkled the varnish over it. The smell caught my lungs and I gagged. I rubbed the material against itself until it was well coated over all of one side. I laid it out carefully over the top of the rounded glazed tiles on the wall between the two roofs. I pushed down on the sacking. It held. Now for the hard bit.

'Airchie, I need you to stand up. I'll help you.' I got behind him and made him stand facing the sacking. 'Hold on to this.' I put his hands on the sacking. 'Now I'm going to give you a leg-up and you're going to fling your right leg over this wee wall and sit astride it. Just like climbing on a bike. OK? Then I'm going to get up behind you and we're going to slide over the other side. OK?'

'That easy, eh? Disnae sound it. Huv you ony rope? Like real climbers?'

'This is kid's stuff. You'll be fine.'

'Aye, right. Ah'm OK, Brodie. Lead me to it.'

I may have overdone force-feeding him the Dutch courage. He might well have been self-medicating before I met him in the graveyard. Bugger. Too late now.

'Right, up you go.' I cupped my hands and gave him a leg-up. As he pushed up I was just able to get behind him and balance him before he tipped the wrong way. I pushed him forward, face down, pointing up the ridge. There was barely enough room for me to get behind him. I jumped up, got my leg over the sacking and swung round and dropped on to the bank roof. Without stopping, I grabbed Airchie and pulled him down beside me. In the course of the manoeuvre the blindfold came off and we lay panting, side by side, backs on the roof, gazing up at the stars.

'It's a braw bricht moonlicht nicht the nicht, eh, Brodie.'

God, he'd be singing next. A drunk on a hundred-foot-high roof.

'Shut up, Airchie. Roll over on to your side and don't look down.'

All his addled brain heard was *look down*. He looked.

'Oh shit! Oh shit!'

He flung himself back and tried to merge with the tiles.

'Airchie! Listen! Turn on to your face. Start sliding along. Do it!'

Inch by inch I made him crawl sideways until he could feel the steel certainty of the fixed ladder going up to the skylight. It seemed to calm him. I kept cajoling him until he'd climbed the half-dozen rungs and his face was just below the skylight. I crawled up beside him and levered back the skylight. Then I hauled up the free ladder and slid most of it into the dark hole. I was holding it by a rung with my head stuck through rungs higher up.

Its weight wrenched at my arm muscles and where it sat on my neck. I couldn't hold it for long without being dragged into the yawning gap. I began to swing it until it banged against the balustrade. The judder ran through my arms. Sweat dripped from my forehead into the pit. I pulled it up one more rung and got the pendulum going again. I could just make out that its tips were now sailing over the wooden rail. I let it perform one last arc out over the drop and then back. Just as it sailed over the balustrade, I ducked my head and grabbed the next rung up, so that it dropped two feet.

It fell back from the apogee of its swing and caught against the balustrade. I paused and caught my breath. Slowly and awkwardly I lowered the ladder rung by rung until it was touching the floor of the landing. I then secured its top rung to the wide hook under the forward lip of the skylight. I pulled my body out of the hole and eased my aching limbs. Airchie was hugging the roof ladder as though his life depended on it. Which it did. His eyes loomed large behind his glasses.

'Airchie, I'm going first. Then you follow.' I eased my lower body inside and searched for my footing on the ladder. I felt it and moved down a couple of rungs.

'Right. Come on.'

'Ah cannae. Ah jist cannae,' he whispered.

'Airchie, you're dead if you stay there. You'll just slide off. This is the easy bit. Move up until you can get your legs inside, then I'll help you down. The worst is over.'

That wasn't what his face said. It said, *I don't believe you. I'm a dead man.*

'You'll deserve your medal. This is what it was like, Airchie. Going over the top. Going into battle was about being afraid, but doing it anyway.'

He searched my eyes for the truth. I don't know what he found but he nodded and began to rise. I pushed and tugged and got him on to the ladder, and guided his steps one by one. Shortly, we were on the landing, collapsed in an exhausted heap. I checked my watch. Midnight.

'Come on, Airchie. Now it's your turn to show me what you can do. Let's go.'

THIRTY-THREE

A s we slunk down the levels on the great spiralling staircase, I kept stopping and listening. There'd been no sign
of nightwatchmen yesterday but maybe they didn't come
in at weekends. Or worse, I'd roused them when they found
the ladder missing, and they were lying in wait. With a pair
of shotguns.

As we descended, I also grew convinced that this was going
to be our one and only chance. I couldn't get Airchie back up
on the roof. He was still shaking. I wasn't sure I had the
strength for it either. I shoved from my mind the horrors of
the return trip. It simply didn't bear thinking about. One step
at a time.

We got to the final landing and Airchie gazed down across
the rows of desks and the walls of filing.

'Christ, Brodie. It's big.'

'I thought you were at the Royal. They're bigger, are they
not?'

'Aye, but I only saw one part of it. This is the lot! All the
branches, the head office branch and the bank-wide books.'

'Well, you're just going to have to narrow it down, aren't
you?'

We stepped into the hall and I found a switch that illumi-
nated the lamps above the cabinets. The soft glow and the
serried ranks of desks turned the accounts hall into a ghostly
reading room. Airchie began to pace his way round the floor,

stopping at each section, reading the spines of the books sideways. He did one full circuit, often stepping back and checking a section he'd just passed. I waited at the front of the class in the big desk that faced the lines of smaller ones. The invigilator's desk. I expected to find a tawse and mortarboard tucked under the lid. I sat and smoked and watched the hands of the big clock saunter round. Half an hour went by and Airchie had just completed his second circuit. He stepped towards me brow creased and rubbing his nose where his specs made a dent.

'Well, Airchie? Can you do it?'

'Oh, aye. If I hud a month.'

I glanced at my watch. It read one o'clock. I reckoned they'd be in at six next morning, the start of the week. We'd work till five.

'You've got four hours.'

'It's no' possible.'

'OK, we'll come back tomorrow night, and every night for a month.'

I saw him consider making the climb again. His face fell. Medal or no.

'Airchie, you'll have to do what you can in four hours. Let's look for the big things. Start at the top. Are the client ledgers alphabetical for the head office branch?'

He nodded.

'Find Gibson. Find his personal accounts. Then we'll take it from there. Oh, and keep an eye out for the account belonging to a certain Douglas Brodie. I'd like to know where my life's savings went.'

'Ony o' that booze left?'

'Empty. Besides, you need all your wits about you. Tell me how I can help.'

He thought for a moment. 'There's a set of the overall head office books ower there. They show transfers between branches and between other banks. Mair important is that there should be a record of the receipt of funds from the Bank of England. The Bank has been spraying cash around to keep up the capital levels of the retail banks. The ledgers might show they came as straight loans or from the sale of gilts.'

'A gilt is a loan issued by the Bank of England?'

'Aye. One of the ways we're keeping the wolf from the door. Borrowing in the international markets, but borrowing backed by the Anglo-American Agreement. See what you can find.'

'Airchie, I'm impressed. You sound like a professor.'

His mouth twisted. 'Aye, well. Ah used to be good at ma job. An' Ah keep an eye on the papers.'

'Good for you. OK, I'll dive in over here. And, Airchie, remember where you got the ledgers. We have to leave this place as we found it. No signs.'

We moved to the shelves. I set myself up on a desk near the back. There were small electric lamps above each desk. I switched mine on and began to bring over the huge books and examine them one by one. Airchie followed suit. For a while, he seemed to be in his element, humming to himself as he thumbed through ledger after ledger. He'd got hold of some scraps of foolscap and a couple of pencils and was making notes. I looked up after an hour or so and saw his head on the desk. Gentle snores seeped from his mouth. I marched over and shook him.

'Airchie! Airchie!'

'Whit? Whit is it? Where am Ah?'

'Airchie, get up. Have a walk round the desks. You need to stay awake.'

We walked together until I was sure he was revived enough to carry on.

'Any progress? Have you found Gibson's statements?'

'Ah huv that. There's some interesting stuff going on. Big sums going out, big sums coming in.'

'Unusually big?'

'For a personal account, aye. A thoosand here, a thoosand there. The odd five thoosand.'

'More than I've ever seen in my life. He's doing well for himself.'

'He is that.'

'Where's it coming from and where's it going to?'

'That's what Ah'm following. That's why Ah'm ower there and there.' He pointed to two other desks, where he'd piled some ledgers from different sections.

'Good work, Airchie.'

'What about you, Brodie?'

'I'm in the big league. I've found entries for transfers of millions of pounds from the Bank of England. Some show them as loans from the sale of gilts. Others as straight loans with a reference to AAA, which I assume is the Anglo-American loan. Others mention Lend-Lease. They're showed as credits.'

'We'll make a bookkeeper out of you yet, Brodie. They're still tying up a' the loose ends o' Lend-Lease. A' they tanks and planes that we got on the never-never from the Yanks we ended up having to pay for.'

'But we got them cheap, I recall.'

'Ten per cent in the pound. Paid off over fifty years at two per cent interest. A bargain, I'd say.'

I had to shake him awake twice more throughout the long hours till dawn. I had him explain some of my own findings and he guided me to further exploration. I'd had some basic training in the army in keeping accounts for soldiers' pay and rations. Between us we were beginning to see a picture emerging. I struggled with my own eyes at times and did a brief jig and short series of exercises to set my blood coursing again.

At four in the morning, Airchie called me over.

'I've found your accounts, Brodie. I thocht you might have been worth mair. No' much to show for a' the years defending the country.'

'You don't say. But I did have a few bob to my name. At least I thought I did.'

'You did.' He pointed to lines in a ledger with my name at the top of the page. 'You had five pounds and ten shillings in your current account, and forty-four pounds, three shillings and sixpence in your savings. Until the ninth of June.'

'That was the Monday *after* Gibson was murdered! Someone in the bank sent forged statements to the court stating I was broke three weeks before!'

'A statement's just a bit o' paper, Brodie. Ye can say anything on it. And put what dates you like on it.'

'It's solid proof I was set up though! Who took it?'

'It shows all your money being withdrawn on the same day plus a five-pound overdraft. There're three chits here, one for the savings account, one for the current, and one an agreed overdraft. All paid out in cash on the ninth.'

'Not to me!'

He waved another bit of paper. 'This is a letter purporting to be signed by you permitting the bearer to access your accounts.'

'Who was the bearer?'

He peered at the heading. 'Miss Pamela McKenzie. A friend of yours?'

'The wee bitch!'

I stood in shock, trying to make sense of it.

'Was it that easy? Anyone could have walked in and slapped a letter on the counter saying they had the right to take someone's money?'

'No' really. It needed bank approval.'

'Did she have it?'

'It was initialled CC – presumably Colin Clarkson, the Finance Director.'

'Bastard,' I said softly.

'It might no' mean anything, Brodie. Heid bummers sign or initial anything put in front o' them.'

'Well, somebody's a bastard.'

I went back to my own analysis with renewed fervour. There were scribbles and boxes with lines drawn between them. I knew what they said – more or less – and Airchie could help me draw the right conclusions. It was a good start. I had traced some of the sources of a sizeable income stream feeding Gibson's account. Airchie seemed to have got some interesting information about his spending habits. Money going to personal accounts and to companies. All we had to do was get out of here and compose the overall picture. In a hurry.

When I next looked at my watch it was five thirty. Some light was filtering through from the high-up windows down into the banking hall. We were cutting it fine. Too fine. I reckoned there would be porters opening up the doors in half an hour. It was time we were on the move. I looked over. Airchie was barely awake, his face white and strained. He looked nearer ninety than fifty. I was never going to get him to make the climb again. He'd get up the ladder, take one look from the skylight at the huge drop and freeze. That was before we'd even tackled the high jump over the ridge wall.

'Airchie, get packed up. All ledgers away. Lights off. It's time to go.' I pointed up to our escape route.

He looked across at me. 'Brodie, Ah've been thinking aboot that. Ah cannae dae it.' His face said it all. 'Even if you had a crate o' whisky, Ah couldnae dae it.'

THIRTY-FOUR

stared at him. I knew when men were trying it on. This was no bluff.

'Leave it to me,' I said with more hope than knowledge. I jogged up the stairs, level by level, until I was breathing heavily on the top landing. I looked up at the open skylight. The rectangle was now grey and would be lightening fast. I could slip out and leave Airchie to face the music. What would another stretch of five years matter to him? Then I thought of his medal hopes and what this work meant to him. A last chance.

I jumped on the ladder and stepped smartly up to the open skylight. I reached out – sorely tempted to climb out and away – and hauled the heavy glass box closed. I all but slid down the ladder and back on to the landing. With my foot on its bottom rung I had to pull it back and unhook it. It was a two-man job. Slowly it came up, but in the process it caught on the long steel arm of the catch that held down the skylight. It clunked, clattered and dangled. Bugger! I stared at the swinging arm. To hell with it. I wasn't going back up there. I hauled the ladder down and on to the landing. I manoeuvred it over to the wall and flung it up in its proper place. I looked up at the errant catch. Who would notice? And when? There was no time to worry about it. If anyone saw it they'd think it had just come loose.

I cast about. There were cupboards and doors running off the landing. I started to go through them. Surely if there was a ladder, there would be other equipment. I found mops and brooms, buckets and a sink. But hanging behind one door was what I was looking for. I grabbed them and a box of tools and headed down the stairs. Airchie was just sliding the last ledger in place.

'Here. Put these on.'

I held out a pair of dungarees, blue cotton and well worn. They came with a matching cap. For the first time in hours, Airchie smiled. I slipped my own pair on and did up the bib and braces. I jammed the flat blue cap on and picked up my gas-mask case. We stowed our notes in it and inspected ourselves. Airchie's dungarees fell over his shoes. We rolled up the cuffs. Mine were halfway up my ankles. I undid the braces as far as possible and pushed them down. We wouldn't pass inspection by a real maintenance crew, especially wearing their gear. But it was the best we could do. The rest was going to be down to brass neck and timing. We sat clutching our bag and toolbox, waiting for the first noises of the day. We had five minutes.

At six o'clock on the dot I heard bolts and chains being unlocked out in the banking hall. Then voices. We stared at the double door that led from the back office along a short corridor to the cash desks. The doors themselves were locked. On the outside. All we could do was wait our turn. At last we heard footsteps. They stopped outside the door. A key fumbled in the lock, and the door started to swing open. I nodded at Airchie and stepped forward into the pool of light.

'Morning!' I called and strode forward. 'All done here.'

The man – in winged collar and tie and tails, presumably a junior manager – stepped back, startled.

'Oh, good morning. I – what? – have you been . . .?'

'Weekend maintenance. Night shift. Had to check all the radiators. Everything fine now.'

Airchie walked behind me, head down, silent behind his glasses. I started whistling and tried to keep my pace normal as we emerged into the grand banking hall and headed for the door. Another man stood nearby screwing in his tie studs. A doorman getting ready for the day. He turned as we walked towards him. I called out gaily:

'Good morning. Looks a fine day.' I nodded to the light-filled windows.

'Aye, it is.' Then his brain said, *Wait a minute*. 'Where did you come frae?'

'Maintenance. Radiators. All OK. Nice bit o' double time.'

'Ah wisnae telt. Wait the noo. Ah need to check ma list.'

'Sorry, pal. We're starving. We're away for a sausage roll and a cup o' tea. Sort it oot wi' yer boss. He kens a' aboot it.'

I walked up to the great front doors and pulled open the small side panel embedded in it. I held it as Airchie stepped out, then followed him. The doorman was transfixed, watching us depart, his head trying to make sense of it, but too slowly. We stepped down into the fresh morning air of St Vincent Street and sucked it in.

'Just keep walking, Airchie. Don't look back. Don't run. We're walking round the corner and down the hill. Keep going.'

We walked steadily down Blythswood Street until I steered us into the cobbles and narrows of Wellington Lane. Behind the Alhambra we stripped off our dungarees and caps and stuffed them in the big bins. We left the toolbox outside the stage door – someone would find a use for it – and emerged on Wellington Street. We walked on and turned into Central Station. A café was just opening for early workers. I filled Airchie with tea and toast until some colour came back. I lifted my mug.

'Archibald Higgins, you're a wee hero. Two medals is what you deserve.'

'Ah don't mind telling you, Brodie, Ah'm fair puggled.'

'Me too. Are you able to brief me on what you've found? I need to pull all this together.'

Airchie straightened up, rubbed his bloodshot eyes and with the aid of his notes and mine, we built up a picture of a managing director robbing his own bank. Gibson had been milking hundreds of thousands of pounds over the last two or three years, especially the last twelve months. He'd been dipping into the golden streams flowing from the Anglo-American Agreement. Loans to help the war effort and its aftermath. Too good an opportunity to miss.

Where required, the various transfers had been authorised by senior officials including Gibson himself and the then Finance Director and now Managing Director, Colin Clarkson. Were Clarkson and the others just doing their boss's bidding? Or were they active accomplices?

There were also records of note-issuing. The Scottish Linen Bank was allowed to produce its own banknotes. Print money. A handy facility if you needed a few bob to make up a short-fall. There were some sizeable issues over the past year or two: hundreds of thousands of pounds in various denominations. I didn't know what checks and balances stopped Scottish Linen from simply running the printing presses when they felt like it. Did it all have to be backed by gold?

Our research covered only the last three years of records, but showed Gibson stealing and disbursing over a million pounds. An amount I struggled to comprehend.

'A million quid, Airchie! What could you do with a million quid?'

He sucked his pencil. 'What do you earn a week, Brodie? About eight pounds?'

'If I get a Sunday shift.'

He did a couple of bits of long division. 'By my calculations you'd have to work for 2,427 years to earn that.'

'So I'll never be a millionaire. It doesn't bother me. How could you spend a million?'

'Ah'd like the chance. See Bearsden?' He scribbled some more.

'You want to live in Bearsden?'

'Why no'? You think it's too posh for the likes of me?'

'For the likes of either of us. But never mind. Everybody needs to aim high. What could you buy for a million?'

He leaned across the greasy Formica. 'Ye could buy a hale street, Brodie. Several *hale* streets. Ah hear the price for wan o' they big detached hooses is getting near two thoosand quid.'

'What would you want with five hundred houses, Airchie? That's not a street. That's *Higginston*.'

'That would be rare.' He beamed. 'Well, maybe Ah'd just buy a couple. One for me, one for ma mither. She'd love that, so she would. And Ah'd just fritter the rest away on women and Rolls-Royces and fine wines.' His eyes went dreamy.

'In the meantime, Airchie, let's figure out what Fraser actually spent a million on, eh?'

Airchie's research showed Gibson steadily syphoning off chunks of cash every month over the past year into a suspense account called 'AAA interest'. Anglo-American Agreement? But it wasn't accruing. Comparing notes with Airchie, we found that each month this account was emptied into one of several personal accounts under the direct control of Sir Fraser Gibson himself.

There were one-off payments from Gibson's accounts as well as regular monthly sums to a small number of named accounts. Among them was a private account in the name of Mungo Gibson at the Maybole branch of the bank. Lady Gibson also received some large dollops of pin money. Just how many furs did one woman need, even in Scotland? The other recipients were companies: 'Silver Dollar' and 'High Times' received irregular but sizeable lump sums.

But over the past year a regular monthly amount of £20,000 had been transferred into the pockets of a company called 'Gulf Stream'. An outfit operating on the Ayrshire coast? Doing what? Some legitimate business at the many ports? Fishing? Or good old-fashioned smuggling with the Irish Republic? Booze and drugs?

It could have been worse, I suppose. We could have found Gibson had been defrauding the bank for *tens* of millions. The amounts pilfered wouldn't break the bank and didn't breach its capital requirements. But it spoke of a stunning lack of controls and corruption and collusion at the highest levels of Scotland's largest financial institution.

I could see the headlines on every newspaper in the country and imagine a bout of handwringing and apoplectic fits at the Treasury. And big question marks in Washington.

THIRTY-FIVE

I left Airchie on his third cup of tea and his second fried-egg roll. I walked out and jumped on a tram. I was too tired to walk and thought I stood as much chance of being spotted and recognised in the street as among the cloud of smoke on the top deck with the red-eyed early risers. I was just another worker slumped in his seat, fag in mouth. I rode down to the Clyde along the Broomielaw to Anderston Quay. Eric was waiting for me. I sidled on board and fell exhausted into my bunk. I slept like the dead man I was supposed to be until noon.

When I at last stirred and clambered on deck I found the *Lorne* anchored down by Dumbarton and rocking on the tide. Eric was sitting quietly smoking his pipe and reading *Great Expectations*. I liked omens. He made us both a late breakfast and I began collating my notes with Airchie's. By late afternoon, Eric and I were sitting on the deck sharing a pot of tea.

'So what now, Brodie?'

I touched the pile of notes in front of me.

'I've got proof that Gibson was stealing from his own bank. I don't know if he was in deep trouble and trying to dig himself out of it or simply building a pension pot. A big pot.'

'Solid proof?' He pointed at the papers.

'The problem is how do I explain how I got the information? These won't count unless we can get the actual bank ledgers in front of a judge and jury.'

'What about your pals at you-know-who?'

'I can tell them what I've found and what to look for. But they're terrified of causing a commotion with all the inevitable questions and public outcry.'

'And it disnae explain why Gibson was kidnapped?'

I shook my head. 'We don't know who these companies are. But even if we did, why bump him off?'

'Failing to pay his debts?'

'There didn't seem to be any shortage of funds. Gibson had a whole bank to plunder and he seemed to have senior staff in his pocket to cover his tracks.'

'So who murdered him? And why?'

'I have no idea. There were entries up to a few days before the kidnap. Why kill the golden goose? Was he going to come clean and face the music? Did his wife know? And if so, did she set me up? Was Sheila trying to get rid of her philandering husband? Did she know about the lovely Pamela?'

'Any news from your man watching her?'

'I need to check with Wullie. And Sam. She's getting in touch with Inspector Duncan Todd. Can you drop me at the Govan Ferry this evening? South bank. I've called for a confab. Wullie and Stewart live in Summertown Road.'

'Are you sure they're not being watched?'

'Why? I'm dead, remember. There's nothing further to be gained from watching my pals.'

After Eric dropped me off that evening I found a box and left a message at Harry's office. Two minutes later he phoned back and I gave him the highlights of what Airchie and I had uncovered. I thought he'd have been more pleased.

'Christ, Brodie, what a God-almighty mess!'

I was miffed. 'But at least the bank's not likely to go under.'

'A small blessing. Assuming you haven't missed anything? But it's hell down here. Our political masters have been climbing the walls. I've been in the office all weekend and the phones have been running red hot. If news gets out about this debacle and causes a banking crisis this week, the political fallout for Attlee could bring down the administration. It's what Churchill and the opposition have been waiting for.'

'Surely the news can be contained?'

'You think so? Imagine the headlines if it gets out that the kidnapped and murdered head of Scottish Linen was also pilfering his own bank? Filling his boots with cash from Lend-Lease or whatever. Can you imagine the speculation about *why* he was killed? Who would believe us if we said the bank was basically sound? It smacks of poor supervision by the B. of E. at the very least.'

'So it's time you moved in, Harry. Got your hands on those books.'

The pause said it all.

'The last thing my masters will authorise is a raid by the Security Service. It will get out. The press will crucify them. Confidence would drop through the floor and cause the very run they're trying to avoid. And the Yanks won't lend.'

I exploded. 'What the hell more can I do, Harry? You've got enough to impound all their accounts and show the Government has a grip. A five-minute embarrassment. And for me – it provides a possible motive for Gibson's kidnap and murder.'

'But it doesn't really, does it? *Au contraire*, in fact. Gibson's death makes no sense. It just suggests there's more dirty business undisclosed.'

I had to admit he was right. 'So what *can* you do? Apart from sitting on your backside and agonising while I take all the risks?'

'Brodie, I'm sorry. I can understand your frustration. Let's first investigate who owns these companies and what they're up to. I'll do a bit of trawling and call you tomorrow. Same time, same call box?'

'Try to get your bosses to see sense. This will come out one way or the other. The sooner the better.'

'You'd never make a politician, Brodie. Their first reaction is the *later* the better. On someone else's watch.'

'I can't keep up this game much longer, Harry. It's only a matter of time before I'm rumbled.'

'I'll press your case, Brodie.'

'And Airchie's. He's earned that medal.'

Stewart welcomed me at his tenement flat door. The smart and spotless McAllister interior belied the dilapidated shared stairwell and the rundown tenement itself. Sam was already waiting for me and got up and hugged me, then drew back, wrinkling her nose.

'You smell of fish.'

'So would you, if you borrowed Eric's sweater.'

Then she hugged me again. 'I could get used to it.'

'Masochist.'

Wullie coughed. 'Should we leave you twa alane?'

'Fine by me,' I said.

'Unhand me, you hairy brute.'

'Fickle, fickle. Right. To business. Let me tell you about my night-time escapades with a crooked accountant.'

At the end of my tale, Wullie and Stewart were laughing. Sam was frowning, her hand up at her mouth.

'You could have been killed on that roof.'

'Tricky for you. A second burial.'

'Don't say that, Douglas! Anyway, I hope you wore gloves?'

I sighed. 'I thought about it too late. I'm new to the life of the cat burglar.'

'Your prints will be everywhere. And they've got some nice recent ones to match them up with.'

'Remind me. Won't they have thrown them away after they closed the case?'

She shook her head. 'They keep them for years. Just in case.'

'In case I'm not dead?'

'In case you've done other bad things. You said you stole dungarees and left a bit of sacking on the roof. And at least two people saw you as you walked out. You're hard to ignore: a big man with a red beard. Smelling of fish.'

'I've worked with these guys. They're not that good. They're certainly not that quick.'

She eyed me quizzically. 'But they'll get there. Eventually. Old bloodhounds.'

'Old poodles, mostly. But you're right, Sam. Time's running through my fingers. So, Wullie, what news from Weasel?'

'Thought you'd never ask. Seems that most days the widow Gibson takes herself off for half a day at a time in her big car.'

'Shopping? Lunch with her pals?'

'Weasel can hardly follow on his broomstick. But two or three times now, he's been down the road a bit and the big car swept past him, heading west.'

'Away from Glasgow? Ayr? A paddle in the sea at Troon?'

'Nae sign of a bucket and spade.'

I thought for moment. 'Sam, could I borrow your car tomorrow? We need to see what she's up to.'

'You're not serious? You're taking enough risks coming here.'

'I'm running out of time. I need to make some real progress. On which topic, I think it's time I met Duncan and put him out of his misery. If he's still in it, in fact?'

'Oh, he's upset all right. But he might be even more upset at meeting your ghost.'

'I need him to hurry up his investigations – if he's doing any.'

'It might stop him all together. What if he turns you in?'

'Duncan? You think he would?'

'He's a policeman. You're not only suspected of murder, but you're part of a grave conspiracy.'

'That's terrible, Sam.'

Wullie chuckled. 'Ah thocht it wisnae bad, Brodie. But Sam's right. Ye cannae trust the polis. If you show yersel' to

196

him, and he disnae clap the cuffs on you, and then it all goes horribly wrong, then he's for the high jump.'

'I know, I know, Wullie. But I've got to raise the tempo. Frankly, I don't care if the British banking system collapses and we're all back to a barter economy. But I still have no clue why Gibson was shot, and any day now I could be back inside facing a trial for his murder.'

Wullie nodded sympathetically. 'By the by, Brodie, Elspeth came up with another nugget about Gibson. I don't know if it's important, but it's about his younger brother, Mungo.'

'I told you Fraser was sending money to Mungo's account. But is Mungo still around? He wasn't mentioned in any of the funeral write-ups.'

'As far as we know. You'll recall both boys were brought up in Maybole. Their mother died young and the father took another woman. But what wasn't said publically was that there was a lot of drinking and rowing. Faither a bit of an alkie. Some of the rammies ended up in the local papers. Fraser came out of it OK. Probably with a wee bit too much drive and ambition for other folk's good. But Mungo went off the rails. Followed in his parents' staggering footsteps. He shows up a couple of times in the court section of the papers just before the war. Drunk, disorderly, fighting the polis. Then silence. Any interviews with Sir Fraser got cut off whenever the topic strayed on to his past.'

'The man had a lot of secrets. Mungo doesn't sound relevant but you never know. Every family has a black sheep. Any way of tracking him down?'

'Elspeth is a wee terrier, as you know. She's casting her net far and wide among the newspaper archives and death registers.'

'Why's she doing this? Does she know I'm alive? You haven't told her, have you, Wullie?'

'Not a bit. Ah think she's been a secret admirer of yours. You and her were the only yins wi' a degree in the entire office. She disnae believe you did it. Nobody in the newsroom does.'

'Strange leap of faith. A higher education doesn't lead to higher morality. Often the opposite. But let's see if we can prove her right. Sam, can you set things up for tomorrow? I mean the car and Duncan?'

She looked at me for a long moment. 'I'll pick you up at nine.'

'I thought you were in the middle of a trial?'

'The prosecution asked for and was given a stay. I'm free as a bird. If Lady Gibson sticks to her pattern, we'll see where she goes. We're going to feel stupid if she just likes the sound of seagulls.'

'I don't want you at risk, Sam.'

'What's more risky? Sheila Gibson looking in her mirror and seeing another woman, or a hulking great Viking who looks awfully familiar?' I'll drive; you keep low in the back. It's either that or I just follow her myself.'

Sometimes there's no point in arguing. In truth, I've learned there's never any point in trying to deflect Samantha Campbell.

THIRTY-SIX

Sam picked me up on the dot of nine on the corner of Highland Lane, on the south side of the Govan Ferry. I slumped down in the back seat. She wheeled the Riley round and headed south down through Pollokshaws towards Whitecraigs. Her blonde hair was hidden by a scarf. I could see her eyes in the mirror.

'I called Duncan this morning. He's meeting me tonight at eight. And you, of course. Though he doesn't know it.'

'Where?'

'Home turf. I'll leave the back gate and door open for you. Try not to look even more like a burglar. Wear a decent hat. You know what the neighbours are like.'

The contrast between the smog-streaked industrial estates of Govan and the leafy lanes of Whitecraigs would be enough to make Churchill turn socialist. I peered out from my back seat over Sam's shoulder, directing her towards the Gibson residence. It was coming up to nine thirty and we parked round the corner once we'd decided which way she'd need to come if she were heading west. The streets were as quiet as a Sunday. Other than our Riley, no cars were parked on the road; all tucked away in their private drives, or outside their city offices.

I'd caught sight of Weasel Watkins loitering in the next street. I wondered what he'd do if he encountered a real corporation sweep. Have a fight? Brooms for swords, dustbin lids for shields? Maybe Weasel had been taken on by the council?

By ten we were beginning to wonder if we'd been unlucky. That today wasn't the day Mrs Gibson went for a ride. Just then we heard the low rumble of a big engine. I ducked as the Humber swept past the end of our road. I didn't have to say anything to Sam. She was already trying to start her Riley. The engine turned and groaned but didn't catch. I leaped out, cranked the handle, the engine caught and we set off after the Humber, catching sight of her well down the Ayr Road. We closed up and then sat behind at a safe distance.

We got out on to the main road running towards Kilmarnock and on to Ayr and points west and south. A few more cars joined us so that we became unnoticeable without losing sight of Lady Gibson. We trundled on via the towns and villages of Ayrshire, as if on a *tour d'horizon* of my youth. Through the cross in the centre of Kilmarnock; maybe on our way back we could call in for tea with my mother in Bonnyton. On down through Symington and Monkton and into the outskirts of Ayr.

Had I not been so focused on the car in front I might have spent more time admiring the handsome town and wishing I lived nearer the sea on one of the wide streets of stone houses. But then I'd have been cheek by jowl with bed and breakfast places and overrun by trippers and holidaymakers. Come to that, weren't we closing in on the Glasgow Fair, when the city shut down and Glasgow hoi polloi decamped 'doon the watter'?

The Humber was about two hundred yards ahead with one car between us. Gradually we left the suburbs behind and began heading along the Dalmellington Road. The signs pointed to Hollybush and Patna. Ahead and on the right I could see a prominent stand of grey buildings. Suddenly I thought I knew where Lady Gibson was going. Sure enough, the Humber stuck out its flashing indicator arm and swung through the high entrance pillars that punctured a long high wall. As we slowed, we saw the car crunching up a long gravel driveway towards a clutch of forbidding stone buildings perched on a hillock. A large sign at the gatepost made its fell business clear: 'Ailsa House, Ayrshire Lunatic Asylum'. The loony bin. Or just 'Ailsa' in these parts: a neat and euphemistic shorthand.

Sam pulled up at the entrance to a field a little further on. We rolled the windows down to drink in the rough country air.

I asked, 'Is she getting some outpatient treatment? Trying to get over her husband's death?'

'Possible. Or she's visiting some daft old auntie of hers. There's plenty of those to go around.'

'How do we find out?'

'Easy. I'll go and ask.'

'Just like that?'

'Why not? I'll leave you somewhere safe. Downwind certainly. Then I'll drive up in my smart motor car, in my smart twin-set, with my smart accent and ask if Lady Gibson's having a breakdown. Or is it just her auntie Peggie.'

I looked at her cool eyes. Of course she could. They'd be jumping to do her bidding.

'And then what? What if they tell you who she's seeing? What use will that be?'

'Depends who it is. I'll ask to see them too. Tell them I'm from the church. Saving sinners or something.'

'You're as daft as me.'

'Oh, Douglas, are you only just recognising that?'

'Maybe we're on the wrong side of that wall.' I nodded towards the tall stone bulwarks around the asylum.

'But who would you trust on this side?'

'Fair point. What if they let you see the inmate? What would you say to her or him?'

'I have absolutely no idea.'

'Oh good, I like a well-thought-out plan. In the meantime, let me buy you an ice-cream and a ride on a donkey.'

'You know how to spoil a girl, don't you?'

We drove back into Ayr and on to the promenade. Though the day was cloudy and a westerly was whipping the waves up into spume, the long stretch of beach was packed with yelling kids running wild and stoic adults huddled behind striped windbreaks. Primus stoves hissed under tin kettles. Sandwiches were spread with marge, paste and sand and devoured anyway. The sun sent surreptitious rays through the clouds to fry fair Celtic skin. I wondered briefly at the crowds on a Tuesday. Of course. It was the second week of July. The factories were out. The schools were closed. Since time immemorial, it *was* the Glasgow Fair.

Sam and I parked and walked down on to the sand. We were a contrasting sight. She in her classy outfit and me in my hand-me-down corduroys, open shirt and full beard. A lady slumming it with a passing matelot from a tramp steamer. But no one was looking or caring. For two weeks they were out of the mills and factories, in the fresh air, by the seaside. Money saved the whole year with the Co-op for candy floss and dancing, beer and ice-cream, singsongs in the pubs and laughter. How I envied them. But I pulled myself up and recalled my determination to enjoy every sunny day as if it were the last. The same could apply to cloudy ones, surely.

I took Sam's hand and dragged her down on to the pale red sand, so fine and soft that after a few steps she had to take her shoes off and go barefoot. She sat, pulled down her stockings and stuck them in her cardigan pocket, along with her scarf. I rolled my trousers up, stuck my socks in my shoes and slung my shoes round my neck. We ran towards the sea like kids, laughter catching in our chests. We splashed through the first sandy pools and Sam shrieked at the cold. Then we hit the sea proper and jumped and cavorted like – I suppose – lunatics. Certainly five-year-olds.

We settled down to a walk along the low waves. The freezing water lapped at our ankles until it convinced us it was really quite warm. We stole glances at each other, not needing to say anything, just holding hands. And we looked out to sea, to Arran, the great slab of rock that dominates the seascapes along the entire Ayrshire coast. *The Sleeping Warrior*.

I wondered if Sam was remembering last year and her own kidnap and my mad chase, and how the wheels had turned and how we were now using the kidnap boat as my safe house. In celebration of our survival, I stopped, turned her towards me and – not caring who was looking – kissed her full on the mouth. Her struggle was brief and only for show. Then we were melting into each other until a wee band of hooligans ran past yipping and whistling, *Gie her a kiss frae me, mister!* So I did.

We walked back up to the sea wall and sat down with our backs against it until hunger drove us up on to the esplanade. We spurned the ice-cream van – for the moment – and queued for fish suppers with all the rest. The broad Glasgow accents spilled over us like a rough benison. Then we sat on a bench and ate the fish piping hot and vinegary, and licked our fingers. In between salty sucking we refined our plan – such as it was – for the visit to the asylum. We splashed our gritty faces in a fountain, and combed our hair in the car. We shook and rubbed off the sand between our toes and donned shoes. I made myself as tidy as possible given my start point. Then we drove off, with me behind the wheel, to inspect a madhouse.

I stopped at the entrance to the asylum and checked the Humber had gone. Sheila Gibson was a person of routine. I drove straight up the drive and parked in front of the sign to reception. Sam checked herself in the mirror, dabbed on fresh lipstick, and got out. As she walked up the steps and in through the front door, I turned the car round and backed up. I'm not sure what we were expecting but I was ready for a quick getaway. I rolled down the window and waited. When Sam didn't come straight out, it seemed safe to assume she'd found something or someone of interest. She appeared after ten minutes, got in the car and I drove off.

'It's Mungo Gibson. He's an alcoholic. Apparently his brother's death tipped him into a big session and he was brought here to dry out.'

'Brought here? By Lady Gibson?'

'His caring sister-in-law.'

'A sister-in-law of mercy?'

'So it seems. Doing the right thing, it appears. The matron was very helpful. I said I was a church visitor and knew the family. That I'd been hoping to catch my friend Sheila before she left.'

'Did you see him?'

She shook her head. 'Matron apologised for not being able to let me talk to him. He'd just been given some electric shock therapy and needed rest. Sheila had come to give her permission.'

'Ouch. I thought he just needed drying out?'

'Apparently it's not just weaning him off the booze. They're concerned about long-term damage. There are signs of underlying depression.'

Another prisoner of his youth. I suppose we all are, to a certain extent. One brother used his tainted childhood to dominate and succeed. The other turned to drink to cope with his demons. I don't know what I'd expected, but I was disappointed. I'd hoped there might have been some new angle to come out, some explanation for Sheila Gibson denying me. But it just seemed a dead end. A woman – whether from affection or for public approval – doing her family duty by looking after her brother-in-law at a time of grief and upheaval.

'Did you find out how often he's been in and out of Ailsa, Sam?'

She shook her head. 'I didn't ask. Is that important?'

'I don't know. I'm looking for patterns. And where the patterns cross over.'

As we headed back across the Fenwick Moors to Glasgow I began mentally preparing myself for my collision with Duncan Todd this evening. I found it hard to concentrate. I'd gone down another dead end and was no closer to unravelling this sorry tale. Just over a month ago, I'd been full of optimism that my life had taken an upward turn. Instead, I'd thrown the dice and landed on a snake.

It was too risky for Sam to take me straight home with her in the daylight. I'd wait till it was dark. She dropped me back off at Govan and I waved her goodbye, all the time wishing we could go back and play at sandcastles on the beach.

THIRTY-SEVEN

I was pacing Sam's dining room again. A caged beast, fighting echoes of my funeral day's wait for the mourners to return and chastise me. As before, I'd slunk in the back gate just after dusk and was now bracing myself for Duncan's appearance. I'd made my rendezvous with the phone box in time to take Harry's call, but it was inconclusive. He had nothing to report about his masters' intent or the background of the companies Airchie and I had identified.

So I was hoping Duncan would open up some new angles of research. But I still hadn't worked out what to say to him. Or rather *how* to say it. Except in books by Algernon Blackwood there were few precedents for a man coming back from the dead for a rendezvous with an old pal. Especially when the pal was a detective inspector and the dead man was an alleged murderer. Maybe I should write it?

He was late. Sam was waiting upstairs in the front lounge, trying to catch up with court papers after her day playing hooky down at the beach. She'd been as anxious as me about this meeting, so that when I slipped in the house there'd been no mood for romance. No snatched passion. A brief hug and a brush of lips was all we could muster. Finally the doorbell went. I listened as she walked down the stairs, opened the door and exchanged greetings with Duncan.

'It's good of you to come round, Duncan.'

'It's nae bother, lassie. Ah'll do all Ah can to help.'

'Hang your coat and hat up, Duncan. Through here.'

I could picture her pointing to the coat-rack and Duncan dutifully hanging up his things. Then the policeman's footsteps started towards me, and Sam was telling him:

'Oh, Duncan, there's someone I want you to meet.'

'Oh aye. Who's that?'

Sam pushed the door open. I was standing in the semi-dark. The only light was from a single table lamp on a side table behind me. Coming from the lit hall, Duncan would only see my outline at first. My beard was further camouflage. Sam stepped inside and held the door open. Duncan followed her in, squinting at me, backlit by the glare of the lamp as he walked forward. His hand was out, expecting to shake someone's. But certainly not mine. Sam pointed at me.

'I think you know each other.'

I came forward so the hall light was on my face.

'Ah don't think we've . . . Good Christ! It's no' . . .'

He wavered and I strode across and grabbed his hand.

'Duncan, it is. It's me, Brodie. Sit down, man. Sit down.'

Sam pushed a chair against the back of his knees. He sank down, still clinging to my hand. I pulled another chair round and sat facing him. He wrenched his hand from mine.

'Whit sort of trickery is this? What *foolery*?' He raised his arm and brushed it across his eyes. I thought he was going to strike me. I wouldn't have minded. I rushed my words.

'Duncan, it is me. We had to fake the death. The funeral. I had to find out who set me up. It was the only way.'

I was desperate to get my explanation out, but even as I said it, it sounded weak. Why had I done this to him?'

'Wis it, indeed? So ye hud to make *me* think you were deid? Ye hud to put me through *that*? Could ye no' have telt me?'

We were both panting and gulping for air.

'I'm sorry, Duncan. I'm sorry. We didn't want to put you in

an impossible situation. Not with Sangster breathing down your neck.'

'So you put me in a different impossible situation? *Ah thocht you were deid, ya bastard!* Ah even said Hail Marys for your thrice-damned soul!'

His fists were clenched and he was on his feet above me. I thought he was about to pound me. He was welcome. I deserved it. I wouldn't hit back. Our verbal flailing at each other was interrupted by the crash of a bottle and three tumblers hitting the table beside us. Sam's voice cut through.

'Here. The pair of you. Take a dram.'

Sam splashed generous amounts into the three glasses. She shoved one at Duncan and one at me. I lifted mine and raised it. Duncan looked poised between throwing that punch and walking out. Finally, thirst won out. He sat down slowly and picked up the glass.

'Here's tae us?' I asked.

'Bugger off.'

I persisted. 'Wha's like us?'

He didn't respond for a second, then: 'Damn few . . .'

'And they're a' deid.'

We clinked glasses and we both took a big spluttering gulp.

He sat back and eyed me up and down. 'But you're no', Brodie. No' you, it seems.'

'No, I'm not, Duncan. I'm truly sorry for not telling you.'

He was nodding. 'Ah can see why. Sangster would have smelt it on me. He would've seen ma look. Ah cannae hide these things. Look at me noo. Up tae high doh.'

'Don't tell me you missed me?'

'Don't go bloody well fishing, Brodie.'

We tossed down our drinks to cauterise the hurt and embarrassment. Sam poured us fresh ones. Big ones. Then she went to the sideboard and brought over the ham sandwiches she'd made earlier. She knew men. Suddenly Duncan and I were ravenous. The three of us made ourselves more comfortable round the table and I explained how Sillitoe's man, Harry, had engineered my escape. Duncan kept shaking his head at the antics.

'And now you're scooting up and doon the Clyde like you were on a pleasure cruise?'

'I'm thinking of moving on to a boat permanently. It's like being a gypsy.'

'A sea rover,' said Sam. 'A Gallowglass.'

'Ah thocht the Gallowglass were Irish?' said Duncan.

'Scottish mercenaries. They were hired by the Irish to fight the Vikings, the English – anyone you care to name. You know the Irish and the Scots. The Gallowglass also fought with Robert the Bruce,' Sam finished.

'How do you know all this, hen?'

'School. We did *Macbeth*. To death.' She shuddered.

'Fought wi' the Bruce, did you say? Show me this fake warrant card again, Brodie.'

I pushed across my Edinburgh police card.

'Ah should confiscate this. Ye couldnae have just been *Inspector* David Bruce. Ye hud to be a chief inspector?'

'If you're going to tell fibs, make them big ones. Rank has its privileges. Helps me get around.'

'Until you're caught. Christ, Brodie, are there any laws you huvnae broken?'

I lifted my glass. 'Other than kidnap or murder? Running my own distillery? But I'm hard pushed to think of much else. Which reminds me. The Scottish Linen Bank. I had a wee keek at the ledgers.'

'Did ye now? And how would you have achieved this wee keek?'

I explained my rooftop adventure without giving away Airchie's name. There was no point in bringing him down with me if things went awry. Further awry. When I was finished Duncan just stared at me.

'It micht have been easier if you'd just gone on pretending you were deid, Brodie. Or went and lived in the South of France. You and Sam. Why didn't you?'

'I'd miss the rain. But it's a good question. It's still an option.' I raised an eyebrow at Sam. She raised hers back. 'But there's a killer or killers out there who're getting away with it. Someone abducted and murdered Fraser Gibson and pinned it on me.'

'Old police habits you cannae shake?'

'Nothing as honourable. I don't like being used, Duncan. They cleaned out my account; such as it was. And had me on remand for murder. Enough reasons to go after them?'

'That rings true. And Ah'm sure masel' you were set up.'

'Tell me more.'

'One o' the good guys Ah know was talking to one of the less good guys, who knows the bad guys under Sangster.'

'Sounds like a shaggy dog story, Duncan.'

'It's ca'd the grapevine. It's how things work, Brodie. Remember your ain days at Tobago Street?'

'Chinese whispers. Send three and fourpence, we're going to a dance. What did you hear?'

'They're out to get you. And they're pleased with themselves that they did.'

'*They?* Sangster? Really? I may have tweaked his nose, but setting me up for murder?'

'Sangster's no' the main one. He was happy enough to see you nabbed, but he didnae initiate it. I might go so far as to say he's feeling a wee bit remorseful at how it all ended up.'

'Tell him to lay some flowers on me.'

'Douglas!'

'Sorry, Sam. Sarcasm's my way of dealing with hypocrisy. If not Sangster, who?'

'That Ah don't know. Someone higher up.'

'God, don't tell me it's McCulloch? Sam and I were speculating. But I can't see any motive. I turned down a couple of job offers from him but that would hardly constitute grounds for getting rid of me. Besides, I did him some good service.'

'Bosom buddies, Ah gather. No' as far as Ah know. You never know wi' heid bummers. They move in mysterious ways to get the top jobs and keep them. But Ah don't have a name.'

'Or a reason?' asked Sam.

'You're right, hen. Motive's always the first thing to look for. In this case, while they wurnae actually queuing up to demolish your boyfriend here, nor was Brodie short of folk wanting to get their ain back on him.'

'But surely I wasn't the target of it all? The whole confection. The kidnap, the ransom, the murder, the frame-up – they weren't all to teach *me* a lesson?'

Sam ventured, 'Opportunistic? Someone knew or heard about the kidnap and intervened?'

'They would have had to move fast. Not like your average copper.'

'Hie!' said Duncan. 'If it is a copper.'

'Good God, have I become such a general nuisance?'

Sam waved a hand. 'Duncan, don't answer that. He's fishing again. Talking of which, you've been kind enough not to comment.'

'That he smells of herring? It's nectar to me. I grew up in Saltcoats.'

I sighed. 'Can we focus on who's out to get me, and why? What else was growing on your grapevine?'

'Money. There's big money behind this. I don't know where it's coming from or who's getting it, but it's oiling wheels.'

'Of a truck. And I'm getting run over. Can you keep your ear to the keyholes, Duncan?'

'With renewed gusto. Ah might even see if Sangster's conscience is bothering him enough to be confessional.'

'Go canny. Don't raise his suspicions. In the meantime, if you think it's coming from outside the force, take a look at these names.' I pulled the folded note from my pocket and handed it to Duncan. 'Two of them – Elliot and Adams – were cronies of Gibson at his golf club and yacht club. We're waiting to find out if they were recipients of Gibson's personal largesse through any of the companies he was funding with bank money. I passed them to Harry to check out. Recognise any of these blokes?'

'Ah know the main pair.' He stabbed the names. 'Roddie Adams, first-choice solicitor for every ne'er-do-well in town. And Frankie Elliot, crook and wide boy. I ken him weil. He'd sell his granny in a whorehouse for tuppence a go. Sorry, hen.'

'A vivid picture, Duncan,' she said. 'As you can imagine, I know Adams. I've seen him in action. Bent as a kirby grip. What does Elliot get up to? What's his line?'

'He's been a thorn in our side for donkeys. Apart from the odd sabbatical at the Bar L. for running prostitutes it's been hard to stick anything on him. His club's a cover. Probably drugs. We know he runs floating gambling dens. Has a string o' lassies that he hires oot by the hour. And has been known to fund some of the bigger jobs around town for a cut. Banks, building societies, department stores. You name it.'

'Is it possible that Fraser Gibson was in hock to Elliot? Ran up a few gambling debts which Gibson was paying off via a wee borrow from his own bank?'

'Could be.'

'Then why would Elliot kill him?'

Duncan shook his head. 'Sometimes these fellas don't need a reason. Frankie Elliot has a temper. Hair trigger.'

'So did Gibson, I hear.'

'There ye go.'

'But surely a bit short-sighted of Frankie to choke off his income stream. Maybe I should meet him. Deal with Adams later.'

Sam and Duncan looked at me as though I were mad. They were right. Mad as hell at being the marionette of a bunch of thugs.

'If you want to put your heid in the lion's mouth Ah know where you can find Frankie. He runs a club ca'd the Silver Dollar.'

'What did you say?'

'The Silver Dollar. A well-known drinking den and cesspit. Why?'

'It's one of the companies getting Fraser's cash.'

'There you go. But what would you do if you paid him a visit? Dive in, guns blazing?'

'I'm trying to give them up. Just a wee chat.'

'Why would he tell you anything?' asked Sam.

'A threat to his business? Do you think your average Glesga hard man would relish a visit from the Edinburgh fraud boys?' I tapped my fake ID. 'They might have a cosy relationship with the local constabulary who'd do anything for a quiet life, but they might well think Edinburgh would close down his operation, bang him up and throw away the key.'

'Always assuming Elliot disnae blow your heid aff at first sight. When do you plan to visit?'

'No time like the present. Who's starring at the Silver Dollar tonight? Hope it's Carmen Miranda.'

THIRTY-EIGHT

For all their aspirations, Glasgow clubs have no obvious counterparts in Las Vegas. Whereas the gangster clientele of the Strip have tastes that run to glitz, glamour and fizz, the hard men of the East End just want somewhere to drink without last orders getting between them and oblivion.

I've never been inside a Vegas or Paris club – something I planned to remedy if ever I got out of this mess. But I've seen the movies, and I've seen the inside of several of the Glasgow pretenders. A cursory glance suggests they're of a different species. The American and French versions seem designed for high-class entertainment and convivial talk; the Scottish for getting blootered. But underneath, the two regimes perform the same service. Exchange the leather seats and cut-glass chandeliers for battered tables, wooden chairs and smoke-yellowed lights. Concentrate on the stained velvet curtain framing a six-by-six stage on which showgirl Elsie – *all the way from Maryhill* – will show off the tops of her nylons and her smoke-roughened voice. The men – and it's mainly men – will ignore her. Their focus is on sinking the booze and reinforcing the camaraderie of the streets and the fitba' stands.

Elsie and her sisters don't make enough to pay for their stockings from singing alone, so they sell their smiles for drinks and tips at the men's tables. Sometimes a smile isn't enough and a more meaningful transaction takes place in which Elsie will spend fifteen minutes with her beau in a back room for a fiver. Out of that fiver, Elsie gets to keep two pounds. The rest goes on the cuts to her pimp and the club's proprietor. Out of the club slice, a further squeeze is made to provide for the local police charity. It's a well-run market in which everyone gets what they want, as long as no one steps out of line or wants more than their fair share. Greedy cops or greedy girls can disrupt trade and lead to hard words and harder deeds until equilibrium is restored.

My leverage was to threaten the stability of the market in exchange for information. Surely that wasn't too much to ask?

After Duncan left, I prepared for my big night out by having a bath and changing into a suit and tie. Studying me as I did up my tie, Sam assured me that even with the beard I might pass as having money to spend on a showgirl or two. But God help me if I did. I smiled. I like a hint of jealousy in a woman; shows they care.

I'd told Duncan *no guns* but that was to avoid upsetting him in advance. While I had no intention of marching in pistol in hand, blasting at anyone who moved, nor did I want to enter a den of iniquity bare naked. As I was unlikely ever to see my service revolver again I borrowed the Webley belonging to Sam's dead father and stuck it into my waistband. The familiar heft of cold steel brought comfort and confidence.

Sam curbed the green-eyed monster long enough to drive me to within a street of the club. I gave her a quick kiss and watched as she turned the car round on the glistening streets and headed for home. I walked round the corner and took stock.

Apart from its name the Silver Dollar exceeded my expectations of the gulf between Vegas and the Gallowgate. It was ten o'clock, the pubs were shutting and the Silver Dollar was the refuge of the partygoer with his mind set on heralding the dawn with a drink in his hand. Duncan had said if the club was open, I'd find Frankie Elliot there. Frankie had a majority stake in the place and managed his investment from a corner seat at the back of the lounge facing the stage. No one could come or go within Frankie's purview without his eyes eating them up. But first I had to get past the janitor.

I touched the hard metal of my gun for luck. Just what I needed squaring up to the gorilla at the door. His face was in shadow with the light behind him. A flight of stairs led up to the promised land. But above him, little or no light escaped from the heavy blackout curtains, and only a whisper of music filtered down the stairwell. I walked up to King Kong.

'Evening, pal.'

'Where d'ye think yer gawin'?'

'Up there. To the flashing lights and sensuous dancing. Where do you think?'

It was clear that thinking wasn't something he did for a living. His Neanderthal brow furrowed. 'Yous a member?'

'I'm here to join.'

'Ye cannae come in if yer no' a member.'

'So how do you become a member if you can't come in to join up? Does this help?' I waved a ten-bob note at him.

He scratched his chin, trying to remember the procedure he'd been taught. Then it came back. With the two times table. 'OK, pal, here's how it works. You go up there and talk to Bert. Tell him you want to join. Bert'll fix it.'

I tucked the ten-bob note into his breast pocket and walked round him – it took a while – and up the stairs. I could feel his eyes on my back and hoped the outline of the Webley wasn't on show from below. I got to the landing at the top. Ahead was a thick black curtain. As I moved to push it aside a man stepped through. The music was suddenly louder. He looked smarter and meaner than the big lout downstairs. He inspected me with fast eyes.

'Are you Bert?'

'Who's askin'?'

'Dave Bruce. I want to join.'

'You just aff a ship?' He stroked his chin to indicate his Holmesian powers of deduction.

'You could say that.'

'Three quid for life membership. One pound entrance. And one for me.'

'I make that a fiver. That's a lot of money and it doesn't even get me a drink. Can I see inside first? See what it's like?'

He measured the odds. 'Come through, take one look and then it's decision time. Yer in luck. Senga's just coming on.'

He held back the curtain and I stepped into the hot smoky darkness. Ahead was the small stage lit by a solitary suspended light. Around me, chairs and tables formed haphazard groups. It was about half full, maybe thirty or so men and a smattering of women. Seekers after the truth – found in the bottom of every bottle and mislaid by morning.

Or maybe I'd find the truth in the songs of Senga who'd just materialised on the scrap of a stage. Senga – so christened by an aspirational tenement mother using the backward spelling of her own name – slunk on stage, all heavy make-up, red satin and bulges. Ageless and wise, Senga knew her audience. Knew they were apathetic bystanders to her possible stardom. But even after twenty years of grinding out love songs to alcoholics, Senga still carried hope in her pendulous bosom that among the deaf drinkers was an agent alerted to her fresh take on 'Pennies from Heaven'.

'Here you go, Bert.' I gave him a big white fiver borrowed from Sam. 'Do I get a membership card?'

'Ye get in. Ah'll mind yer face if ye want to come back.'

Fair enough. Trust between gentlemen wasn't dead. I looked casually round the room while Senga began to belt it out. A big girl with a big voice that filled the low-ceilinged room. The punters had to shout louder to hear their own bons mots. I let my gaze drift casually across the room to the dark corner table at the rear. Sure enough, I met a pair of questioning eyes. They belonged to a small man with a centre parting and a thin 'tache: the spiv's trademarks. When I say he was small, that was only in relation to the two beef-steaks sitting either side. They didn't look taller than the central figure but neither had necks, and both looked ready to break someone in two at a nod from Frankie Elliot. I moved to the far side of the room away from Frankie and found a tiny table for two. I sat down and lit a fag and waited. It didn't take long.

A girl who might as well have been Senga's daughter slid into the seat next to me and asked for a light.

'You in on a ship?' she asked.

'More a yacht.'

She looked puzzled, as her catalogue of boats flashed across her mind. It didn't take long.

'Ah'm drinking lemonade but you'll have to pay for Baby-cham. Ma name's Rena.'

I studied her. Barely of drinking age, possibly pretty beneath the layers, and already with the wary hardness that comes from dealing with much older men.

'I'm not here for a girl. I want to talk.'

'Ah'm fine wi' talking. What do you want to talk aboot?'

I smiled. 'Much as I'd like to chat with you, Rena, I'm here to have a wee word with your boss.'

Her face froze. 'Which boss? Ah mean the boss of the club, or ma – you know . . .'

I didn't want her to say the word, didn't want to think of her pimp. 'Frankie. Mr Elliot. Here, tell him I'd like a quiet word.'

I took out my police warrant card and showed it to her. Her eyes widened further and I thought she'd bolt.

'Take it easy, Rena. This isn't a raid. I just want a friendly word. Will you please tell him?'

Her face was drawn; her lips had tightened. I saw her gulp.

'Aye. Ah will. Ah wisnae doin' anything wrong, wis Ah?'

I shook my head. 'No, Rena. Absolutely not. I'm sorry I couldn't buy you a drink.'

She was nodding and nodding and then she was scampering away. I waited. I didn't look round. Just listened to the steady murder of one of my favourite songs . . .

> *A cigarette that bears a lipstick's traces,*
> *An airline ticket to romantic places,*
> *And still my heart has wings:*
> *These foolish things*
> *Remind me of you . . .*

I sensed his presence as he came up on me from behind. I kept still, all my nerves jangling, trusting that no one would cosh a senior cop, not even in the Silver Dollar. Then fag-laden breath warmed my ear, and a deep rasping voice whispered, 'Mr Elliot will see you now.'

THIRTY-NINE

I stubbed out my cigarette and got up. I'd been right; he was short but about the same width across. The shoulders and biceps were stretching the stitching of his cheap suit. He looked up at me, clearly hoping I'd punch him to show how much pain he could take, before exploding all over me. He nodded towards the far corner. I went ahead of him, praying he didn't frisk me. I got to the table and looked down on Frankie Elliot. His eyes were ferrets running up and down my face and body, then they stilled and bored into mine. I don't know if it was anger or madness that fuelled him but I didn't want to find out.

'Sit doon, *Chief Inspector*. Looking for some fun? A girl for the night? Free drinks? We're always happy to look after our pals in blue. Especially if they're playing away frae hame.'

Rena, smart girl, despite all her terror, had picked up the rank and the location. I sat down opposite him, with my back to Senga. I hope she didn't think I was being rude.

'Call me Dave. If I can call you Frankie?'

'Only ma friends get that honour. Are we gontae be pals – Dave?'

'Why not?'

He nodded. 'Depends why yer here. So what's it to be, Dave? Girls or booze. Or do you want something a wee bit stronger. Hell, maybe boys are your thing? Eh, lads?' He turned to his Praetorian Guard and got their dutiful laughs.

'I appreciate your kind offer, Frankie, but not tonight, thanks. I'm here about a murder. I need your help.'

His dark eyes were dancing again. Did it reflect his mental gymnastics or what he was taking? Methadone? Coke?

'A murder? That's a weighty deed. Whose? Is this a murder that's happened or one you'd like to see happen?' He got his laughs again.

'Could we maybe have a wee chat, just the two of us?'

He looked at me for a while. 'You twa, fuck off. Don't go far though.'

The short heavies grappled with gravity and hauled their bodies upright. Then they meandered off and stood on the far side, arms folded, watching us and waiting for a signal to run back and pulp me. Cop or no cop. I hoped it wouldn't come to that. I got up and moved round to sit beside him. The chair was hot. I saw out of the corner of my eye the bodyguards unfold their arms and twitch, like bulldogs. A cop had just taken their seat. Frankie didn't blink or move back. We were now both looking to the stage. Senga was making love to the front tables.

> *'I'll never smile again,*
> *Until I smile at you.*
> *I'll never laugh again,*
> *What good would it do?*
> *For tears would fill my eyes,*
> *My heart would realize*
> *That our romance is through . . .'*

The front tables were trying to ignore her.

'She's not bad,' I said, tactfully.

'She's shite, but she's cheap and naebody listens. Tell me about murder.' He turned his head and smiled a dirty smile at me. It seems murder was a subject that took the chill off his stone-cold heart.

'A man called Gibson. Fraser Gibson.'

Frankie's smile disappeared. He looked rueful. Guilt? 'Who?'

'Your pal, the banker. *Sir* Fraser. The bloke you played golf with. Spliced the mainbrace with.'

'Oh, him. Single shot to the forehead,' he said professionally. 'A .38.'

I nodded. 'Close up or good shooting. It would have been quick. The bullet spun on entry and mangled up his brains.'

'Better quick.'

'You don't seem very upset at losing a pal.'

He shrugged. 'I hear they got the guy. The *Gazette* man. Then *he* took a fall.'

'So he did.'

'That's an end to it then.'

'No, Frankie, just the start. Why was he sending you money?'

The smile returned. 'Who telt you that?'

'You're not denying it.'

'Ah'm not saying anything, except who telt ye?'

He really wanted to know. I could see him pointing his guard dogs at the 'someone' and smiling as they tore him to bits.

I shook my head. 'It's all in the books, Frankie. The bank books. The books of account. The Silver Dollar accounts for twenty-three thousand pounds of Fraser Gibson's spending over the past year. We're pretty sure it wasn't interest on your savings account.'

'You arresting me?'

'Not if you're helpful.'

Frankie looked up and about, then snapped his fingers. A waitress appeared by the table and leaned close. Frankie spoke and she left, only to return in a moment with a bottle of Bell's and two glasses. Frankie poured three fingers in each and pushed one to me.

'I don't squeal, copper. Frankie Elliot disnae squeal.'

'Understood. Code of honour and all that.'

He glanced at me to check if I was taking the piss. I went on.

'It's a simple question: why was Gibson paying you so handsomely?'

He grinned, then he called the waitress again and whispered to her. She looked up at me, nodded and disappeared through a side curtain. I waited. Frankie waited. The curtains twitched and a woman came out. A different species to Senga and her ilk. The best thing I'd seen all night since leaving Sam. She was slender, dark-haired and doe-eyed, and way too classy for this sticky-floored joint. She sashayed over to our table, smiled at Frankie, then me, and sat down. Her dress was a dark wrap-round and exposed her smooth throat in a gash of curving white. Her smile rocked me. I hoped she wouldn't say anything; how could her voice live up to the rest of her?

'Sindy, this is Mr Bruce. You can ca' him Dave.'

Sindy stretched out her slim bare arm and I pressed her warm fingers. She used her middle finger to brush the palm of my hand. It sent a shock up my body.

'That's Sindy with an "S". As in *sin*.'

It was a well-honed line but it sounded fresh in my biased ears. Her voice was deeper and more exciting than I could have hoped. East coast perhaps, educated, enticing. Sindy, not Candy. I'm surprised the Gourock yacht club secretary didn't remember it right. But then his blood only boiled for mermaids.

'Nice to meet you – *Dave*.'

'And you, Sindy. Do you sing?'

She flashed a row of small white teeth. 'Only when I'm happy. Or taking a bath.'

She put the emphasis on *bath,* slowing it down and stretching it out to conjure an image of her naked in a hot tub, glistening with soap and bubbles, hair carelessly pinned up, proffering a sponge and inviting me to scrub her back. Or her front. I turned to Frankie, waiting for an explanation.

'This is what he was paying for. You can see how a man could run up a bill. A big bill.'

His grin said, *And I ken fine you'd run up some debts too, Mr Chief Inspector.*

He could be right. At that moment, all I wanted to do was spring up, grab Sindy by the hand, run out the door, set her up in a flat in Hyndland, and run her a bath.

'Your point's well made, Frankie. I have one last question for you.'

Frankie nodded his head at Sindy. She rose in one lithe motion, smiled at me as though she was genuinely sad to say goodbye, and swayed out between the curtains.

'Ye can put your e'en back in, Mr Polisman.'

I blinked. 'Quite a girl.'

'A wee jewel. Ask it, then I'm going to ask *you* to leave. You're bad for business.'

I leaned over the table to get his attention. We locked eyes.

'Gibson was shot in the head after being kidnapped by two men. If this reporter from the *Gazette* was one of them, that leaves at least one other still out there. We also think there was a ransom, a big one. It's missing. The whole thing doesn't add up.'

'What's your question?'

'Why did you kill Gibson?'

For one second his intensely focused gaze broke. He blinked in obvious surprise. Then he smiled.

'Yer aff your fuckin' heid, Dave. Why the fuck would *I* shoot one of ma best customers?'

I sat back. He was telling the truth.

'So who did, Frankie? If there were at least two kidnappers, who was the second one?'

'Ye've had your quota o' questions. Ah'm no a clype. And Ah'm certainly no' a copper's nark. Drink up, Chief Inspector, and bugger off.'

I got to my feet, and suddenly two gargoyles were on either

side of me. Both had hands in their tight jacket pockets. Digging for something. Their hands formed fists. Chunky fists. Deformed with knuckledusters.

'It's OK, boys, I can find my own way out. By the way, Frankie, after Senga's performance I think I deserve a refund.'

He looked at me and laughed. 'The entertainment comes free. Except for Sindy, and a' ye got from her was a smile. And I paid for yer drink.' Nevertheless he stood up, reached inside his jacket and pulled out a wad. He peeled off a fiver and stuffed it in my top pocket. 'There. Now you're on the payroll, like a' the rest.' He smirked. 'See him oot, boys. Watch the stairs, Dave.'

I walked towards the curtains to find them being pulled back by Bert. I stepped through on to the landing above the steep flight. I sensed the twins crowding through the curtain as I reached the top step. There was a sudden rush behind me. I dropped to a crouch just as a weighted fist flew over my head. I reached up, grabbed the wrist and hauled forward. His weight fell across my shoulders – like a live sack of coal – and I kept on pulling through, using his own momentum. He somersaulted over me in a tumble of limbs down into the stairwell.

By the time I let go he was travelling so fast that he did a full 360-degree flip before hitting the stairs halfway down with his feet. It could have been a miraculous recovery, deserving applause, but he was no acrobat. He bounced as though he'd hit a trampoline and went sailing on into a second mid-air tumble. This time he ran out of momentum and landed flat on his back across the bottom steps. He yelped twice, then settled into a steady stream of oh fucks.

I sprang round with my gun in hand. Bert and the fallen man's twin were gawping past me at their pal lying moaning at the bottom.

'Back off!' I shouted.

I pointed the big Webley at them. Gun trumps knuckle-duster. Their expressions shifted from wonder to anger. They retreated until they got tangled up in the curtain. I turned and jumped down the stairs, gun still in hand. I was halfway down when the bouncer stumbled in to see what the ruckus was. His small brain struggled to take in the sight of his tough pal, spread-eagled, writhing on his back and holding his dislocated shoulder. The brass knuckles dangled limp from his useless arm.

I took the last couple of stairs and pressed the muzzle of the Webley against the bouncer's chest. I pushed him back and stepped delicately round his supine colleague. I looked down at him. He gasped out a few words.

'Ye've broke ma fuckin' back. And ma airm.'

'You should have used the handrail.'

I stepped out into the cool night air, tucked the gun into my waistband and hauled off into the night.

FORTY

A s I shadow-slipped through the quiet streets, side-step-
ping coppers on the beat, I had an overwhelming urge to
return to Park Terrace and wake up Sam with at least a
kiss. Residue of the feelings stirred up by Sindy? It's a good
job we can't read minds; especially our own at times. Besides,
I didn't want to expose Sam to more than I had already. Being
a fugitive didn't play well with me, but I had to stick it out.

My mind was racing with what I'd found. I had several of
the pieces of the jigsaw in front of me but couldn't work out
how they fitted together or how many bits were missing. I
could see people in motion, some doing wicked or stupid
deeds. But I had no idea of scale. I didn't know if I was
looking at scenes at a bowling green or an international at
Hampden Park.

Frankie Elliot was on the fringe of the picture; he'd played
no direct part in Gibson's abduction and death. I was sure of
that. However, £23,000 was a lot of money to pay for sexual
favours, even from the lovely Sindy. Were there other girls
like Sindy for hire? Twosomes? I might have to start saving.
I wonder if Frankie had been putting the screw on Gibson? A
little light blackmail with the threat of telling Lady Gibson or
going public about his loose morals?

The same might apply for the other corporate recipients of
Gibson's generosity. But unless Gibson had Pan-like stamina,
Gulf Stream must have been providing services other than

sexual. If he was in hock to them or being blackmailed in some way, he seemed to be having no problem paying them off. So, who *did* want rid of him? And why? It always came back to Sheila. Lady Gibson. Revenge on a straying husband? The punishment seemed high. Yet who was I to judge how someone responds to scorn and betrayal? The same emotion – revenge – was driving me to take stupid risks. But then I'd been locked up, my name dragged through the mud, my mother and Sam put through fire, and I still might end up on the gallows.

Then there were Duncan's revelations about some big players in the shadows intent on framing me. If bringing me down was the overall objective, it was a pretty convoluted way of doing it. Why not just have me shot? Or a stiletto in the back in a crowded pub? Why did Gibson have to die?

It was one in the morning. A night tram passed me, rumbling through the city like a ghost train, but otherwise I was alone. I was at the appointed spot by Anderston Quay but there was no sign of my water taxi. Eric was the most reliable of friends and yachtsmen. He knew the estuary flows and currents well enough to be here on time. I sat and smoked, then got up and paced. By two o'clock I was seriously worried, and thinking about joining the vagrants in one of the bombed-out warehouses along the Clyde. I twice had to merge with the misfits under the railway arches to avoid policemen on their beat.

Then, suddenly, my boat came in. Her sleek profile stood out against the night sky, and her lantern blinked a welcome. I jumped on and we were off back downstream.

'Sorry I'm late, Brodie.'

'What happened?'

'We got stopped. River police. They wanted to know what I was doing at this time in the morning. They assumed I was up to no good.'

'Fair question. And they were right, I suppose. What did you say?'

'I'd missed the tide and was heading upstream to moor for the night. They searched the boat but there was nothing to find apart from empty bottles.'

'So there's no problem?'

'Weeell, they said they'd seen me plying the river a few times over the past few days. Said they'd had reports that I was offering some sort of unlicensed ferry service. Thing is, Brodie, we're being watched and I'd hate to be stopped and them to find you below.'

I had a troubled sleep despite rocking in our moorings down by Dumbarton. My brain whirled with images of blowsy tarts and wee hard men coming at me with knives and brass knuckles. I wasn't sure which repelled me most. I woke exhausted at first light and sat and smoked a fag staring out across the sluggish tide. I was feeling doubly like a hunted man after Eric's encounter with the river police. Maybe it was time to take his offer of French leave. But I hated the idea of running away.

The bile kept rising in my chest at what had happened to me. I felt like a wee boy, given the tawse for some crime his pal had committed. *It wasn't fair.* Neither on me nor my friends. They were all putting themselves at risk for me. But unlike that wee boy, I was prepared to make it fair. And I didn't care who among my enemies got badly hurt as I did so. I did some thinking.

When Eric awoke and joined me, I told him to take a couple of days off to throw the river police off the scent and, more important, see his wife. I was meeting Sam early at Shimon's and I'd hole up there for a while and hope not to be spotted coming and going. Eric argued, but he saw the point, and in his mind he was already running up Kildonan beach. He sailed me up to Govan and I descended into the subway at Govan Cross, losing myself among the early-morning commuters.

We rattled and roared round to Buchanan Street and I walked down to Candleriggs. I tried not to look shifty, even as I prowled down the back alley and nipped into Shimon's storeroom. Sam was sipping tea with Shimon himself as though they were at the Willow Tea Rooms. A good china teapot and matching cups and saucers were set out – appropriately – on an old tea chest.

'No cucumber sandwiches, Shimon?'

'Come in, Douglas. Sit. Enjoy.'

Sam smiled her brightest and the world felt safer and better for having these two in it.

'Did you enjoy the nightclub, Douglas?' Sam asked, all innocence.

'It was enlightening. But let's say Marlene Dietrich has nothing to worry about.'

I told them about my wee chat with Frankie Elliot, and how his neds tried to evict me unceremoniously. Sam rubbed her face.

'You shouldn't draw attention to yourself like that.'

'By the way, I didn't need this, but it gave immoral support.' I pulled up my sweater and brought out the Webley. 'I'll put it over here for safe keeping, if that's all right by you, Shimon?' I found a heating pipe high up and secreted it behind it.

'No problem, Douglas. I'm glad you didn't have to use it. But you don't think Elliot killed Gibson?'

'No motive. In fact a strong financial motive for keeping him alive.'

'I agree,' said Sam. 'Now what?'

'I can't get past the idea that Lady Gibson is involved. And who else knew about me? Her chauffeur, Cammie. He even deposited me at the first drop point when I was running around with twenty thousand pounds in my hand. They could be a team. We need to apply some pressure. Get them to reveal their hand.'

r Dollar. Are you

w sorry I am

ter?'

life. Wine, women

sex. Top quality,

first names. I

ed.

'the standards set

e talked a lot

e a very high-class

nd her too much.

d I held our

esan?' I could see

ging. She waited.

called me.'

bson. I'd like to set

houted it out.

ccepts the line you

sn't ... well ...'

rendered.'

early know my

could listen in.'

anyway why

o take?'

art – and her

? And if I don't

oreroom and the

the papers.'

for an answer she

up.'

heard the call go

wn interest to

onded in an accent

come to some

soft and genteel;

Scots. In the court-

ut ever sounding

, and always worth

asgow in it.

n old friend of her

furniture shop

other side of the

a familiar voice

'Yes, hello. To whom am I speaking?'

I gave a thumbs-up to Sam.

'Hello, Sheila. I wanted to start by saying about your husband.'

'Thank you, but who is this? Are you a re

'No, Sheila. I'm an old friend of Fraser.'

'I don't recall giving you permission to u don't think we've met.'

'Oh, *we* haven't. But Fraser and I have. about you.'

There was a painful silence and Sam breath.

'Look, who is this?'

'You can call me Mandy. That's what Fras

The implication was as clear as if she'd There was a further silence.

'What do you want?'

'I'm owed money. From Fraser. For service

'This is an extremely upsetting call. You husband is dead. His debts died with him. A on earth should I believe some faceless – demand for money.'

'Because I wasn't the first *tart*, was I, Shei get the money from you, I'll have to get it fro

'Look, I won't be blackmailed. I'm hanging

'Suit yourself. But I suggest it's in your meet me and have a wee chat. I'm sure we ca arrangement. Keep it all nice and quiet.'

Again the silence. I was biting my knuckl

'When?'

'Today. Four o'clock.'

'Where?' No hesitation.

'Somewhere public but discreet. Belsinger' in Candleriggs.'

'The *Jewish* shop?'

'Do you have a problem with Jews, Sheila?'

The line went dead.

I gazed at Sam in admiration. 'You soon got into the swing of things, *Mandy*.'

'She annoyed me. *Tart* indeed.'

'Well, if nothing else, it proves *Sheila* knows about Fraser's peccadilloes.'

'And is prepared to hush them up. Clearly not for the first time.'

'On which subject, are you going to dress for it?'

'Whatever do you mean?'

'Slinky dress, high heels . . .'

'In your dreams!'

'Exactly.'

There was a discreet cough behind us. Shimon was waiting.

'How do you want to play this, Douglas?' he asked.

'Let her come in your front door. Sam will be waiting to pounce. Then she'll bring her through here. I'll be waiting behind a suitable pile of boxes. Like a French farce.'

'Huh,' said Sam. 'Just keep your trousers on.'

FORTY-ONE

I spent the time till the rendezvous going over the papers that Airchie and I had scribbled down from our night at the bank. I made neater versions showing the key flows of cash. Some of the transactions were convoluted, like the circuitous route taken by £10,000 that ended up in the account of High Times. I also flagged up the outstanding questions such as the extent of collusion with Gibson inside the bank. It would have been bizarre for the top man to be popping in and out of his back office dealing directly with chits and ledgers. Indeed the ledgers had showed all the transactions being counter-initialled, often by CC – the Finance Director, Colin Clarkson – and sometimes by others. Were they accomplices or merely dupes, signing papers that they hadn't read, as Airchie had said? *Heid bummers sign or initial anything put in front o' them.* I assumed that beneath Clarkson and the other senior managers, the clerks were simply pawns, doing what their bosses told them, making entries in ledgers without seeing the bigger picture or even questioning the instructions.

Like Gibson's blousy PA, Pamela McKenzie, for example. I kept returning to the scribbles Airchie had made about the pilfering of my own meagre current and savings accounts. Counter-initialled by Clarkson, now the MD. It made my heart thump with anger that with some neat strokes of a pen, they'd made me a pauper. And made Gibson's girlfriend richer. A lover's wee gift or payment for services rendered? It was time I had a word with our Pam.

When I had all the paperwork together I stuffed it in an envelope and asked Shimon to get one of his lads to post it to Harry. He'd get it first thing.

At three thirty, Sam came through to my den. She was wearing a coat and looked both taller and lovelier. Also more indignant, as though she'd already heard my words before I'd formed the thoughts.

'Don't you say a damned thing, Douglas Brodie.'

'I hadn't opened my mouth, *Mandy*.' I smiled. 'Show me.'

'It's not a beauty parade.'

'Call it a kit inspection.'

She pursed her reddened lips and came further into the light. Her normal subtle make-up – a dab here, a dab there – had been . . . enhanced somehow. Her eyes were a more vivid blue, her cheeks more sharply defined and her sweet mouth more curved.

'You look fantastic.'

She frowned but I knew she was pleased. She unbelted her coat and opened it. Underneath was a clingy dress of some maroon material. A belt cinched her slim waist and pulled the hem up just above the knee. Her new-found height was due to the perilous heels she wore.

'Tarty enough?' she asked, daring me.

'Skirt could go higher. But you're *my* kind of tart.'

'Get your hands off, sailor. And don't you dare smudge my lipstick.'

'You never wear that red for me.'

'I worry about your blood pressure.'

I took my hand from her waist and stood back. I put on my serious face.

'You look lovely, Samantha. Are you ready for this?'

She took a deep breath. 'It's a performance. I do it every day in court.'

At five minutes to four she left me and marched through into the showroom, heels clicking on the wood floor. I took up position behind a double height of crates in a dark corner. We'd cleared away my camp bed and all other signs of anyone living here. There was just one dangling bulb above a small open space bounded by low crates. An arena. A stage.

At a little after four I heard clattering footsteps and a voice raised querulously. A voice last aimed at me, asking me to deliver the ransom money.

'Where are we going? It's dark.'

'It's quiet. Here. I'll put the light on. I've bribed the owner for an hour's use of his storeroom.'

'Is that how you conduct your business? By the hour?'

The heels stopped. I could imagine Sam turning.

She replied coolly, 'More honest than some arrangements, *Sheila*. No hypocrisy.' The steps started again and light spilled from the dim bulb. 'Shall we sit?'

The crates creaked and then I heard a lighter clicking. Soft cigarette fumes drifted up, mixed with perfume. Heady.

'Can we get to the point, *Mandy*? If that's your real name?'

'Fraser liked it. I work for myself. I have a contract – among others – with a company called the Silver Dollar. Ever heard of it?'

'Not my sort of place, I expect.'

'Not exactly Whitecraigs Golf Club, if that's what you mean. Though we get the odd member popping in.'

Sam let the silence build.

'I see.'

'I'm sure you do, Sheila.'

'Stop calling me that!'

'It's your name.'

'It's not for *you* to use.'

'I'm damned if I'll call you *Lady* Gibson. You earned that title the same way I earn a living!'

There was a long pause.

'Can we get to the point?'

'Fraser – such a fun chap – I'll miss him. We all will. Fraser popped in to the Silver Dollar quite often. And I'm afraid he ran up quite a tab.'

'On you!'

'Me. Other girls. Drinks. You know how it adds up.'

'No, I don't. But you want *me* to pay it off? My husband screws around with some little – *nothing* – and you expect me to pick up the tab? You're mad!'

'Oh Sheila, you wouldn't be here if you *really* thought that, would you?'

Again a pause.

'Well, it can't be *much.*' Her voice dripped with sarcasm.

'What did *you* charge, Sheila? Diamonds? A title? It's just business, dear. I always like to get that side sorted first. Give or take a few quid here and there, call it ten thousand.'

'Ten thousand pounds! You're mad! I don't believe you.'

'Are you saying I look cheap?'

I had to stick my knuckles in my mouth.

'No. Yes. That's not what I meant. Look, I just don't have that sort of cash. It's impossible.'

'Really? I heard there was a big insurance payment. And I'm sure the bank is looking after you.'

'That's none of your business.'

'Ah, but you see it is. And we don't want it to become a public business, do we? Fraser was always very concerned about that. Terribly discreet, he was.'

'Stop talking about him like that!'

'Well, I feel I know him. *Knew* him. He talked about you, Sheila.'

Sam left a space. Sheila didn't jump into it but didn't close it out either. She wanted to know.

'Yes, he said you had an open marriage.'

'*What?*'

'You had your little flings and he had his. Wild nights at the golf club, eh?'

There was a scrape. Sheila was on her feet.

'How dare you!'

'I'm not making judgements, dear. Not in my line of business. Just passing on what I was told. Are you saying you weren't having a little fun on the side? One of Fraser's pals? That *would* be a waste. Especially if Fraser was getting his.'

'Oh God. This is such a mess.' I heard the crate scrape as she took her seat again and the lighter clicked once more. 'It doesn't matter, does it?'

'What?'

'Morality. Standards. They've all been ditched. Perhaps you never noticed – *in your line?*'

'Morals are a luxury of the rich, Sheila. They mean nothing to Frankie Elliot.'

'Who the hell is he?'

'I thought you might have bumped into him at the golf club? He owns the Silver Dollar. He's not only got unpaid debts but he's lost a good client. So have I, but there's plenty more out there.'

'So what? I don't follow.'

'Well, Frankie knows a bit about the nasty side of things. He knows how these things work.'

'What things?'

'Husband being naughty. Becoming a real pain. New man around. The pair of you come up with a dodge to get rid of the nuisance. He reckons you and one of Fraser's other golf buddies did for poor old Fraser.'

'That's preposterous!'

Sam gave a big theatrical sigh. 'No, it's not, Sheila. It's life. Where I live anyway. Join the all-too-human race.'

'Enough, really, enough. It wasn't like that. At all.' She sounded exhausted.

'Suit yourself. However it was, Frankie wants compensation for future income. That's how he put it.'

'You're utterly without scruples, aren't you?'

'Takes one to know one.'

Silence.

'I can't pay you ten thousand pounds. I don't have it.'

'Don't say you've spent the insurance money?'

'It hasn't come through.'

'What about the ransom money?'

'*How. . .?* I mean, what makes you think there was one? It's not in the papers.' Her voice was panicky.

'Just a guess. An experienced guess, shall we say? Seems we were right. So, about this compensation? Or do we just take this to the press?'

'I don't have such an amount.'

'That's all right. You're one of us now. Pay on the never-never. A thousand down and the rest later. Nominal interest. What do you say, Sheila?'

FORTY-TWO

'll say this for Sheila Gibson, she was a tough nut. Apart from the odd loss of control she stood up well to Sam's royal command performance. Sam and I sat for a while after she'd left.

'You were magnificent.'

'I was a bitch.'

'A tart. With a heart. I loved the hire-purchase idea.'

'She's actually thinking it over. It's a pity it was only you listening in. We should have had the Procurator Fiscal, the Chief Constable and Sangster lurking there with you. Or at least a recording device.'

'She didn't say enough to hang herself,' I pointed out.

'Not quite. But we now know she knew about Fraser's wild side.'

'And despite what the police said, there was a ransom,' I said. 'But we don't know who's got it.'

'And she has a lover?'

'Quite possibly. Who arranged to kill Fraser and set me up.'

'One of Gibson's Chanty Wrastlers? Roddie Adams? Maybe. But why *you*, Douglas?'

'Just convenient? They needed someone with a reputation for taking on daft challenges?'

'They came to the right guy. But Duncan said he'd heard someone was out to get you. Someone senior.'

'Douglas?' It was Shimon. 'Phone for you. It's Templeton.'

240

I'd signalled to Harry I would be at the furniture store all day if he had any news. I went out into the corridor and took the phone from Shimon.

'Brodie, we've got a bit more gen for you. About one of the companies mentioned in the SLB ledgers: the so-called High Times, who were getting significant payments from Gibson's secret accounts. Well, it's an outfit owned wholly by a Mrs Annie Fulton.'

'Who's she?'

'The wife of Angus Fulton, usually known as Gus.'

'Gus? I know Gus Fulton. Or did. A bad lad in the thirties. GBH, robbery with plenty of violence. Is he still around? Still being bad?'

'He's around. He finished a long spell in Barlinnie about a year ago.'

'What does he do now? Or rather what does Annie's company do?'

'On paper it's a number of market stalls, but in reality it's a front for illegal bingo. They use a network of Catholic church halls, changing venues every week. Gus manages it and the market stalls show a sliver of a profit. But of course what's not on the books is Gus's earnings from the bingo games and some off-course bookmaking on anything with four legs.'

'And High Times is suddenly showing a healthy profit. Fraser Gibson's gambling debts? I can't see him calling out housey, housey.'

'I don't expect the money to show up in the next company accounts.'

'But it raises a big question. I was just tidying up the paperwork from my night out with wee Airchie. A copy is on its way to you. The ledgers show cash being remitted to High Times over several months. A few hundred here, a few hundred there. Nothing regular. Nothing out of the ordinary. But then there's a windfall of ten thousand, three days *after* Gibson was murdered.'

'I know. It says someone in the bank is *still* fiddling. Unless it was part of Fraser's will. A post-mortem instruction.'

'Surely now you'll send in the heavy mob? A bunch of accountants with Tommy guns or something?'

'I'm working on it. The minister is like a rabbit at a greyhound track. The PM's on notice too. We have less than a week to go before the balloons go up. The double whammy of sterling convertibility and loan decisions for the Marshall Plan. If we leap in and there's a big fuss and it spills into the public arena, then at best Britain gets egg on its face.'

'At worst?'

'We go into a financial tailspin. You've no idea how close we are to bankruptcy, Brodie.'

'Meanwhile, I'm a ghost in my own town!'

'I know, I know. Keep moving – and if I can help, just shout.'

'Here's how, Harry. The ten grand to High Times didn't go directly from Gibson's head office account. You'll see in my notes that there were several transactions culminating in a banker's draft made out by an SLB branch.'

'Which?'

'Maybole.'

'Where Fraser's brother Mungo has an account? Does that mean Mungo's directly involved? I thought he's a drunk in Ailsa Asylum.'

'Drunks sometimes sober up. And it's a great cover. I need to pay a visit to Maybole, Harry. Chief Inspector David Bruce needs a look at the books. Can you provide me with a search warrant?'

'Not a real one. That needs to come from a local judge, or sheriff, or whatever it is you call them up there.'

'It can be as real as my police warrant card.'

'Fair point. Consider it done. We'll get it couriered up to you first thing. Where will we find you?'

'Shimon's. The boat was searched last night by the river police. I wasn't on it, thank God. But I thought it best to move my base. On which point, Harry, if I can show that someone in the top echelons of SLB is still remitting cash to High Times, will that get you to send in your troops? Until now we couldn't prove whether the counter-signature and initialling of Gibson's instructions that went on were rubber stamps or criminal collusion. This might be a breakthrough. Time's running out.'

'For all of us, Brodie. I'm working on it.'

'Can you please work faster! I can't afford any more close shaves.'

I needed some expertise alongside me if I were to make sense of the transactions at the Maybole bank. I had Wullie McAllister locate Airchie Higgins with a view to his joining me first thing at Central Station the next morning.

I was sitting on the platform at nine o'clock in suit and specs, equipped with the necessary forged documents. The train for Maybole was due to leave in five minutes and there was no sign of my dodgy bookkeeper. The guard had his whistle in his mouth and the train was belching steam when Higgins trundled up looking hot and sweaty. I shoved him in an empty carriage I'd been keeping an eye on and jumped in beside him as the train edged out.

'I'm sorry, Brodie. I'm no' used to an early start.' He took off his grubby specs and wiped his wet brow with a stained hankie.

'I can see that. Away to the toilet and put your tie on and wash your face. Have you got a comb? See if you can get the stain off your jacket. We've got over an hour to go. It should dry out by then.'

He shambled off to reappear just short of Paisley, looking if not exactly Savile Row at least less like a tramp I'd found in a ditch. I told him what we were looking for at Maybole. His eyes glittered.

'It'll be somebody in the finance unit. Yin o' my former compadres. Gibson will have been looking efter him and feeding him instructions.'

'Even from the grave, it seems.'

We puffed and whistled our way through Kilwinning and Ayr and I wished I was with Sam sitting on the beach again, counting the waves. We clattered out of Ayr and passed close to the grey buildings of Ailsa Asylum. I wondered at Mungo Gibson's life, how it must have been bounded by parental rages and drink. Was he born with the taste of it, inherited from his father? Or did he learn by example that the booze rage gave moments of control over his life, made him the big man in a brief reign of terror. Or was it just for the sanctuary of oblivion, which turned to dependence?

There were too many like him in this post-war Scotland. Too many fights on mean streets outside the pub on a Friday night after the pay packet had been hammered. Too many beatings of wife and wean in shell-shocked houses as men struggled with the pitch-black space inside them, hollowed out by the bestiality of war. None of us talked about it, this national disease that struck men down. All of us too ashamed, too afraid of looking weak.

I'd understood that Mungo had never made it into uniform, unfit through drink and the concomitant mental and physical illness. No one wants a shaky finger on the trigger next to you if you're fighting for your life. But that didn't mean he hadn't experienced his own battles. And who was I to say they were less bloody than mine?

'You a' right, there, Brodie?' asked Airchie.

I looked up from my introspection to find we were deep among the green rolling hills of darkest Ayrshire.

'I'm fine, Airchie. Just enjoying the trip. A train ride's a rare treat.'

I smiled and for the first time I saw this wee man properly. Outwardly a bit of flotsam tossed around in currents of his own making. But here he was, by my side, in a madcap enterprise that offered him a few quid and maybe a silly medal. Not silly to him. Airchie's last chance for redemption? I knew nothing about his earlier life, where he came from, how he went off the rails. Was there a woman in his life? Kids even? Before I could ask him who he was and how he'd got here, we were drawing into Maybole.

'You ready, Airchie?'

'Ready as can be. I know my way roon a bank, Brodie. This is my forte.' He grinned, but I could see it was to bolster his nerve. I'd heard variations on such wisecracks from my platoon as we waited for the barrage to stop and for it to be our turn.

The brakes squealed; the train ground to a halt. I nodded at Private Higgins.

'Let's go.'

FORTY-THREE

We marched along Culzean Street before turning off and down to the High Street. Maybole is a bonny town, the main streets unchanged in decades, perhaps centuries. The houses and shops are in good local stone and are kempt and polished. In the distance, at the foot of the street, the turrets of Maybole Castle thrust assuredly into the calm blue sky. The branch of the Scottish Linen Bank sits proud and with an air of permanence in a prime location opposite the butcher's.

'Right, Airchie, remember today you are *Mr* Higgins. You're an accountant from the Scottish Office seconded to assist the Edinburgh police – namely, me – with my investigations. I'll do the talking. Jacket buttoned. Shoulders straight. Look keen. Your medal's on the way.'

His little round face beamed and he made an effort to pull his shoulders back and puff out his chest. Like a mating pigeon. It was the best I could hope for. We pushed in the door and marched to the counter.

'I'd like to see the manager please.'

The girl behind the counter was immediately into *oh, I'm afraid that's not possible without an appointment* mode. Then I showed her my warrant card. She disappeared into the back and came out a moment later and lifted the hinged counter. She ushered us through.

Mr Alexander McCutcheon had his name emblazoned on the glass panel of his door above the title 'Branch Manager'.

The timid lass knocked on the door; we heard 'Come' and went in. McCutcheon was standing behind his cleared desk, pulling down his waistcoat, buttoning his jacket and putting on his important face. A bowler hung just so on a coat-stand in the corner. Big man, small pond.

'Mr McCutcheon, it's good of you to see us so promptly. I'm Chief Inspector David Bruce from the Financial Services Special Unit of Edinburgh police, and this is Mr Archibald Higgins, seconded to me from the Scottish Office.'

I flashed my identity card at him long enough for him to see how official this visit was. I saw him swallow. He was in his middle years, undoubtedly born and bred in Maybole and reaching the pinnacle of professional success in the last few years. Senior member of the Rotary Club and golf club, and with a wife who knew a thing or two about finger buffets and the inner machinations of the Women's Institute. The last thing he needed was a lightning visit by a senior detective from the capital on *special financial services* business.

'Good morning, Chief Inspector. Allison, dear, can you please bring us some tea. And plenty of ginger biscuits.' His voice was strong Ayrshire, with a good country burr.

'Certainly, Mr McCutcheon.' Allison all but curtsied and left us alone.

'Now, gentlemen, please be seated and tell me how I can help. Head office didn't warn me about your visit.' He said it with pain in his voice.

'That's because they don't know. I'm afraid I need your utmost discretion on this matter. It relates to the death of Sir Fraser Gibson.'

He shook his head. 'A tragedy. A terrible tragedy. One of Maybole's most famous sons.'

'It is indeed. However, we have reason to believe that there are some irregularities at St Vincent Street.'

The word *irregularities* struck him like a harpoon. An irregularity for Alexander McCutcheon was being sixpence out at the end of the day's reckoning. Not some debacle involving head office and a murdered managing director.

'My goodness! But what has that to do with my wee corner of the universe, Chief Inspector?'

I put on my gravest voice. 'Transactions, Mr McCutcheon. Transactions. Money flowing in and out of accounts at head office which are – how shall we put this? – *not fully accounted for*. And some of them have wound their way through here. To this little corner of the bank. And then found their way back out again to destinations which *may not be wholly above board.*'

I might as well have come out and said embezzlement. The manager's eyes were wide and I'm sure his pulse was off the chart. I felt sorry for him and quickly went on.

'I should say we have no reason to believe that any blame or hint of wrongdoing attaches to the Maybole branch. It – *you* – may have been unwitting assistants to these . . . irregularities.'

He gulped for air as his brain digested the possibility that he was about to be frogmarched into a Black Maria and whistled off to sin city and its dungeons.

'Right, I see. So, again, how can I help?'

'Mr Higgins and I would like to examine some of your accounts; indeed, one in particular. The account belonging to Mr Mungo Gibson, brother of the late Sir Fraser.'

'Ahhh. Of course, Mr Mungo Gibson. We were proud to have Sir Fraser's brother here.'

'Did he come into the bank in person?'

'Oh no, no. Not for some time, now. Except . . . But I'm afraid I can't say any more than that. Client confidentiality, Chief Inspector. I'm sure you understand.'

'Normally, yes. But these are unusual circumstances. I have here' – I produced the very official-looking search warrant – 'the power to investigate all accounts and all ledgers of your bank.'

I let him read and digest the document, let him finger the red sealing wax imprinted with the official stamp of the High Court of Glasgow. How did Harry manage that in a hurry?

McCutcheon looked up. 'I see. This all seems in order. So where do you want to start?'

'Mr Higgins and I would like immediate access to the ledgers.' I stood up to impress on him that I meant immediate. He got up too, tugged down his waistcoat, checked his tie was tight and walked out from behind the desk. I wondered if he was going to put on his bowler.

'Gentlemen, please follow me.'

We did, into the back office. The dozen or so clerks began getting to their feet, but McCutcheon waved them down. He led us over to a large-bosomed lady with glasses on a cord round her neck, sitting at a desk at the back. He introduced us.

'Miss Mathews, can you please provide these police officers with access to any file and account they wish. You have my full authority to assist in any way they wish.'

Miss Mathews put on her specs and appraised us. I might pass muster in my good suit and glasses, despite my beard. But Mr Higgins still looked like less like a Scottish Office bookkeeper than a down-at-heel bookie's runner. He smiled encouragingly at her, which was enough to startle her into motion. She found him a spare desk as far from her own as possible and cleared it. He took up position and began issuing instructions. Miss Mathews brought the first folders to him and as she leaned over to place them on the desk Airchie looked as though he was about to sink his head into her big cushiony chest. I made him a throat-cutting sign to behave. He grinned and got down to work. We left him to it and went back to McCutcheon's office. He closed the door behind us.

'Exactly what's going on, Chief Inspector? Can you tell me?'

Why not? I know Harry didn't want news to get out about top-level shenanigans, but it was *my* neck on the line. I was past caring if it embarrassed the Government – and maybe it would ginger some action. I waited till we were both seated and sipping the tea brought by Allison. McCutcheon was shifting in his seat as though he had piles. Our arrival was a big boulder in his small calm pond. I chucked another one in.

'Someone at head office is diverting funds to some company accounts. These companies are almost certainly fronts for various forms of illegal financial trading. Money laundering, gambling, tax evasion. There was one major transfer three days before Sir Fraser's murder to his brother's account. And then three days after the death, a reverse transaction took place from Mungo Gibson's account to a company called High Times, which operates illegal bingo games in Glasgow.'

McCutcheon looked as though he was having a barely stifled heart attack. His neck and cheeks flushed. As I spelled it out he was nodding his head in time to each new revelation. 'Yes, yes. I know about those, Chief Inspector. The amount was ten thousand pounds and I personally had to authorise it. Any transactions over a hundred pounds have to be authorised by me, personally.'

'Mr Higgins will find a record of these transactions?' I enquired. That was presumably why McCutcheon was suddenly loquacious.

'He will, but I can save you time in your search for the head office authority.'

I inclined my head to hear.

'We received a credit note of that amount deposited at St Vincent Street and transferred to this branch just – as you say – three days before the terrible events.'

'This took the form of a written credit?'

'Mr Higgins will find it in the file.'

'Who signed it?'

'Sir Fraser himself.'

'Was this unusual?'

'No. Over the years, Sir Fraser has deposited similarly large amounts to his brother's account to cover the care.'

'The care?'

'You are aware that Mungo had some – problems?'

'Alcoholism and depression, yes.'

'It has required constant care and special protection for many years. The money was to pay for the care home and the private treatment.' He hesitated. 'Sometimes it was to pay for him to be found. Private detectives were called in after he'd gone missing from the . . .'

'Asylum?'

'Exactly.'

'This was Ailsa, the Ayrshire Asylum.'

'Oh no, Mr Mungo Gibson was always kept at a home in Glasgow. A private mental institution.'

'Constantly?'

'No. The bills we received and paid showed irregular stays, some a few weeks, some days. That's when he would go missing. Over the past ten years I'd say he was committed about half the time. The rest of the time, I believe he stayed with Sir Fraser and Lady Gibson.'

'Committed? He was that bad?'

'Sir Fraser had medical power of attorney.'

'You said that the authority for the cash coming into the account came directly from Sir Fraser. Who authorised the money leaving it? Was Mungo out of care at the time? Did he come into the bank?'

'No. It was authorised at head office.'

He didn't say more; he knew what was implied.

'Mr McCutcheon, who authorised the transfer of ten thousand pounds to the company called High Times?'

'Mr Clarkson. Mr Colin Clarkson, our new chief.'

FORTY-FOUR

Airchie duly appeared, flushed with success and the proximity to Miss Mathews. I doubted it was reciprocal. Airchie clutched the documents that confirmed the manager's statement. I insisted on borrowing them, together with a strong foolscap envelope. Before we left I also got the Gibson boys' old address in Maybole. I thought I might walk round there. But first I escorted Airchie to the train.

'Apart from leering at the bank staff, you've done well today, Archibald Higgins. Here's a fiver bonus for your time. Buy yourself a new suit.' Harry was paying him a retainer directly but had given me funds for any eventuality. This seemed a good use. As I was closing the carriage door on him, he leaned forward.

'Brodie, Ah just wanted to tell you, Ah'm fair enjoying masel'. It's no' just about havin' fun wi yon lassie back there. Nor the medal – though that would be nice. Ah'm liking working for something – something real. Do ye un'erstaun'?'

'I do, Airchie.'

'Is there ony chance? Ah mean efter this is a' by wi'. Is there ony chance of mair work for – you know who?'

I grinned. 'I'll put in a word. Let's see.'

I closed the door, the whistle went and the train wheezed out of the station. I turned and walked back into town. My first stop was the post office. I addressed my big envelope to Harry Templeton in London and popped the incriminating documents inside. I asked for special delivery. They'd arrive either late tonight or first post in the morning. Then I called him.

'I don't know if you got my package this morning, but I'm at Maybole and just sending you some more interesting material. Clarkson is your man. I don't know if he's been doing all the illicit transactions for Fraser over the last year or two, but he certainly authorised the ten thousand quid to High Times.'

'It's a timely call, Brodie.' He sounded excited. 'I got your notes this morning, had them typed and talked them through with Sir Percy half an hour ago. It did the trick. We're going in tomorrow. Quietly, but in force. Your find today caps it. Want to join the party?'

'Is it a bring your own masks and guns?'

'Not a bit. Suits and briefcases. We will politely walk in and ask to speak to the boss. Very low key. Those are my instructions.'

'Can I bring my wee friend? He'd be useful.'

'Consider him invited. I'll leave a message confirming the time with . . . who's best?'

'Inspector Duncan Todd, Central Division. He knows all about it, and he's on our side. *My* side.'

I hung up and ran my hands over my face. Real action at last! Things were moving my way. I thought for a minute about whether I needed to do any more digging in Maybole but decided it couldn't harm. The more I could build the case the better.

The Gibsons' old home was – inevitably, if I were to believe the stories of poverty and dissipation – in the less salubrious part of town. The streets were late-nineteenth-century rows of council tenements; solid stone, but with the worn and neglected air that clings to the properties of councils with limited funds. Some mustered bits of turf either side of their front path. Some stretched to clumps of weed and plants and a few rocks pillaged from the beaches down by Turnberry. I gazed up at Number 29 wondering what I could glean from this visit.

'Hello?'

A small, white-haired woman peered out from her open window. It looked like her regular haunt. She was leaning on a faded cushion.

'Oh, hello. Fine day.'

'No' bad. Who are you looking for?'

'The Gibsons.'

'Och, they're long since away.'

'Have you been here a while?'

'Fifty-five years, nigh on. Ma first hame when Ah got married. Jimmie died ten year ago. Ah kent the Gibsons fine. What were you after them for?'

She was old, wanted company, why not?

'I'm a policeman. Could I have a wee chat?'

I was scarcely in the door when the kettle was boiling and the best china dragged out from the back of the sideboard and given a quick wipe with a tea towel from Millport. As I sat sipping, I let her talk.

'Always rows, that's how Ah remember them. Stan and Jean. Fighting day and night, then making up a' lovey dovey. It was the drink, ye ken. Always fu'. You should hae seen the piles o' empties. It was thae boys that Ah was worried for.'

'Fraser and Mungo?'

'Aye. Sometimes they'd come in here to get oot the way o' the rowin'. Pair wee things. Then as they got older they got into trouble mair and mair. Wee Mungo was always trying to keep up. Two years makes a difference at that age. Fraser got him to take dares and the wee fella did his best.'

'Like what?'

'Och, jumping off o' high wa's. He broke an ankle once. Smoking, drinking, lassies. Fraser got Mungo fu' when he was only twelve or thereabouts. It's nae wunner he ended up wi' problems. It a' stopped for a while when pair Jeannie Gibson died. She was only in her forties. They say it was an accident. Fell doon the stairs. Ah'm no' so sure. Cigarettes and alcohol, Ah reckon.'

'Then Stan took a new wife?'

'Aye. Worse than ever. She was younger. And didnae get on with the weans. Mair screaming. Till Fraser just left one day. Ah think he was only fifteen. But he didnae dae too bad.' She sighed. 'Until the noo.'

'What happened to Mungo?'

'He went intae himsel'. Couldnae get a word oot o' him. Left school at fourteen and hud a few jobs. Never stuck tae them. Got mixed up wi' a gang in Ayr. And just drifted away, so he did. It was a shame. He came back a few years ago but by then he was a real boozer. Dossed wi' pals or in a flat his brother paid for. Then he was in and oot of hospitals.'

'Hospitals?'

'Loony bins. For his drinking. Look, Ah've got a photo or twa put by.'

She levered herself up and went to the old sideboard. She pulled out three thick albums, glanced at each and selected one. She brought it over and flicked through, sucking her teeth at times and smiling at others. Finally, she pulled out a black and white family photo: a man, a woman and two boys aged about ten and eight. Same dark hair and light eyes shared among the mother and her sons.

'That's them. An' here's the boys again.'

She passed me a black and white of the boys, older, well into their teens. They looked happy. And suddenly it came back. The very pale eyes. Staring up at me from the dead man's face. The memory shuttled through my brain like a burst of slides from a projector . . .

. . . the hot, deserted street. Marr Street. Everyone at the Govan Fair. Walking into the dark close, feet echoing.

Climbing the stairs, heavy briefcase in left hand, gun in right. Reaching the top landing. Two doors. Music from the left:

> *'Don't sit under the apple tree,*
> *With anyone else but me . . .'*

I step forward and strike the door with the butt of my gun. Twice. I push, and the door swings open. A hall with two doors. I place the briefcase on the floor and push open the first. Gun up. Empty. A scullery.

Down the short corridor comes the singing. The Andrews Sisters.

> *'. . . anyone else but me,*
> *Till I come marching home.'*

I walk towards it, revolver high and cocked. I turn the handle and fling the door wide. A wireless burbling on a mantelpiece. Bare wood floor. A broken wooden table tilted on its side. Some rope next to it. A slight movement of the door. A loud creak from behind me. I whip round. Gun up. The blow takes me on the back of my head as though the ceiling is falling in.

Waking in pain. Trying to focus. The ropes and the wireless gone. The table upright on all four legs. The dead man on the floor, staring up at the ceiling. My gun lying near where I'd fallen . . .

I left the old woman before she ran out of tea and I ran out of composure. I mooched back to the station, thinking, assembling the picture in my head. I'd been hit from behind. By someone in the room. Someone else was coming down the hall. A simple trap by two kidnappers? If so, it removed the last lingering doubt that I'd somehow fired my gun accidentally and blown a hole in Gibson's forehead. Bang in the centre.

But the broken table and the scattered rope I saw before I

was knocked out suggested something else. Fraser Gibson had been tied up, had got free and broken off a table leg as a weapon. It was *Gibson* who'd felled me, shortly before the kidnapper or kidnappers had returned. Had they been waiting next door? And if Gibson had hit me from behind, only the most unlikely of ricochets could have put a bullet in his head. Whoever had shot him had tidied the place including propping up the table with the broken leg.

When I got back to Glasgow at midday I took the risk of calling Duncan Todd to tell him of my revelations.

'Great, Brodie, but of course Sangster would say it was awfie convenient to have your memory back.'

'I know. But it makes me feel better. Besides, we might not care what Sangster thinks. Harry Templeton and his merry men are raiding the bank tomorrow. I'm joining him. He'll call you first thing with timings and I'll call you when I can get to a phone.'

'Maybe I should tag along, eh?'

'I would steer clear, Duncan. You might find it awkward to explain how you knew about it. Keep pretending you know nothing. Be my fifth column. We don't want Sangster's suspicions raised. Speaking of which, any news?'

'Some. Some good, some bad.'

'Good first.'

'Well, even the good isnae *that* good. But it's joining a few more dots. Your pal Cammie, the elusive chauffeur, is Cammie Millar.'

'So?'

'Son of Meg Fulton.'

'Fulton? You're kidding me. Related to . . .'

'You've guessed it: Angus Fulton. Cammie's mammie is Gus Fulton's sister. Uncle Gus.'

'And Uncle Gus and his wife Annie own this bingo enterprise that just received a windfall from SLB. "What a tangled web we weave . . ." What's the really bad news?'

'The prints. The Scottish Linen Bank finally realised that somebody had broken in. They've had our forensic boys round to take prints.'

'Shit.'

'Shortly to hit the fan.'

'When?'

'They went in yesterday. It'll take them a few days to look through the files.'

'We're safe until at least end of tomorrow?' My first thought was the return of Airchie Higgins and me to the scene of the crime in the morning. We might as well go straight to jail without passing Go.

'The forensic boys huvnae got any faster since your day, Brodie.'

'Higgins is safe for twenty-four hours?'

'Should be nae bother. But I'd get him off the streets after that.'

'What about me? They'll check mine, even though I'm dead?'

'They will, my friend. Slow but diligent wee bureaucrats so they are.'

'Then what?'

'Well, at first they'll no' believe it. Why should they? You're deid. Then Sangster will get them to check everything again. Couple of days at least. They won't want to look stupid.'

'Then?'

'They might decide to dig you up.'

FORTY-FIVE

Before I hung up on Duncan I asked him to round up my pals. It was time for a confab. Likely the last one before my resurrection and subsequent incarceration. I needed to pool what we knew and to decide where we went next. A number of threads were becoming visible but all running in different directions and crisscrossing. I needed help disentangling them, finding out where they led.

After Shimon had closed up that evening and wished me a good meeting, the conspirators began convening in the storeroom. As each one arrived through the open back door I welcomed them with a handshake. Except for Sam: she got an embrace and a kiss. Duncan Todd slouched in. A little later I heard crashing and cursing and Wullie appeared in his wheelchair, steered by Stewart.

'Push him in the Clyde if he's a nuisance, Stewart.'

'It was a close-run thing. Wasn't it, Billie boy?'

'Ah'm just getting a wee bit frustrated no' being quite ma' independent self.'

'How are the legs coming on, Wullie?'

'Stronger every day. Ah can get up and walk about a bit. It's coming back.'

'That sounds good enough to outflank yon new winger for St Mirren, Wullie,' said Duncan.

I let them banter for a while and get settled on their crate of choice. Examining them in the faint light from the bulb, I felt a sudden empathy with Guy Fawkes sitting in the bowels of Parliament with his fellow plotters. I hoped I wouldn't let these good people down.

'Thanks for coming, folks. I wanted to give you my news and make sure we were all au fait with what's going on. You've all been busy. Thank you. I've also got some hypotheses about who's behind all this. I'd like to give them an airing to make sure I'm not going mad.'

Nodding agreement all round.

'First, you'd better know that the police are about to launch a manhunt. For Airchie Higgins and me. Duncan tells me that Scottish Linen is now aware that there was a break-in the other night. The police have taken dabs. Airchie's and mine are all over the skylight and roof and on a ladder. They might also be scattered around the back office. They'll take prints from all the staff and separate out the ones that don't belong.'

'But you're deid, Brodie,' said Wullie.

'Seems my fingerprints are still on file. It might make them stop and think. Maybe double-check. But when there's no other likely solution, someone might decide to think the impossible and break out the shovels. Sangster's convinced I'm some sort of Machiavelli as it is. Houdini isn't too big a stretch. So, we need to move fast.'

I brought Wullie and Stewart up to date with what Airchie and I had found in our midnight rambles at the bank. Then I told them all of my visit to Maybole and what I'd found out about Clarkson, the new head man at SLB, and the cash transfer three days after Gibson's death to High Times.

'We also found out that Clarkson had authorised the emptying of my poor wee bank accounts on the same day. You met the beneficiary, Wullie. The curvaceous Miss Pamela McKenzie.'

Wullie whistled. 'A femme fatale right enough. But slim pickings, Brodie, or she'd be on a roon-the-world cruise by now.'

'Peanuts. But they were *my* peanuts. The crucial thing is that the bank provided a false statement to the courts saying I'd been in debt more than three weeks before the actual date they stole my money.'

'You think Clarkson is the brains?' asked Duncan.

'All the signs say so. As Finance Director he'd also have known about Gibson's pilfering. Higgins says there needed to be someone inside the finance unit helping.'

'Then why would he arrange this last transfer after his old boss was murdered?'

'A double-cross? Clarkson behind the murder and then paying off the villains? I'm planning to ask him that tomorrow when MI5 goes in. Harry Templeton has asked me to join him.'

'But that's going to blow your cover, Douglas!' said Sam.

'Clarkson's never seen me other than in old photos in the paper. I'll still be Chief Inspector David Bruce, Edinburgh division.'

'But you were spotted leaving the bank. The doorman will recognise you,' she persisted.

'I was in dungarees and flat cap. I'm going in wearing suit and tie and glasses.'

She wouldn't let go. 'The beard stands out. A red flag; says *look at me.*'

'It might have to come off, then. Will you miss it? I'll keep the specs, though.'

Wullie leaned forward. 'Maybe you shouldnae be worried, hen. This could be the end o' it. If Brodie and the secret service boys are going in the front door to put the cuffs on Clarkson, does that no' tie it all up?'

I shrugged. 'Maybe. Assuming we can get our hands on all the ledgers Airchie and I examined, and Clarkson plays ball, we can demonstrate chicanery at the bank. But unless Clarkson confesses it doesn't explain Gibson's killing.'

'It will be hard for Clarkson to account for authorising the transfer of ten thousand pounds to Gus Fulton other than pay-off for services rendered,' said Sam. 'Getting the top job is certainly motivation.'

'You met Clarkson, Wullie. Is he capable of it?'

'No' at first sight. The words *criminal mastermind* don't easily fit the picture. When I interviewed him, I thought here's a man over-promoted if ever there was one. He seemed a timid wee thing who'd just got lucky. Always a number two till the top door suddenly opened and he fell through. But, to massacre a metaphor, still waters run deep in a wee man wi' a chip on his shoulder.'

'The other question is how Sheila fits in to all this?' I asked. 'Either she's being threatened with her life – her and her staff – to deny ever meeting me. Or she's up to her perfumed oxters in a plot to put a noose round my neck.'

Sam responded: 'Threatened or bought? But by whom? How about Fraser's gangster pals?'

'Possible. But again I don't see any motive on the part of the gangsters. You put Sheila through her paces yesterday, Sam. She knew about Fraser's gambling and womanising. Enough to get rid of him?'

Sam screwed up her mouth. 'By making an ally of Clarkson? Possibly. An alliance of convenience. She's not a woman to be crossed. And as Wullie says, who knows what ambition was burning up Clarkson? Maybe Sheila lured Clarkson with the promise of a route to promotion.'

'And what about Mungo?' asked Duncan. 'How does he fit in?'

I shook my head. 'He sounds like a sad sideshow. In and out of mental homes. A drunk and a depressive. Though it's not clear why he was moved from his Glasgow asylum to Ailsa. Maybe Sheila just wanted to dump him out of sight now she had the chance.'

Sam said, 'It's also not clear why they picked on you, Douglas.'

Duncan intervened. 'Ah'm following that up, lass. Now we have some sort of link with Gus Fulton we're checking who Gus is connected to. The tentacles of crime. It sounds like there was a favour called in. You know how many gangsters your man has upset.'

'OK, so we're saying that we've got a conspiracy. That it might start with Clarkson and could involve the vengeful Sheila. At a stroke she gets rid of her faithless husband and gets a big insurance payout and maybe the ransom money; which gives me another question for Clarkson tomorrow. Twenty grand is more than pocket money. It could tie him and Lady Gibson together. We just have to prove it.'

'How, Douglas?' asked Sam.

'If there is a conspiracy we need to put pressure on the weakest link.'

'Clarkson?' said Wullie immediately.

'Certainly not Sheila,' said Sam. 'A tough old boot.'

'I've never met Clarkson but agree about Sheila,' I said. 'I was thinking more about Cammie and Uncle Gus. If they provided the muscle for the kidnap either one could have shot Fraser. There was only one shot, one finger on the trigger. One of them should hang. Maybe the other would prefer not to.'

'King's evidence?' said Sam. 'It could work, Douglas. Let me take a look at precedents. It may not matter who pulled the trigger. They'd both blame each other, blood tie or not. They might both hang. But if you're looking for a bargaining counter, this could be it.'

'Do you think there's room for a real policeman to do his job?'

'A real policeman? Who did you have in mind, Duncan?'

'Awfie funny, Brodie. If you're in at Scottish Linen the morn, and Clarkson sings his song, then we have grounds for arresting Gus Fulton for receiving misappropriated funds and running an illegal gambling den. To wit, a series of bingo halls. Ah could then have a wee side conversation with him about adding a murder to the charge sheet.'

'I like the sound of that, Dunc. But what about your boss, Sangster? Can you side-step him?'

'Wi' my eyes closed usually. But you're right, Brodie. We don't know who's pulling Sangster's strings and whether there's a connection to Gus Fulton for example.'

Wullie squinted through the smoke from the fag jammed in the corner of his mouth.

'Are you saying that Detective Chief Inspector Walter Sangster is *bent* as well as stupid?'

Wullie's rasping elongation of the word put bent coppers down there with pederasts and perjurers. Which of course they were. It stung Duncan.

'Let's no' be hasty, Wullie. Ah don't want to see any lurid headlines before we get some proof one way or the other. A' we know is that he was celebrating putting our pal here in the slammer, if not in the grave. And Ah've heard there's some big man in the background who wanted to see Brodie swing.'

'Good job my suicide pre-empted that, Duncan. Right, folks, next steps. I'll call you first thing, Duncan. You'll have received confirmation from Harry Templeton about the time and arrangements for raiding the Scottish Linen Bank. Can you ask Harry to phone Airchie Higgins – Harry has his contact details – to meet me on the corner just before the time of the raid? Tell him to tell Airchie to get his suit to the steamie. With him in it. Sam, you're following up the King's evidence question. Wullie, could you have a word with your pal Weasel Watkins?'

'Aye, sure. What do you want him to do?'

'We've got all we can from his road-sweeping outside Sheila's house. And he's going to get caught at this rate. Or get in a fight with the council about overtime. What about setting him loose on the Govan streets? To try to track down the kids who provided me with the paper trail to the kidnap house? They must have been paid. Who gave them the job? Descriptions, car used, anything at all.'

Wullie shook his head. 'Needles in the haystack. There's a wheen o' gangs knocking about Govan.'

'Brodie?'

'Yes, Stewart.'

'You know I'm a teacher. In Govan.'

Of course. Why didn't I think of that?

'You might know these kids?'

'I know lots of kids. But more importantly, I know who to ask and where to find them. Let me make enquiries. I'd be glad to help.'

'I'd really be glad if you did, Stewart. Thank you.'

He beamed. Wullie patted his arm.

One by one they left, leaving Sam for last.

'It's quite snug in here, Douglas.'

'So it is. Have you seen my wee bed? It's quite snug too.'

'Show me.'

FORTY-SIX

Sam didn't stay the night. But she stayed long enough for me to recall the aphrodisiac effect of proximity to danger. Like a wartime love affair. It was as though my brush with the graveyard had given urgency and spice to our relationship.

In the morning I squared up to myself in one of the stored, tall mirrors with a bowl of water and a fresh razor blade. Reluctantly I started hacking away at my beard; I'd grown fond of it. But I left a thick dark-red moustache. Slowly I emerged from my disguise. Thinner and greyer round the gills compared to the rest of my face. I hadn't realised how much Scottish sun had been filtering through the clouds.

Besides, I was done skulking in the shadows. I was ready to confront my enemies, and see who blinked first. I donned my suit and tie. I flattened my mop of dark hair with Brylcreem and parted it in the middle. Finally, on went the glasses. Every inch the accountant. Or rent collector.

As agreed with Harry, I called Duncan from the corridor phone in Shimon's store and got his confirmation they were going in at 9 a.m. Harry sent his compliments; would I care to join him? I would.

I was heading out the storeroom when I had a thought and turned back. I fumbled above one of the most out-of-reach crates and retrieved the Webley. I fingered its cold contours, enjoying the feel of the smooth metal. Engineered precisely and solely to maim or kill. Then I put it back. I was going to ask questions at a major Scottish bank, not rob it. Or shoot Clarkson, despite what he'd done to me. I wondered at my first reaction. Heightened sense of risk? Threat of attack? In a bank?

I took a deep breath and marched out through the show-room. Shimon glanced round, nodded, and then ignored me. I stepped into the sunshine and walked up to Ingram Street. I could have hopped on a tram which would have taken me up and round to St Vincent Street, but it wouldn't have taken me all the way. Forbye, I had time and was enjoying the air. I'd been cooped up too long. It was time to come out into the open. I felt invulnerable in my new persona. At the corner of West Nile I walked past two police constables without either batting an eyelid. I was any other businessman strolling through the city centre.

I was within sight of Scottish Linen at five minutes to nine. Skulking by the corner was Archibald Higgins. He was trying to look nonchalant while stepping from foot to foot and peeking round the corner. As I got closer I could see he'd been spring-cleaned.

'Good morning, Airchie.'

He jumped. 'Christ, Brodie, it's you.'

'New suit, Airchie?'

'No' exactly new. I got it at the Barras.'

The turn-ups were longer than normal, but otherwise Mr Burton would have been proud. I looked him up and down. Shoes gleaming, face red raw from a close shave and his hair plastered to his head. Even his specs were nearly transparent.

'You'll do. Come on.'

I marched into St Vincent Street, Airchie trotting along-side. Everything seemed normal. A bus was grinding up the hill and a couple of cars heading down. A few pedestrians meandered past. No sign of anything untoward. Then suddenly two identical saloons appeared from the west –

Morris Tens – one behind each other. They drew up outside the bank and four people got out of each. Six men and two women, all in dark two-pieces. One of the men was Harry Templeton. He looked around, saw us crossing the road and smiled. I reached him and we shook hands.

He said, 'You're looking well, for a corpse.'

'I'll feel even better at my resurrection. This is Archibald Higgins, the man you've been sending into danger.'

'Mr Higgins, you've done your country proud. You will be rewarded.'

Airchie glowed and stood an inch taller.

'Shall we?' said Harry, pointing up at the bank. 'And remember, chaps, this is all low key. No fuss. Our masters don't want this in the papers.'

As he spoke, the big doors at the top of the flight of stairs began swinging open on the dot of nine. Harry led the way, with me alongside. Airchie and the rest of Harry's team swept up behind us. A bit of me – the soldier – wanted to call out the rhythm and get them in step. As bank raids went this was pretty civilised.

The doorman was the one Airchie and I had brushed past in our dungarees. There was no spark of recognition from him for either of us, just a 'Good morning, gentlemen, ladies' as we sailed past. Clerks were already in position behind counters. A manager in tails and bowler was fussing about with his watch fob to makes sure it hung straight. Harry went straight up to him and showed him a pass. The manager's face blanched.

'Please ask your staff to stay exactly where they are. And kindly have your doorman close and lock the doors. No customers. You're closed for the day.'

The manager's mouth opened and shut. He pulled at his winged collar and looked round at the polished faces of Harry's MI5 team standing in a ring around him and absorbed their air of intent and professionalism. Even Airchie looked the part. Sort of. The manager nodded and walked over to the doorman to give him instructions. As the doors swung shut he came back. Harry gave him new orders.

'What's your name, please?'

'Smyth. With a "y",' he gulped, face stretched with shock.

'Well, Mr Smyth with a "y", please show my team into your back office. Where the ledgers are. Then I'd like you to take me and one of my colleagues to meet Mr Clarkson, your Managing Director. Come on, Smyth. Hurry up. We are on Crown business.'

We were led through the counter and into the short corridor leading to the back room. We emerged into the great room and found it already filled with clerks who'd piled their desks with ledgers and the first paperwork of the day. The odd bit of chatter stilled and died as we poured in and took up position at the front of the hall. Harry stood forward.

'Good morning, all. My name is Templeton. My colleagues and I are from the Government.' He held up his identity card and brandished it. 'There is no need for alarm. My team and I will be spending some time with you today examining the books. We require your assistance to do so. Your help will be appreciated.' He looked round. 'And noted.'

He nodded to me. I turned to Airchie.

'Mr Higgins, you know where everything is filed. Take these agents with you and leave one at each point of interest. Tell them as you do so what to concentrate on.'

He puffed up his chest, and nodded. 'Yes, sir!'

I signalled to his colleagues to follow him. Harry and I watched as Airchie led a clockwise procession round the tall shelves of ledgers. Once or twice he paused to confirm with a nervous clerk which shelves were which and then dropped a team member at that point.

'I hope that medal is struck. Higgins has earned it.'

'We're going to do better than that. As well as a medal – the Double Entry Cross, do you think? – he'll have a job. We have need of reformed crooks like Higgins. He is reformed, isn't he?'

'A medal and a job? I think you'll find you've bought undying loyalty.'

While we waited I glanced round the room. On one side was a bank of typists, on general secretarial duties. I wondered. I walked over and flourished my warrant card.

'Is there a Miss Pamela McKenzie here?'

The women's eyes flickered and glanced at each other, all trying to avoid focusing on one young woman who was turning pink and had suddenly become fascinated with her typewriter. I walked over. Her mane of hair sat like a black helmet framing her face.

'Miss McKenzie?'

She looked up at me. Huge blue eyes ringed with mascara and thick lashes. Mask of make-up and vivid lips. I smiled encouragingly at her. She nodded.

'Please step this way. I just want a word.'

I walked to one side of the room and waited, arms folded. Pamela got up from her desk, pulled down her tight skirt and walked towards me, head high, chest thrust out. Wullie hadn't exaggerated his use of an hourglass to describe her figure, but I'm sure I was more appreciative. Pamela clicked across the lino and stood in front of me, her lips pressed together, ready for anything. She crossed her arms under her splendid bosoms as if they needed lifting or accentuating. They didn't.

'Miss McKenzie, I am led to believe that you wrongfully emptied the bank account of one of the bank's customers. A certain Douglas Brodie.'

Her mouth opened and shut like a red sea anemone. Her arms dropped. Her eyes darted round the hall, looking for an escape route. She brought her gaze back to mine and lifted her head up.

'Ah did as Ah was telt, so Ah did.'

'*Who* told you?'

'Ma boss.'

'Who's your boss?'

'Well, it came doon from above. From the tap flair.' She raised her eyes up to the executive levels. 'Ma boss – Miss Carmichael, over there – said she'd been instructed. And Ah wis just tae follow orders. So Ah did.'

'Are you aware that the accounts belonged to the man – the reporter – who was accused of the kidnap and murder of Sir Fraser Gibson?'

Pamela's face lost its hardness. I thought she was going to break down.

'Ah didnae know at the time. How could I? Am Ah in a lot of trouble?'

Pamela McKenzie probably hadn't looked innocent since she turned fourteen, but there was an honesty about her face that couldn't be contrived.

'That depends, Pamela. What did you do with the money?'

She shook her head. Her hair didn't move. 'Nothing. It's still there. In my account. Ah knew it wis . . .' She searched for the right word.

'Stolen?'

She tossed her head. 'Well, Ah knew it wisnae mine. So it's just sitting there, so it is.'

'Good. Keep it there. We'll be in touch. Thank you, Miss McKenzie.'

I tried not to watch her swaying back to her seat. I walked back to join Harry. Airchie had just completed the full circuit of the hall and was now solo. The MI5 boys and girls were already pulling down ledgers from the shelves and making themselves at home. Airchie came up to us and barely supressed a salute. His wee face was flushed.

'Good work, Mr Higgins. Your job now is to supervise the team. Walk round. Keep an eye on them. Give them directions. Answer their questions. They need your guidance. Is that OK?'

'Aye, it is. Yes, Brodie. Yes, sir.'

He executed a terrible about-turn and started his duties. We turned to the manager. His face was miserable. Harry was smiling.

'Right, Smyth with a "y", take us to Mr Clarkson.'

'I need to call ahead. He won't know you're coming.'

'Good. Let's go.'

FORTY-SEVEN

We declined the lift and headed for the wide staircase. Harry and I took them two at a time, while Smyth puffed after us. We got to what I recognised were the executive offices on the top floor. Suddenly the lino became carpet, good quality. I hoped it came from Blackwood and Morton in Kilmarnock. If it was good enough for the *Titanic* it was good enough for the Scottish Linen Bank.

Smyth opened the glass-paned door into a long corridor. The hush was profound. The walls were burnished wood panels. Former chiefs of the bank scowled down at us in dull oils. We walked past the doors marked 'Finance Director', 'Treasurer' and 'Gentlemen'. We stopped outside a door bearing the legend 'Managing Director'. Smyth's eyes filled with terror. It might as well have said 'Pearly Gates'.

'After you, Smyth,' said Harry.

Smyth tapped timidly on the opaque glass panel, turned the handle and half opened the door. A female voice asked, 'Yes?' As in, *How dare you open my door without advance notice?* Gingerly, he pushed his head round, expecting to have it chopped off.

'Sorry to bother you, Miss Pringle, but . . .'

By this stage Harry had had enough. He pushed the door the rest of the way back and shouldered Smyth aside. I followed. Miss Pringle was halfway to her feet, glowering at us from above her specs.

'You cannot just barge in here. Who do you think you are?'

Full on Kelvinside. I recalled Wullie saying that Clarkson had brought his own 'girl' with him. But I doubted he had much choice. She seemed more like his jailer.

'Good morning. Miss Pringle, is it? This is who I am.'

Harry handed over his card and let her read and digest. Her face slid and she dropped back into her chair. A frown became a look of fear, then something else. Acceptance? Of what? She fought back.

'Would you like me to make an appointment, Mr Templeton?'

It was a game effort. Harry smiled back.

'That won't be necessary. We'll just stick our heads round the door.'

She half rose, but subsided, and nodded. Harry marched to the door, gave it a smart rap and opened it. I was barely two seconds behind him. There was a yelp and I was in time to see a small man leaping to his feet out of his much-too-big chair. There was a look of panic and guilt on his face, like a wee boy caught playing with himself. Maybe that's what he did in this grand room, overcome with his own exalted status.

'Who are *you*? What's the meaning of this?'

I answered before Harry could. 'Your nemesis, Clarkson.'

Clarkson's brow furrowed on the word. Harry explained.

'To put it more simply, my name is Harry Templeton and I'm from MI5. This is my colleague, Chief Inspector David Bruce. We have some questions for you.'

Like his secretary, Clarkson subsided in his chair, punctured. Then I noticed how red his eyes were, as though from lack of sleep. Was he expecting this? I suddenly felt sorry for him. A wee bit. He gathered himself.

'What's this about, gentlemen?'

Harry nodded to me. I took the cue.

'I think you know, Clarkson. It's about stolen money. It's about secret accounts. It's about pay-offs to crooked businesses. And, finally, it's about kidnap and murder. Shall we sit over here?'

274

I walked across to the comfy armchairs surrounding the gleaming low table. Harry followed me. We stood waiting. Clarkson had no choice but to drag himself over to join us. We sat, Harry and I on one side, Clarkson on the other.

'Nice office,' I said.

'Aye, so it is.' He looked around, perhaps sensing that he ought to enjoy every last minute in it. I followed his eyes and took in the painting on the wall. The one described by Wullie. Sir Fraser Gibson in his pomp. His piercing eyes stared at me, daring me to sully his office with accusations.

'Is this the pay-off? Is this what Fraser Gibson promised you if you did what you were told?'

'I don't understand.'

'Sure you do. Downstairs in the accounts department, Mr Templeton's team of highly trained investigators are ploughing through your ledgers. Are you really suggesting they won't find anything?'

His eyes were all over the place. His knuckles clenched white on the chair arms.

'What sort of thing?'

'Money being drained from the bank's main loan accounts into your old boss's account so he could pay off his gambling and whoring debts. That sort of thing.'

Clarkson grasped his knees and pulled them up. He sat rocking like a child who'd gone into a dwam.

'Mr Clarkson,' prompted Harry. 'What do you have to say?'

'What's it got to do wi' me?'

'We expect to prove you were the counter-signature to this embezzlement,' Harry went on. 'It will go easier with you if you confess now, rather than deny it.'

He looked at us in turn, his head on one side. Then he nodded in some sort of acceptance. All the denial left his face.

'Will it? Will it really? Ah don't expect so. Ah think it will all go awfie badly.'

FORTY-EIGHT

We looked at him, saw resignation. This was going to be easy. Unpleasant but easy. His accent had shed its veneer. Dropped back into the Ayrshire of his youth.

I asked, 'Why did you do it? What did you get out of it?'

He snorted. 'Ah wis nuthin'. Just another wee boy stuck in Maybole.'

'Maybole? Like the Gibson boys?'

'Oh, aye. Do you think Ah was born with this accent? Ah used to run aroon' with Fraser and his gang. Ah got away. Ah had an uncle who took me on in Ayr. Ah did my articles and Fraser ca'ed me up and gave me a job. Kept promoting me. A' the way up.'

'The branch manager in Maybole didn't mention you. Didn't say you were a local boy. Why was that?'

'Why do ye think, Chief Inspector?'

'He's in on this? Good God! Why didn't he warn you?'

He shook his head. 'Ah didnae mean that. McCutcheon hates the idea that Ah made it this far. Jealous, Ah suppose. He phoned me yesterday to say he'd had a visit. He probably enjoyed that.'

'Did he say what we were looking for?'

'Naw. Just that the polis had been asking questions.'

'But you didn't make a run for it?'

'Where to? Ah don't have a passport. Ah don't have a stash

of money. Just some savings from my salary. A good salary, mind. Ah didnae do it for the money. Fraser was hard to say no to. Ah owed everything to him. But Ah always knew it would end like this.'

He said it wistfully as though three witches had stopped him on a blasted heath one day and forecast the whole pattern of his life. He'd accepted that it would be his fate, while all the time hoping to avoid it. I turned to Templeton.

'Harry, it looks like you've got the makings of the embezzlement case. Can we turn to the kidnap?'

'Help yourself.'

'Colin Clarkson, let me ask you directly: were you involved in the kidnap and murder of Sir Fraser Gibson?'

He looked me straight in the eye. 'Naw. Naw, Ah wisnae. Why would Ah? What was the possible benefit to me?'

I blinked. I cast a hand round the room. 'All this. You got the top job. That will seem a strong enough motive to any jury.'

'They'd be wrang. Did you ever meet Fraser? Big guy with a big ego. A steamroller.'

He glanced up at the painting. Why hadn't he had it removed? Still under Gibson's thrall?

'So?'

'Look at me. Do you think Ah could follow in his footsteps? Ah'm scared shitless, Chief Inspector. Ah'm no' sleeping. Ah'm oot of my depth. Ah would have been found out soon enough.'

'That's easy to say now. It wouldn't have stopped you wanting the job. Wanting it so badly you'd conspire to get rid of Gibson.'

'Well, Ah didnae.' His small jaw was set.

'What about the ransom? Sheila Gibson called you and you promptly sent round twenty thousand pounds. A ransom apparently. By day's end her husband was dead and the ransom had vanished.'

'You're no' going to believe me, but Ah didnae ken it was ransom money. In fact Ah didnae ken Fraser had been kidnapped.'

'You're right. It's unbelievable.'

He sighed. 'You don't un'erstaun'. Ower the years Ah've had to accept that a request from Sheila Gibson – Lady Gibson – was as good as a request from Sir Fraser himself. Twenty thoosand was a great deal of money. But it wisnae that unusual. She phoned me and Ah arranged it without question. Fraser had plenty in his account.'

'Regardless where it came from?'

He pursed his lips. I pressed on.

'When did you first hear of the kidnap?'

'Later that day. That afternoon. My secretary came in and told me about the murder. Then the whole story came oot.'

I studied him. I was minded to believe him.

'What about the earlier payments? The one-offs and the regular amounts from Fraser's many accounts to dodgy companies? You initialled those transactions.'

'How could you . . .? How did you . . .?'

Confusion mounted in his face. I piled it on to get the breakthrough confession.

'What about the money you sent three days *after* the murder? That's why we were in Maybole asking questions. The ten thousand was credited to a bank account in Maybole in the name of Mungo Gibson. It was then transmitted to the bank account of a company called High Times. You authorised it.'

He put his hands up to his face and then pulled them down, as though washing it. His shoulders jerked and his breathing became a pant. Then the tears started. They turned into sobs that racked his skinny body.

'Sorry, sorry. Ah'm that sorry.'

Harry and I could barely look at each other, far less at Clarkson. Finally the sobs stopped. He pulled a big hankie out of his pocket and blew his nose.

'Ah need the toilet. Ah'll no' be a minute.' He got up and went out.

'Should we follow him? Is he going to run?' I asked.

'As Clarkson himself said, where to? No. Give him a chance to get his composure back.'

I nodded. The Gents was just outside. We waited. I wondered if this was the end of the story for me. All the evidence that I'd been framed was beginning to pile up. That Gibson had been kidnapped and murdered by an unholy alliance of a jealous wife, an over-ambitious number two and some petty gangsters. I still needed to find out why Clarkson had sent money to High Life *after* his boss's murder. But the overall picture was taking shape. Clarkson would fill in most of the blanks and then we'd start on Sheila and Gus Fulton.

The shriek from outside cut through my hope-tinged reverie. Harry and I shot to our feet and launched ourselves at the door. We ran through the secretary's office and into the corridor. At the far end where the stairs and balcony were, people were already clustering.

'Oh, shit!' I said as I ran towards them. I barged through the growing crowd and looked down. Far far below, another crowd was gathering. Women were screaming. At the centre of the eddying wave of people lay a small body, spread-eagled across one of the large desks in the ledger hall. Some of the people were looking up at us and pointing at the flight path Clarkson had taken to meet his fate. I saw Airchie Higgins staring up at me. His mouth was open and he was shaking his head.

Then I saw movement on the edge of the scene. Newcomers sweeping in. In blue uniforms. I was transfixed by the eddies. They pushed aside the clerks and the MI5 agents and gathered round the body. Then one man, wearing the full uniform of a real chief inspector looked up. A detective overly fond of the trappings of rank who never missed a chance of swapping

279

shabby civvies for silver pips on tailored black. He searched the faces ranged along the balcony until he found what he was looking for. *Who* he was looking for. Sangster stared straight at me.

FORTY-NINE

had time enough to see Sangster point at Airchie and issue an order. Two constables grabbed him. Then Sangster started barking new commands to deploy the rest of his unit. He directed three officers towards the signs to the emergency exit and the back stairs, and another two towards the lift. He personally led the charge towards the wide main staircase. They knew what they were after; *whom* they were after. All my exits were blocked.

'Harry, I've just lost my get-out-of-jail-free card. Unless you have powers that override the local police, I'm heading back to prison.'

'I can argue with them but I can't trump them, Brodie. You know that.'

'We still can't prove who killed Gibson. Until we can, I'm in the frame. I need time. Give me a hand.'

I pulled him with me and we grabbed the skylight ladder from the wall. We hauled it to the balcony edge and raised it up against its catch on the skylight. It was much easier with two of us. As I moved to put my foot on the first rung Harry slipped something into my pocket.

'Keys. The lead Morris.'

'I'll be in touch,' I shouted as I started up. 'Move this back when I've gone, Harry!'

It was a variation on the Indian rope trick. I scrambled up the ladder and shoved the skylight open. I dragged myself through it and slammed it shut behind me. I peered through the glass and could see the ladder swinging back down. No sign yet of the boys in blue. Harry would use his authority to clear the bank officials away from the landing and back into their offices. He could then stall Sangster and his crew long enough for me to get away. Maybe.

I slid down the roof to the wide gutter and walked quickly to the dividing wall. The efficient maintenance staff had removed my patented skid-proof mat and rubbed off the varnish. Rain from a brief summer shower glistened on the smooth curved flanks. I had no time to size it up or think about how far I'd slide to my death. I jumped up and on to it. Even as my weight began to drag me down I flung my leg over and pushed. It wouldn't have won a gymnastics gold medal on the horse, but it got me sailing through the air. I hit the wet tiles on the roof of the furniture store and crashed to my hands and knees, slithering and sliding until I hit the gulley. And stopped.

I lay panting for a moment, the adrenalin coursing through my body. I shoved myself to my feet and found myself shaking. I stepped along the roof edge and grabbed the top of the fire escape. Quickly I clambered round on to it and began my descent. When I reached the last piece of ladder, I unclipped it and let it run to the ground. I was half down when the Alsatian leaped at me, barking with fury and clashing its teeth. My break-ins had been reported and they'd increased their security. Bastards.

I hung above the slavering hound for one second, then jumped. It was him or me. I landed with a foot striking its head and the other bouncing off its back. It howled and rolled away. I hit the ground and fell over. I was on my feet in an instant and running for the wall. Once more, sheer fear gave me spring heels. I could see myself as a cartoon figure, practically running up the wall. However I did it, I was just in time to avoid the furious onslaught from the angered hound.

Clearly I hadn't broken any of its bloody bones. Its teeth snapped an inch short of my trailing foot as I got my body over the top of the wall. I pivoted round and dropped, sprawling, into the back alley, not knowing if Sangster had had the nous to station a couple of coppers there. He hadn't.

I got to my feet, my body dented by the cobbles. I hobbled off down the lane into the downhill street. I stopped and brushed my suit down. It was damp down the front and scuffed, but not torn. I wiped the beads of sweat from my brow and adjusted my tie and smoothed my hair. I'd lost the specs somewhere en route. Not that I needed such a simple disguise any longer. The hunt was on, the game afoot.

I took a deep breath, and calmly walked round the corner into St Vincent Street. Ahead was one police car and a Black Maria parked askew just behind the two Morris Tens of MI5. A growing crowd was gathered on the pavement, peering up at the part-open doors. So much for keeping the raid low key and out of the papers. My stomach was churning as I walked towards them listening for police whistles and the sounds of hue and cry behind me or from inside the bank. At any moment I expected the doors to crash open and a platoon of coppers to burst out on the hunt for me.

I kept my pace steady until I was past the police wagons. Then I walked out into the road between the two Morris Tens. The door to the lead car was unlocked. I got in and inserted the key in the ignition. I released the handbrake and let the car begin to move. I put my foot down on the clutch, turned on the ignition, and waited till I had enough speed up. Then I slotted into second gear and let the clutch out. The engine jerked, coughed and spluttered into life. I accelerated down St Vincent Street, across Hope Street and was on my way.

But to where? Sangster now knew I was alive. He'd have police watching Sam and my few good friends like Wullie. I couldn't risk going back to Shimon's store and I had no way of contacting Eric in a hurry. The plan was for him to phone into Wullie at noon and get my directions. It was just after ten o'clock.

I had a little while before Sangster would put out the order to look for this car. Percy Sillitoe had introduced radio cars, damn him. Then I'd be ducking every police motorcycle in the area. But that assumed Sangster would notice one of the MI5 cars had gone. Harry wouldn't tell him. Whatever, I needed to warn Sam and Duncan. I needed a phone box.

I found myself driving across Glasgow Bridge. The road signs for the A77 triggered my homing instinct. I could keep the car pointed south, towards Kilmarnock. But I had no intention of holing up at my mother's. The last thing I'd do was put her in harm's way. She'd put up a fight but the thought of her being hauled away by the polis for harbouring a fugitive was simply unbearable. I found a box on Pollokshaws Road. I called the house. I knew Sam was at home today, waiting to hear how our bank assault went.

'Sam? It's me. The balloon's gone up.'

'Thank God! I had a call from Duncan. He was panicking. Said there's a police raid on.'

'There sure as hell is. Clarkson began confessing everything. He wanted a toilet break and took the chance to throw himself off the top floor.'

'Oh God! Poor wee man!'

'Shame he didn't wait a couple more seconds. He could have landed on Sangster. The bank is flooded with police. They're not as slow as we thought. Sangster was looking out for me and saw me. He knows I'm alive and he's after me.'

'But you got away! Where are you now? What are you doing?'

'I haven't decided yet. I borrowed a car from Harry.'

'Do you want me to meet you? Shall I pack for us both? We can be in England by tonight, France tomorrow. Come get me!'

'Oh, sweetheart, you're a wee marvel. But I'm not putting you through that. We're not going on the run. I'm close to a solution. I just need to buy time. Look, can you get a message to Wullie? Eric will call him at midday. Tell Eric to steer clear of Glasgow. He's to lie low on Arran until I get in touch.'

'Where will you go, then?'

'I'm going to seek sanctuary.' I explained my plan, such as it was.

'"As ye sow ..."' she began.

'"... so shall ye reap." I hope so. Can you call Shimon and arrange it? Take care. Don't answer the door to Sangster.'

I replaced the receiver and let the spare coppers run through. Then I dialled Central Division and asked for Inspector Duncan Todd.

'Duncan, it's me.'

'Ah'm all ears.'

'Sangster's just raided the bank and I got away.'

'Ah knew aboot the first and Ah'm glad to hear aboot the second. Ah left a message with your lady friend. They had a wee look below a certain tombstone.'

'Shame it's not Easter. That would have thrown them.'

'That's quite enough blasphemy for one day. What can I do for you?'

'We're going to have to flush out Sheila Gibson. Face to face. But first I'm going to ground. I need some thinking time. Can you be on standby tomorrow? With a squad car?'

'That can be arranged. Anything else I should know?'

'Clarkson killed himself. Jumped off his fourth-floor balcony into the ledger room. He didn't bounce.'

'Oh, shit!'

'Just missed Sangster.'

'Pity.'

'You live by the books, you die by the books.'

'Glad you've still got a sense of humour.'

'It keeps me going.'

'Ah could do with a drop masel' when my boss gets back with no arrests and a top executive's suicide to explain.'

'One arrest. He picked up Airchie Higgins. See what you can do to help. He's a wee hero.'

'Airchie Higgins, a hero? You'll be telling me next you've seen the light and you've converted to the true faith.'

'Things aren't that bad, Duncan. Got to go.'

'Keep in touch.'

FIFTY

I turned the car round and headed back into the city praying the word wasn't yet out to the patrol bikes and cars. I took the long way round avoiding the centre and was soon climbing Thistle Street. I crested on to Hill Street, drove along it and turned into the side street that served Garnethill Synagogue. Shimon Belsinger was waiting along with Rabbi Leveson. As I stepped out of the car the two men threw a tarpaulin over it and tied it down.

'Welcome, Douglas,' said the rabbi. 'Come in and take tea with us. Or maybe something stronger, eh? I imagine you need it.'

As they shepherded me before them, I was thanking them.

'This is good of you both. I am indebted.'

'Ach, it is nothing compared to the debts we owe you. This barely makes a dent. Come in, come in.'

They fed me and watered me, and even found a welcome glass of brandy for me. They told me the wireless was full of the news of the drama enacted at Scottish Linen Bank. A Government spokesman was playing it down; but how do you play down the violent loss of two managing directors in a month? Or explain how a dead man is suddenly on the run again suspected of everything from bank robbery to double murder? It wasn't the outcome Harry or Sir Percy had hoped for. Far less their political masters. But when the flack is exploding all round you, all you can do is grit your teeth and fly through it. Ducking and diving was just as likely to put you in harm's way.

I asked Shimon to do one last thing: let Harry Templeton know where I was. Then I retired for the night in a makeshift bed in the rabbi's robing room under the great hall of the synagogue. It was a Friday, and up above they were holding prayers and singing. It sounded jolly.

Eventually it grew quiet. Shimon and the rabbi came by with a towel, soap, a toothbrush and a razor. They wished me goodnight and left me lying in the light from a guttering candle. I lay far from sleep, trying to plan my next steps. But I kept coming back to poor Clarkson's face: the look of utter desolation. I should have seen it coming. I'd recognised that look on soldiers who'd been pushed one battle too far. They knew the next bullet was for them, or the next shell. It tended to be self-fulfilling.

And still I hadn't unlocked the full story. Clarkson had taken us most of the way there but there were still too many missing pieces. We didn't know what Roddie Adams's role was, for instance, or what the company Gulf Stream did other than suck in large sums of money from Gibson's accounts. As I lay there, my frustration boiled. So close to an answer, but it had been snatched away from me with Clarkson's plunge. But Adams's office might hold the key.

Just then, I heard a noise. An outside door opened and I felt the movement of air. Someone was padding towards me down the corridor. I rolled out from under my blankets and got silently to my feet. I stood behind the partly open door. It wasn't Shimon or the rabbi. They had no reason to be furtive. As the door eased open, I readied myself.

'Brodie?' he hissed.

'McLeod! What the bloody hell are you doing here?'

I faced Eric in the faint light from my candle. His big grin was catching. I grinned back and we shook hands.

'I'm here to help.'

'No, no. I sent the message out for you to go home. To your wife and weans.'

'Brodie, I've been sailing up and down the Clyde for a fortnight. Your personal taxi service. And I've been proud to help. But I heard on the boat's wireless what was going on. And I got the message from McAllister. You were in trouble. Again.'

'And I don't want anyone else to be.'

'Listen, a year past, you were in bother. Deep bother. I found you trying to steal one of my boats so you could sail off and save your girlfriend.'

'And you helped, Eric.'

He waved his hand dismissively. 'I gave you a better engine. In return you gave me the *Lorne*. It's transformed my life. *Our* lives.'

'What would I have done with a yacht? I'd have sunk it by now. You know me and boats.'

'That's no' the point. I wished then I'd gone with you. I've regretted it since. Well, this time, I'm coming. And that's an end to it. You'll be going after that Roddie Adams fella?'

'How did you know that?'

'We've talked enough about it all. Adams was the last bit to look at. I figured you'd have a go.'

I shook my head. 'You seem to know me better than I know myself, Eric.'

'Good. What's the plan?'

I gazed at him. He was unbending. I smiled.

'A plan? Not much of one. But I'm always happy to have the Black Watch on my flank.'

We shook hands again, and I outlined what we needed to do. The objective was vague and we'd have to make it up as we went along. But as Eric realised, it might fill in the last missing piece.

'Are you armed?' I asked.

'Just this.' Eric drew out his hefty knife from the boat. It could slice through a tangled rope in a second. Or a man's heart.

'Leave it. Breaking and entering is bad enough. Armed robbery adds ten years.'

I reached for my jacket and felt the inside pocket. The bent nails I'd used to get into the yard behind the bank were still there. The luminous dial of my army Omega said one thirty. We slipped out of the side door of the synagogue and headed down through the silent streets, taking back alleys where we could. In some ways the dangers had multiplied: we were more conspicuous. Two big men wandering the streets in the middle of the night carrying house-breaking tools. But it felt good not to be alone.

FIFTY-ONE

A dams & Co. Solicitors were housed in a smart former mansion on Blythswood Square. Each property had three or four storeys above ground and a basement with stairs leading down from the pavement. We did one casual circuit of the central gardens and then tiptoed down the stone steps to Roddie Adams's lower office.

I soon found I lacked Danny McRae's expertise with a rusty nail. I jabbed away at the Yale lock and the bigger bolt, getting nowhere. I was also making too much noise scrabbling away in the dark. Eric was keeping lookout from halfway up the steps, his head jutting out over the square. I waved at him and touched my ear. He signalled all was quiet. So far.

I summoned him down and indicated what we had to do. The pair of us put out shoulders to the door and braced. I raised three fingers. I lowered one after the other, at one-second intervals. When the last finger dropped, we both heaved. The door cracked open.

We let the noise die away and waited for shouts or lights to come on. Nothing. We pushed open the splintered door and walked in. It was pitch dark but we couldn't risk putting lights on. The basement was a storage area. Great shelves of files filled the rooms. We moved up to the ground floor. Here, some light filtered through dusty windows from the street lamps and the moon. We ghosted through the reception area and checked the names on doors. Secretaries and junior clerks.

We took to the stairs again, kneeling in front of every door looking for one name. Not this floor. We climbed to the top floor. Eric found the gold lettering proclaiming which was the office of 'Roderick Adams Esq.' and how many qualifications he had. It was bolted, but I was past caring about the niceties of lock-picking. We did the double shoulder trick and barged into a grand office overlooking Blythswood Square. Very nice. All wood and fine books and leather. The shelves held exquisite vases and glass ornaments. The wages of sin.

We looked around. Against one wall was a run of cupboards. On the desk sat a couple of framed photos and a desk light. Also a brass pencil holder, a paper spike like mine in the *Gazette* newsroom, and a letter opener in the shape of a dagger. I chose the dagger and plunged it into the door locks on the cupboard. They splintered and sprang open. Eric started one end, I the other. We could easily read the file names in the moonlight. But we couldn't find what we were looking for. As Eric did some final checks of the shelves I walked round the huge wooden desk and sat in the leather chair. Its cool depths sucked me in.

I looked down. The desk sat on two pedestals either side of my legs. I switched on the desk light. Using the now bent letter opener I broke open the locks and started rifling through the folders. I found two of interest, considerable interest. One was simply marked 'Gibson F.', the other 'Gulf Stream'. I waved them at Eric and gave the thumbs-up sign. I placed them on the desktop, gave the Gibson file to Eric and we began sifting through them in the pool of yellow light.

From the Gulf Stream folder I took out a set of papers for a property. There was a deed of sale dated eighteen months ago, registering the house in the name of one Fraser Bell. The house had a name – surprise, surprise: Gulf Stream. The accompanying photograph showed why: a white bungalow with a full-width veranda framed by exotic trees and shrubs.

Palm trees. Tropical shrubs. This wasn't a house that backed on to Glasgow's Botanical Gardens. Gulf Stream was in Martinique. I showed them to Eric. His eyes and teeth gleamed. It looked like he too was finding gold in his folder.

I kept laying out the papers from my file. Banks statements in the name of Bell going back over the same period. The headed notepaper on the statements showed a palm tree either side of the bank's name: Bank of Martinique. This chap Bell was in clover; at the last statement date in June his account held £657,000. Enough to keep anyone in coconuts and rum punch for the rest of their lives.

Eric began passing me documents from the Gibson folder. Letters between Fraser Gibson and Roddie Adams confirming arrangements for cash transfers between them. There were also two passports: one for a man, one for his wife. Mr and Mrs Fraser Bell. Their black and white photos gazed unblinking and unsmiling at me. Unsurprisingly, Mr Bell looked just like the oil painting of Sir Fraser hanging in Clarkson's office. Fraser clearly thought he didn't have to change his Christian name for his Caribbean hideaway.

And Mrs Bell had chosen to keep her first name. Pamela was trying to keep to Foreign Office rules by not smiling in her passport photo. But it was hard to hide the delight and anticipation in her large, made-up eyes. Even though she'd cleaned out my bank accounts, I felt a small pang of sympathy for Pam. She'd so nearly had it all.

> *The best laid schemes o' mice an' men*
> *Gang aft agley,*
> *An lea'e us naught but grief an' pain,*
> *For promis'd joy.*

They sure do, Rabbie. They sure do. We gathered up the whole set of wonderfully incriminating papers and passports and stuffed them in our jacket pockets. It was time to go.

Then a door crashed. Downstairs. The front door. Voices and running feet.

'Upstairs! The light's upstairs!'

I motioned to Eric. We walked over to the heavy office door and crowded behind it. I pulled it back on us so that we were mostly shielded behind it. I left the light on over the desk. It should draw their attention. Moths. The feet thumped up the stairs. It sounded like three of them. I hoped one was Roddie. Next thing a figure ran into the room followed closely by two others.

'Shite! He's got the papers!'

'He's gone, sir!'

'I can see that, ya eejit!'

They would turn round any second. One of them was close enough to the door. I took a deep breath and gave a mighty shove. It smashed into him and sent him flying against the second man. Eric and I leaped out and we followed through with a banshee scream and a charge. It was the style of the 51st. Minus the bayonets. And the kilts.

The man I'd struck with the door was tangled up with his pal and both were floundering across the desk, flailing pickaxe handles. The third man was standing by the desk brandishing the empty folders in his left hand. He held a gun in his right. By his glasses I assumed this was Roddie.

I hit him with my shoulder and we crashed over the corner of the desk and on to the floor. The folders and the gun went flying. He was wriggling like an eel until I lifted my head up and smashed my forehead down on his nose. I rolled off his limp body just as the club descended. It missed my head and caught poor Roddie on the chest. He bellowed and I rolled once more and shot to my feet. On the other side of the desk, Eric was in a wrestling match with one of them.

Roddie's bully boy, the one who'd tried to decapitate me, lunged at me – his boxer's face contorted with rage – with another mighty swing that would have staved in my skull if

I hadn't wrenched a standard lamp between us. He roared as the club splintered the wood and caught in the cable and material. It gave me enough time to reach for the nearest ornament on the glass shelves. It took two hands to grab the tall vase and sweep it across the shaven skull. It shattered with a satisfying bang and the man collapsed.

I glanced up in time to see Eric administering his own nutting. A Black Watch speciality honed in every pub in every garrison town in the world. The first strike distracts the opponent; it's impossible to ignore the pain of a broken nose. It opens up the defences to a couple of fast stomach punches. As he doubled up, winded, Eric's kneecap drove up and into his head. He went down with a quiet oof.

I turned to my own growling opponent, rising from the debris clutching his club. I pretended I was taking a penalty to win the match for Scotland, and drove my boot into his head, just under the jaw. His head snapped up, his eyes looked surprised, and he went back and over. He lay still among the splintered porcelain.

Beyond him, Adams had got to his knees. His face was a mass of blood and he was picking broken glass out of his cheeks with his left hand. But the gun was in the right. He brought it up and tried to steady it on the corner of the desk. He was blinking and wiping at his eyes to clear them. To take aim.

I took one step and grabbed the spike glinting provocatively on the desk. I slammed it down, skewering his hand deeply to the wood. He shrieked. I knocked the gun out of his reach and put my face down to his.

'Roddie? Roddie Adams?'

'Yes! Yes! For the love of God! Take it out! Take it out!'

'We haven't been introduced. And it appears we can't shake hands. I'm Douglas Brodie. It's been a pleasure.'

I nodded to Eric. We turned and walked out, leaving Roddie trying to free his nailed hand without ripping it apart.

His unconscious minions were in no shape to help for quite a while. This time we left through the front door, pockets full of evidence of plans that had gone awry. We walked smartly away, adrenalin pumping through our bodies.

'I enjoyed that, Brodie.'

I didn't want to agree with him, to admit that I felt the same. Too much. What had come over me? It was like a switch being thrown in my head. Was this how the war left the pair of us?

'You shouldn't. It could get you the jile.'

'Worth it.' He rubbed his forehead, savouring the memory.

I patted my pockets. 'Worth it indeed. Fraser established a lush wee bolthole in the sun for himself and Pamela. His bank account filled to the brim. Shangri-La.'

'Poor bugger'll never get to enjoy it.'

'I guess Lady Gibson found out. Then arranged for his dream to be punctured. A woman scorned, eh?'

'What will Roddie do after he frees his hand, do you think? Call the police?'

'And say what? Maybe I shouldn't have given him my name. But I'm fed up with folk I've never met trying to wreck my life.'

'Do you have all you need now?

'To prove my innocence? Just about, Eric. We can prove Gibson was a baddie and that Adams was helping him. But we haven't got proof of who killed him. It's time I had a wee chat with Sheila.'

'I'll join you.'

I stopped. I shook my head. 'You've done wonders, Eric. Just what I needed. But the next bit isn't going to need the heavy mob. We'll try the legal route. I'll get Duncan to join me at Lady Gibson's house in the morning. We'll do this bit by the book.'

'Shame.'

'And you should go back to the *Lorne*. Head for Arran. You've done a good night's work.'

He agreed, reluctantly. He handed me all the documents we'd snaffled. We separated, and I made it back to Garnethill without incident.

Surprisingly, I fell asleep as though I'd been felled, exhausted by the day's events and my nocturnal adventures. But I woke before dawn, staring into the dark.

I'd been stupid. Everything had happened too fast. I'd missed two vital clues. First: everything about Clarkson's partial confession rang true. He'd been the puppet of Fraser Gibson. So if the strings had been cut by Fraser's murder, why pay off High Times three days later? More important, why arrange to clean out my account?

Second: in my mind's eye I saw clearly the lifelike colour oil painting of Sir Fraser Gibson in his former office. Saw his intense blue eyes staring at me. Taunting me.

FIFTY-TWO

I washed as best I could in a sink in the small kitchen of the synagogue. I took some painful pleasure in removing the moustache with the borrowed blade. Better. The time for disguise was well and truly over. I was about to depart when Rabbi Leveson came in.

'Ah, Brodie, you are leaving us?'

'I must, Rabbi. Besides, I don't want you to be in trouble with the police.'

He waved his hand dismissively. 'It is nothing new for us. But I came to bring you these.'

He held out a slim package wrapped in brown paper. I took it and pulled out two car licence plates.

'It was left with us late last night by a man called Harry. He sent his regards and said he'd be in Glasgow for a few days. He's staying at the Central. I assume it all makes sense?'

I grinned. 'It does. Great sense. Do you have a screwdriver, Rabbi?'

As I swapped the plates on the car I thought I could recall seeing the new ones on the second Morris Ten parked outside the bank yesterday. Good man, Harry. It was barely gone six. Too early for my next steps. I was easily persuaded to share fried eggs and toast with the rabbi.

As I wolfed down the last eggy morsel, I pushed across the bundle of papers liberated from Roddie Adams' office.

'Rabbi, this is evidence that will go a very long way to proving my innocence. Can you please call Advocate Samantha Campbell and ask her to pick them up from you? She'll know what to do with them.'

'I know Miss Campbell well. She has been a friend to us. It will be my pleasure.'

I set out in my car with its innocuous number plates at eight o'clock. I drove down through the city and across the Clyde out on to the Kilmarnock Road.

I opened up across the open moors, enjoying the feel of the Harry's car. It was more solid than Sam's Riley and not as fast but I was in no hurry and it gave a smoother ride. All the time I kept an eye in my mirror waiting to see a chasing police car or motorbike. The plates would help but maybe they would be checking all Morris Tens.

I toured round and through Ayr and emerged on the Dalmellington Road. Quickly, I found myself coming up on the grey mass of Ailsa Asylum. I turned in, drove up the long drive and parked on the gravel in front of the big house. It was time I had a word with Mungo Gibson. Eyeball to eyeball. There were too many unexplained threads linked to him. The bank account in his name at Maybole used as a vehicle to transfer cash to a bingo hall. The puzzling switch of asylum to Ailsa away from his usual care home in Glasgow. And the timing of his latest confinement, immediately after his brother's murder.

I gave a last brush-down of my mangled suit, fingered my naked chin and lip and straightened my tie. I pushed through the doors into the reception. Unless Sangster had passed a warning throughout Scotland, my police warrant card should still work for me, even minus the beard and the specs. I'd soon see.

I waited twenty minutes, trying not to keep glancing at the door or my watch, fearful of the clanging bell of a police car crunching up the drive. Finally a doctor appeared. A man, in his fifties I'd say, in a smart three-piece suit with a gold fob watch strung across his waistcoat. His moustache and hair were a matching shade of salt and pepper. His gold-rimmed glasses glinted in the light-filled reception hall. Under his arm he carried a slim folder.

'Chief Inspector Bruce? Dr Arnold Prentiss. I'm head psychiatrist here. Sorry to keep you. I was with a patient.'

'I'm sorry to bother you like this, Doctor. I'm grateful for your time.'

We shook hands and he asked me to follow him to his office down a corridor. It was exactly how I imagined Siggie Freud's den: books covering two walls, and dark wood panelling the others. The smell of pipe tobacco and maleness. Neat piles of papers and files on every surface. Wooden and ivory figures and bowls neatly arrayed on shelves and his desk, presumably marking his travels and his interests. No doubt spelling out the character of the man, if only I had the language. I was relieved at the absence of skulls. Too blatant a statement about his line of work.

Prentiss took his seat behind his desk and I sat in front of him. I wanted him to be Dr Andrew Baird. My few sessions with Baird in Sam's library seemed a lifetime ago. I wanted Prentiss to pick up the baton and say, *Now what seems to be the problem, Douglas?* And for me to pour out my soul. And for him to nod and suck his pipe and pose perceptive questions that would get to the bottom of my fractured existence and make everything all right. I needed either psychiatry or a bottle of Scotch.

He placed the folder between us and pointed at the file cover. It read 'Mungo Gibson' and had the date on it – the start date of Mungo's latest commitment. Prentiss sat back in his big leather chair, filled his pipe and lit up. I retaliated with my puny cigarette.

'You wanted to speak with Mr Gibson, Chief Inspector? Might I ask why?'

'We are hoping he might be able to help us in our investigation into the death of his brother, Fraser.'

'Hmmm. That's very difficult. Our fear is that his brother's murder is at the very heart of Mungo's problem. The last thing we want is to dig over that ground and drive him further into confusion.'

'I can see that. Tell me, Doctor, who committed Mungo to your care on this date?' I pointed at the file.

'His sister-in-law, Lady Gibson. She and her late husband had joint powers of attorney. A very caring woman, I might add. She was at great pains to make sure he was given a good room, and pays for little luxuries such as biscuits and sweets. It helps the patient to know he's loved.'

'I'm sure it does. The one thing that puzzles me is that hitherto, Mungo Gibson has been cared for in an asylum in Glasgow. Do you know why Lady Gibson brought him here? I would have thought he would have been better off in a care home where his case is known.'

'Lady Gibson explained that it was precisely because they were so familiar with his case that she wanted to try a different approach. Something fresh. Especially as Mungo had been so strongly affected by his brother's death.'

'I can see that. Tell me, Doctor, while I don't want to breach patient-doctor confidences, may I ask exactly how Mungo's problems manifest themselves? Apart from alcoholism of course.'

Prentiss inclined his head. 'It is important for us to draw a line, Chief Inspector. But perhaps I need to explain things a little so that you might better understand why it would be traumatic for you to visit him and talk about his brother.'

'Thank you, Doctor.' I waited while he sucked at his pipe for the right words.

'The grief of the knowledge that someone close to you has died is sometimes so great that the mind refuses to accept it. The mind insists that the person lives on. In very rare cases, such is the strength of conviction that the mind takes on the personality of the deceased so as to gather up and protect the dead person within the griever's own mind.'

'I'm not sure I follow.' In fact I was sure I didn't.

Prentiss leaned across the desk and pointed his pipe at me.

'Let me put it simply: Mungo thinks he *is* his brother Fraser.'

FIFTY-THREE

I sat back, relieved in a way, but my head buzzing with annoyance that it had taken me so long.

'Poor man. Does he make an issue of it? I mean is he always Fraser or does it come and go? Is it like schizophrenia?'

'You ask a good question, Chief Inspector. But schizophrenia is a very difficult term. There are many forms of it. In one sense, this could certainly be classed as a type of split personality. But with Mungo, he does not switch between minds. He is always Fraser.'

'Do you tell him he isn't?'

He shook his head. 'That would be a mistake. It might make him more entrenched in his new identity. We humour him while at the same time trying to get him talking about his life as Mungo. I'm afraid, however, that that doesn't satisfy him. He seems to have taken on some of the attributes of his brother.'

'Which?'

'From what I've read in the press, and from talking with Lady Gibson, Sir Fraser seems to have been a very arrogant man. A tendency to expect to get his own way. A tendency to bully and shout.'

'And Mungo is now acting like this?'

'And getting somewhat violent. We are administering electroconvulsive therapy – ECT. With the permission of Lady Gibson, of course. There. I've said enough.'

'Could I at least see him?'

Prentiss was quiet for moment. Then he rose.

'Come.'

We walked through the dark halls and into a long corridor, like a hotel's, but each door had a little grill panel, making the effect more like a prison cell. I shuddered inside. We stopped halfway along and Prentiss stood poised to slide the panel.

'I should warn you, Chief Inspector, this is not a pleasant sight.'

I nodded and Prentiss drew back the flap. I stepped closer. The room held a bed, a small table and a deep armchair. A man sat in the chair. He was wearing a straitjacket. He seemed to be drowsing. The click of the panel woke him. He straightened up and looked around. His eyes were red and mad. He saw us and before we could close the panel he was on his feet and shouting at us. At me.

'Help! Help! I need help. Whoever you are, get the police. I'll tell them everything.'

Prentiss moved to shut the panel. I jammed my hand against it. He stopped, curious to see what might happen, I suppose. I moved closer. So did the man inside. Our faces were about two feet apart. I was staring into the face of the dead man in Marr Street. But I was staring into *blue* eyes, not grey. *Blue,* like the oil painting in the chief's office of Scottish Linen. The black and white photos taken by their old neighbour in Maybole showed two young men who could only be brothers. But they'd just showed *pale* eyes. As had the newspapers.

'Please. You must believe me. I'm Fraser Gibson.' He looked mad, but angry-mad, not demented.

'Then what are you doing here, *Fraser*?'

His jaw clenched and I thought he was going to have a fit.

'*She* did it! That bitch did it!'

'She?'

'My wife! Sheila. She got me committed. They'll never let me out. They're giving me shocks. Frying my brain! I'll die here. No one will believe me.'

'Perhaps if you told me your story I could find someone who'd believe. Let's start with the most obvious question: if you're Fraser, where's Mungo?'

His face went into new contortions. 'Dead. He's dead.' Tears started running. 'My wee brother. He's dead.'

'Did he die in your place, Fraser?'

'The pair wee bugger. He wis oot o' it these past years, so he wis.'

'Did you put him *oot o' it*, Fraser?'

'Naw, naw it wisnae me.'

'You mean you didn't pull the trigger. But you arranged it, didn't you?'

His face was a blubbery mass of tears. He just nodded and kept nodding. This was the second man who'd snivelled on me in twenty-four hours. What was wrong with this country?

'Will you testify in court?'

'Aye, Ah will. Ah don't care if they string me up. Anything's better than this hell!'

'Not quite Gulf Stream, is it?'

He stared at me, shocked. 'How did you ken that? Who are you, pal? Can you really get me oot?'

'How remiss of me. My name is Brodie. Douglas Brodie. You framed me for the murder of your brother.'

His mouth flapped. I wondered if he was beginning to think he *had* lost his mind. Banquo's ghost come to haunt him.

'But you're—'

I slammed the flap shut on his face and turned to Arnold Prentiss. The good doctor's mouth was open. He looked like he'd been hit by a mallet. His theory of transposition of minds looked decidedly flawed. I was supportive.

'It's clear the man is mad as a hatter. Lady Gibson identi-fied the body of her husband personally. Your diagnosis is

305

absolutely right, Dr Prentiss. Delusional. I doubt if he'll ever get better.'

Prentiss looked relieved and nodded, sagely.

'What was all that about, Chief Inspector? Saying you were someone else. And the murder?'

'Trick questions, Doctor. To check who he is and what he knew. I discussed it beforehand with his former physician. It confirms your diagnosis. And your ECT treatment.'

'Thank you, Chief Inspector. One has doubts at times, but that's most helpful. Most helpful.'

'I'll see myself out, Doctor. Thank you for your time.'

I walked smartly through the corridors and into the reception area. There was a phone booth to one side. I phoned Turnbull Street, not caring who might recognise my voice. I was put through.

'Duncan, has Sam been in touch?'

'Aye, she has. Says she's got some interesting material from Roddie Adams. Which was generous of him. He must have handed it over before he went to the hospital.'

'Did he call the police?'

'No. But the hospital did. He's one of three beaten up and saying nothing.'

'The papers speak for themselves. And I've got more proof. Can you meet me at Gibson's house at Whitecraigs in half an hour?'

'What have you found?'

'It's not what, it's *who*. There seems to be an epidemic of resurrections. I've found Sir Fraser Gibson, very much alive. The man in Ailsa isn't the man I saw in Marr Street, just before he was shot. They killed Mungo.'

'God, Brodie! I'd better have an ambulance standing by when we tell Sangster. His heid's going to boil.'

'Don't tell him yet. Not till you and I have had a word with Lady Gibson.'

'Fair enough. See you shortly.'

FIFTY-FOUR

I drove back to Glasgow in a mounting rage. Rage at my idiocy. It wasn't until I'd seen the oil painting that my slow brain had joined the dots. But I should have made the connection earlier. Airchie's search of the ledgers had showed that Fraser's mistress, Pamela, had emptied my account *after* the kidnap and murder. The transactions had been authorised by Clarkson who seemed – and claimed – to be Fraser's puppet. Ergo: Fraser set the whole thing up. Set *me* up.

But I raged too about Fraser himself. How could a man arrange to have his own brother murdered? I wouldn't do it to a friend, far less kith or kin. It made me think about my old pal Hugh Donovan and how he'd been stitched up by the police, accused of murdering his own son. It was over a year ago now, but there wasn't a day I didn't think about him dying on the gallows an innocent man. That's what these bastards would happily have ensured happened to me! That train of thought led to others. Things started slotting into place. But suddenly I was coming up to the Whitecraigs turn-off. Funny how time passes when you're seething.

I tried to think how I'd approach the pitiless Sheila. If Fraser's soul was stained by his brother's blood, hers must be poisoned by revenge to have her husband committed, never to come out. Or was it love for Clarkson? A betrayed woman easing past her prime, but still attractive, taking up with someone who worshipped her? Clarkson was no Cary Grant but I never underestimate the allure of *being* loved. Or having money. All that lovely insurance money to share between them. How would she be taking Clarkson's suicide?

I drove into the leafy suburbs and stopped in a side street just along from her house. There was no car in the drive. Was she out? Or just Cammie? What was the best way to confront her? Should I wait for Duncan to join me?

I smiled at myself. I knew only one way. Duncan would be here soon. I walked up the long drive and stood in the grand porch. I pressed the bell and listened to it echoing away through the hall. A short while later I heard footsteps. The door opened and Janice, the maid, stood there. She seemed a little dazed. She didn't recognise me. She smiled, but it was a put-on smile. What did she know?

'Good morning, sir. How can I help?'

'I'd like to speak to Lady Gibson, please.' I held up the much abused warrant card. 'I'm Chief Inspector David Bruce.'

Her eyes boggled. 'Oh, right, sir. Please come in. If you'd like to wait in the library, I'll see if Madam is available.'

I followed her along the familiar hall, my feet clicking on the parquet floor. I winked at Lady Gibson's portrait glowing on the far wall. Janice showed me into the room where I'd listened to the kidnappers making their demands on Sheila Gibson by phone. It seemed like a dream now. Death and resurrection. I looked round the room and saw the sideboard covered with photos. I walked over.

Most were of her and him, or her alone. But obscured by a lamp was a colour photo of two youngish men, maybe early thirties. I lifted it out and peered at it. Their features were very similar. There was no doubt they were brothers. There was also no doubt which was which. Grey eyes and blue eyes. I'd found the grey-eyed Mungo lying dead in a flat in Marr Street. I'd just left his older brother in Ailsa Asylum. The double pair of footsteps came towards me: the maid's and someone wearing heels.

I didn't turn, kept my eyes on the mirror. Watched the maid open the door and let her mistress enter. Sheila Gibson looked smart in a pretty blue linen dress, belted at the waist. Her dark mane was newly brushed and shining. Layers of make-up took years off her. Echoing her picture in the hall. Maybe there was a really bad one in the attic.

She sailed towards me with her face set in a pose that tried to suggest, *How interesting, I wonder what this policeman can possibly want from me, for I am innocent of all things*. But as she got closer I saw the strain round her eyes, as though she was only just holding it together.

'Chief Inspector? Good day to you. How can I help?'

I turned round, waving the photo at her.

'You can stop lying, for one thing. Don't you remember me, Sheila?'

Her eyes widened. Her mouth fell open. She stopped dead in her tracks and her outstretched hand slowly dropped to her side. She turned to her maid.

'That'll be all.'

Janice's mouth gaped open too. Maybe it was seeing me in the lounge that jolted her memory. When the maid had left us and closed the door, Sheila's nerve finally broke and she swayed. I didn't rush to catch her.

'That's right, Sheila. Douglas Brodie. Back to haunt you. Shall we sit?'

Her eyes were wild, like a startled horse. She gulped and put her hands to her face. Then, with sheer willpower, she pulled her hands down. She smoothed her skirt round her hips and walked over to the couch. She sank into it and dug out a cigarette from the box on the low table. I stood. She took several goes at getting her lighter to work. Her hands were shaking.

'I heard . . . The wireless . . . How did you . . .?'

'Come back from the dead? Well, obviously, I didn't actually die. Some friends helped me.'

'They said you'd escaped. That Colin Clarkson is dead.'

'Yes, I did. And yes, your friend Clarkson is dead.' She didn't seem too distraught about Clarkson. Interesting. 'We confronted him yesterday morning. He confessed. Then his conscience got the better of him. How's yours, Sheila? I've just been to see Fraser.'

She stilled. 'What?'

'Very smart he looks too in his straitjacket. He knows you've betrayed him. It's become second nature to you, hasn't it?'

She took a deep breath and got up. She walked to the drinks tray and filled a glass. She didn't offer me one. Ghosts don't drink.

'You don't understand.' She waved her hand with the cigarette as though it was – *I was* – inconsequential.

'Try me.'

'Fraser was in trouble. Big trouble. Horrible debts. It couldn't go on. Everything was out of control. We couldn't just let it all go to pot. Everything we'd worked for.'

'He had enough money. The bank's money. Why didn't you just run off into the sunset?'

She squeezed her eyes tight shut, a little girl playing hide and seek. Then she opened them and found I was still here.

'Blackmail. He was being blackmailed by all the *whores* he slept with! And by that little *shit*, Frankie Elliot. Another one of his whores came out of the woodwork last week. It was never going to end.'

I smiled inwardly; Sam would be amused.

'What was wrong with America, or Canada? Somewhere that small-town thugs like Frankie wouldn't follow?'

She smiled, a lopsided smile, and emptied her glass. She splashed in some more.

''Cos wee Colin said he'd had enough. Clarkson was always snivelling. He'd have blabbed and they would have found out about the money Fraser was stealing. They'd come after us. We'd always be looking over our shoulder.'

'So Mungo was your fall guy. You arranged *his* kidnap and murder. Then you and Fraser were going to slip away. The Caribbean. To your little plantation in the sun. Gulf Stream.'

'How did you know that?' She wavered, then got a grip. She was getting her confidence back with every mouthful. She gulped some more. 'It wasn't like that. Mungo was dying. His liver was shot. Terrible stuff, booze. Cheers!' She raised her glass at me. 'He had months – weeks to live. It was no life, anyway. Stuck in an asylum. The poor man was demented.'

'Oh, I see. It was a mercy, really? I saw Mungo's face. His dead face. He died in terror.'

She didn't hear my last words. 'Sort of. If you like. It was hopeless. And this way . . .'

'Fraser – pretending to be Mungo – could lie low in Ailsa till the dust had settled; then you and he would disappear. No one in the world would care what happened to Mungo once he got out. Certainly not his brother or sister-in-law!'

'Was a good plan,' she slurred. 'Till I found out the bastard wasn't taking me!'

'Who told you?'

'Someone. Our lawyer confirmed it.'

I nodded. 'Roddie playing both sides, I suppose, until he was sure who'd win. Did you promise a bigger tip than Pamela?'

'That was never going to happen!' Even now, Sheila couldn't resist a sneer. Nor could I.

'You can't blame Fraser. Pamela's very pretty. And so young.'

'Bastard!'

I ducked as she heaved the glass at me. It shattered against the wall.

'But wasn't it a bit stupid of Fraser? Once you'd found out he'd gone off with Pam and not you, wouldn't you just have told the police?'

She stood, reeling, laid bare. 'Told them what? That we'd swapped Mungo for Fraser? Anything I said would incrim . . .

would get me jailed. Besides . . .' A look of cunning came over her face.

'Besides – you had a better plan. A better offer. You keep the insurance money, Gulf Stream passes to you once the probate is through, and Fraser gets locked up for life?'

Her lips pursed. She filled a fresh crystal glass. Gulped at it.

'Serves him bloody well right.'

'With a little electroshock therapy to complete the punishment?'

'For his whoring!' she snarled.

'What a shame you and Fraser have split up. You were made for each other. But you've got something better lined up. If it's not Clarkson, can I guess?'

'I can answer that, pal.'

The door had opened silently on its top-quality hinges. Framed at the entrance was Cammie Millar. Holding a gun. Pointed at me.

FIFTY-FIVE

'**O**ne murder not enough for you, Cammie?'

'Shut up. Sheila, let's go. You all packed?'

She tried to put her glass down, relief flooding her face. She missed. The glass tumbled to the floor. She ignored it. She walked over to him and slipped her arm through his.

'All packed.'

'You pissed already?'

'Course not. Just needed a drink, cos of him.' She pointed at me.

'You packed the money too?'

'Course, darling.'

'Darling?' I asked. 'How very sweet.'

'Shut up, you.' He raised his gun again.

Sheila wrinkled her forehead. 'You're not going to kill him, are you, darling? Just tie him up or something.'

'Seems to me he's already dead. They've already put a stone up. Just need to change the date, is all.' His finger tightened.

I forced a smile. 'Cammie, Cammie, did you really think I'd come alone? The game's over. The police are on their way.'

'Naw. Why would they? I heard the wireless. They're looking for *you*, Brodie. What I think is that we could kill you now in self-defence. Say you attacked Sheila here. It'll give us time to get going.'

'Martinique?'

'None o' your fuckin' business. Let's put it this way, it'll be first class all the way.'

'They'll come after you, Cammie. I broke into Roddie Adams's place last night. I've handed all the evidence of the love nest to the police. They'll catch you and you'll swing for *two* murders if you kill me. But you might get away with your neck if you don't shoot me.'

He blinked. 'You're a tricky sod, aren't you, Brodie?'

Sheila tugged at his arm. 'Wait, wait, Cammie, dear. What do you mean, Brodie?'

'There were two of them, weren't there? Two kidnappers. I assume Fraser himself wasn't one. Too risky. He'd be lying low, prior to being committed to Ailsa. That makes it just you and Uncle Gus Fulton? But there was only one shot. Which of you pulled the trigger? Who shot poor Mungo? You or Uncle Gus? You could turn King's evidence and save your neck.'

His confidence faltered. His brain digested the implications. But:

He turned to Sheila. 'Get your stuff. Now! Let's go.'

'You're not going to . . .?'

'There's no need. Every cop in Scotland's looking for him. They still think he murdered Gibson. Disnae matter if it's Mungo or Fraser.'

He walked across the room and picked up the phone. He dialled, all the while keeping his gun trained on me.

'Detective Chief Inspector Sangster, please.'

He waited.

'Walter? It's me. You're looking for Brodie? Well, he's here. Whitecraigs. Naw, he'll be no trouble.' He glanced at me and smiled. A dirty smile. 'Aye, right. Right. It'll be my pleasure.'

He hung up. Then he tore the phone cable out the wall. He smiled at Sheila.

'Cops are on the way and this yin cannae call any pals. Janice says he must have walked here. Nae sign of a car. It'll take days for Sangster to work oot what's going on. If ever. We'll be long gone.'

Sheila squeezed his arm in silent adoration. He faced me.

'You! Turn round, or I put a bullet in you, right now.'

He shifted his gun to his left hand and aimed it at my head. He reached into his jacket. Slowly, I turned round. I heard him take two steps towards me then a rush of air. It was just enough warning to shift my head to one side, but I still took much of the blow. Like a soft hammer smashing into my skull. A lead cosh. It drove me to my knees and I heard him move forward to administer the knock-out blow. I fell flat forward and heard the cosh whistle past my head. I kept falling face down and played dead. It didn't take much acting. I lay there with my brain exploding, slipping in and out of consciousness for what seemed like eons.

FIFTY-SIX

There were no more blows but the pain lashed through me. I opened my eyes. I could see light and colour again. A mishmash. I heard someone come in. I stiffened, ready for another pasting, but whoever it was knelt beside me.

'Sir, sir! Are you a'right?'

I groaned. 'Water. Get water.'

I pushed myself on to my side and let my eyes focus. Outside I heard a car's engine revving up, then wheels spinning across the gravel. I struggled to my knees. Janice darted back into the room with a glass of water. I grabbed it and poured it over my head. The water cascaded off me.

'Show me to the bathroom.'

She helped me up on to my feet. With her support under my arm, I staggered to the door, bouncing off a lamp and an armchair. In the hall, she steered me towards a white door. I limped inside the bathroom and ran cold water. I slunged it on my face several times until my head cleared. It still hurt like blazes but I was awake. Janice passed me a towel and dried myself.

'Do you know who I am, Janice?'

'Aye. Ah ken fine. You're that pair man they blamed. Ah thocht you were deid.'

'So did everybody. Why did you lie about me?'

Her face crumpled. 'Ah was feart. For ma job. For ma life.'

'Have they gone?'

316

She just nodded, face a picture of misery.

'Just ran oot, sir. Narry a thanks or onything. Efter five years.'

'Where did they go, do you know?'

'Ah saw tickets the other day. The *Queen Mary*, so it was. Ah thocht it was a wee holiday. But Ah didnae think they were kinda eloping.'

'You knew about them?'

'Oh aye. That's no' something you hide.'

'Right, lassie. If a policeman arrives in the next wee while, tell him to follow me. Tell him to meet me at the docks, the passenger dock for the *Queen Mary*. Got that?'

She nodded and I stumbled for the door, head splitting with every movement. I lurched down the drive, my head feeling like the top had come off and my brains were hanging out. I clambered into the Morris, fired her up and set off. By the end of the road my head was clearing and I put my foot down. As I swept round the corner I nearly crashed head-on into the big police Wolseley filled with cops. We swerved and squealed to a halt. Duncan jumped out of the front passenger seat and ran over. I rolled my window down.

'Sheila Gibson and Cammie are on the run. He's got a gun. They're heading to the docks. The *Queen Mary*.'

'Go!' he shouted and ran back to his squad car. The pair of us set off, revving and crashing through the gears to get to top speed as fast as possible. The police car had its bell going now. It must have looked and sounded like I was a desperado being chased by the cops.

We broke out on to the main Kilmarnock Road running into Glasgow. The road was quiet. The big police Wolseley, with its top speed of about 75 mph, soon swept past me, bell clanging away. I cranked up my speed until my dial was quivering around the 60 mark. I wished I had Sam's Kestrel. It would have been a match. I swept round a long curve and

317

entered the long straight through Pollokshaws. As yet, Cammie would have no idea that he was being hunted. He wouldn't risk breaking the speed limit.

My answer was far ahead; the solid shape of the big Humber was just sailing out of sight and the police car was gaining. I hunched over the steering wheel, my foot hard to the floor, willing more speed from the Morris. But the dial only flickered above its max when the slope was in my favour.

A bit of me knew that the elopers weren't going to leap on to the liner and sail off laughing into the sunset. Not unless it was poised to set off the moment they shot on to the passenger pier. But my cold anger had warmed up to melting point. This bastard had casually coshed me and left me to Sangster's tender mercies. It was the second time Cammie had set me up. I was going to knock his teeth out. Simple as that. There was the small matter of his having a gun and my Webley lying in Shimon's back room, but that wasn't part of my red-misted judgement.

They were heading straight as a die towards Glasgow Bridge. Ahead of them the traffic was beginning to thicken. But the police bell was carving a hole. And the Humber was accelerating. Cammie must have realized he was being chased. Cars began pulling to the kerb as if pushed aside by a long bow wave from some invisible craft. I began catching up and hammered along in their wake. The Humber was now in plain sight, weaving in and out of the traffic, the Wolseley right on its tail.

They blasted over the bridge, closely followed by me. Where would they go? They couldn't swing left and down to the docks. We'd catch them when they stopped. They ran on past the turn-off and up Jamaica Street. They were heading north. Refuge in the hills?

They screeched round a left turn on two wheels and took off up the Great Western Road. Where would that get them? Dumbarton? The Highlands? The police car was now right behind them. It drew out to overtake. If they worked it well they could get in front and I could ram them from behind. But as Duncan drew alongside, I saw one of his side windows shatter. I'd forgotten the gun. Cammie had shot at them. The Wolseley swerved and slowed and pulled over on the wrong side of the road. As I drew alongside I peered over. Duncan waved and gave the thumbs up and flagged me on. I left him picking glass from his jacket. Both cars regathered speed and we set after the runaways.

I assumed Cammie would keep heading west and north, but then his car swung left into the maze of streets of Hillhead. Hoping to lose us, backtrack to the docks? We raced through the streets, skidding round corners, dancing round cars. Cammie's Humber bounced off another car and came off best. An innocent Model T ended up smacking into a wall. I saw the driver's head bounce off the windscreen. At least he had his hat on; it would take some of the impact. Where the hell were they going?

We shot into Bank Street, a road I'd walked most days in my university period. Then we were on even more familiar ground: University Avenue itself. He must be trying to head back down to the docks. But he threw another fit and drove, tyres squealing, into the Glasgow University grounds. I'd spent four years here studying and wandering the precincts every day. I knew every inch. There was no way out. All we had to do was box him in.

And not get shot.

The Humber went right with the cop car tight on its bumper. I went left to cut him off. While they would be shooting across Professors' Square, I would whip down past the lodge and round the side of the East Quadrangle. We should meet smack in front of the central tower on Gilmore Hill, with its high wide views of the Kelvingrove Park and the city far below. On the opposite hill, in Park Terrace, Sam would be sitting in her lounge fretting about what was happening to me. She'd be fretting more if she were on the roof with a set of binoculars.

I swung round the corner and saw them dead ahead, coming straight at me. There was nowhere to go. The choice was the steep drop to my left or the solid flanks of the university frontage to my right. If they wanted to escape they'd have to get past me or through me. And I wasn't going to let that happen. No matter what.

I began bracing myself for the impact. We were belting towards each other at a closing speed of 50 or 60 miles an hour. I didn't care about my car; MI5 would foot the bill. But I doubted they could put me back together. The Humber's straight six engine probably weighed as much as the whole Morris Ten. But I was counting on Cammie and Sheila not wanting to risk the uncertain outcome of a head-on crash.

Suddenly Cammie's arm poked out. With his gun in it. He let rip with one shot, then another. My windscreen shattered but the bullets missed my head. I just had time to punch the jagged screen aside and see their faces clearly. He was shouting in fury. She was screaming. I gritted my teeth ready for the crash.

That's when Sheila Gibson threw herself across Cammie and grabbed the wheel. She shoved it away from her and the car slewed sharply to my left, towards the drop. The whole passenger side of the car dipped as the forward impetus was transferred to a sideways motion. For a long second I thought it was going to roll, and smash into me side-on. But the low centre of gravity of the heavy chassis and engine block kept it on all four wheels. Kept it on the road just long enough to sail over the edge of Gilmore Hill.

I slammed on the brakes and juddered to a stop, nose to nose with the police car. We all leaped out and ran to the edge. The heavy Humber was still smashing its way down the steep slope. For a while it looked like it would make it in one piece to the Kelvingrove footpath at the bottom of the hill. But then an axle gave out and a wheel flew off on its own trajectory, bouncing over a tree. The wing dug in and the car began to cartwheel. More bits started to fly off until with one final shocking crunch the Humber threw itself in fury against a tree.

Silence settled on the slope. The eye followed the swathe of ripped bushes and gouged grass to the tangle of metal and tree. Steam rose from the burst radiator.

'Christ,' said Duncan softly.

I set off down the slope. Duncan and his three uniformed colleagues slithered after me. We skidded and ran, tumbled and crashed through bushes until we reached the wreck. We approached gingerly in case the fuel tank went up, or a gunman started blasting away. We crouched, inspecting it for long seconds, but there was no sign of life from the engine or the occupants. I got up and walked closer. I could see inside.

Cammie's head and shoulders jutted through the windscreen. His face was lacerated to the bone. His head lay funnily to one side. I couldn't see Sheila until I got to the door and peered down. She was bent over, a jumbled set of limbs in the passenger footwell, a broken manikin. A soft moan escaped her lips. Duncan joined me and peered in.

He shouted to his constables. 'Get an ambulance. Fast.' He stood up. 'Rough justice, Brodie, eh?'

'And not the final tally. Come on, Duncan. Let's finish the job. Leave these boys to clean up the mess. We've got a date with Sangster.'

FIFTY-SEVEN

We walked down to the path and then on through the park. On a summer's day like this, it was lovely to walk in dappled light past flower beds filled with blooms. This was my life before my untimely death, and I wanted it back. I wanted to stroll though here and over to the Western Baths and plough up and down a swimming lane until my shoulders ached.

We crossed the Kelvin at the footbridge and began zigzagging up the side opposite the university.

'You're peching, Duncan. Time you gave up the fags.'

'And the booze. And this job. Are we going to Sam's, Brodie?'

'I need some legal advice. And I need to make some phone calls.'

We were both out of puff by the time we reached the terrace. We stopped and looked back across the tree-filled park. We couldn't quite make out the wreck. Only a faint tendril or two of smoke indicated its resting place. We could hear the bell of an ambulance at the far end of the park, coming from the Western Infirmary. I wondered if Sheila Gibson would make it? It didn't matter. Not now. We turned and walked towards Sam's.

'Oh God, Douglas! Oh God!' She flung herself into my arms as I stepped inside.

I held her long and hard until she'd settled.

'It's all right now, Sam. Everything's going to be all right.'

She pushed back from me, her eyes shining. 'You might have to grow that beard again.'

I kissed her. Then we heard Duncan's ahem and split up.

She grabbed my hand. 'Come through. Tell me everything. The wireless has been going non stop about the Scottish Linen Bank. Suicide of the Managing Director, police all over it, and a manhunt for a murderer.'

'Sangster's a terrier. Doesn't let go.'

Anxiety swept her bonny face again. 'How are we going to stop him?'

'By resurrecting Fraser Gibson. Duncan, can you fill Sam in on what's been happening? I need to make some phone calls.'

'Ah'm no' one hunner per cent sure masel', frankly. But Ah'll have a go.'

Though it was Saturday, my calls provoked instant results. Duncan, Sam and I then sat down and mapped out our plans. Two hours later, Sam was drawing up in the Riley outside Turnbull Street. I was in the back, Duncan in the front. My heart was pounding. The last time I was here I was being carried out on a stretcher with a sheet over my face. Sam turned to me.

'Are you sure everyone is on our side?'

'Nope. I haven't spoken to McCulloch. He worries me.'

'It's hard to believe.'

'So is the last five weeks. We'll soon see. Let's go.'

The three of us marched towards the front door: Sam dressed in her smart business suit, and carrying a slim leather folder under her arm to look even more the top-flight advocate; me, bathed and in a fresh suit; Duncan, well, Duncan his crumpled self. As we walked into the police reception hall, he took my arm. He could claim to have me under arrest if there was no kindly reception committee.

At first I thought the place was empty apart from the desk sergeant. Then a woman rose from a chair near the door. It was Miss MacDonald, personal secretary to Chief Constable Malcolm McCulloch. She walked straight over to us.

'Miss Campbell, gentlemen, this way please.'

She strode off and we followed her through the side door and up the stairs to her outer office.

She knocked on her boss's door and poked her head round the corner.

'Your guests, sir.'

I heard the gruff, familiar voice call out, 'Come.'

Was he standing there, shoulder to shoulder with Sangster, guns pointed at the door and handcuffs at the ready? We walked in. The Chief Constable was already walking towards us, hand outstretched.

'Brodie, it's good to see you. I mean it.'

'It's good to be here, sir. I assume you've had a call from Sir Percy?'

'A long one. Followed by a visit by one of his staff. I think you know this gentleman.'

Harry Templeton strode forward and shook my hand as though he'd never let it go.

'Well done, man,' he said. 'You've done a remarkable job.'

I'd phoned Harry at the Central Station Hotel. He was then going to phone Sir Percy Sillitoe and get Sillitoe to sort things out with his successor to the chief constable role. It looked like it had all come off.

'What's happening at Scottish Linen?

'We've issued press statements announcing the tragic death of the Managing Director and a temporary closure of the head office today. The Bank of England will have to fill some of the big holes in the balance sheet, but it's not structural and there will be no public ruckus.'

'Any knock-on effect? Sterling on the slide? Flack hitting the Marshall Plan funding?'

'Embarrassing but not fatal. So far. The phones have been running hot across the Atlantic soothing nerves in Washington. We should get our Marshall loan. Just as well: signs are we're seeing the start of a major run on our dollar reserves.'

'What about Airchie Higgins? Where's he?'

Harry smiled. 'I claimed him from Sangster. He's holed up at the Central, abusing room service. We'll make use of his talents.'

'Don't forget his medal.'

McCulloch touched my arm. 'Brodie, Miss Campbell, come and take a seat. I imagine you could do with a drink. I know I could. Just the one, mind. We have some nasty work to do. But first I want a full briefing. The whole wretched story, from start to finish.'

It took a while, with plenty of interrupts. For much of the time Duncan left us. He had work to do. Relevant work. At the end of my explanation, our glasses were as dry as my throat. McCulloch looked bleak.

'Dirty business, Brodie. Dirty. I'm ashamed of my people.'

'Let's hope this is the final clearout.'

He nodded and gazed into his empty crystal glass wondering about having the other half. Then he rose and walked to the door.

'Miss MacDonald, please ask Chief Inspector Sangster to join me. Don't tell him who else is here. Right away, please.'

McCulloch tidied away the decanter and the glasses and invited us to stand to one side. He took up position in front of his desk and waited. Before Sangster arrived, Duncan rejoined us. He barely had time to nod at me and smile before we heard voices, then a knock on the door.

'Come,' McCulloch called out.

The door opened and Chief Inspector Walter Sangster came in.

'You wanted to see me, sir. Is it about the bank . . .?'

His eyes registered there were others in the room. Then he paused. He'd met all us before. Harry, for the first time, yesterday at the bank. Todd, who worked for him. Samantha Campbell, advocate, who'd crossed swords with him several times, usually over me. And me. His gaze stopped on me. Then he turned to face his boss, his mouth open to start his defence.

FIFTY-EIGHT

McCulloch got in first. 'Yes, Chief Inspector, it's about the Scottish Linen Bank. But it's also about kidnap and murder. And last but by no means least, it's about framing an innocent man.'

At this he turned to me and nodded. I stepped forward and faced the lonely figure.

'Why did you do it, Sangster? Money? Did you get a slice of the ransom?'

'I don't have to answer *your* questions. You have to answer mine!'

McCulloch said quietly, 'You're wrong, Sangster. And by the way, as of this moment, you are formally suspended from duty. Furthermore, I am formally arresting you on suspicion of conspiracy to pervert the course of justice, aiding and abetting the kidnap and murder of Mungo Gibson—'

'Wait! Wait a minute, ye cannae dae this! And why are you saying Mungo Gibson? You're confused, sir. It wisnae him, it was his brother that got killed. And *he* did it! Douglas Brodie did it! Ah know nothing aboot a ransom!'

I studied him. He really seemed convinced that Fraser had died.

'I thought you knew Fraser Gibson? You were quick enough to identify him.'

'Ah've never seen the man in the flesh. Ah've seen his face

327

in the papers and his wife said he was missing. She identified the body! But whoever it was, *you* killed him!'

'It's interesting that you still think that, Sangster. It might just save your neck. But you haven't answered my question. Why did you frame me?'

Sangster was looking wildly around him, a cornered rat. McCulloch spoke again, his voice harder than ever.

'Sangster, this is going to go ill for you. You might – as Brodie here suggests – just save your worthless skin. But your one hope to do that is to make a clean breast of your part in this miserable affair.'

'Sir? Excuse me for interrupting,' said Duncan.

'Yes, Todd?'

'While Brodie was explaining things to you, my men were picking up Angus Fulton – Cammie Millar's uncle – and he's singing like a lintie. His wee nephew Cammie is dead but Lady Gibson might live long enough to confess. Gus Fulton is prepared to sign a sworn testimony which includes the part played by Chief Inspector – *sorry* – the former Chief Inspector Walter Sangster in setting up Brodie.'

All eyes focused on the diminished figure standing in front of us. He blinked a couple of times as the accusation sank in and then suddenly jolted into life.

'Ah never knew about the kidnap till it happened. Ah jist got a call from Gus Fulton telling me to send a squad car to Marr Street. That's where we found Brodie.'

'Really? So an old lag phoned you out of the blue and you jumped into action?' I asked. 'Just like you jumped when Cammie phoned you this morning to say I was at Lady Gibson's house. And you'd find me – how shall we put it? Indisposed.'

His jaw clenched. 'Gus had been in touch before. He said there was something going down, and it would be in my interest to respond. Ah didnae know it involved you. No' till later.'

My raw anger at the man drained away and I was left with something close to pity. But no more than I might have for a mangy dog breathing its last.

'But when you found me there, you were quick to assume I was guilty and happy to concoct a story that framed me. Then, acting with Sheila Fraser, Cammie and his Uncle Gus, you and your squad went on to build a watertight case against me.'

He was silent and his silence convicted him.

'Sangster, let me help you. Here's my theory. Inspector Todd tells me that it's common knowledge around the station that someone – how was it put? – someone in a senior position wanted to see me at the very least jailed, but preferably dead. Hanging was the preference. But my suicide would do. Is that correct?'

Sangster's eyes were bulging and his head was shaking. He seemed to be shrivelling up inside. His shoulders drew in on his chest as though his innards were being sucked out. I went on.

'I think I know who he is. I also think he *used* to be in a senior position. Used to be your boss, Sangster. Am I getting warm?'

It was plain from his face that I was boiling hot.

'Did you hate me that much, Sangster?' I asked softly. 'Hated me enough to see me swing?'

I thought he wasn't going to answer but finally he found some moisture in his mouth. He answered just as softly at first. As though it were just the two of us in the room.

'Hate you? Ah suppose that's what it was. Always making me look an eejit, Brodie. You, wi' your fine education, looking doon on me. On all of us wee folk. Thinking you were better than us. Too good to wear a uniform. To get your hands dirty doon among ordinary folk. It's no' easy, doon here. Trying to clean up a shite-hoose while the stuff keeps pouring in through the roof and through the windaes and unner the door

. . . And a' the time, there you are, sitting on the sidelines like bloody Sherlock Holmes, sneering at us. Treating *us* like shite!'

His voice had risen to a shout. I kept mine low.

'So you were prepared to send *another* innocent man to the gallows because I made you feel small?'

He looked puzzled. I jogged his memory.

'A year ago, last spring, you and your fellow *officers* framed my pal Hugh Donovan for murder. Advocate Campbell and I tried to save him, but it was too late. You and your high-up friends had already fixed the evidence. But afterwards, when Hugh was dead and buried, I found out who did it, didn't I? I found out who among the high command in the Glasgow police force put the rope around his neck. But it seems we didn't dig out all the pus. The sore went on festering. It seems policemen like you, Sangster, can't shake off the dirty habits.'

He didn't answer. There was nothing more he could say in his shocked state. McCulloch saw it too. He stepped towards Sangster.

'Hand over your warrant card.'

Sangster reached inside his uniform pocket and pulled out the slim folder. He looked at it once, fondly, wistfully, knowing he'd never see it again. Then he handed it over. McCulloch turned to Duncan.

'Inspector Todd, take this man into custody. No visitors except his lawyer. And while you're at it, arrest every officer that worked with him on the Gibson case. With immediate effect, every man jack of them is suspended. If anyone argues, tell them to come see me.'

Duncan moved forward, unsure exactly how to go about this, but keen enough. He reached out and put a hand on Sangster's shoulder. Sangster winced as though Duncan's hand was red hot.

'Let's go, Sangster.'

Duncan steered him out of the door and away. I looked round the room. Sam had her hand up to her mouth. Harry raised his eyebrows at me: *What can you say?* McCulloch looked old and beaten.

'Malcolm, thank you. That wasn't easy,' I said.

He took a deep breath and pulled his shoulders back.

'You're wrong, Brodie. It *was* easy. I never have a problem rooting out rotten apples. The hard bit's to come. We've got a police force to rebuild.'

He looked me straight in the eye and continued.

'In a way, Sangster has a point. If Miss Campbell will excuse me, we *are* down in the shit. Glasgow's a midden and we're the only ones with a shovel. It's dirty and it's nonstop. It corrupts good men. I think Sangster was once a good copper. So, I don't blame you for not wanting to be down among it. But I need help.'

'Malcolm, *you* of all people can hardly say I've been standing on the sidelines! Not just this time, but for the last year and a half.'

'I know that. But you've chosen not to be part of the team. Officers like Duncan Todd need leaders. Men like you. Men they can look up to. I've asked you this before. Join me. You've been masquerading as a chief inspector for a few weeks now. I can make it real.'

It was so unexpected that I had no sensible response. I turned to Sam. She was into the eyebrow-raising business like Harry. I turned back.

'I'm going to play hard to get, Malcolm. I'll think about it and I'll give you my answer in one week. But before all that, there are some formalities. Miss Campbell is my lawyer. She needs to make sure all charges against me are dropped. Sam?'

'I've already alerted the Procurator Fiscal we might need some urgent help. He should be on the premises. Can I call him to join us, Chief Constable, and get you to confirm that Douglas Brodie is . . .'

I smiled at her. 'Alive is a good start, Sam.'

'Quite. Alive and exonerated. Amongst other things we'll need a warrant to arrest Fraser Gibson.'

'By all means, Miss Campbell. It will be my pleasure. Anything else, Brodie?'

'I have unfinished business.'

'The man behind Sangster?'

I nodded.

'What do you need?'

'Two things. First, a letter from you and a loan of Inspector Todd early Monday morning.'

'Done. What's the second?'

'A word with Gus Fulton.'

McCulloch eyed me up. 'As long as it's just a word.'

Duncan and I walked down into the body of the police station, down along the familiar corridors, past my former temporary home. My mouth was dry and my heart was racing. Duncan gripped me by the shoulder as we marched past the cells. We strode on and into the interview room.

Gus Fulton was hunched over the desk, pencil held in his claw, tongue sticking out. He stopped scribbling. Duncan nodded to the uniformed sergeant and picked up the sheets of lined foolscap bearing the part-written confession. He handed them to me and turned to Gus.

'Hello, Gus. You no' finished yet?'

Fulton's thin face blazed at Duncan. 'Ah'm daen ma best. It's no easy efter whit you did.' He held up both hands and showed torn knuckles and welts, and then pointed at a black eye and swollen cheek.

Duncan sighed. 'Ye shouldnae have resisted arrest, then. Ah'm forgetting myself. You two huvnae been introduced. Or huv ye?'

Fulton's sallow features twitched and tensed. I saved his memory the trouble.

'Oh, I think we've met. Haven't we, Gus? Before the war and again more recently. In a wee flat in Marr Street.'

Fulton's face took on a look of panic. He turned back to Duncan.

'Yer no' gontae lea' me wi' him, are ye?'

Duncan smiled. 'Depends on whether you answer his questions nicely or not. Ah'll just stand here. Mr Brodie, he's all yours.'

I sat down opposite Fulton and held his gaze.

'Are you going to be helpful, Gus?'

He nodded, several times, and gulped. His big Adam's apple shot up and down his skinny neck like the gong on a test-your-strength machine at the shows. I then – very deliberately – read through his confession. It confirmed my suspicion about who was behind my frame-up. And why.

I finished. I tidied up the sheets, laid them down between us and pointed at them.

'This is going well, Gus, but there are some details missing. I'm going to ask you some specific questions, you're going to answer, and then you're going to add them to this confession. OK?'

He nodded.

'Why did you chose the Govan Fair day?'

He shrugged. 'It kept everybody away at the other side o' Govan. Nae witnesses. And we could keep an eye on you.'

'Why did you send me on the wild-goose chase?'

'Foot ferries. Cammie had the car. It meant you had to get oot and walk.'

'And gave Cammie time to get back to Marr Street?'

He nodded.

'Don't nod. Speak it out loud. We all want to hear.'

'Aye. That's right.'

'Who owns the flats?'

He wiped his mouth. 'Ma wife.'

'Investment of profits from the bingo?'

'Aye. Her pension, she ca'd them.'

'Were you and Cammie waiting for me in the flat next door to Gibson?'

'Aye, ahint the door. In oor stocking feet.'

'Very professional. What was the plan?'

'We tied up Gibson and then we was waiting till we heard you go in and then we was gontae clobber you.'

'Then shoot Mungo and make it look like I'd shot him?'

He gulped. 'Aye. We were gontae leave a gun by you where the polis would find it.'

'What happened?'

'We heard you go in. We began to come efter you. Then we heard a crash and you fell oot the far door. Mungo had got free and hit you. Yer gun went clattering. We didnae ken you had a gun.'

'What happened then?'

'We ran doon the hall . . .' He stopped.

'Go on.'

'Gibson came oot.'

'Then?'

'Then Cammie grabbed your gun and shot him.'

'Convenient. And you're sure it was Cammie that shot him?'

'As God's ma judge.'

'Oh, you won't need God for that, Gus.'

FIFTY-NINE

I suppose Duncan and I could have made the visit on the Sunday. Every day's the same where we were going. But on no account was I going to spoil my first day as a free man. And I had more important business. Sam and I rose early and went for a walk through the park along by the Kelvin. On the way, we bought a pile of the Sunday papers. They were full of wild stories. The *Post* even had my photo under a headline: 'Danger Man on the Run'.

We sat on a bench as the sun struggled through to take off the chill off the day. Sitting in the dappled shade, surrounded by birdsong and bidding good morning to other walkers, we flicked through the papers, laughing at the outlandish speculation and distortions. Somehow it made it easier to hold a long review of the last few days. Already the events were shuttling into the past, happening to someone else. We dumped the papers in the bin and walked up the long slope, hand in hand, ready to dress for the kirk.

'You should wear your uniform.'

'Too much, surely, Sam.'

'Not for this morning. It's exactly what's needed. You still see a lot of uniforms on a Sunday. Anyway, you should be proud. As far as Sillitoe is concerned you're still in the Service.'

So I did. I had to polish the Sam Browne belting and press the jacket, but soon I was marching out of the door in the dress uniform of a lieutenant colonel in the Royal Tank Corps, black beret at a jaunty angle. I could have wished it had been my old regiment, the Seaforth Highlanders, but any man would be proud to sport the tank badge. I had a momentary pang that my holster was empty; I wondered if I'd ever see my service revolver again? But who needed a gun in church? Not even the dullest sermoniser deserved that.

Together we drove down to Kilmarnock and whisked my mother off to her kirk. I briefed her beforehand.

'Just tell them you can't really talk about it. That it's all a bit hush-hush.'

'*Need to know*? That sort of thing?' She was grinning a wee secret smile.

'You've got it, Mum. Don't overdo it, now.'

'Me? As if . . .'

She could barely contain her glee, like a wee girl who'd just been told she was off to the circus at Kelvin Hall for her birthday. It was a small recompense for the weeks of frowns and headshaking that she'd had to put up with. Kilmarnock folk were quick to forgive, but quicker to judge.

We were in good time to mingle with her fellow worshippers outside. Apart from my height and the uniform, and Sam's blonde hair and sparkling eyes, my renaissance itself would have drawn some attention. I'd been headlining the wireless and newspapers for days. My mum waltzed through the crowd smiling and chatting as if it was an everyday occurrence for her boy to come back from the dead looking every inch the hero. Even the minister came over and shook my hand, vigorously. He looked as embarrassed as only a man could who'd declined to officiate at my funeral.

'It's good to see you, Douglas. And this is . . .?'

'Miss Samantha Campbell, advocate.'

'Right, right. Well, it's good to see you both here. With your mother. So everything is well then, Douglas?'

'Just fine, Minister. Don't believe everything you read in the papers, eh?'

'Aye, quite so. Good. Good. Well done . . .' He all but asked for absolution.

Mum's pew was in the front row of the gallery, looking down on the pulpit. It meant we were in full view of most of the kirk when we stood to sing. It was as if we'd switched on a big magnet. Eyes were drawn inexorably to Sam's blonde cap under the little blue pillbox hat. To Mum between us, silver hair gleaming under her bonnet, and her occasional big smile up at me. And to me, reformed murderer, risen-again suicide, and army colonel in full uniform and medal ribbons.

After more glad-handing at the end of the service, we whisked Mum off to Troon for a full-blown, slap-up lunch at the Rowantree Hotel on the seafront. It was my first chance to recount to her all the recent machinations. Her disbelief was matched only by mine.

Later, when we left her outside her tenement in Bonnyton, we made as much noise as possible to ensure we had all the neighbours' curtains twitching.

Come the Monday, I'd asked to be picked up at ten. It gave me time for a long, shoulder-busting swim at the Western, followed by tea, boiled eggs and toast with Sam. Once more, I was in uniform. It seemed appropriate. I knew Duncan would be wearing his. The squad car was waiting for me as I stepped out of the door. Duncan was standing by the Wolseley, tunic unbuttoned, tie undone, cap off, smoking.

'Well, *Colonel*, before we get going, I want you to promise something.'

'What?'

'You'll no' hit him.'

I laughed, but he was serious. Was I such a loose cannon?

'I'll let the law hit him.'

'You don't have anything in yon holster?'

'If you recall, Sangster took it.' I flipped up the flap to show it was empty.

'Just checking. You're a man that always seems able to lay his hand on a gun, Brodie.'

He slid into the driver's seat. I took the passenger seat alongside him.

'Have you been demoted, Duncan?'

'Naw. I assumed we'd need to talk. The station is in enough of an uproar without giving out more gossip.'

'How's Sangster?'

'Are you really asking after his health?'

'Just morbid curiosity.'

'On suicide watch. Not that Ah think he's got the bottle for it.'

'You can never tell. Look at poor wee Clarkson.'

'True enough. Sangster's no' sayin' much, apparently. Ah think the shock's driven him doolally.'

'His men?'

'We've got five of them locked up. A' protesting their innocence and assuring me Ah'm a dead man when this is a' cleared up.'

'Which suggests they're guilty of something.'

'Exactly my thought.'

'You enjoying it, Duncan?'

'Mixed. It fair scunners me to run into dirty coppers. On the other hand, these particular gents deserve a' they get.'

'Doesn't your lot absolve sinners?'

'Only if they confess and are truly repentant. Sangster's minions have a fair way to go. Speaking of sinners: how do you want to handle this meeting? And before Ah forget, here're the letters from McCulloch.'

He pulled out an envelope from his inside pocket and gave it to me. It was addressed to the Governor, HM Prison Barlinnie. It wasn't sealed. I flipped it open and found two letters addressed to the Governor. I read them, one from the Chief Constable and one from the Procurator Fiscal.

'These should do it.'

We drove north-east out of Glasgow until we got to the sparsely built-up area of Riddrie. Towering over the scattered rows of houses stood the massive grey walls and bleak buildings of Barlinnie. It took me back eighteen months to my first visit with Hugh Donovan.

We parked, did up our tunics and adjusted beret and cap respectively. With our uniforms, Duncan's warrant card and my letters of introduction, we were soon in front of the Governor. He remembered me from over a year ago when I'd first asked to see Hugh in the condemned cell. At the time I'd found Colin Hislop – then Deputy Governor – a twitchy bureaucrat terrified of taking a decision. He'd been particularly leery of letting me see Hugh once he found out I was both an ex-Glasgow copper and a current freelance reporter down in London. It appeared my latest incarnation – *reincarnation* – as an army colonel had sent him back to biting his nails.

'This is so irregular. I mean it was in all the papers that you . . . that you're . . .'

'A murderer and dead? Exaggerations, Governor. Now I'm here with Inspector Todd. Do you doubt his credentials?'

He looked over at Duncan, and eyed him up and down, clearly suspecting some trickery.

'I suppose not. I mean of course not.'

'Good. And unless you believe in ghosts, I am sitting here as solid as Inspector Todd. Is that also correct?'

He gnawed away at another piece of nail, indicating his clear preference, if it was all the same to me, that I was a visitor from the spirit world.

'Yes, yes. I can see that. But . . .'

'And you don't think I've stolen this uniform, or that I'm impersonating an officer?'

'No, no. of course not . . . *Colonel.*'

'Well done, Governor. We're nearly there. Now, those letters you have in your hand.' I pointed at them. 'Do you think they are forgeries? And if so, would you like to pick up the phone and speak to both the Chief Constable and the Procurator Fiscal?'

I fully expected him to self-combust at being forced to take a decision on something that wasn't written down in the three-volume manual about a governor's duties that sat on his desk. We waited, curious to see if he'd plunge his paper knife into his own chest rather than take a personal initiative. He pored over the short missives twice more. Finally he shot to his feet clutching the letters. He called for his secretary.

His pale assistant materialised, certain we were about to murder her boss and chop him into small pieces. She must have been reading my mind.

'Please get my deputy to arrange for these – *gentlemen* – to see the prisoner. In the side room. The secure room. Right away.'

Then he sat down and stared at his desk. We crept out, leaving him to his three volumes and his paper knife.

SIXTY

As Duncan and I walked down the long corridors, the smell instantly evoked the memories of meeting Hugh for the first time here. I hadn't seen him since we were both seventeen, half my lifetime ago. Not since he'd waltzed off with my first love. Back then, he was black-haired and dashing, the epitome of the Celtic poet and soldier. He'd torn my heart out by taking my girl. Our ways had parted and then came the war. I'd heard he was dead. Until I got a call from him, from here, from the condemned cell. Four weeks before his appointed date with the hangman for the abuse and murder of a wee boy.

I'd grudgingly answered the call and met the stuck-up but desperate advocate Samantha Campbell, Hugh's defence counsel. I was her last throw. My first sight of Hugh in his prison grey erased every image I had of my handsome rival. It expunged all my hatred too. Hugh had been a rear gunner in a Lancaster. The death rate was atrocious. So was the wound rate and the wound type. Like many airmen fighting beneath canopies of Perspex, when the plane caught fire he'd been horribly burnt. As the plastic had melted, so had his face.

Four weeks hadn't been long enough for Sam and me to find out the truth. Hugh died an innocent man, and I had gone after the real killers and the policemen who'd conspired with them. Including the senior officer we were about to interview: former Chief Superintendent George Muncie.

Duncan and I marched along the corridor behind the new deputy governor himself. We were in step, a guard of honour.

'Brodie, you get me into some helluva situations, so you do.'

'Keeps life interesting, Duncan.'

'How do you think he'll react?'

'Depends if word has reached him about the events of the last couple of days.'

'With any luck we banged up all his contacts before they knew what was happening: his pal Gus Fulton and his old bodyguard from Turnbull Street.'

We'd stopped outside a metal door. The Deputy Governor nodded to the guard and he began opening it.

'We'll soon find out. After you, Inspector.'

'Ah think it's your privilege, *Colonel.*'

It was a small room, not like the huge airless vault in which I used to meet Hugh. That chamber was for all visitor contact and there was a wire mesh running across the room separating prisoners from visitors.

This room was just as airless but about twelve feet square. There was a metal table screwed to the floor and two chairs facing each other across the table. A guard stood in one corner, his eyes on the prisoner sitting at the table. For an instant I thought they'd brought the wrong man. George Muncie had been big-bellied and florid, with red hair and a temper to match. This man's hair was white and his skin matched the colour and texture of the grey walls. But there was no gut. The shoulders and chest were heavy with muscle. I was glad of the short chain linking the metal cuffs round each wrist.

Then the stranger looked up and the loose wet lips and the big hooked nose were unmistakeable. Though now the nose had a scar and a new kink, like a careless boxer's. The eyes were still heavy-lashed but were now veined and bulging.

'Hello, George. It's been a while.'

He squinted at me like a malevolent bear woken too early from its hibernation. No recognition.

'Whit's the army doin' here? Am Ah being ca'd up?'

'Called to account, certainly.'

'Ah don't know you. Who ur you?'

'Maybe you remember my colleague here?' I stood to one side to let him see Inspector Duncan Todd. Duncan stared at him and waited.

'Wait a minute, wait a wee minute. You're Todd, are ye no'? Sergeant Todd.'

'Detective Inspector Duncan Todd. Hello, George. You've lost some weight.'

He stared at us both before finding a reply. 'Prison porridge. Prison gym.' He flexed his shoulders to show the effects. *Look at me. I can take this shit. Nae bother.*

Duncan replied, 'Ah'll remember that, next time I need to lose a few pounds. Talking of remembering, do ye no' remember this man?'

Muncie shook his head, and the anger surged in me. After what he'd done to me, he didn't even know me. Maybe he couldn't see past the uniform. I sat down at the table and looked at him. I saw light beginning to dawn in his bloodshot eyes.

'That's right, George. Douglas Brodie. The man who put you in here. The man you arranged to frame for the murder of Sir Fraser Gibson.'

Muncie rose out of his seat. A rumbling volcano. Was he planning to jump over the table at me? The prison guard called out sharply.

'Sit doon, Muncie!'

He subsided. 'But you're . . .'

'Dead? Everybody says that. Not yet, George. And I'm here with Detective Inspector Todd to tell you that you will soon be back in court charged with conspiracy to murder.'

His lined cheeks flushed. Some of the old choler gave it life.

'You cunt.'

343

'I see you've expanded your vocabulary in here, as well as your jacket size. Have you anything more witty to say before Inspector Todd reads you your rights?'

A sneer curled his wet lips. 'Ye cannae prove a thing. How am Ah supposed to have tried to frame you when Ah'm banged up here? Eh?'

'Your pal Gus. He's in a cell down at Turnbull Street, writing out his life story, including the time he spent here. Sharing a cell with you. Planning the kidnap, the murder and setting me up for it.'

'Gus isnae a squealer.'

'Everybody's a squealer if they think it'll save their neck. He might just get away with it. Might. He claims his nephew Cammie Millar shot Fraser Gibson. But as Cammie himself is dead it's going to be hard to prove either way. Bad car accident on Saturday.'

Muncie's eyes were now avoiding mine. The sneer had gone. He was rubbing his mouth with the back of his hand.

'It's his word against mine. There's nae proof. Nae connection.'

I leaned across the table and said quietly, 'We've also got Sangster, George. And a few more of your old team. You're going to have company soon. Just like old times. Without the whisky, but the same bum boys.'

He roared and leaped at me, kicking his chair back and into the path of the guard. I lurched back and up to my feet. My chair crashed behind me. Muncie dived round the table, both fists wrapped round the two-foot chain. He'd done this before. If he got the chain round my throat they'd have to club him off me. By then it might be too late.

I ducked right and swung my left fist up and into his midriff. It bounced off. But he staggered and then he came at me again, roaring, his yellow teeth wide. He flung his arms up to swing the chain over my head and drag me to him. It gave me the split second I needed. I drove a right straight into his gaping maw with all my pent-up rage. His head snapped back and he crashed over the chair. He got on to his hands and knees and started spitting blood and teeth on the floor. My fist hurt. My knuckles were cut and bruised. But I hoped he'd get back up so I could hit him again.

He was too slow. The guard had kicked aside the chair and had his truncheon out. He pushed past me and brought it down on the back of Muncie's head. Muncie went down. The guard stepped forward to hit him again and I caught his arm.

'Enough! You'll kill him!'

The guard turned to me with wild eyes. We were both panting. He nodded. Duncan was already kneeling next to Muncie. There was a groan. Duncan and the guard dragged Muncie to his feet and stuck him on a chair. He placed his chained forearms on the table and sat, head bent, dripping blood from his mouth. The back of his white skull had a thick weal across it.

I picked up my beret and screwed it back on my head. I pulled down my tunic and let the adrenalin begin to seep away. I stepped forward and leaned down on the table.

'Thanks, George. I enjoyed that. One last question.'

He brought his head up. His eyes were dulled. Gore and saliva coated his chin.

'If you wanted revenge it would have been easier to have me shot or knifed. Why go to all this trouble?'

He opened his mouth and I saw at least two bloody gaps. He fought for words.

'Ah wanted you inside. In here. Wi' me.'

He tried to look menacing but it's hard when you've lost your front teeth.

'Wrong choice. As you've just seen.'

'Fuck off,' he slurred.

'Glad to. Which is more than you'll be able to do, George.

You would have been up for parole in six months.' I leaned closer so we were almost nose to nose. 'I wouldn't count on it.'

The rage died in his old man's face. Even as I said it I wished I could pull it back. It's more unkind to take away a man's hope than his life. I left him and stood outside while Duncan read him his rights. When he came out he was shaking his head.

'You promised you wouldnae hit him.'

'What was I supposed to do? Keep dancing?'

'You provoked him.'

'I provoked *him*!'

We marched through the metal gates side by side. Duncan was shaking his head again.

'What a bloody waste,' he said.

'Of a good copper? He was never that, Duncan. He was a drunken bully. He sent my pal to the gallows. And then he tried to do the same to me.'

'Ah didnae mean that. It's a waste of a life. Nursing a' that spleen.'

'You know what they say, "Before you embark on a journey of revenge, dig two graves."'

'Who said that?'

'Confucius.'

'He wid.'

We walked on through the clanging doors until we were out in the sunshine of the courtyard again.

'This revenge thing, Brodie?'

'Yes?'

'You wouldnae say that's why *you're* here, would you? Ah mean, no' to the same extent of course.'

'Are you thinking of training for the priesthood, Duncan?'

'Jist askin'. That's all.'

We stepped through the outer door and heard it slam shut and the bolts get thrown as we walked to the car. We stopped either side of the car and pulled out cigarettes. We took our hats off and rubbed our scalps. I licked my knuckles. We leaned over the car's roof and looked at each other and back at the high walls.

'Don't think I haven't thought of it, Duncan. Just now. In there. What was I doing? I didn't have to come. I didn't have to see Muncie's face fall. You could have gone yourself.'

Duncan didn't say anything. A good priest.

I went on: 'I admit it. I goaded him deliberately. It was pure and simple retribution. If it's any consolation I don't feel any better for it.'

He nodded and waited.

'I've been like this all my days, Duncan. Harm me or mine and I'll harm you. It carried me through the war. It made me pursue the Slattery brothers and put Muncie and co. away. Same with the Nazis here in Glasgow. I don't know any way of changing me. Do you?'

He thought for minute.

'Ah huvnae been tested like you, Brodie. Ah've nae right tae comment.'

'But . . .?'

'The war's over. We won. The boys have been demobbed. They've handed in their uniforms and their guns. By any standards, Douglas Brodie, *you've* won.'

'I can hand back my uniform – if Sillitoe lets me. But what about this?' I tapped my skull.

'You need to draw a line, Brodie.'

'Is that it? I think I knew that. How?'

'Ah know you're no' a believer. And a' that Protestant brainwashing that went on—'

'That's rich from a left-footer!'

'Exactly. Ma church is fu' o' ceremonies. The Latin, the incense, the wafer and the wine. But they have a use. Humans need symbols.'

'You want me to go to confession? The booth would explode.'

'Naw, naw. But we need a ceremony.'

I gazed at him, thoughtfully. '"A ceremony of innocence"?'
'Who said *that*?'
'Yeats. "The Second Coming".'
'That sounds about right.'

SIXTY-ONE

It was the perfect morning. A few soft clouds and a gentle westerly. A day to savour. I started it with a stroll though Kelvingrove Park and a swim. Sam had the day off and we took breakfast together. We smiled a lot.

The drive down to Kilmarnock was smooth and easy. Sam was humming away and looking pleased with herself, as well she might. She'd steered a brilliant and dogged path through the legal contortions surrounding my case, and as of yesterday, I was officially exonerated. It was helped by Gus Fulton's full confession and a series of witnesses being found. Stewart had showed up at Turnbull Street police station with a pack of grubby boys, one stumping in wearing callipers. Through his teacher contacts Stewart had tracked them down and the wee ruffians were clamouring to tell their story. They were still excited about the sweets and silver sixpences they'd got from the man in the big car. Just for playing a game of hide and seek with the silly man with a briefcase.

At the same time, Duncan found the memories of the ticket men at the ferry booths were pinpoint clear. Of course they remembered a hot sweaty man with a briefcase running around like a dafty. That's what they'd have said – if anyone had bothered to ask them. Another charge against Sangster and his crew. Duncan even found Sticky, plying his trade back on George Square. Sure, he remembered the soldier laddie who always saluted him and overpaid for his mushy apple.

I'd given him enough extra to let him catch the subway and see the Govan Fair the next day.

A public apology was made by Malcolm McCulloch. He announced at the same time that a number of members of his force would stand trial for everything from drinking on duty to conspiracy to commit murder. Sangster's name headed the list.

I took the Dean Castle turn-off just outside Kilmarnock. A trickle of brown water ran across the ford and we bumped over and took the back road past the Kay Park to the cemetery. I glanced over to the right at the lake – big pond, really – and remembered as a wee boy being taken on the rowing boats by my dad. A million years ago. Now my father lay under the green grass on the hill ahead, just one of the lines of headstones marching away over the rise. Continuity.

We drove towards the small crowd gathered nattering at the gate. A coach was parked just along from them. A single-decker with the roof off. Later – at my request – there would be streamers fluttering from the windows, like a Sunday-school jaunt. The trippers were dressed for summer, the women in bright frocks and the men in shirtsleeves or gaudy ties with hankies drooping from breast pockets.

Duncan was the first to see us and got the others' heads turning round. Shimon Belsinger grinned and waved from among a small group of men sporting yarmulkes. Shimon had his big arm round his shy wife, whom I'd last seen at another cemetery when we were burying Isaac Feldmann, a mere five months ago. In the worst winter in memory, they'd had to build fires on the ground to get a shovel into the frozen earth. Today, Isaac's daughter had come, but not his son. Amos and his family were on a kibbutz in Palestine holding the land until it became theirs – if the UN ever agreed.

Wullie, ensconced in his wheelchair, raised a languid hand with a fag in it. I was surprised he wasn't sipping from a cele-bratory half-bottle. Behind him, Stewart grinned. Gathered round them were my friends from the *Gazette*: Big Eddie, Sandy, two of the secretaries, and brainy Elspeth peeping shyly through her glasses and the thicket of strawberry-blond hair.

My new pal Harry Templeton gave a nod and a smile. Alongside him and looking like he'd robbed a bank and spent the lot on a bespoke tailor, an optician and a barber, was a beaming Archibald Higgins. Even from a distance I could see the ribbon and medal dangling from his breast pocket. He shoogled it at me as I approached.

There was also a big blonde woman sheltering among them, carrying a baby in a shawl and holding a small girl by the hand. Mairi McLeod, Eric's much put-upon wife. I owed her a huge apology and a million thanks for giving me so much of her husband's precious time.

But best of all was the beaming smile I got from the small white-haired woman who stepped towards us. She wore a blue summer frock with big flowers on it and a bonnet that would have won the Kilmarnock Easter parade. If they had one. I lifted my mother up and gave her a birl.

'Put me down this minute, you big silly man.'

But she didn't mean it. There were no neighbours around. Sam and I were hugged and our hands shaken off until we'd done the rounds. We got to Mairi.

'Where's Eric?' asked Sam of the blushing Mrs McLeod. Sam had lifted the wee girl in her arms and they were inspecting each other.

Mairi raised her brows at me. I smiled.

'He's waiting inside, Sam,' I said.

'Shall we go?' asked Duncan.

We filed through and I walked slowly enough that I could keep my arm round Sam and my mother. It had been a while – too long – since I'd walked with Mum and laid flowers on my father's grave. I was relieved to see we were nowhere near his. She must have read my thoughts.

'It just wouldn't have been right to have put you next to him, Douglas. I mean it's no' as if . . .'

'Not as if it *was* me.'

'Besides, the space left beside him is for me.'

'Och, Mum, don't talk like that. You've a few miles left in you yet.'

We were making our smiling procession up the slope to the newest and unfinished line of gravestones when the sounds of a lone piper filling his bag came shrilling over the far hillside. Wullie would say it was a decent distance for the ear. Quickly, the piper had enough air and broke into a fast jaunty tune. As the melody took shape Sam burst out laughing. I smiled at her.

'He's playing your song, Sam.'

My mother tugged at my arm. 'I ken that tune, son. What is it?'

'"The Campbells Are Coming".'

It set the lot of them off and we marched arm in arm up the slope. Eric McLeod, sometime soldier and pipe major, got there before us from the opposite direction. He stood there in all the finery of the Black Watch – kilt and sporran and great buckled belt – sending the blood pounding through us.

> *'The Campbells are comin', Oho! Oho!*
> *The Campbells are comin', Oho! Oho!*
> *The Campbells are comin' to bonnie Lochleven,*
> *The Campbells are comin', Ho-ro! Ho-ro!'*

No one except Sam knew the other verses so we repeated the lines in high good humour until we stood breathless in front of Eric. His pipes droned flat and then fell silent. I walked over and pumped his hand. His family joined him.

We all turned to face a polished black stone. The ground in front had been recently dug over and now dipped in a six-foot hollow. Duncan told me that after the exhumation they'd carted away 'my' coffin as evidence. Well, we wouldn't be asking for it back. I had other plans today.

SIXTY-TWO

stepped forward with my mother and Sam, holding their hands, and read the stone words to myself.

Douglas Brodie

Born 25 January 1912
Died 26 June 1947

'A man's a man for a' that.'

They should have sent a chill down my spine but they were just words. They had no relevance. Someone else with that name had died.

'Is that all you could come up with?' I asked the pair of them.

'As I recall, Douglas, you chose the words.'

'Ah, so I did, Sam. So I did. How pompous of me. And can I just say again, to both of you, how sorry I am to have put you through this.'

Sam looked at me with eyes that were filling up. Why? This was no moment for tears.

'Just don't let it happen again, Douglas Brodie. OK?'

'I'll do my best.'

My mother butted in. 'I'll second that. It's not in the order of things.'

'Wheesht, Mum.'

I hugged them both and we dabbed our respective eyes with hankies.

'Enough o' the watterworks,' said Duncan, standing forward. 'In the absence of a good priest or even a bad minister, it fa's on me to say a few words.'

There were good-natured groans from the mourners.

'A few words. I meant it. We're gathered here today to reverse a crime done to our good friend, Douglas Brodie. Ah think we can all see why villains want rid of the man. He is fearless in his quest for justice. He is a true friend. And he sets an impossible example of guts and determination.'

'It's fair wearying at times,' said Wullie and drew a laugh.

'What we hope for you, Douglas Brodie – and for us too, please – is a period of tranquillity. Naebody shooting at you or bearing false witness against you.'

Duncan paused and stared intently at me. He dropped his voice so that some of the listeners had to strain their ears.

'We want you to have peace in your life, Douglas. Let others carry the load for a bit. And savour the sunny days like this, surrounded by your friends.'

He reached out and shook my hand. There was a quick chorus of hear, hear, a round of applause and a flush of embarrassment all down my neck.

Duncan finished with a flourish. 'We don't want a wordy reply, Brodie. Spare us your fine prose. Give us action!'

I turned to Eric. 'Did you bring it?'

The day goes quiet. Far beyond the lines of headstones, the green hills shimmer in the heat. Eric hands his pipes to Duncan, who holds them as though they'll bite. Eric walks round the back of my gravestone and heaves up a massive sledgehammer. He lays it ceremoniously across his arms and bears it to me like a king's mace. I take it and feel the dead weight dragging to one side. I let its head fall to the earth

355

with a thud. I take a good hold of the handle and step forward. I take one long, last look at the forlorn words, swing the hammer up behind me and bring it through, like a good drive down the fairway. In that short arc . . .

the bullets from a tank's machine gun kick up a path towards me

a rickle of bones drops at my feet in a camp of barbed wire

Hugh's ruined face turns towards the girl and they smile

Samantha Campbell seeks my arms the first time, the night they hanged him

a military court pronounces death sentences on a line of housewives with huge numbers on their chest

Sam and I stand shivering, holding each other, looking out across the frozen lake in Hamburg

Lieutenant Will Collins dies in my arms saying, 'It was worth it, wasn't it?'

Danny McRae's face lights up even as she betrays him

. . . and then the metal head strikes the stone in its black heart with a loud crack. The whole top half, bearing my name and birth date, crashes behind the jutting remnants. I take another swing to erase my death. And another, until there are just broken shards of marble scattered over an empty grave.

I turn back, panting slightly. My little gang are staring at me, wide-eyed and shocked. It's some sort of desecration, isn't it? Then their rational minds take over and applause bursts out again. Time restarts . . .

I walked over to Sam and my mother and embraced them again.

'Much better,' whispered Sam.

Wullie coughed theatrically. 'Funerals are gie thirsty affairs. Resurrections even worse. Is it no time for the wake, Brodie?'

'The *awake*, surely?' suggested Harry. 'By the way, Brodie, I'd like to add my little bit of sunshine to this joyous event.'

'Just your being here is enough, Harry. Without your help' – I pointed at the smashed stone – 'that might have been for real.'

'That's as may be. But you have some compensation coming to you for what you've been put through.'

He put his hand inside his blazer pocket and drew out two envelopes. He selected one and handed it to me. I took it and opened it. There was a typed note:

Dear Mr Brodie,
I just want to say I'm very sorry for taking your money. As you can see, I kept it safe.
Yours truly . . .

It was signed, in a great looping scrawl, 'Pamela McKenzie'.

I dug in the envelope again and pulled out a cheque for £50 to be drawn against the Scottish Linen Bank.

Harry grinned. 'There's more. Gibson's insurance company is *very* grateful. You saved them a very significant sum of money.'

He handed me the second envelope. I opened it and pulled out another cheque, for a sum that a man could retire on. Or a couple.

'Harry, this is ridiculous.'

He shook his head. 'It's ridiculous what was done to you and the risks you took. I'm also expecting some recompense from Scottish Linen itself. You stopped them haemorrhaging money.'

'But not the pound collapsing.' The papers were full of it.

'Nothing was going to prop us up against the dollar. We've had our day, Brodie.'

'I hope you're looking after Airchie Higgins?' I nodded at Airchie, fondling his medal.

'In every sense. After this we're whisking him off to London to work for us.' He drew closer and lowered his voice. 'We daren't leave him alone up here with cash burning a hole in his pocket.'

'Or his liver. Thank you, Harry.' I shook his hand. I looked round at them all. 'Thank you. Thank you, all. I'm sorry that it's taken my own demise to appreciate what good friends I have. I'll try to make up for it, starting with sausage rolls, and strawberries and cream back at Sam's house. And maybe a wee dram, eh, Wullie? Eric, will you lead the way?'

Eric took back his pipes and began warming them up. My mother took charge of Wullie's wheelchair. He grinned up at her.

'Come on, Agnes, gie me a hurl! Pretend this is ma bogie!' he called out. And they set off down the hill as though on their way to a wedding. Eric found his key and suddenly the air was rent with the skirl of the pipes. I held Sam back as we watched them descend.

'What's he playing now, Douglas?'

'"*Cabar Feidh*". "The Antlers of the Deer". It's the marching tune of the Seaforths. He's playing it pretty well for a Black Watch man.'

'He must be. You're getting teary.'

'Naw, just dust from my gravestone. The last time I heard it was when the regiment was dismissed outside Bremen. They went home without me. And I went off to interrogate some Nazis.'

Sam raised her hand with a hankie in it and dabbed my eyes like a mother with her wee boy.

'Silly how it hits you.' I pulled her hand down and took her shoulders. 'Do you know the size of that cheque from the insurance company? It changes everything, Sam.'

She shook her head and waved her hand dismissively. She looked solemn. 'Cheque or no cheque, Douglas, there's something I need to ask you.'

Oh God, just when things were on the up. Not only was I in funds, McCulloch had written a formal letter inviting me to rejoin the force in Glasgow with the rank of Chief Inspector. Was she going to tell me she'd been invited to take silk, move to Edinburgh? Was she going to dash the wine cup from my lips? She continued.

'A few months ago, you asked me to marry you.'

'I did. You told me you were a career girl. Are you getting your KC?'

She shook her head and smiled up at me. 'Is it still on offer?' she asked.

I flushed. 'Of course.'

'Oh, good. In that case, I accept. On one condition.'

'What? Name it.'

'That we do it soon.'

Her blue eyes were dancing now. She'd never looked better. Her skin was flushed and shining with health. Blooming, in fact . . .

Big thanks to:

Richenda Todd, my assiduous editor, for coaxing the best from me. Ian Marshall, visiting professor of Cass Business School, for his pre-computer banking insights. Bryan McLaughlan for the glorious story of 'Sticky'. Sarah Ferris, first reviewer, cheerleader and fellow plotter.

Read on to discover more titles

in the *Glasgow Quartet*...

DOUGLAS BRODIE BOOK 1

THE HANGING SHED

Glasgow, 1946: The war is over, but victory is anything but sweet. Ex-policeman Douglas Brodie is back in Scotland to try and save childhood friend Hugh Donovan from the gallows.

Donovan returned from war unrecognizable: mutilated, horribly burned. It's no surprise that he keeps his own company, only venturing out for heroin to deaden the pain of his wounds. When a local boy is found raped and murdered, there is only one suspect...

A mountain of evidence says Donovan is guilty, but Brodie feels compelled to help his one-time friend. Working with Donovan's advocate, Samantha Campbell, Brodie trawls the mean streets of the Gorbals and the green hills of western Scotland, confronting an unholy alliance of church, police and Glasgow's deadliest razor gang along the way.

Can Brodie save his childhood friend from the gallows? Or will Donovan meet his fate in the notorious hanging shed?

Praise for *The Hanging Shed*:

'The word-of-mouth hit that is leaving its fellow thrillers in its wake. Ferris is a wonderfully evocative writer'

Observer

DOUGLAS BRODIE BOOK 2

BITTER WATER

Summer in Glasgow. When the tarmac bubbles, and the tenement windows bounce back the light. When lust boils up and tempers fray.

When suddenly, it's *bring out your dead*...

Glasgow's melting. The temperature is rising and so is the murder rate. Douglas Brodie, ex-policeman, ex-soldier and newest reporter on the *Glasgow Gazette*, has no shortage of material for his crime column.

But even Brodie baulks at his latest subject – a rapist who has been tarred and feathered by a balaclava-clad group. Brodie soon discovers a link between this horrific act and a series of brutal beatings.

As violence spreads and the bodies pile up, Brodie and advocate Samantha Campbell are entangled in a web of deception and savagery. Brodie is swamped with stories for the *Gazette*. But how long before he and Sam become the headline?

Praise for Gordon Ferris:

'Electrifies readers...a rising star of Scottish literature'
Scotsman

DOUGLAS BRODIE BOOK 3

PILGRIM SOUL

It's 1947 and the worst winter in memory: Glasgow is buried in snow, killers stalk the streets – and Douglas Brodie's past is engulfing him.

It starts small. The Jewish community in Glasgow asks Douglas Brodie, ex-policeman turned journalist, to solve a series of burglaries. The police don't care and Brodie needs the cash. Brodie solves the crime but the thief is found dead, butchered by the owner of the house he was robbing. When the householder in turn is murdered, the whole community is in uproar – and Brodie's simple case of theft disintegrates into chaos.

Into the mayhem strides Danny McRae – Brodie's old sparring partner from when they policed Glasgow's mean streets. Does Danny bring with him the seeds of redemption or retribution?

As the murder tally mounts, Brodie discovers tainted gold and a blood-stained trail back to the concentration camps. Back to the horrors that haunt his dreams. Glasgow is overflowing with Jewish refugees. But have their persecutors pursued them? And who will be next to die?

Praise for Gordon Ferris:

'Ferris is a writer of real authority, immersing the reader into his nightmare world…everything speaks of an original voice'

Independent

Read on to discover titles in the
Danny McRae series...

DANNY McRAE BOOK 1

TRUTH DARE KILL

The war is over. But there are no medals for Danny McRae. Just amnesia and blackouts; twin handicaps for a private investigator with an upper-class client on the hook for murder.

Danny's blackouts mean that hours, sometimes days, are a complete blank. So when news of a brutal killer stalking London's red-light district starts to stir grisly memories, Danny is terrified about what he might discover if he delves deeper into his fractured mind.

Will his past catch up with him before his enemies can? And which would be worse?

A fast-paced thriller by the author of the Kindle sensation *The Hanging Shed*, a Douglas Brodie investigation.

Praise for Gordon Ferris:

'Great feel and authenticity... terrific'
Val McDermid

DANNY McRAE BOOK 2

THE UNQUIET HEART

London, 1946. Danny McRae is a private detective scraping a living in ration-card London. Eve Copeland, crime reporter, is looking for new angles to save her career. It's a match made in heaven... until Eve disappears, one of McRae's contacts dies violently and an old adversary presents him with some unpalatable truths.

McRae's desperate search for his lover draws him into a web of black marketeers, double agents and assassins, and hurls him into the shattered remains of Berlin, where terrorism and espionage foreshadow the bleakness of the Cold War. And McRae begins to lose sight of the thin line between good and evil...

The thrilling sequel to *Truth Dare Kill* by the author of the Kindle publishing sensation, *The Hanging Shed*.

Praise for Gordon Ferris:

'Evocative, beautifully told...Ferris might just become the new Ian Rankin'
Daily Mail